Holding the Baby

Rosie Milne lives in Hong Kong.
Her novel *How to Change Your Life*
is also published by Pan.

Also by Rosie Milne

How to Change Your Life

Rosie Milne
Holding the Baby

PAN BOOKS

First published 2005 by Pan Books
an imprint of Pan Macmillan Ltd
Pan Macmillan, 20 New Wharf Road, London N1 9RR
Basingstoke and Oxford
Associated companies throughout the world
www.panmacmillan.com

ISBN 0 330 49005 2

1 3 5 7 9 8 6 4 2

A CIP catalogue record for this book is available
from the British Library.

Typeset by IntypeLibra London Ltd
Printed and bound in Great Britain by
Mackays of Chatham plc, Chatham, Kent

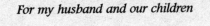

For my husband and our children

One

Annie glanced down at her newly sparkly ring finger, and thought, yet again, how much she disliked rubies. Then she glanced across to William, and thought, yet again, how much she disliked blond men. Blond men were exactly what their description said they were: blond. And bland, and boring – like blond wood. Although, Annie chided herself, it wasn't as if William were dull. It wasn't as if she'd wake up every morning for the rest of her life, turn to him in the half-light of their bedroom, and at once picture Scandinavian kitchens. No, she'd wake up every morning, turn to him and . . .

'There you are!'

Annie's thoughts were interrupted by the arrival of Jo, her second-oldest sister. Jo lived in New York, where she was a Wall Street *über maven*, but as a sister she was a pussy cat, and the two women warmly embraced.

'You made it! How was the flight?'

'Awful.' Jo grimaced. 'Airsick all the way.'

'Airsick?' Annie looked concerned. 'But are you okay now? Can I get you anything?'

Jo shook her head. 'I showered at Liz's. Now I feel almost human.'

'You don't want to go upstairs to lie down? And where *is* Liz?'

'Got waylaid by Mum.'

'Ha! So how did you escape?'

'I used your whirlwind romance as an excuse.' Jo reached for her sister's left hand, and raised it to eye level. 'Argued that since I'd come all this way, it stood to reason I had to see the ring, pronto. Not to mention meet the man.' She examined Annie's ruby, nestling in its protective setting of diamonds. 'My, my! Very pretty.'

To Annie, the stone seemed to pulse like a tiny, mocking heart.

'A ruby.' She sighed. 'So hard to match to nail varnish.'

Jo thought her sister was being deliberately deflationary, to hide the true depth of her emotions.

'So that's why you went for complete contrast,' she teased, playing along.

'Yeah. I tried shimmery white first, but this was much better.'

Both sisters studied Annie's nails. They were painted silver, and shaped like spear tips. The colour not only contrasted with her ruby, it complemented her Chinese-style dress just beautifully. Her silk cheongsam was every shade of grey; it could have been woven from cloud, or smoke. After a moment, Jo, who was head to toe in black, woven from the night, smiled and released her sister's hand.

'So much for the ring. Now, where's the man?'

They both looked around. Annie craned over to where she'd last seen William's blond head bobbing amongst their guests, but he'd moved on, and she couldn't spot him.

'He's somewhere about.'

'Yes,' said Jo, gesturing around the crowded room. 'I can quite understand it'd be easy to lose a guy in here. This place is *huge*.'

Jo was used to the petits fours apartments of Manhattan, but William lived in one of those wedding-cake creations that line the squares in the better parts of London: six highty, haughty storeys of privilege and power, all iced in white. His drawing room was easily big enough to hold seventy or eighty people. But today it was a crush; he and Annie had invited nearly 150 of their closest friends to help celebrate their happiness. The room swelled with the confidence of success-ful people, and billowed with the chatter of voices so plummy you could have made jam from them and spread them on your toast. Tall, well-fed, well-dressed bodies loomed every-where: they lingered on the sofas, lounged against the piano, and leaned against the antiques William had inherited from a bachelor uncle, along with the house. Tiny, smiling Filipina waitresses, dressed in black and white, slid amongst the guests. They carried trays of champagne and platters of food, bearing them so carefully the wine and the itty-bitty bites of this and that might have been offerings to Eastern gods.

'Huge?' queried Annie. 'I s'pose it's pretty biggish.'

'It's just to die for.'

'To die for?' Annie again spoke uncertainly.

'I'll say! Or, at least, to marry for. You'll be *quite* the lady of the house.'

Both women knew Jo was teasing. She'd never suspect her own sister of marrying for a house. And, in truth, Annie wasn't a gold-digger; William's house, and his wealth, had not figured in her acceptance of him. Not at all! It was just that she'd thought if she couldn't have her Anglo-Chinese ex, Ming Kwan, it didn't much matter who she'd have. Or what she'd have. So, since it didn't matter anyway, she'd decided she might as well have money.

'Me? The lady of the house?' Annie mugged astonishment. 'Don't let Henrietta hear a whisper of that!'

Henrietta was William's mother, and she lived in his house ex-officio, as it were.

'Oh, Henrietta!' laughed Jo, who'd not yet met her, but who had heard all about her. 'Never mind! The old bat can't live for ever. You'll be able to do exactly as you like.'

'Hmmm . . .'

'All-night parties! A family of refugees in every bathroom! And just think of all the fun you'll have redecorating!'

At the mention of redecorating, Annie perked up, and grinned. 'I've planned it all. Right from the kitchen – in the basement, and very nasty, a dingy shade of grease spattered on fat – to the guest suite on the fifth floor.'

'The guest *suite*? On the *fifth* floor?'

Annie nodded complacently.

'It's all right for some!' sneered Jo. Resentment was clear in her voice, and Annie was having none of it.

'Oh come *on*! Who d'you think you're kidding? You could buy this place a dozen times, if you chose.'

She exaggerated, but her words held a kernel of truth. As a swashbuckling buccaneer of the global markets, Jo pulled down more pieces of eight than any pirate ever had.

'Maybe . . . But you know full well I wasn't really thinking of the house.' Jo sighed heavily and nodded at Annie's left hand.

'Yeah,' disparaged Annie, 'and I'm sure you could have a ring, too, if you wanted.'

No she couldn't, thought Jo bitterly. Not unless Brett divorced Marcie. But she could scarcely say so. Divorce was surely the filthiest word anybody could toss into conversation at an engagement party. Especially if their interlocutor was the bride-to-be.

Jo and Annie's mother, Ursula, wasn't a divorcee, she was a widow. By now, fifteen years after her husband had died, she was a very merry widow, to boot. In her youth she'd been a knockout, and she still had a terrific figure – from behind, she could pass for twenty. She tinted her stylishly plucked

---

eyebrows, as well as her stylishly cut hair. She made herself up skilfully, and point blank refused to dress in old women's weeds. Today she was in kingfisher-blue silk – a long and flattering jacket over slim trousers.

'God, this is yum!' she said, speaking through a mouthful of mouthful-sized Yorkshire pudding, topped with rare roast beef and horseradish sauce, a morsel that she'd just claimed from a hovering Filipina. 'Have one, everybody!'

By everybody, she meant Liz, Jason, and Zack, who formed a little group around her and who, in her mind, orbited her as planets orbit the sun. Jason, her lover – twenty years her junior, and a resting actor daaarling – and Zack, her son-in-both-law-and-love, quickly helped themselves, but Liz, her eldest daughter, held back.

'Not dieting, are you?' Ursula spoke sharply, worried about Liz's extreme thinness.

'Diiieeeting?' Jason never talked if he could drawl, and he pulled the word out, like cling-film from a roll. 'Look at her! She's so skinny, she's positively stringy!'

'You really should eat more,' pressed Ursula. 'No need for *you* to worry about the old tee ay ef.' *Tee ay ef* was her private code for *ef ay tee*. Fat.

Liz got very fed up with people commenting on her scragginess; fat, or more precisely the impossibility of attaining it, was more than a sore point, it was a wound. Her relationship with her body was as deranged as any anorexic's. How horribly slender she was! How she detested her resolutely flat belly, her obstinately pert breasts! Yes, and how well she hid her self-loathing. She laughed a fairy bells laugh.

'Mum! Don't be fattist.'

'Never! It's just you're not eating.'

Zack slid his arm around his wife's thin shoulders. 'Yes, love. Are you okay? You do seem a bit quiet.'

Liz smiled up at him. 'I'm fine,' she lied, trying to pretend she didn't feel terrible – giddy and aching. And sick with the suspicion that she knew why.

Annie and Jo made slow progress across the room, since every couple of steps someone grabbed at Annie. The timid air-kissed her half a centimetre from each cheek, but braver souls allowed actual bodily contact, and touched their dry, their powdery, their soft, their sweaty flesh to hers as their lips puckered on nothing. Despite all the social kissing, the sisters gradually eeled their way through the crush until they were standing directly in front of William. Both women gulped at his clothes. He was dressed, inoffensively enough, in a blue and white checked shirt, and baggy, brown cords. But, dear oh dear, his blazer. William's blazer was navy, staidly cut, and decorated with shiny, brass buttons. It filled Jo with alarm, and put her in mind of golf courses. It filled Annie with despair, and put her in mind of things she was determined to put right out of her mind.

'Darling!' she squealed, 'best beloved!' She flung her arms around him, and kissed him lingeringly, full on the mouth. He kissed her right back, swaying slightly, as she pressed her body into his.

Jo didn't smell a rat. As Annie kissed William, she smelled nothing but lilies, beating out their incense sweetness from a big, fussy arrangement just behind her. It would have been different at work. At work she would have sniffed out fraud in seconds. At work she snarled: wanna friend? Gedda dog! But even an *über maven* had to be soppy sometimes, and anyway, Jo wanted to believe in Annie's happiness, for her own sake, as well as for her sister's.

'Aaaah!' she sighed, whilst inwardly reminding herself not to judge a man by his blazer.

Across the ocean of the floor, Henrietta was trying to dissuade a small child – who *could* it belong to? – from shredding one of her flower arrangements. This flower arrangement, this floral pagoda, this foliate extravaganza, entirely filled one of the room's two ornate fireplaces, and Henrietta was very proud of it. Few people could get as excited about the precise position of a twig of eucalyptus as could Henrietta, and she'd spent an absolute age over all the many flowers that decked the drawing room today. She knew Annie liked delicate, lacy sprays, small flowers, misty colours, lots of blues. So she'd gone for big, blowsy blooms, heavy things, tall spikes in hot colours. Now the naughty child, a boy of about two, was sitting on the cold, white, marble hearth, tugging at a tiger lily.

'No!' said Henrietta, bending down towards him. 'No! We don't pull the pretty petals off, do we.'

It wasn't a question, so the child, who was sensible as well as naughty, didn't bother to answer. Instead he jiggled a bit on his nappy-padded bottom, then put a fistful of lily petals in his mouth. He chewed a moment, before spitting an orange mush all over a pair of high-heeled, strappy sandals. The elegantly clad woman to whom the sandals belonged exclaimed crossly, tossed her expensively mussed up hair, and minced away.

'Noool' repeated Henrietta, and she reached for the boy's hand. As she did so, a slight shift in the arrangement of the room's legs rippled before her, and she was afforded a brief but clear upwards-slanting glimpse of William kissing Annie. This transient view made her want to take the lily-eating child's hand, and slap it. Annie as her daughter-in-law? The prospect was simply frightful.

Henrietta had welcomed Annie into William's house as warmly as she'd have welcomed mice – or as warmly as mice would have welcomed a cat. She sensed that Annie, the woman her son loved, didn't love her son, but that didn't bother her unduly. After all, she hadn't much loved William's father, now ten years dead, and their marriage had been happy enough. The problem wasn't love – it was absolutely everything else about her future daughter-in-law. Politics? Henrietta would brook no criticism of the dear, dear Queen, but Annie scoffed at the monarchy and said of course she was a republican, she'd much rather be a citizen than a subject, thanks very much. Attitude? Henrietta often started her sentences with *I'm sorry, but I think,* whilst Annie never, ever apologized for her beliefs. Taste? Henrietta had loved her portraits of the dear, dear pugs . . . *and Annie had moved them!*

Throughout her life, Henrietta had very often felt happier in the presence of dogs than of humans, and pugs had always been her chosen breed: so loyal, so trusting, so absolutely sweet. Her current darlings, Bonnie and Clyde, were about the party somewhere, probably trying to snuffle up a few canapés. Until very recently, seven or eight of their goggle-eyed predecessors had stared down from the walls of the drawing room, their crushed-up doggy visages immortalized in badly executed pastels. But one by one Annie had removed the pugtraits and replaced them with abstract no-traits of her own. When the first one had appeared Henrietta had instructed William to instruct Annie to replace it, immediately, but he'd astonished her by saying he rather liked the new picture – a landscape so abstract Henrietta could discern no land in its swirls and loops and whorls of thickly textured paint. Although that was perhaps no surprise, since the artist came from Beijing, and China no doubt looked very different from Hampshire, where Henrietta had her cottage. Not that she'd looked at the picture very closely; she'd had so much more to worry about than art criticism. Defeat in the battle of walls was surely a sign of things to come. Over the past couple of months she'd watched in silent fury as Annie had one by one removed all her other pugtraits. Now the drawing room was almost entirely hung with ghastly, gaudy daubs. It was too infuriating! Was it any wonder Henrietta had wanted to slap the little chap who'd been eating her flowers?

Not that the little chap was the sort to be cowed. He was a cheeky chappie. And a hungry one, too. Since lilies tasted yukky, he now reached for a margarine-coloured carnation, and tried to pluck it from its oasis base. Henrietta was too quick for him: she shot out her own claw-like hand and encircled his soft, podgy wrist with her scrawny fingers.

'Noo!' she said again. 'Let's find Mummy. Shall we? Where's Mummy?'

The boy was suddenly scared. He'd been snatched by a witch! She had talons for fingers, and bird of prey eyes.

'Muummy!' he wailed. 'Muuummy! M-u-u-u-u-ummy!'

Simon was sixty feet away, near the rear windows, where he was crouched by the skirting board, using his handkerchief to rub at one corner of a sprawling purple scribble on the magnolia-tinted walls. Despite his preoccupation, and all the racket of a party in full swing, the wail of his son's distress twanged into his consciousness, and set up a jealous vibration: Mummy. Louis had called for Mummy, not Daddy. His boys always did that. It was always Mummy first, and Daddy a long way second. Still, he couldn't just drop everything and rush to the rescue.

'Not now, Louis,' he muttered. 'Please not now.'

'Nat do it,' announced Nat proudly, wonderingly, touching one finger to the purple scrawl.

Nat was Louis's identical twin, and right now Simon could cheerfully have brained him.

'Don't sound so pleased with yourself! I know you did it. The point is, you shouldn't have done!'

'Nat do it,' repeated Nat. He reached into one of the many pockets of his dungarees, and pulled out a stump of crayon, which he offered to his father. 'Pretty,' he boasted, with shining eyes.

Despite himself, Simon half-smiled at Nat's misplaced pride. Whatever careless or destructive things his boys did, he found it impossible to remain cross with them for long. They were so lovely, so adorable, and so much fun. And, he thought, with a jolt of pain, they were rushing away from him at such a helter-skelter rate. He had half made them, and here they were, shooting away from his body at the terrifying speed of life.

'Muuummy.' From across the room, Louis wailed again, and the timbre of his wail held the warning of imminent meltdown. For the first time, it fully dawned on Simon that Louis had gone and got away from him.

'Shit!'

'Shit!' mimicked Nat, doing a joyful little jig. 'Shit! Shit!'

'No!' said Simon, forcefully. 'Daddy meant . . .'

'Muuummy.'

Simon hastily scrambled to his feet and held out his hand to Nat. 'Come on, butterbean. We'd better go and find him!'

'I s'pose I really should go and find her,' said Ursula, as she helped herself to yet another mini morsel – a tiny spring roll, proffered by yet another smiling Filipina.

'Annie?' asked Liz, who was still feeling unwell.

'No. I can see her anytime.' Ursula pouted slightly. 'I meant Jo. She scarcely even said hello!'

'New York manners for you,' soothed Jason. 'D'you know, I was once walking down Fifth Avenue, and I stopped someone to ask the way. He gave me directions, then I asked for clarification. And he said . . .'

'What is this? A conversation?' supplied Ursula. 'Darling, you trot that out any time anyone mentions Jo.'

'I know. It's irresistible.'

Zack smiled, but the smile did not reach his eyes, which were zeroed on his wife. He briefly flicked them to Ursula.

'Why don't you two go and find her?' he ordered. 'We'll follow after.'

Ursula popped the spring roll into her mouth and chewed a moment. She glanced from her son-in-law to her daughter, who looked drawn and wan. A virus? Perhaps. But Ursula, a shrewd woman and a shrewd mother, had her suspicions. She began to regret her tactless remark about the improbability of Liz's falling victim to the old tee ay ef. Should she enquire? But no! That would be prying, and Ursula prided herself on not prying. Her own mother had been greedy, and needy, and she'd spent years trying to escape her shadow. When her girls had been little, she'd dreaded the pattern repeating itself. She'd always done her best to grant each child a loving, respectful distance. She still did. It was often hard, but now that her four daughters were adults, she did a lot of not asking, and quite a bit of not admitting, too. One thing she was determined not to admit, especially not today, was that she had her doubts about Annie's true feelings for William. Annie had committed to her betrothed so hastily, after such pain, and though she tried, Ursula could sense no depth behind her baby's facade of happiness. Likewise, she could sense sadness behind her eldest's pale complexion. Still, she firmly told herself as she swallowed her spring roll, best not to ask.

Caroline, who was also nibbling canapés, was quite certain about her own happiness. She was wallowing in the luxury of not being a mummy, if only for an hour or two. In the car, on the way up to town from Ryleford, she'd laid down the law to Simon.

'I'm going to enjoy myself this afternoon. You'll have to do twins duty.'

Simon, who'd been driving, hadn't demurred.

'Okay, love. I don't get to see them nearly enough. And you have had them all week.'

'All week, *every* week.'

'Uh-huh. So take an afternoon off.'

Caroline had taken him at his word. She'd seen neither her husband nor her sons since they'd arrived. Bliss! God, she thought, as she stretched for yet another glass of champagne, it was wonderful to be back with the proper grown-ups. She'd been drinking, she'd been smoking, she'd been *talking*. These days, she rarely talked about anything other than breast milk and organic carrots, but this afternoon she'd had a lengthy conversation with a diplomat about North Korea, and another with a theatre lighting designer about shape, colour, and shade. And she'd flirted outrageously with both men. Caroline giggled, and took a sip of her champagne – it was light and dry, and flooded her with the taste of dancing. God, what fun it would be to dance! She'd love to raise her arms above her head, roll her wrists and hips, and stamp her feet. How her skirt would swish and sway! Caroline caressed it, briefly. She had been determined not to look homespun or mumsy this afternoon – not in front of her glamorous mother, and her glamorous sisters, and William and Annie's glamorous friends. Luckily, her body hadn't been completely trashed by bearing and nursing the twins – at least, not on the outside, where it mattered. She'd have liked to have clothed her still shapely curves in something new, but finances wouldn't run to it, so she'd dug out one of her pre-pregnancy party frocks. Sure, it looked a little dated, but it didn't look *dull*. How could it, since it was a lovely, buttery gold? Buttery gold and dullness didn't mix. This dress reeked with the promise of excitement. The clingy, synthetic fabric was low cut and skin-tight over the bodice, then it flared into a soft, full skirt. In the past, when wearing it, she'd always walked as if she were on a red carpet . . .

. . . But even a red carpet could wrinkle, and cause a trip.

'Excuse me,' said a headmistressy voice.

Caroline froze, and tried not to feel like a slouchy fifth-former who'd been caught with contraceptives in her pencil case. She turned round and came face to face with an elderly woman in flat brown shoes, a brown tweed skirt, a cream silk shirt, and pearls. The next moment, Louis launched himself at her knees.

'Hello, poppet,' she said, tonelessly. At once she felt guilty for her lack of enthusiasm, so she bent down to drop a kiss on her son's soft head – it did the trick, it reminded her she loved him.

'So, he is yours,' said Henrietta. 'I found him in the fire-place, trying to eat the flowers.'

Bloody hell! thought Caroline. She couldn't even trust Simon with the boys for one measly afternoon.

'Oh,' she said. 'Well. Thanks for returning him.'

The two women looked at one another appraisingly.

'You must be one of Annie's friends!' accused Henrietta.

Caroline was taken aback by the hostility of her tone. 'Her sister, actually.'

'Her sister?' Henrietta paused a moment. 'Ah, yes. The stay-at-home mum, with twins?'

Luckily Caroline was in the mood to find this patronage funny, not offensive. 'That's right,' she smiled. 'And you are . . .?'

'William's mother. Henrietta.'

Like Jo, Caroline had heard plenty about Henrietta, and she suddenly understood her hostility. But before she could say anything bland and emollient, Simon materialized at her elbow – and Nat at her knee.

'So you found him,' said Simon, nodding down at Louis, and speaking in a relieved tone.

'Mummy!' yelled Nat, his face suffused with adoration.

Liz was suffused with supplication. She had been praying hard, all afternoon: *Please don't let this be . . . please let me be . . .* But her prayers were not to be answered, this month. She felt wreathed in sorrow and loss as she perched on the porcelain in William's loo. The drawing room was on the first floor, and she'd had to descend a wide flight of stairs to reach this little guest loo. Like all loos it was a very private place, also dark, and chilly. It felt, to Liz, subterranean – an outpost of the classical underworld, with the addition of modern plumbing. Even the floor was classical, laid with black and white marble tesserae, in a Greek key design. No, a diamond pattern. Or was it checks? The bothersome tesserae just wouldn't keep still. As Liz stared at them, they blurred and resolved, scurried and revolved, and hopped about from here to there. Their motion made her feel sick. Although not nearly so sick as the sight of her own blood had made her feel. She was a woman cursed by the curse. Again. And again, and again. How many months, now? Liz didn't want to count. She stood up, too sharply. The floor scurried away from her in all directions, forcing her to reach for the wall – thankfully it stayed solid and upright beneath her fingers. After a few deep breaths she told herself to get a grip. This was Annie's party, and she'd better damn well get out there, and celebrate! She dutifully forced herself out of the loo. As she ascended the stairs to the drawing room, she felt like a bat, flitting between worlds, a creature of the dark, with eyes ill-fitted to the light.

Upstairs, Caroline was just thinking how motherhood very often felt like a cavern.

'Good gracious!' she said, drawing back in horrified surprise from the wide purple scribble on William's wall.

'Nat do it,' boasted Nat.

'Simon!' reproved Caroline. 'How could you have let this happen?'

'Um,' gulped Simon. 'Um. Er.'

'Nat do it!' sang Louis. 'Nat do it.'

Caroline batted at her sons, to shush them.

'It only needs a drop of white spirit,' blustered Simon. 'Or a touch-up with emulsion.'

Caroline glared at him. Granted, he'd always been the sort of man to show her he loved her by fixing a dripping tap, or rewiring the wall lights, and once she'd gloried in his practicality. She'd never been able to tell a spanner from a . . . any other tool, but he tossed around drills and hammers with an easy confidence. His skill had seemed so sexy, once. My lover is a shelf bracket, and I am a shelf. But now the suggestion of white spirit or emulsion just infuriated her. She was trying to think of a cutting reply when her mother and Jason walked up.

'Granny!' Nat and Louis shouted their greeting in unison and began jumping up and down with excitement.

Ursula frowned.

'Caroline, sweetheart, how many times have I told you they're not to call me Granny? It's one of the ugliest words in the language, and so ageing!' She kneeled down and held out her arms. 'Come on then, boys. Who wants a kiss from *Ursula*?'

'Ursula's so hard for them, Mum,' objected Caroline, her irritation with Simon giving a very grumpy edge to her voice.

'Rubbish!' Ursula bestowed a kiss on each boy's nose. 'Say *Ursula*, boys.'

'Granny,' the twins chorused.

'You see!' crowed Caroline.

Ursula sighed, and stood up. Sometimes she thought grandmotherhood suited her about as well as sneakers and a puffball skirt would have done. True, it was great revenge – but what woman wanted revenge on her own daughter?

'Have you seen Jo?' she asked, deliberately changing the subject.

'Ages ago. Annie was about to give her a tour of the house.'

'Ah! The grand tour!' Ursula paused. 'D'you know, sitting on the stairs there's a girl who reads palms. We've both had ours done. I've got a foreign adventure coming up, and Jason's in for a windfall, apparently.'

'Fingers crossed!' said Caroline, glumly holding up crossed fingers and simultaneously nodding at the purple scribble. 'We've been dealing with this.'

Jason bent down to facilitate closer inspection. 'Oops!' he said.

'Nat do it!' chirruped the boys gleefully.

'Nat do what?' asked Annie, unluckily choosing this moment to arrive, arm-in-arm with Jo. She spotted the scribble at once, and blanched slightly. But then she recovered herself and laughed. 'It could have been a lot worse! He could have got to *that*.' She pointed to one of her pictures, which was hanging a few feet away. The canvas was painted in only two colours, a flat sky-blue, and a flat Pepto-Bismol pink. From a distance, it looked like a very traditional Chinese painting of peach blossom against the sky, but close up, the blossom could be seen to be composed of helicopters and Barbie dolls, hamburgers and Cadillacs. A collective shudder went round the adults as they all imagined pink and blue enhanced with purple.

'So, let's be grateful he didn't touch it!' Ursula firmly closed discussion of the putative *enfant terrible* of the art world, and held out her arms to Jo. 'Now, no escaping! You and I really must say a proper hello, darling.'

After Jo had embraced her mother, she hugged Jason. Unlike her sisters, she saw these two so rarely the age difference still gave her a bit of a jolt. Jason was much closer to her own age than he was to her mum's. But so what? Mum was fond of remarking that a woman was not old so long as she loved and was loved, and certainly she and Jason lit each other up like the spotlights they both so adored. Lucky them, thought Jo, jealously thinking of herself and Brett skulking in the shadows for fear of Marcie and their colleagues. But she didn't have time to sink too far into self pity, because Liz and Zack just then appeared.

Zack looked strained, and Liz looked crumpled. Her greenish-hazel eyes were flecked with distress, and her creamy complexion had developed a rancid sheen.

'Liz!' her mother and sisters cried, in consternation.

'What is it?'

'Is everything okay?'

'Can I do anything?'

'Everything's fine,' said Zack, replying to them all on his wife's behalf. 'But Liz isn't feeling too well, so we're going to head for home.' He turned to Jo, who was staying with them. 'D'you want to come now, or would you rather get a taxi?'

'We'll drop you off,' volunteered Simon.

'No!' objected Jason. 'It's the opposite direction for you. We'll do it.'

'Thanks, Jason,' said Jo. She turned to Zack. 'I'll come later.' She turned to Liz. 'Are you sure . . .'

'Yes,' confirmed Liz. The two oldest sisters had always been particularly close, and often communicated in a telegraphic, near telepathic code.

Zack smiled at Annie. 'How about a quick toast before we go?' He waved over one of the Filipina waitresses. 'Except, where's William?'

'Caught up with some old school chums,' replied Annie. 'Never mind him. Toast away!'

The Filipina glided across, and each of the adults took a flute of champagne.

Zack held his aloft. 'To Annie and William – in his absence.'

They all clinked glasses.

'Nat want,' demanded Nat, stretching up for his mother's glass.

'Louis want toclate,' whined Louis, whose tastes were not as advanced as his twin's.

Everyone laughed, except Liz, who threw back her head and drained her champagne in one long gulp. Then, in a fluid motion that made her blue-green swirl skirt billow, she sank to the twins' level, and held out her arms to her nephews. They obligingly clambered onto her lap, where they giggled and squirmed and twisted. Liz hugged them tight, rubbing her face in their coppery curls and breathing the scent of cleanish baby boys. Her face was white, but in her heart and in her ears, the blood rushed and pounded, red as longing, red as pain.

Two

Jo wriggled to get more comfortable. She and Liz were slobbing on Liz's intricately carved, exuberantly be-cushioned Indonesian day-bed, which, like everything else in this house, was a riot of colour, pattern, and texture. From the outside, Liz and Zack's house looked unremarkable, a pretty, mid-Victorian cottage in the middle of a North London terrace, but Liz's style in interior design was all tribal prints and ethnic weaves, and walking through the front door was like walking into a psychedelic souk. Jo, in her customary black, felt like an oil slick poured over a rainbow. She quite liked the clashing reds and purples and yellows of Liz's Native American throws, her cushions of Thai silk, her bits and pieces of patchwork and batik, but she much preferred the sleek minimalism of her own Upper East Side apartment, where the mood was quiet, and the colours were mostly green and grey.

Liz felt as colourless as the mineral water she was drinking, though not as fizzy. The water was strategic. She was a wine woman, really, but her bedside table was gravid with guides to getting pregnant, and all of them advised cutting out alcohol before even attempting to conceive.

'So,' she said, 'a year of fucking to the calendar, and still no joy, outcome wise.' She scarcely dared let herself think about any other wise. But given all the pressure, and all the planning, any other wise hadn't been so great, either. Thank God Zack was so supportive. Thank God he wanted a child just as badly as she did.

'A year's not so long,' soothed Jo.

'Not so long?' repeated Liz, blankly.

'Okay, it might seem an age to you. But . . .' Jo trailed into silence and absent-mindedly massaged her breasts, which were vaguely hurting, again.

'But what?' pressed Liz.

Jo shrugged, and took a sip of her wine. After all, what did she know about how long it took to get pregnant? The one time it had happened to her, it had taken, oh, all of three minutes. She'd been nineteen, and she'd had an abortion, of course – not exactly casually – the secrecy and the subterfuge had seen to that – but there'd been no moral anguish. If she'd had the baby, her own life, just beginning, would have been over. That would have been that. So she'd done what she'd had to do to save her own life, and she'd never allowed herself to feel guilty. True, she sometimes felt a pair of ghostly eyes upon her, especially as what would have been her baby's due date rolled around each year. For her, 23 February was a day of the unborn dead, a day on which she was haunted by a pair of eyes as old as time, and yet as young as each new second. These disembodied eyes were huge, dark with resentment, and focused both on nothing and on her. Jo's imagination was not gothic, nevertheless she fancied these eyes came from a land of not-being, a land of blank, a place, she imagined, not unlike an airport lounge, a waiting place, stuffed with souls, all waiting to leave, all yearning to come to be, in the world of being, the world of not-blank. And who, or what, determined when a soul came to be, in the world of things and happenings? Jo hadn't a clue. She was a banker, not a mystic. Yet in the particular case of her own haunting eyes, she knew who'd put a stop to their yearning for actuality. Still, she'd never truly regretted her abortion. Not really. And in all the years since, she'd done everything she could to avoid conceiving for a second time. She took her pill religiously every morning and, as she swallowed, she told herself babies were other women's territory. And not other women who were Other Women either – not mistresses, like her. Babies belonged to an entirely different breed.

Babies fascinated Liz. Babies were irresistible to her, and enchanting.

'I'm thirty-six,' she said, sadly.

'So?' replied Jo. 'It's not old. Loads of women have babies well into their forties.'

'Mostly ones who don't want them. The ones who want to, can't.'

'Bullshit!' Jo gestured with her wine glass. 'Celebrity older mothers fill the gossip rags.'

'Ha! Name one!'

Jo was sure there were hundreds of famous, late-starter mums, but she couldn't think of one offhand, so she remained silent, and massaged her breasts a bit more vigorously than before. She supposed this soreness must be down to ill-fitting bras. She had two criteria for choosing bras. They must either be invisible under clothes, seamless, and in the sheerest of fabrics, or they must be screamingly visible under whatever she happened to be wearing. Either way, her bras had to be the sort Brett would want to remove with his teeth. Comfort didn't come into it. And nor would it. Let her breasts tingle! She'd rather put up with discomfort than change her lingerie allegiance to an *underwear* allegiance. For Christ's sake! Big, comfy, cantilevered bras in reinforced fabrics? She'd as soon wear orange – in her opinion the tackiest of colours. Though Liz probably liked it. Liz, with her eclectic taste, liked everything. Jo touched one of Liz's Thai silk cushions – sludge green, not orange – and reprimanded herself, sharply, for letting her mind wander.

'Have you seen anybody?' she asked. 'A doctor?'

'That's what Zack says. See a doctor!'

'He's probably right.'

'I know.' Liz paused to sip her water. 'But I haven't, yet.'

'Why? It's probably something really simple, like . . .'

'Like what? Get the timing right – I told you, I've been counting days, taking my temperature, you name it – and get the mechanics right. What else is there?'

'Don't your books have any suggestions?'

Liz grunted. She wasn't prepared to remember all the possible causes of delayed conception, as listed in her guides to getting pregnant.

Jo ran her eye over her sister's body.

'You're even skinnier than me! Maybe you need to put on weight? Or to take vitamin supplements?'

'Vitamins?' Liz shook her head. 'And I eat like a horse, you know that. It just never shows.'

'So are you . . .?' Jo blushed.

'What?'

'Well, you did say . . . y'know. Get the mechanics right?'

Liz looked at her sister incredulously, and laughed, properly laughed, for the first time that evening.

'*What?* What d'you think we could be doing wrong?'

Jo decided it had been a mistake to probe the mechanics of sex. She picked up a patchwork cushion, and used it to hit her sister.

'Perhaps you're stressed?' she said.

'Of course I'm stressed! I'm trying to get pregnant, and I can't.'

'Precisely.' Jo paused to sip her wine. 'It's a vicious circle! I really do think you ought to see a doctor, if you're so worried.'

'Mm.'

'Phone tomorrow, and book the next available appointment!'

Liz met her sister's eye, and held it. 'You know what's really stopping me? I'm scared of being given bad news. All those years of taking the pill so I *wouldn't* get pregnant, and now I might be told I'm infertile, not a proper woman . . .'

'Not a proper woman!' If Liz hadn't looked so sad, Jo would have thumped the day-bed and shouted, but she restrained herself, and spoke gently. 'Come off it, Lizzie. You know that's all fiddlesticks!'

'I can't help these thoughts. I don't think any woman could – not if she'd been trying for a baby for a year. I feel . . . *broken.*'

There was silence whilst the semi-telepathic sisters both imagined Liz as a broken doll, lying abandoned in a gutter.

'Perhaps it's Zack?' suggested Jo, after a beat.

Liz seemed not to hear. 'I don't want to be turned into just another medical case. Just another social statistic – one of the whatever per cent of women who leave it too late.'

'Exactly! Of course you don't. That's why you have to go to a doctor. To get help so you *don't* become one of those statistics.'

'So I can be repaired?'

'So you can be *helped.*'

'What if I go through God knows what medical procedures, and end up a statistic anyway?'

Jo took a good pull on her wine, to hide the beginnings of irritation.

'Honey, I hate to be harsh, or to sound unsympathetic. But you must know all this worrying in the dark is pointless. It's self-indulgent. And it can't be fair on Zack . . .'

'Yeah. I must be driving him nuts about all this.'

'W-e-l-l . . .'

'And each month he's just as disappointed as me. He's just as keen for a child.'

'Then go to a doctor! find out if there's a problem, and if there is . . .'

Liz made to interrupt, but Jo cut her off.

'. . . I said *if* there is, *if*, then you and the doctor can come up with a plan to do something about it.'

'Easy! And easy for you to say!'

'I'm sorry. I really am. But if there's a problem, you'd surely feel happier to know than to stumble on in ignorance?'

'That's what I'm saying. I'd rather not know.'

Jo sniffed dismissively. 'And *if* there's a problem,' she repeated firmly, 'I'm sure there must be a solution. Medicine can do so much these days.' *Can't it?* she silently added in her head.

'What do you know about it?' taunted Liz. Then she relented. 'I know you're right, really. And Zack's right. Enough time's passed. Now I'm being stupid. I should do something.'

'Yes, you should,' agreed Jo, 'but *will* you?'

*

Henrietta heard the ticking of her biological clock almost as loudly as Liz. Granted, she'd packed William off to boarding school as soon as she decently could, at age seven. But that she'd packed him off to grow up didn't mean she expected him to pack her off to die in an old people's home – or that she didn't welcome the general *idea* of children. And she badly wanted one *specific* child: a grandchild. Henrietta was a groody granabee – a broody, wanabee granny. It was, she thought, absolutely selfish of William to have postponed parenthood so far beyond the first bloom of his youth. A son who refused to become a father did a terrible thing to his mother. Not that Henrietta was utterly without hope. Indeed, for all the years William had been dating dear Penelope, Henrietta had been constantly hopeful that he'd plant his seed in the mystical garden which was Penelope's . . . yes well, even in her thoughts Henrietta stumbled over the word *womb*, just like a shy reader at nine lessons and carols. Anyway, whatever her thoughts, William had constantly disappointed her. And constantly disappointed Penelope, too. Not that Henrietta had been appraised of the details, but she rather assumed the sensible girl must have eventually got fed up with her swain's unromantic refusal to swoon, and issued an ultimatum: marriage, or else. He'd called her bluff; she'd dumped him. Quite right too! Except now Henrietta was landed with Annie as a future daughter-in-law. Could her hopes of posterity possibly be in worse hands? Absolutely not! Or so Henrietta had persuaded herself. Unlike Penelope, Annie was so very far from sensible! She simply didn't know her place. She was vain, flighty, and selfish. She was indolent and insolent. Annie with a baby? Henrietta found it impossible to imagine. Annie become mumsy? Pliant? Biddable? Ha! It was so unfair! How could William have inflicted such a trollop on her? Was she to begin the long and lonely descent into oblivion without the least scrap of evidence that some part of her was consecrated to the future? Had William no pity? No compunction? Annie had none, but then, what else could you expect? And even if Annie did deign to bear a child, she'd probably wait until her mother-in-law was safely dead.

Henrietta raged against her fate. Not that she'd dream of saying so to William. Honesty with men had never been her style. Her style had been to manoeuvre, and to manipulate. Her husband's style had been to patronize, and to stray. Henrietta had known he'd been an adulterer, but she'd smiled, and flattered, and pretended ignorance of his affairs. What had she had to lose? Her marriage had been courteous. She'd trusted her husband not to inflict on her the gross public humiliation of divorce. It had been enough.

Or, if it hadn't, Henrietta was not about to admit it. And at least her husband had been easy to manage; to compensate her for the one big thing in which he'd done just as he liked, he'd let her have her way on all the little things. William had been equally compliant, until he'd met Annie. But recently his compliant nature had gone the way of the pugtraits. Henrietta had yielded, however gracelessly, over the drawing-room walls, but no mother would yield her son without a fight.

'So,' she said, brandishing a stiff, white oblong over her toast and her pot of tea, 'I suppose it won't be long until it's yours and Annie's turn for these?'

William merely grunted. He and Henrietta were having a leisurely breakfast, whilst Bonnie and Clyde, ever hopeful of crumbs, foraged under the table. Annie liked to be out of the house by 7.20 in order to make it to work for 8.00, so her arrival on the domestic scene had scarcely disrupted the Frobishers' cosy morning ritual. Neither William nor Henrietta needed to dash. Henrietta did courses, organized charity dos, and spent hours over her flower arrangements, but she'd never worked, and William, who had very few ambitions, had never had a career, he'd only ever dabbled. After Oxford (geography – a third), he'd dabbled in the City, but everyone else had been so much smarter than him, he'd never got beyond counting paperclips. Then he'd dabbled in the restaurant business, and been taken to the butcher's by his clever, unscrupulous partners. Next, at the height of the dotcom bubble, he'd dabbled in wine e-tailing. If he'd taken his company public in time, he'd have made paper millions, but he'd left it too late, and his business had gone pop along with so many others. Just at the moment he was between dabbles, but thinking of going into property development once the moribund economy turned around.

'Did you hear me?' pressed Henrietta, as if to a recalcitrant schoolboy.

William glanced up from his *Telegraph*, and took in the stiff, white oblong.

'Wedding invitations? I'm leaving all that side of things to Annie and Ursula.'

Henrietta narrowed her eyes, but refrained from comment.

'It's not an invitation.' She began to read aloud from the card. 'Charles and Clarissa Carrington-Boothe are delighted to announce the birth of Edward Richard Henry . . .'

'Good heavens!' cut in William. 'I didn't know she was preggers.'

'I told you, months back.'

'It slipped my mind. Good for Charles!'

Henrietta fixed her son with a gimlet eye. 'And good for Clarissa.' She paused. 'Excellent stock, those girls.'

William blushed. Those girls meant Clarissa, and her younger sister, Penelope. 'Mummy,' he sighed, 'do stop it. They're not brood mares.'

Henrietta decided not to argue the point.

'Serena is such a good friend,' she said, invoking Clarissa and Penelope's mother, with whom she'd been at school. 'And I am so very fond of Penelope.'

'As am I, but . . .' William trailed off, mentally comparing Penelope, with her pleated navy skirts, her candy-striped shirts, her pearls and her padded velvet Alice bands, with Annie and her fuck-me shoes, her jangly earrings, and her nails. He shivered, slightly, to remember Annie's nails on his back, but then suppressed the memory. This was, after all, breakfast. With his mother. He sighed. At least Penelope had never discomforted him at breakfast. 'Things have changed,' he finished lamely.

'Perhaps,' acknowledged Henrietta, 'but the point is: is Annie?'

William was thrown. 'Is Annie what?'

'Good stock.'

'Mummy!' William's tone was sharp with rebuke.

'No hips, to speak of,' replied Henrietta, unperturbed. She patted her own scrawny chest. 'No bosom.'

William frowned, and put down his paper. Again he mentally contrasted Annie and Penelope. The one as delicious as an oyster, the other as comforting as chicken soup. 'There's nothing wrong with Annie's bosom,' he said.

Henrietta pressed her lips together, and once more narrowed her eyes.

'You know, William, I would so like to become a grand-mother. Not immediately, but I do have expectations of your union with Annie.'

William glared at her a moment, then picked up his paper, and ostentatiously shook it out.

'Terrible what's going on in Russia,' he said. It was the closest he'd ever come to telling his own mother to fuck off.

*

Caroline was interested in world events, just not in the middle of the night. Right now her house should have been dark and silent, and she should have been snuggled under her duvet, in Simon's arms. Not that her husband was the object of her desire. Sleep! How she hungered for it! How her body and her mind screamed for it! But the twins were both wide awake, and Caroline was groggily stumbling around the nightlight-lit semi-gloom of their bedroom, sincerely wishing she could thump someone.

'Nat make pooey,' said Nat, standing up in his bed, and pointing at his nappy.

'Oh, God,' groaned Caroline. Shit at 2 a.m.? Had she really signed up for this?

Well, yes, she had. She had become a mother by *choice*, and now there was no point in moaning; she just had to get on with being one.

'Milk!' demanded Louis, who was on the floor trying to tie a piece of string to a plastic toolbox. 'Milk!'

'No!' snapped Caroline. 'No milk until breakfast. And get back into bed, this minute!'

'Miiiiilllkkk,' wailed Louis, on a rising pitch. 'Miiiiilllkkk.'

Caroline knew, because everybody told her so, that consistency was the thing when dealing with children.

'Oh, all right,' she said, scratching her stomach through the thin cotton of her nightie, which was old, and shabby, and sexy as dental floss. 'Just this once. I'll get you a cup when I've changed Nat.'

A few minutes later Caroline yawned and bent down to dispose of a soggy, reeking nappy in the NappieSan – and she was very, very lucky to be able to do so, she firmly reminded herself. Every moment was a blessing. So what if it was sometimes – nearly always – impossible to remember that? She was very, very lucky that her life revolved around wiping up shit and vomit, cooking endless meals the boys refused to eat, singing about the wheels on that sodding bus, and all the rest of it. After all, look at Liz!

Caroline often looked at Liz, or at Annie, or at Jo. These days, she tended to live her life vicariously, through her sisters. Not that she wanted *Liz*'s life. Poor Liz! Caroline didn't know for sure, but she was beginning to suspect Liz and Zack must be having problems starting a family. Five years married, and no children? And it wasn't as if they'd married young, like her and Simon. Liz and Zack couldn't afford to wait; for both of them forty loomed. Of course, reasoned Caroline, they might not *want* children; they had a very nice, unencumbered life. They complained about their mortgage, but they took two holidays a year, plus lots of weekend breaks. They shopped in interesting shops, ate interesting food, and did interesting things – and they shopped, ate and did them spontaneously – whereas, for her, even the weekly trip to Cooper's to stock up on fish fingers and pasta was a major hassle, requiring meticulous planning. And Liz and Zack could still fool themselves they were young. At thirty-two, Caroline could no longer do that. She had kids, so she had to be one of the boring stiffs, a prig putting a stop to fun. She was one of the grown-ups, disenchanted, disappointed, and bossy . . . although, if her suspicions were right, she couldn't be as disenchanted and as disappointed as Liz. It was so unfair! Liz would make such a great mother. She was so kind, so gentle, and so endlessly, endlessly patient. Caroline had zero patience. She often shouted at the twins non-stop, all day. Liz wouldn't. Liz would remain calm even in the face of a full bottle of black ink, shattered against a newly painted, white wall. When Louis had pulled his Rorschach blot stunt, Caroline had shouted loud enough to make the windows rattle – and then felt ashamed enough to make her insides rattle. But Liz, being Liz, would probably have used the explosion of black on white to make an educational point about colour contrast. And Zack! He doted on the twins. He would be so involved as a father, in a way Simon just couldn't manage because of his hours.

Nat and Louis eyed their mother anxiously. Had she forgotten her promise? Nat reached up from the floor and tugged at her nightie.

'Milk,' he reminded her.

'Milk,' agreed Louis, who was by now sawing at the clasp of his toolbox with a plastic saw.

'You both have to get into bed first.'

'No!' chorused the boys.

'I mean it! Bed!'

'No!'

Caroline scowled, and ran her hands down her nightie.

Back when her nights had been dedicated to sleep, and to pleasure – or rather, in those days, to pleasure and to sleep – she had slept naked except for her scent and, sometimes, the odd scrap of lingerie. Nighties were almost worse, she now decided, than her daytime uniform of baggy jerseys and saggy leggings. Jerseys and leggings were just unflattering and unstylish, but nighties were truly repulsive. They were the sartorial equivalent of the white flag of defeat. Don't shoot! I surrender!

The boys, an army of two, sensed weakness – and went for it.

'No bed,' said Louis, vigorously shaking his head.

'Video?' suggested Nat.

'Video!' seconded Louis, flinging out his arms for emphasis.

'You can have a video on Tuesday,' said Caroline, briskly. Very often, when her boys wanted something she didn't want them to have, she'd tell them they could have it on Tuesday. They had, as yet, no concept of time, and it quite often satisfied them. But never at 2 a.m.

''Itty 'Itty Bang Bang,' the boys yelled, in unison.

Caroline, who felt dizzy and light-headed from lack of sleep, knew, because everybody told her so, that a parent's role was to discipline, not to placate. She gazed at her sons forlornly. It was so hard, always to be outnumbered one to two. True, she'd been thrilled to learn she was carrying twins but, since they'd been born, she'd very often wished they'd come one at a time, decently spaced with an interval of a couple of years. Quite apart from anything else, if they'd come singly she could probably have afforded to go back to work once she'd discovered how little she enjoyed the day to day business of caring for them. Work! She hungered for it almost as much as she hungered for sleep.

In another life, Caroline had had a very good job, as a corporate communications specialist. Corporate communications was a blend of financial PR and HR, and she had fallen into it at West McKee, the management consultants, straight after she'd graduated. Then she'd moved to Holland, Blaine & Murphy, the accountants, and stayed with them through their high-profile merger with Haskey Twigge. She'd been on a good package. Her salary would have covered childcare for one child. But childcare for two? Ha bloody ha! And, anyway, there'd been the commute to consider.

Ryleford was way beyond the M25. Back in the days when Caroline had still thought she wanted to be a non-working wife and mother, that had been part of its attraction – she and Simon had *both* fallen for the green wellies, waxed-jacket dream of country living. Not that Ryleford was the country. The centre of town had a chocolate-box, tea-caddy prettiness which screamed of the burbs, rather than of the heath, or farm. And as befitted a burb, the place had no economy of its own, beyond quaint little shops selling twiddle-de-dee junk, and outrageously expensive boutiques serving the pampered wives of businessmen far more successful than Simon. Hardly anybody actually *worked* in Ryleford. Most Rylefordians depended on London for their livelihood. When the trains were running smoothly, the commute up to town took forty minutes. Allegedly. But nobody in Ryleford could vouch for this, since the trains were never running smoothly. In fact, it took an average of an hour and a half for Simon to get into his City office. He caught the 6.20 each morning – which was why he was let off night duty with the twins – and he was never home before 9.00. Caroline's working hours wouldn't have been so very different, if she'd gone back.

So Caroline hadn't gone back. She hadn't thought she'd want to. As she stood in the grey pre-dawn of another kiddy day, outnumbered by her kiddies, she remembered discussing work, with Simon. They'd talked it all over, even before she'd conceived.

'What's the point of having children if you never see them?' she'd asked, rhetorically. 'And anyway, it'll only be a few years of sacrifice. They aren't tiny for ever.'

'Mm-hmm.'

'And surely it would be better for our baby to be looked after by me, than by some flighty, ill-educated girl who'd mostly be interested in finding a man?'

Caroline's arguments had seemed conclusive. And she was still willing to grant they probably were conclusive, considered from the point of view of the universe. But not from her own. The problem, she now knew, was that she'd been mouthing the pieties from a position of ignorance. How could she not have been? Did any childless woman, contemplating trying for a baby, ever realize how grotty motherhood could be? Or was it just her? Had she been uniquely unimaginative? For that matter, was she a uniquely horrible person? Was she a uniquely selfish bitch, because it so often felt as if she was allergic to motherhood?

Probably, thought Caroline gloomily. But self-loathing would get her nowhere. And nor would self-pity. She crossly reminded herself that, for her, the shock of motherhood should have been softened by the Surrey factor. True, she couldn't, right this minute, remember motherhood's rewards, but her life was a doddle compared to many women's. Sure, she missed work, but at least she wasn't bringing up the twins alone, in a high rise on a council estate, with no man in sight, and no supportive family to help her out. And she was lucky to be spared the double load that was so many mothers' lot: house-work and real work; nursing, and nursing the figures; cuddling, and cuddling up with the clients. Multi-tasking. Followed by collapsing. But for her there'd be no collapse. No, she repeated to herself, very sternly, there would not. Simon was willing to keep her, and he could afford to do so, just about. She knew she damn well ought to be grateful. She was, in so many ways, one of the lucky ones.

Liz would have agreed. She had finally taken the plunge and made an appointment with her GP. She sat amongst the coughs and sniffles in the waiting room, and flipped through an ancient magazine, with unseeing eyes. She was right to be here. How many times had she been through the arguments? Jo and Zack were right; it really was time to seek help. Fate, her thermometer, and a distasteful attention to the state of her cervical mucus had all let her down; it was silly to be nervous about what science might now have to say. Yet she was nervous – very nervous. What if science said: *tough luck, lady, but all your eggs are blasted, your ovaries are blighted, and your uterus is blind to the procreative light?*

Liz shuddered, and snapped shut her magazine. She would not let herself think like this! She would remain optimistic. Positive thinking was the thing. Except Liz didn't believe in positive thinking; it was all New Age mumbo jumbo. What next, if she went down that route? A sub-neo-feminist reinterpretation of some ancient, near-Eastern fertility rite?

Liz's GP, Dr Kent, always carried a lump of rose quartz about her person, to ward off radiation from computers and mobile phones. She was a short, plump woman in her early forties, and she looked like a Teletubby at the best of times. Now Liz was disconcerted to see she was, of all things, pregnant. She warily eyed her doctor's swollen stomach, bulging under some hideous navy maternity dress. Could it be right that the woman she was consulting about her own fertility should be so obviously fecund? Liz felt like a prune in the presence of a plum. On the other hand, why shouldn't Dr Kent be fruitful?

And at least her relatively advanced age offered hope. Liz told herself not to be envious, clamped a broad smile on her face, and congratulated Dr Kent far more effusively than was strictly necessary.

'A-ha,' said Dr Kent, a few minutes later. 'You've been taking your temperature for a year now?'

'Yes.'

'Not orally, I assume?'

'No!'

'I do have to check these things.'

'Mm . . . and I've been counting days.'

'Um-hmm.'

Did medical schools offer courses in cocking your head in doctorly fashion, and saying a-ha, and um-hmm? Liz resisted the urge to ask. 'It's been very stressful,' she said, instead.

'Of course. But no menstrual irregularities?'

'No.'

'Pain? Pain on intercourse?'

'No.'

'And your general health's good?'

'Yes.'

'Um-hmm. It sounds to me like a matter of timing. However careful you think you've been, it's possible you've simply been missing the monthly window of opportunity. Let's just rule that out, shall we?'

Dr Kent didn't wait for a reply, but launched into a long spiel about hormones. Horrormones, thought Liz, dejectedly.

How come the damn things had such power over her? She twisted her wedding ring and stared down at the surgery floor, which was covered with tatty, brown lino. *Follicle stimulating hormone,* she heard. *Luteinizing hormone.* She vaguely remembered the names from the books she'd read. Luteinizing hormone seemed to be the key. Dr Kent was going on about its surges, and how its surges were linked to ovulation, and how a woman could only get pregnant if she had sex when it surged. Or just after it had surged. Or something. Liz glanced up, nodded, and hoped she looked intelligent. How different it all was from the last time she'd been given a lecture on getting pregnant. Then she'd been thirteen, and giggly, and the school nurse had given the general impression that a quick snog would get her charges pregnant. Which it probably would have done, given the way pregnancy would have wrecked their lives. But now Liz was nearly three times as old, and she no longer snogged, instead she kissed Zack. But kissing Zack was clearly neither here nor there, and that, she thought, was truly sad.

'So I think you should use ovulation prediction kits for the next three months,' concluded Dr Kent. 'They'll let you time sex to egg release very accurately.'

'Do you prescribe them?'

'We haven't the funding. But they're available everywhere, at any pharmacy. A bit pricey, but worth it, if you get pregnant.'

'If.'

Dr Kent glossed over that.

'Give yourself three months. If you're still not pregnant after that, then come back.'

'Three months?' queried Liz. Three *more* months, she thought. Now that she'd forced herself to seek help, surely things should move quickly? Shouldn't today's visit have led at once to some kind of high-tech tests, or treatment? But over the counter kits were low-tech stuff. Would they even work? And was it fair to put her through three *more* months of trying, and of failing? She took a deep breath of the surgery's antiseptic air. 'And then what?'

Dr Kent smiled at her kindly.

'Buy yourself a prediction kit, Mrs Fielding, and let's just see what happens.'

William was thinking of his friend Charles's future, and also of his own. He stared at the jaunty card that lay on the desk in front of him, and thought, glumly, of the great joy it celebrated. The card showed a blue teddy bear, sprinkled with glitter, and holding a banner urging *enjoy your new baby boy!* William didn't much like this card, but then none of the others in the shop had been any better; he'd had a choice between twee, twee-er, twee-est. Someone else might have known where to get nicer ones, but he'd had no practice at buying cards, of any type. For years his mother had dealt with his social stationery, and all he'd had to do was sign it. Later, Penelope had taken over where Henrietta had left off. But

Annie was quite useless on the card front. She hadn't even sent cards at Christmas: *Too much to do!* she'd said airily, and, since they'd only just met, he'd found her attitude endearing. But then, nor had she bothered to give him a Valentine's card. He'd been the teeniest bit hurt about that, and had found her insouciance very surprising, given all the fuss Penelope had made about the annual orgy of red roses and choccy hearts. With such a track record, he'd decided he'd better buy Charles and Clarissa's card himself . . . Not that Annie's breezy attitude had been his sole consideration. Even if she'd been the sort to write her Christmas cards in August, he couldn't have asked her to buy this particular card. Nor could he now sign it in their joint names: *with love from William and Annie.* No. It simply wouldn't do. Charles was one of his oldest friends, and his own family and Clarissa's went way back. But Clarissa's family was also Penelope's, since they were sisters. Alas, things had been very awkward since the big split. It hadn't escaped his notice that Clarissa had sent the birth announcement to his mother, and not to him, and he guessed she'd probably be surprised to receive his glittery teddy bear. But he wanted to be friendly towards people he'd still like to count as friends . . . Yes, and his gesture of friendly intent would be quite ruined by the addition of Annie's name. It was such a pity! William sighed, and briefly pressed one hand to his eyes. Then he picked up his sleek fountain pen in readiness for signing his name, and *only* his name. But he became distracted, and instead traced the teddy with his finger. What was it about babies, he wondered, which made card designers go ga-ga?

Silly question! Didn't he know? William put down his pen, and leaned back against his leather padded chair. Of course he knew! It was just that he hadn't yet got used to the idea – which was the alarming idea of himself as broody. It was only very, very recently that William had started admitting to himself that he'd like a child. Perhaps, he mused, it was the season? Green forces always thrust strongest in spring. William glanced out of the window. His study was on the third floor of the Knightsbridge house, and it looked out over a garden square, to which only a resident's key gave access. Down in the semi-secret garden the fresh sap was rising. Seeds were sprouting, blossom was blooming, and bulbs were putting forth their shoots. The garden thrusted and thrummed with the thrill of beginnings; was it so very unlikely that his body should do the same?

Not that it really mattered, thought William, *why* this broodiness had crept upon him; it was the fact of it that would change his life. He hoped. He looked back to Charles and Clarissa's card, and mouthed the words emblazoned on the teddy's banner: enjoy your new baby boy! A boy! A baby boy! How William wanted to chase a little boy, and then to hear him squeal with glee as he caught him, and gave him a tickle. He wanted to kick a ball around with his son. He wanted a soft, small hand in his big, old, rough one. He wanted to be used as a climbing frame, to turn his knees into mountains, to look on innocence, adoringly, and to be looked at with trusting, defenceless adoration; unlike his own father, he wanted to tell his son he loved him.

William quite gave himself up to soft-focus images of himself as a father – and also to a glow of congratulatory self-satisfaction. Wasn't he noble, to relish these images! Wasn't he good for wanting fatherhood, when so many men of his generation just didn't! How grown-up he was, how mature, how adult! Not for him the empty, laddish hedonism of no commitment except to beer and football, fast cars, and porn. What a transformation Annie had wrought in him! William briefly recalled his pre-transformed state. He blushed at the memory of how he'd treated Penelope – but squashed the memory, flat. Penelope was his past. His future lay with Annie.

Thus far, William and Annie had been too busy screwing to discuss reproduction but, unlike Henrietta, William had no problem imagining his beloved cradling a baby. He pictured her happily crooning to a bundle wrapped in white, whilst he looked on fondly . . . and his mother looked on triumphantly. He was no longer offended by Henrietta's maternal impertinence, but chuckled to remember it: *I do expect grandchildren from your union.* Well, there was no reason she wouldn't get them! How nice it was that his grown-up desire to become a father would produce such pleasure in the two women he loved best in the world!

Mind you, Penelope would certainly get a shock when he became a father. William pursed his lips, and frowned. He didn't want to think about Penelope. But how could he not? After all, she was the one who'd first set him thinking about commitment, and about babies – cruel joke, that.

'What about children?' Penelope had asked him the afternoon of their putting asunder.

'*Children?*' he'd said, in tones of utter astonishment.

'Yes. Children. How do you feel about them? Do you want them?'

'Good God! No!'

'Well, I do.'

'Oh.'

Oh? Even at the time he'd recognized it as an inadequate response, but what else was he supposed to have said? Penelope had wanted children. He hadn't. They'd been like two people shouting at each other from opposite sides of an abyss. And children hadn't been the only issue on which they'd taken incompatible positions.

'After all,' Penelope had continued, 'children are what marriage is all about.'

'Marriage?' he'd squeaked.

'Yes,' Penelope had replied, her eyes like bayonets. '*Marriage.*'

William had remained silent in the face of the dreaded M word. *Oh, God!* He'd thought, *Mr and Mrs and then mummy and daddy* . . .

At the time it had seemed like a death sentence. He'd had to dump Penelope, of course. No choice. What else was a man to do when he sensed the matrimonial trap closing? . . . The strange thing was, the minute he'd put her aside, he'd met Annie. Now, a few months on, he could quite understand that marriage was an honourable estate, ordained for the procreation of children. Soon he was going to be a husband, and then a father: his family's bulwark against the world. That was certainly honourable. And Annie would look so pretty when she was pregnant, so glowing, so radiant, so plumply content. William's eyes grew moist to think of it . . . but this was no good! He had no time to indulge in fancy; he was meeting a couple of chaps for lunch, and he really ought to leave soon. He pulled himself together, sharpish, and picked up his pen. *Dear Charles and Clarissa,* he wrote, *welcome to little Edward. I do hope he's a good baby, and that you are managing to get some sleep . . .*

Caroline never got enough sleep, and she rarely lunched; she was a lady who coffee-morninged, a paid up member of one of Ryleford's many coffee covens. Her fellow coven members, Lucy, Emma, and Sophie, were all sweetie-pies – kind, generous, and forgiving. Nevertheless, their coffee mornings very often made grouchy, ungrateful Caroline want to scream. In her meaner moods, after a bad few days with Nat and Louis, she was wont to wonder whether there was any being more consciously respectable, self-satisfied and unambitious than the non-working mother? Granted, her friends had reason to be smug – yes, yes, they were doing right by their kids. Possibly

– but that was simply no excuse. And what could excuse the pleasure with which they donned the mantle of martyrs? Martyred mothers should, she thought, have gone out with the Ark, and yet, this morning, full blown martyrdom was being served along with coffee and biscuits.

Sophie's, Lucy's and Emma's husbands all worked similar hours to Simon, and the martyrs were discussing one of their favourite torments: absentee fathers.

'It all falls to us,' sighed Sophie.

'You know we really are effectively single mums,' agreed Emma, rolling her eyes.

'Yes,' added Lucy, 'we're the ones who ensure they don't drink bleach, or play with razor blades, or swallow marbles.'

The mothers were sitting in Emma's big sunroom-cum-playroom, and they all now involuntarily glanced out into the garden, where five toddlers were variously occupied. Nat and Louis were chucking grass cuttings at each other. Lucy's Tabitha was poking at the ground with a stick. Emma's Phoebe was on the slide, and Sophie's Hector was hiding in the playhouse.

'Yeah,' said Caroline, after the mothers had established that their offspring were safe, for the moment. 'We're the ones who tell them what's important, and what's trash; what to believe, and what not to; how to behave, and how not to.'

The other three mothers looked at her, unsure what to make of her belligerent tone.

'We're always *there* for them,' said Sophie, after a beat.

'Doing the most important job in the world.'

'And it's not as if we're paid for it. Why not a wage for full-time mothers?'

'Because,' snorted Caroline, 'any fool can become a mother. Or almost any fool. You don't need qualifications. There's never any shortage of volunteers for the job. Why pay us, when you don't have to? And *who'd* pay? The State? Higher taxes – how would *that* go down round here?'

This was met by stunned silence. Lucy was the first to recover.

'It's not just a matter of economics!'

'It's the most important job in the world!'

'Except being the President of the United States, or something?' flashed Caroline.

'Surely you don't think that's more important than raising your own children!'

'And we get no thanks for it!'

'No appreciation!'

Emma decided it was time to circle back to her original refrain.

'We're just like single mums,' she sighed.

'Ha!' objected Caroline. 'How many single mums live in houses costing hundreds of thousands of pounds? How many have personal trainers?' She looked at Sophie. 'Or dog walkers.' She looked at Lucy. 'Or cleaners.' She didn't bother to fix anyone in her glare – all four of them had cleaners, if only for an hour or two a week.

'Gosh!' said Sophie brightly. 'Quite the socialist, aren't we?'

'Well, we do have choices!' Caroline was by now starting to wave her arms. 'At any moment all of us could demand our husbands pack in their jobs. We could tell them to find something more family friendly. But none of us will.'

'No,' agreed Lucy, very sternly. 'Indeed we won't.'

She didn't bother to spell out why not – it was obvious to all of them. The drop in income would be too great. They might get behind with their mortgages, and they'd have to give up their dreams of moving into even bigger properties. The toddlers now playing in the garden, all of whom were down for private nurseries, might have to go to *state schools*. Horrors! State schools made a nosedive down the socio-economic ladder a dead cert. Or so thought Sophie, Emma and Lucy. And also Caroline. She was bolshie, but she didn't kid herself: she was completely at one with all the other Ryleford mums on the income/schooling/status triangle, and the importance of aspiring to its pinnacle. But at least, she thought, indulging in her own off-putting smugness, she was open about it. Although what was the value of honesty? This morning, all honesty did was make her long to grab a knife and run amok in an orgy of suburban blood.

Jo would have called it going postal – for some reason, postal workers in the States were very prone to running amok, although usually with guns, not with knives. Despite the ever-present danger that she'd be mown down by a loon with an Uzi, Jo was very eager to get back to her adopted homeland. Would this flight never be over? She flew often, and she was usually an excellent flier. It helped that, like tonight – or today, or whatever it was – she nearly always flew business class. Her routine was to put on her eyeshade, put in her earplugs, and snuggle under her blanket the very moment the plane left the ground. Meals? Movies? Wine? She turned them all down in favour of a good sleep. But this flight was different. Tonight – this afternoon, in New York – she simply couldn't switch off her thoughts, which were swirling around Brett, like dust around a vortex. Anyway, she felt far too sick to sleep, just as she had on the trip over – strange, since she never normally got airsick.

Jo threw off her blanket, and pushed up her eyeshade. The cabin was quiet and dimly lit; the man seated next to her was asleep, snoring slightly, his mouth agape. How unattractive he looked, thought Jo, and what a strange intimacy, to stare down onto the face of a sleeping stranger. What would he think, if he woke up now? Jo quickly glanced away and looked around the cabin. Most of her fellow passengers were also sleeping, although here and there someone tapped away at a laptop, and the cabin crew glided around like nurses on a night ward. Jo wished they were real nurses; she felt dreadful. The recycled air was dry and fusty, and she could almost feel germs reproducing all around her. But what to do? She could scarcely stop breathing, although she *could* protect herself from deep vein thrombosis, and with that in mind, she began to circle her ankles, vigorously. Her eyes followed her shoeless feet as they turned first clockwise, then anti-clockwise. She could see her toes through the fine mesh of her stockings, her nails varnished a deep plum. Brett had never painted her toes, nor had he ever complimented her on her feet – although that was scarcely surprising. Personally Jo thought feet, though necessary, were deeply unattractive. Hers were no exception, and nor were his, although the rest of him could easily have featured in an advert for male underwear. True, he was in his late thirties, and so too old to be a model, but he'd bought into the American dream of eternal youth, and he'd looked after himself very well – he worked out, ate right, didn't smoke, didn't drink much. No, he hadn't let himself down, and Jo felt sure that even New York's hardest bitten women would have stepped oblivious into the paths of trucks and taxis on catching a glimpse of his firm, toned body rearing on a Times Square billboard. Thirty feet of abs and pecs, and perfect teeth? There'd have been squashed women all over the place. Jo abruptly stopped circling her feet. A squashed woman? Was that what she was?

No! Certainly not! She was an *Other* woman, that was all. And, sure, an Other woman was something no rational woman would ever choose to be, but it couldn't be helped, it was just the way life was. *Marcie* was the squashed woman, if anyone was. Yes, and someday soon, Marcie would have to be confronted with the new reality . . . or would she? Would Brett ever take his wife aside and say, *Sorry, babe, but now it's like this* . . . Perhaps. And then again, perhaps not. There were, after all, those three little girls. Jo shivered; she suddenly felt cold as a ghost. Which was fair enough. She *was* a sort of ghost, a shade haunting Brett's relationship with Marcie, and with his daughters . . . How could she fail to feel insubstantial, when the relationship at the core of her life did not officially exist? She felt as if she were being airbrushed out of her own present, as surely as some old-style communist leader, airbrushed out of the past. Except she was colluding with her airbrushing. She was as careful about hiding her relationship with Brett as he was. It wasn't just Marcie, it was that Brett was her boss. He had to worry about charges of sexual harassment, but she had her worries, too: screwing the boss just wasn't on. It was cheesy. It was tacky. It was clichéd and undignified.

Brett and Jo both worked at United American Bank, where Brett, the head of trading, was first among raptors. Even in an environment where most people would have sold their grannies to turn a quick buck, he was known for his ruthless-ness. His attitude to the competition was simple: crush 'em. He didn't moderate it much for his colleagues, but came at them with a knife in the stomach. On The Floor – the trading floor – they called him either The Extra Terrestrial, because of his alien eyes, or The Verminator, because verminating was what he did best. He shot at vermin. Bang!

Brett's aim at women was as true as it was at vermin. It was as if he had some divinely conferred power to inspire female devotion. Last autumn, Jo had been felled by his charismatic, alien gaze, directed solely at her. She'd briefly told herself not to get involved with a married man: He'll only use you, a voice within her head had hissed. Think of his wife! Think of his children! But her resolve had dissolved in the solvent of Brett's ruthless intensity. And she was glad it had. She'd quickly discovered his ruthless intensity did not stop at the bedroom door. Between the sheets all that violence, all that vehemence was focused on *her*. Jo remembered it, and shivered again. Brett could sear her soul to flesh, and blast her flesh to mush. He could turn her body inside out, as easily as if it were a rubber glove, and expose her shiny, quivering guts to the world . . .

But so what, if she couldn't openly acknowledge him? And it wasn't just a matter of scrupulousness around her colleagues. She hadn't even dared admit she was dating him to Liz, her closest confidante, let alone to her other sisters, or to Ursula. Why was this? Why had she kept silent? Was it simply that an adulterous relationship was scarcely a fit topic of conversation when her family was celebrating an engagement? Or was it because she'd known, only too well, precisely what her mother and her sisters would have said? Jo scowled. In theory, she, her mother, and her sisters, all believed women should show solidarity – and you didn't do that by nicking another woman's man. In theory, they all believed children should be at the centre of the moral universe – and you couldn't put them there if you were prepared to snatch a child's father from his home. In actual fact, they all knew that love made you vulnerable. Jo knew that her mum and her sisters would have worried that by becoming a man's mistress she'd made herself *extra* vulnerable to pain and disappointment. They'd have offered lectures or, at the very least, unwanted advice. Jo had known these things, so instead of owning up to Brett, she'd lied that she was between men, right now.

That lie had felt much falser to her than any of the lies she'd told at work. It had almost made her wonder whether Brett was worth all the deception, and the secrecy. And *almost* wondering, she now reflected sourly, was pretty much the same as wondering. The trip home had been so unsettling. In New York, the walls between her and other people were of brick, or of stone, and it was liberating. In New York she was free to be whoever she wanted to be, and to behave however she chose to behave, without fear of censure or even of comment. But the walls between herself and her mother, and herself and her sisters, were of translucent glass. And there was just so much you couldn't get away with when you were semi-visible to other people. Jo sighed. Surely this confusion was temporary, a short-lived product of all the turmoil she had felt – and still felt – over Annie's engagement?

The plane began to bounce a bit, and the 'fasten seatbelts' light flashed up. Jo checked that hers was clunked shut, and wished she could buy a seatbelt to protect her against worse types of bumpiness. Her life was a veritable mogul field of inconsistencies and contradictions. Here she was, one of Wall

Street's finest, and a total mess. She had the veneer of cynicism essential to life in New York, but she didn't *want* to be cynical, she wanted to be a romantic. She was a mistress, but she wanted to believe in marriage. She looked askance at cookie-cutter brides, all billowing in white, but she wanted to believe in the promise of the big white wedding, all billowing with glamour, romance, and hope. I'll be with you, and hold your hand, until we both grow old. That was how it should be, and how it was for her sisters. One man, one woman, two souls linked for all eternity, two people, once young, growing old together and then being buried in the same grave. Caroline and Simon. Liz and Zack. And now even baby Annie, and her William. Jo began to circle her feet again, more maniacally than before, and reminded herself that she was delighted for her youngest sister. Delighted. And she was. But she was also jealous. Annie was five years her junior, and yet she was the one getting married. Was that fair? Not that Jo had felt resentful when Caroline, also her junior, had married Simon, but then, Caroline and Simon had married so young the only possible reaction had been alarm – misplaced alarm, as things had turned out, since Caroline and Simon seemed very happy. And now Annie, too, looked set for happiness. Jo scowled, and consoled herself that Annie's choice seemed very surprising: William, with his ruddy, fleshy, English looks, and his horrible navy blazer was not the man she'd have picked out for her sister. He was so unlike Annie's ex, Ming Kwan. Ming Kwan's face had been all planes, with cheekbones sharp enough to kill.

He had been so fluid, where William was so solid. Ming Kwan had been so lithe; he'd padded and prowled, he'd been louche and farouche. Jo could have gone for him herself, if he hadn't been Annie's. And so *obviously* Annie's – the two of them had seemed perfect for each other. But so what? That was love for you, thought Jo resentfully, love, the four-letter thing that brought people together, however unsuited they seemed, and which spat them out, mangled, even if they seemed an ideal match.

Was Jo one of love's victims? It was not a question she could face without alcohol, so she called over a trolly dolly. Wine was dehydrating at 30,000 feet, and dehydration was very bad for her skin, nevertheless she asked for a glass. Whilst she waited for it, she remembered something she spent much of her waking life trying to forget: Brett had never taken her in his arms and whispered, or sobbed, or screamed *I love you.* He'd said flattering things – extremely flattering things – about her body, and about sex. But he'd never said *I love you.* And she'd never asked. She'd often wanted to – she was a trader, just as averse to uncertainty as the markets, which invariably plummeted at its merest whiff. And she was also a woman, who needed to know. But she'd never asked: *Brett, do you love me?* Something about his extra-terrestrial eyes had always stilled her tongue. Although what, precisely? Jo closed her own eyes and tried not to answer the question. Perhaps she'd have succeeded at ground level, but she wasn't on the ground. She was high above the earth, whizzing along in a tiny tube of metal, a speck suspended in all the vastness of the sky, and all of a sudden, she could *see*. Up here the air was thin and pure, and the view was clear – even with her eyes shut. She hadn't asked Brett, *Do you love me?* because the question invited a lie.

Do you love me?

Sure I love you, silly.

No, not silly: sensible as a teapot. Jo groaned and slammed down her hands on her arm-rests, completely unmindful that she risked waking the stranger who slept beside her.

Three

Annie was in bed, staring at the ceiling, willing William to get on with it. His grunts were getting louder, and she hoped he was undergoing an increase in psychic volume, too, since she hungered for the rapid decrease that would inevitably follow. She truly wished she could get just a little more excited by her lover's evident excitement, but the problem was, she just didn't love him.

No! No! No!

Annie would not let herself think like this! She would not! Instead, she'd try. She moaned, a bit, and thrashed her limbs, a bit. Loving William, she told herself, between theatrical gasps, was neither here nor there. And, okay, it was a bit strange to be telling herself this in the middle of sex but, after all, men were only genitals on legs, what did it matter if those genitals were caramel-coloured, or pastry-coloured? It surely didn't matter a jot whether they were attached to William, or to Ming Kwan?

Oh, God, Ming Kwan! Annie genuinely groaned, and

surrendered to memories of his velvet kisses, his silken taste, his satin scent, his skin. Oh, his skin! William's skin was just a hide. But Ming Kwan's skin had been like some cloth of heaven. Annie remembered it draped over her body, and arched her back, trying to recapture the way it had fallen, its particular ripples and graceful folds. She clawed her fingers along William's spine, and clawed for Ming Kwan. She stretched her mouth to William's, and encountered Ming Kwan's. Soon her gasps stopped sounding like they'd been dubbed, and she began to gasp in earnest.

A few minutes later William was cradling his sobbing beloved in his arms, stroking her hair, and thinking sex with her was the best he'd ever had – of course it was, otherwise he wouldn't be marrying her. He grinned to himself in the dark, thinking of all the nights to come, and of the way in which Annie was his, now, and his alone. And she'd be even more his when she had their baby – a prize not only won, but branded with his ownership. William licked her delicious ear, then bit it.

'Darling,' he whispered, offering her, or so he thought, the greatest gift, a gift consecrated to their joint future, 'how about trying for a baby?'

The effect was not at all as William had anticipated; Annie abruptly stopped crying, and went rigid in his arms.

'A baby?' she managed, at last.

'Well, not immediately,' blustered William, realizing he'd bungled. 'But, y'know, when we're married.'

Annie stickily unpeeled herself from his chest, and sat up. 'Why?' she asked.

'Why?' parroted William. 'Y'mean, why a baby?'

'Yes.'

William blinked a couple of times. 'Well,' he began. 'Y'know . . . uh, we are getting married . . . uh, it's what life's all about, isn't it? I mean, y'know, I do want children. And, uh, we are getting married.'

'You already said that.'

'What?'

'That we are getting married.'

'Well, y'know . . . I mean, we *are*.'

Annie flopped back against her pillows. She puffed her cheeks and blew out the air on a long breath.

'God, William,' she said. 'I'll have to think about this.'

It didn't cross William's mind that Annie might mean she'd have to think about whether or not she wanted to go through with the wedding; he assumed she meant she'd have to think about whether or not to try for a baby. He felt mortified! Humiliated! Crestfallen! He had revealed to Annie his secret – and admirable, and adult – broodiness. How could she have rejected it so roundly? And how could he not have foreseen that she would? He loved her – so shouldn't he know her all through? Shouldn't he know her the way he knew blue, just by looking at it? Quite evidently, he didn't. What if Annie didn't want children at all? William sniffed, in the dark. Don't be stupid! he chided himself, of course she wants children! It was just that he'd surprised her. It was just that she wasn't ready yet. Surely it was simply that Annie wanted some time alone with him before they got swamped by nappies. William cheered up. Time alone together was fine. After all, he wanted some time alone with Annie, too. And they had time. They were to be married. They had time, in spades.

Time was running out. Liz knew that. The days were sliding by, quicker and quicker. This one, too, was almost over. She'd already dished up supper, a nursery-style meal of shepherd's pie followed by ice-cream, but with no kids to eat it. Now she and Zack were alone in their multi-coloured, crazily patterned sitting room, where she was trying to make sense of the instructions leaflet that had come with her OvuTrue ovulation prediction kit. Zack, meanwhile, was pretending to watch football on the telly, although he was actually watching his wife.

Liz knew Zack was watching her, and she was unnerved by his attention. And by the football. Despite fairy-boots players with pop-stars for wives, she persisted in believing the beautiful game was nothing but an excuse for mob behaviour – men getting together, secreting yobosterone and then surging out of the ground to terrify women unlucky enough to cross their psyched-up paths. No wonder she couldn't concentrate.

'Turn that off!' she snapped.

Zack, who had mastery of the remote, immediately obliged.

'So?' he asked, after the screen went dead.

'What d'you mean, *so?*' asked Liz, who knew the answer.

Zack nodded with studied casualness at the OvuTrue leaflet in Liz's hand.

'What's it say?'

'This might as well be written in Japanese,' Liz grumbled. 'You'd need a degree in chemistry to understand it.'

'It can't be that bad,' soothed Zack. 'It must've been written with lay people in mind. People like us, who don't know much about science.'

'So you'd think, but listen! "Bottle B must be prepared for use prior to using the test kit. To prepare bottle B, remove the cap. Also remove the cap from bottle one. Squeeze all the liquid from bottle B into bottle one. Shake gently. After preparation bottle B should sit at room temperature for ten minutes before first use."'

'So bottle B goes into bottle one, which then becomes bottle B?'

Liz re-read the instructions. 'Dunno,' she said. 'But there's bottles A, C, and D, too. I have to collect my urine between 10 a.m. and 8 p.m. There's a test pad, and a pipette. I have to add six drops of urine, three at a time, and then add the stuff from bottles A, B, C, and D at very precise time intervals. *One* minute or *three* minutes. I have to use a watch with a second hand to time myself.'

Zack tapped his own watch. 'Precision timing? I'll help with that.'

Zack's watch was of steel and leather; it looked well-fed

and comfortable, like a fat cat C.E.O. But it was a fake, a sham. Liz had picked it up very cheaply, on Canal Street, in New York's China Town, one time when she'd been visiting Jo. Now she dared not look at it. During their honeymoon years, she and Zack had often teased each other they were Mr and Mrs Smug. *You can take me for granted*, they'd assured each other. But was it true? All at once Liz felt as sick as if she actually were pregnant, and had just walked into a kitchen reeking of meat. What if she were barren? It was a biblical sort of word, not the sort of word you heard very often these days, just like you didn't see Old Testament prophets wandering down the street, but nevertheless it was a useful word, thought Liz: it would describe exactly how she'd feel if she couldn't conceive. And also how she'd feel if, in consequence, Zack left her for some more fertile woman. Would he do that? Would he? Liz still dared not look at her husband's watch, let alone his face, so instead she stared at her shoes – new ballet pumps in a hot pink suede.

Jo's watch was a neat, discreet little Cartier – real, not fake – and her shoes were block heels, in black patent leather. Both her shoes and her watch looked professional and sexy – but not *too* sexy. There were working girls, and then there were working girls – Jo didn't want to look like a hooker on the job as she went about the daily tasks of her own job. For work, she wore clothes that were simple, elegant, and black. She wore divine little dresses, and delightful little suits. Her silkily slinky shirts were an exception to the all-black rule – they were in eye-catching, jewel colours: emerald green, ruby red, amethyst, citrine.

Jo was undoubtedly a very clothes-conscious woman, but today, even by her own high standards, she felt terribly aware of her skirt – for some reason, it was uncomfortably snug around her waist. Why could that be? Jo hadn't changed her diet, or her exercise routine. She knew she couldn't be pregnant, since she was so careful about the pill, so she must be bloating with sadness, she supposed – sadness and all this dead time for brooding on it. Today she had very little to distract her; things were dull on the trading floor, the markets were quiet, and would remain so until the Fed made a much anticipated announcement about interest rates. Jo had sat all morning at her screen, her head full of personal stuff, rather than the dollar/yen exchange rate, or the dollar/euro. Once, a few years back, she'd lost 60 million bucks on a trade – not through incompetence, or she'd have been fired, but as a result of market turmoil, caused by turmoil in Washington. You couldn't always hedge against these things, and the huge loss had in no way been her fault, but still she'd felt sick, and panicky, and cold – just like she felt today. She couldn't ask Brett, *Do you love me?* Not her fault. Because the question invited a lie. A huge loss. And a lie could only mean Brett didn't love her. No hedge.

Fortunately, having no hedge was not the same as having no strategy. On Wall Street, the rule was: you gotta problem, you deal. Jo was determined to introduce some of that steeliness into her private life; she'd fire Brett. But when? And where? And how? Jo leaned back in her ergonomically designed swivel chair, and stared at the market information displayed on her screen. She supposed she could always send Brett an e-mail: u r sakd ☺. But no. A workplace renunciation was out of the question. And she certainly didn't want to break the news at home. At home, she'd probably cry, whilst Brett would probably try to seduce her – and he'd probably succeed. Jo needed somewhere public, but anonymous. A place where strangers would act as a brake on tears – hers – and shouting. A stroll in Central Park, perhaps? Or a restaurant? The possibilities foodwise were endless: Thai; Chinese; French; Mexican. And the advantages of a restaurant were many. The other diners would discourage histrionics. Wine would ease potential difficulties. Jo hesitated, stretched to her keyboard, withdrew her hand – then stretched it out again. She typed one word, and clicked the mouse. There would be an e-mail, after all. Her electronic billet-doux to Brett contained a command disguised as a deceptively simple invitation: *Dinner?*

As usual, Simon had skipped breakfast. Another day, another doleur. He was inching towards Waterloo on the 6.20. Yup, the train had been delayed. Yup, the ancient carriage was stinky and shaky, but at least Simon had managed to bag a coveted window seat, and at least he was safe from the hostile eyes of the less fortunate. He knew those forced to stand were jealous, and he was grateful to be hidden behind the rosy pages of the *Financial Times*, even though the economic news was grey as newsprint.

Simon read the *FT* everyday. Like Jo, he worked for an investment bank – Global Commerce Bank, or GCB. But though employed in the same industry, Jo and Simon worked in different worlds. Jo was front office; Simon was back office. In any bank, front and back office could have been on different planets. Jo was one of the high-rollers gambling millions with one click of a computer mouse, whereas Simon dealt with the settlement of transactions generated by her type. Settlement involved sending confirmations of deals to clients, and paying and collecting money. Grunt administration was dull and dun-coloured, lowly and relatively poorly paid, but Simon had no desire to join his sister-in-law on the hurly-burly of the trading floor; the risks she took would have shattered him. Unlike Jo, he'd always been risk-averse, always valued safety. So had Caroline. It was one of the things that had brought them together.

Caroline and Simon had met at university – a dozy, cosy academic backwater. Caroline had been reading business studies, and Simon accountancy. They'd both been quiet, cautious students. Neither of them had ever experimented with drugs or unsuitable partners, they'd never dabbled in politics, or heartbreak, they'd never gone to raves, dressed from skips, dyed their hair blue, or pierced their noses. Then, one morning in their second year, they'd happened to sit next to each other at an economics lecture entitled 'Futures: understanding the basics'. The lecturer had meant the financial futures markets, which neither Caroline, nor even Simon, if he were honest, had ever properly understood, but after that morning they'd often joked that they'd come away understanding something very basic about their own futures; they were meant to be.

And so they were – or so Simon still thought. His mind slid to his wife, as his eyes stared at the doom-laden headlines of the *FT*. He was so proud of Caroline, and of the life he and she had built together. The ordinarily miraculous happiness of a wife, a house, and children was all he'd ever wanted. And he'd got his heart's desire – knock on wood. Simon superstitiously, and surreptitiously, stretched out his hand to touch the carriage's wooden window frame. So what if, these days, Caroline's bad moods dragged from one end of the week to the other? It was only because she was tired. Shopping, cooking, cleaning, she did all that. Of course she did. That was the deal they'd made. She got domesticity, he got commuting. Ancient trains. Delays. Horrible fellow commuters. This morning he'd left the house in the chilly dark, and he wouldn't return until chilly darkness yet again descended. It was like that every day. Simon sighed. What a life! Especially for a father. He knew he was missing out. He'd been there for the drama of Nat's and Louis's births, but had he been there when they'd started to crawl? Or to walk? Or when they'd tried ice-cream for the first time? No. No. No. And the boys were missing out, too, for the same reason: he was never there. Still, no point in complaining. He had kids, and he just had to get on with it. A good husband and father provided for his family, and that was that. His job might be boring and repetitive, but at least it put the bacon on the table.

And at least he *had* a job. These days, jobs came and went with far more regularity than the Ryleford trains. Simon gloomily shook out his paper. The *FT* was no place for sentiment. Unlucky office fodder who were about to be given the bullet often learned of their fate through its pages. *No Name Bank is focusing on core competencies and improving efficiency by responding to customer needs.* Oh yeah? It wasn't quite that bleak this morning, but it was still dreary. Simon frowned as he read. The R word throbbed up at him from every other paragraph. Recession. And the D words, too, were much in evidence. Devaluation. Deflation. Even – whisper it not – depression. Simon sighed and shut his paper. Outside, through the grimy windows, Canary Wharf was just coming into view. The tower was such an optimistic, show-off, times-are-good sort of building, that at the sight of it he couldn't help but succumb to a shiver of fear.

Liz's career was subject to the economy just as much as Simon's. As a child she'd been drawn to anything textile-related, from her grandmother's antique table linens, to her mother's shiny PVC mackintosh, to her own candlewick bedcover. She'd collected scraps of fabric the way some girls had collected dolls: velvet; broderie anglais; linen; lace; crimpolene;

nylon – she'd stowed shoeboxes full of oddments under her bed. Her vocation had been clear; she'd followed it, and become a textile designer. All had gone swimmingly until, in her late twenties, her career had taken a slightly strange turn. She'd been working for a once-mighty retail consortium, which had been brought to the brink of collapse by weak markets and bad management. The consortium had been sold off to a slicker one, and Liz had thought she was going to be made redundant in the shake-out. But no. Her new employers had owned Noodle O'Doodle, a chain specializing in children's wear. Liz, who was in no position to argue, had been seconded to Noodle O'Doodle, where it had been discovered very quickly that she had a flair for drawing cute little animals – bunnies, piggies, doggies, quack-quacks, kitties, moo-moos and lambkins. Drawing animal motifs for children's clothes was a highly specialist job; Liz had found her niche. Or else she'd been pigeonholed. Either way, she'd been locked in a big-eyed, floppy-eared menagerie ever since, and the dominant colours of her working days were baby blue, pale pink, and soft yellow.

Today was a soft yellow day. Liz was at her drawing board, concentrating so hard on a family of ducks that she hadn't thought about getting pregnant for all of five minutes. But then her phone rang.

'Liz? It's Miranda.'

For Liz, soft yellow deepened to ochre, and deepened again to brown. Her happy family of ducks went out of focus, and their webbed feet and feathers morphed into a sharp-edged

OvuTrue box. All at once she was reclaimed by the familiar ache of absence, and of emptiness. She took a deep breath.

'Hi, Miranda,' she said.

Miranda was Noodle O'Doodle's design director, and Liz's boss. She was a good boss, quick to praise where praise was due, and quick to take the blame where it wasn't. She and Liz were of similar ages, and their shared interests in colour, design, and texture were usually a glue between them, but recently their friendliness had been replaced by tension and embarrassment. The miasma had wafted in a few weeks back, when Miranda had taken Liz aside, and confided that she and her husband had been trying for a baby for almost a year now. Liz had confided absolutely nothing, just nodded briskly.

'Under the circs,' Miranda had added, 'this job can be a bit depressing. All the baby products, y'know?'

'I can imagine.'

'Most of the time I'm okay, but your work . . . I do find it especially upsetting. So I was wondering . . . would you mind clearing your drawings away whenever I have to visit your office?'

Liz had flushed, and her flush had spread until it covered her whole body, a prickly, itchy rash of distress.

'Of course,' she'd said. 'No problem. I quite understand.'

'I thought I might come down,' Miranda now suggested, a note of apology in her voice. 'I mean, if it's not too much trouble?'

Liz merely grunted.

'Or else you could come up, if you'd rather?'

'What d'you need to see me about?' Liz spoke gracelessly, and gracelessly added a quick stroke to her mother duck's beak – what a mistake! The thing now looked more duck-billed platypus than duck.

'Its the dyers,' explained Miranda. 'The autumn greens are causing them terrible problems. I've got the swatches – all in shades of piss.'

'Oh dear!' sighed Liz. 'You'd better bring them down.' She paused a moment, sniffed, and blinked hard. 'And don't worry. I'll clear my stuff away.'

Jo was determined not to cry so early in the evening, but she simply couldn't get into the dress she'd planned to wear. She angrily yanked it off, and held it at arms' length. It was a silver sheath which was supposed to ripple down her body like water, and which, when worn properly, shimmered with shark appeal. *Look what you're losing!* That was the message she'd intended to send to Brett – and to herself, too. But how could she say anything reassuring to herself now? Tonight her dress hadn't rippled, it had strained and stretched. She was fat! Whatever she wore, she'd look a rag! Jo crossly tossed the dress onto her bed, and turned to contemplate her wardrobe. What *did* a fat woman wear for rightsizing her lover? Rightsizing. That was a current euphemism for sacking. Jo imagined a nameless, faceless trader returning home from work, and greeting his wife.

Darling, I've been rightsized.

Oh yes? And which particular part of you would that have been, then?

Jo grinned to herself and felt slightly better – up to contemplating her body in the full-length mirror which hung inside her wardrobe door. She was naked but for her thong knickers, and there was no denying her tits seemed to have risen like bread dough. Still, since there was nothing she could do about it, she decided she might as well work with the situation and wear something low-cut and revealing. And black. She'd always worn black because she liked it, but now she gloomily predicted she'd be forced to wear it for its slimming properties. Well, at least she had plenty of choice. She riffled through her mourner's wardrobe, and dug out a clinging black top, cut so that it would have given a steam iron a cleavage. Next she pulled out a black skirt in tiered silk chiffon; it had always been too big for her, but now it fitted perfectly. She decided to wear pointy, slingback shoes, in scarlet ostrich leather, just for the hell of it. Moonstone jewellery finished off her outfit. This set, necklace, bracelet and earrings, had been a gift from Annie, and she'd always liked the way the pale stones glimmered mysteriously at her throat and wrist and ears. Jo twisted this way and that before her mirror. Not too bad, she decided, uncertainly. Not quite diva, but probably a wow.

*

Jo regretted her skirt the moment she stepped through the door of Hispano. Chiffon tiers, bodega frills just made for dancing, would have been fine Uptown, but they were not, she thought, quite the thing in a Downtown tapas bar. How could she have been so silly? It was as if she'd worn a sombrero to Mexico. Still, the ambience in Hispano was just as she'd hoped it would be. The place had been hotter than jalapeño until a few months back, but now it was padded out with Midwesterners, looking for an authentic New York experience. Nobody, including herself, could make a scene in front of these plaid-shirted whales, and there was absolutely no chance she and Brett would run into anybody they knew.

Brett was already perched at the bar, behind which a sweating Latino chef presided over a gas grill – occasionally alarming geysers of flame shot towards the ceiling. Brett had often dumped women in restaurants, their advantages as settings in which to pull the ripcord had been conveyed to him by osmosis in the male locker room back in high school. He guessed what was coming tonight; nevertheless, his pose was relaxed. He was dressed in the most elegant of suits – not the suit of a suit, but the suit of a predator at the top of the food chain, who lived by the maxim: eat what you kill, and bury the bones. He oozed confidence, extruded arrogance, and generally gave the impression that he might, at any moment, whip his cock out and ask his date to suck it.

Not that Jo could see this. Now that she was actually in Brett's presence, she found herself once more a victim of his eyes – those eyes with the magical power to inspire devotion. And it wasn't just his eyes that got to her. As she crossed the room towards her lover she was acutely aware of his whole body, and of his tiniest movement. He brushed his hand across his knee; she felt him brush it over her thigh, and her flesh rose in goosebumps. He tapped his foot to the rhythm of the background flamenco music; she felt her innards twang to another rhythm. He smiled; so did she. He was a master of the universe and she was enthralled, a slave girl, unable to flee.

No she *wasn't*! Jo *wasn't* a slave girl, and she *would* flee. Brett gave her a low wolf-whistle as she slid onto the stool next to his.

'Don't give me that!' she snapped, taking them both aback by the suddenness with which she'd initiated hostilities. 'Sorry,' she modified, dashing at her skirt. 'This thing was a mistake.'

Brett wasn't fooled. He looked at Jo a moment, then shrugged, and poured her a glass of red wine – he'd already started on the bottle.

'So,' he said, 'dinner?' He spoke pure gedouddahere-Noo-York, but even now, Jo heard arias, in Italian.

'Yes,' she muttered.

'But we're not here for the food, I guess?'

'No.'

'So what's the skinny?'

Jo drew herself up and folded her arms across her chest. Her desire for certainty glowed bright. Why beat about the bush? She wanted to say something irrevocable. She didn't want to give herself room for last-minute dithering.

'I'm retrenching.'

Brett knew that when banks rightsized their employees they did it in the name of retrenchment. He pursed his lips, and nodded.

'I see.'

'You *see*?' True, Jo hadn't expected him to weep. She hadn't expected him to prostrate himself before her, clasp her knees, and beg. Anyway, the point of the Midwesterners was to prevent that sort of carry on. But *I see*?

'You're de-hiring me,' clarified Brett.

Jo nodded, and Brett drew a bead on her with his eyes.

'Well, babe, remember what I always say about de-hiring.'

What Brett – The Verminator, The Extra-Terrestrial – always said about de-hiring was that the trick was to persuade the de-hiree that his retrenchment was a good idea, to get him to agree that United American Bank was doing him a favour by rightsizing him, and that he ought to be grateful.

'I haven't forgotten.'

'It would certainly be awkward if our affair got out at work.'

'Uh-huh.'

'You knew all along I was married.'

'And a father.'

'Yup.'

Jo took a breath, steadying herself to deliver some verbal

killer blow, but she couldn't think of one. Instead she looked at Brett's mouth, and remembered his kisses. She remembered his tongue, exploring, probing, showing off, and promising. Then she raised her eyes, and fell into his alien gaze. The two of them stared at each other a long, long moment.

'D'you love me, Brett?'

Brett wasn't a misogynist; he didn't hate women, he was just indifferent to them. But he wasn't indifferent to sex. Indeed, one of his two most cherished ambitions was that his life should be one long orgasm. The other was that he should remain young enough to enjoy sex, for ever. And why shouldn't he? He was a master of the universe; he'd never turn to dust. Women's bodies helped convince him – not – of this falsehood. And it didn't matter who the women were, since women were fungible.

Fungible is a technical term used on Wall Street to describe financial products. It means interchangeable. Bonds, for example, are often interchangeable, just like oranges on a deli shelf. And so, thought Brett, were women. They were replaceable. As soon as one started to whine about love or commitment, he dumped her and reached for another. And so, now, he would have to do with Jo. But he hadn't yet got her replacement lined up. There was, as yet, no glistening piece of candy ready and waiting in his candy jar. And until there was, he surely couldn't be expected to survive on pedestrian sex with Marcie? She was his *wife*, ferchrissakes!

'C'mon, babe,' he reassured his lover, 'sure I love you. Sure I do.'

Zack truly loved Liz. She was as necessary to him as oxygen or water, and as lovely as the breeze, the sea. He felt terrible for his wife over the baby business – and terrible for himself, too. How he longed to cradle a newborn child, to kiss his own nose in miniature, to worship his own tiny eyes. How he longed to breathe in his own baby's scent of talcum, and milk, and hope – and, underlying all these, the elusive scent of his own blood. And, oh, how he wished he could feel more hopeful that one day he would do these things, but the OvuTrue kit had really, really depressed him. A baby would be the culmination of his and Liz's love. It had been bad enough that their love had been subject to calendars, temperatures, and the state of Liz's secretions, but to Zack it seemed much, much worse that it was now subject to bottle A and bottle B, to pipettes, and urine test pads, and stopwatch timing. Science had no place in the bedroom, no place at all, and he felt bloody miserable that it had intruded.

This afternoon he felt particularly glum. His PA, Karen, was seven and a half months pregnant, and about to go on maternity leave. There was going to be a do for her in a few days, at which Zack would be expected to make a hearty, avuncular speech. Zack was good at this sort of thing. He was an adman, a creative, a copywriter. *Ooops! Saucy!* had been one of his; so had *Germs squirm when you blast 'em with Skjerm!* *(Cleanliness from Sweden)*. Zack could switch charm on and off like a tap in a strictly professional capacity, and for an ad he could conjure almost any mood. But in his personal life he didn't like to charm, to manipulate moods; at home he preferred wysiwyg – what you see is what you get – just as at home he preferred unpretentious jeans and T-shirts to the adman's sharp suits, self-consciously zany shirts, and silly eyewear. For him, Karen's bloated belly blurred the personal/professional distinction. It was an enormous reminder of his home life, throbbing around the office, and he didn't at all look forward to being hearty and avuncular in its grotesquely swollen presence.

But Karen had worked for him for three years, and there was no wriggling out of his speech-making responsibility. There'd been a whip-round for her, of course, and her gift was also too close to home for Zack's comfort. Linda, another of the PAs, had just brought it into his office together with a card for his signature.

'We thought she'd like the smellies,' she said, of a big, wicker basket packed with toiletries. 'Something for her, when everyone's thinking about the baby. And we got the clothes from Noodle O'Doodle, specially.'

A pile of baby clothes lay on Zack's desk. He picked up a pair of dungarees at random. They were of red corduroy, and embellished with an appliqué panda.

'Very nice.'

'Yes. D'you think Liz did them? We hoped she might have done.'

Zack traced the panda with his finger.

'Must have. She's the only one they've got doing animals.'

'Oh *good*,' said Linda. 'Karen'll be *so* pleased.'

Zack put down the dungarees and reached for a pen so he could sign Karen's card. 'I'll tell Liz,' he lied. 'She'll be delighted to think of Karen enjoying her stuff.'

Simon was determined to lie to Caroline, tonight. When she asked him if he'd had a good day, he'd smile, and say: yes, darling. But one of Global Commerce Bank's competitors had just announced it was axing 6,000 jobs across Europe, and his own company was now rife with rumours of a headcount squeeze. It was unsettling – but Simon didn't want to bother his wife with his fears. Why alarm her with talk of cuts? She'd only worry, and she really didn't have to. He hoped . . .

But Simon's hope was weak, and sickly. He and Caroline lived in a detached faux cottage in the Ryleford vernacular – all red brick, wisteria round the leaded windows, and pantiles circa 1955. As he turned the key in the solidly real lock, he suddenly imagined himself jobless, the mortgage falling into arrears, his wife and children destitute. Imagine it! The boys, homeless: shoeless, ragged street-children!

Despite the troubles at work, or perhaps because of them, Simon had made a superhuman effort to leave the office early, to give himself a fighting chance of seeing his snugly pyjama-ed boys before they went to bed. As soon as he stepped into the hall, he knew he'd failed. The house was quiet, which meant the twins were asleep. Simon sighed, and put down his briefcase.

'Hi Honey,' he yelled, hoping he might wake his sons, 'I'm home!'

Caroline was slumped on the sofa in the sitting room, trying to ignore the chaos of books and toys and biscuit crumbs strewn all over the carpet. She had a glass of wine in her hand. Though she'd never really drunk before she'd had children, she had a theory that motherhood would have made an alcoholic of the strictest teetotaller, and she was more than happy to set about proving it in her own case.

'I've had a shitty day!' she snarked, the moment her husband appeared in the doorway.

Simon realized at once that his wife was in a foul temper, but at the sight of her reclining amidst all the evidence of boisterous family life, his resolve to lie vanished. She, not the house, was his home, and tonight he needed the comforts of home.

'Me too!' he said piteously.

Alas, Caroline wasn't in the mood for wrapping her arms around her husband, neither literally nor metaphorically.

'I waited in all morning for the washing-machine man, who didn't show up. So I had to lug a bag of washing to the launderette. Wouldn't you know it: no service wash! The only good bit was this notice: "Please refrain from laundering horse blankets in our machines."' Caroline gave a quick snort of derision, then continued with her tale of woe. 'The boys were a nightmare, Nat threw a tantrum . . . and Louis took advantage of it to chuck laundry powder everywhere. I mean *everywhere*. They've both been vile all day!'

Vile? His beautiful, adorable boys *vile?* It was a corrosive word, and Simon felt it smoke through him, like sulphuric acid. All day he'd been suppressing anxiety and frustration, and now his feelings vented.

'For God's sake! You don't know you're born! It's not as if you're living in a cardboard box.'

'A cardboard box?' Caroline was puzzled.

'Street life! Diseases! Drugs! Prostitution!'

Caroline swung her legs onto the floor, and sat up. 'Simon,' she said calmly, 'what on earth are you talking about?'

'My hard work pays for you to lead a life of luxury!'

'Luxury? I just told you I spent today at the launderette!' Caroline smiled, but her smile did not diffuse the tension.

'Only because the washing machine I paid for's broken. Mostly you've got all day to play with the boys! To take them to birthday parties, go to coffee mornings and silly salad lunches!'

'I never do lunch – or hardly ever.'

'Ha! And what am *I* doing, whilst you're gallivanting? I'm sitting at a screen, plugging in data, pulling out data, getting shouted at, answering endless stupid, stupid questions . . .'

Caroline stood up. 'Of course, darling . . .' She spoke in a conciliatory tone, preparing to acknowledge she had no monopoly on exhaustion, or tedium, but Simon wouldn't let her.

'And then there's the commute! Four hellish hours a day, give or take!'

'Darling . . .'

'I'm just a wage slave, but for you life's one long round of fun!'

Fun? The word acted on Caroline's psyche as *vile* had on Simon's.

'*Fun?*' she repeated, recoiling as if from a snake. 'You think my life's *fun?*'

'Reading to the boys, singing to them, playing with them!'

Caroline laughed mirthlessly. 'Running around after them, clearing up after them, cooking for them, cleaning for them . . .'

'How can you complain?'

'How can you think my life's *fun?*'

'Anyway,' shouted Simon, executing a complete volte-face. 'Who wants fun?'

Caroline glared at her husband a long moment. 'I do!' she yelled back. 'And if you think my life's fun, you can try living it!'

Caroline realized what she'd said scarcely made sense, even before she'd slammed the front door behind her. How could Simon live her life? He was a man. She was a woman. He was he and she was she. Still, she hadn't got time for meta-physical niggles. She climbed into the Volvo and zoomed off in the general direction of anywhere that wasn't Ryleford. Driving wasn't her thing, and usually made her very nervous, but not tonight. Tonight she slammed through the gears with the casualness of a boy racer. *Slow down!* she told herself, as she did a hundred down a dark and twisty country lane, *you don't want to end up wrapped around a tree.* Thank God that was true! She really, really didn't want to end up dead – it just wasn't an option, now she had kids – and she pulled into the next available passing-place to save herself from the dangers of road rage. But the passing-place was unlit, deserted, and screened by trees. Was she now in danger from a lurking psychopath? Caroline hurriedly clicked down the door locks. This everyday action, this sensible precaution, only served to make her feel more than ever trapped. The car had got her. Life had got her. And what escape routes were available to a woman locked into her self, by marriage and twins? Not work. She'd been over those arguments a thousand times. Childcare. The commute. Blah, blah, blah. So what else? Escapist books? Escapist movies? Ha! How could she sink into either, when she never got ten minutes to herself? How could she slip into some character's engrossing life, when she was so firmly rooted in her own? And that was what she really wanted to do: she wanted to slip into somebody else's life . . .

No she didn't! Nat and Louis would have to come along, too! Caroline thumped the steering wheel in frustration. Somebody else's life would be no good to her, after all. She couldn't *be* anybody else with the boys in tow. She was their mother. And because she was their mother, she just had to make do with being her own boring self. Caroline thumped the steering wheel again . . . and as she thumped, she was thumped by a thumping great idea: why not escape, both her self and her life, by having an affair?

Well, why not? God, thought Caroline, she could really be herself with a secret lover. No role – except that of femme fatale, which any woman would want. No rules. No expectations. The bed she shared with a lover would provide a wide open space in which, after years of limping, she could at last run free. But it wasn't just that. There was regret to contend with, too. Her youth was slipping away, and in lots of ways she felt she'd never had it. She'd never been a rebel, a tearaway, a bad girl. What a prissy little goody two-shoes she had been! What sort of an eighteen-year-old chose to take a degree in *business studies* for God's sake? What had she been thinking of? Why not Assyriology, or astrophysics? Something wild, wonderful, and pretty much useless? But worse even than bloody business studies were all the men she'd never had. Caroline hunkered down in the driving seat, and seethed. How many men had she ever slept with? Four. Three of them before she was twenty! It seemed a shamefully low tally, and she blushed, unseen, in the dark.

But what was this? Caroline jerked upright again. She'd slept with only four men, because she'd met Simon, when she was very young. And that was a good thing. She'd been *lucky* . . .

Oh no she hadn't. True, the feelings that had got her and Simon started had been overwhelming, but how depressing to think she'd never have feelings like those again. Not with Simon. That intense, obsessive, drunken dizziness was in their past. That breathlessness. Now she could breathe easy in her husband's presence. What they had now was . . . nice, safe, comfortable. Like old cotton sheets. Caroline groaned. She didn't want cotton sheets, she wanted satin. She'd always thought she valued security, but tonight security looked like missed opportunity. She'd always thought *promiscuous* meant *lonely*, but tonight promiscuity whispered that it was generous and joyful. So why not make a grab for a dangerous excitement before it was too late? Offhand, Caroline couldn't think of any good reasons. Not that she tried very hard. She sniffed and snuffled to herself, a bit, as she finally, resentfully, pulled out of the passing-place, and turned the car for home. It was, she argued, definitely time she had an affair . . .

Maybe . . .

Perhaps.

Annie's workplace discouraged agitation. A few years back she'd gone into business with two of her oldest friends – Isabelle and Camilla. Together they'd opened Zenses, a swanky emporium of Eastern delights. Chinese ceramics? Korean cabinets? Burmese silver? Cambodian bronze? Silks and carpets? Jade and coral and pearls? All of these things were to be found at Zenses, a temple of commerce with something of the peacefulness of a Buddhist monastery. From the fish pool set into the floor, just inside the door, to the incense sticks burning smokily, to the Chinese opera warbling in the background, everything possible had been done to promote tranquillity. This morning, the shop was steeped in an almost Mogadon serenity. Though she knew she shouldn't be, Annie was grateful for the lack of customers; it was good to be alone – all except for the dragons.

Dragons were everywhere in Zenses. These sinuous Sinophiles were embodiments of celestial power, potent symbols of balance and harmony, and they disdained the horrible beasts imagined by the west. They twined in blue around white pottery, they curved gracefully across rainbow silks, they slithered in silver, and twisted across rosewood, oak, and elm. Annie was even kneeling on one – a becoming Tibetan dragon woven into a rug, along with a phoenix.

The dragons watched Annie impassively as she unpacked a shipment of Vietnamese lacquer ware. They watched as, one by one, bowls and platters, trays, and boxes emerged from an artificial snow of Styrofoam Ss. It was such *messy* protection, they thought. Annie agreed. She swept a handful of Ss from her skirt, and decided she'd have to get the vacuum out later; she couldn't have the place looking a tip.

Annie took pride in her shop. She was knowledgeable and enthusiastic about the stock, and she loved working with her two friends. But still, Zenses didn't fully satisfy her. What she really wanted to do was to open a gallery specializing in edgy, contemporary art from Shanghai and Beijing – portraits of Mao taking off Elvis, pop art PLA soldiers shaking their little booties, and wotnot – but she lacked the necessary capital. She intended to ask William for it, once they were married. He'd be able to invite his chums to openings, she thought. *Come and join us*, she imagined him scrawling across the invitations, *my wife's hobby!* Annie wasn't sure what she thought about becoming a hobbyist, but she supposed she'd be able to put up with it for the sake of the pictures, and of the artists. Anyway, she reassured herself, Isabelle was more or less a hobbyist, and it didn't seem to worry her.

Isabelle's hobby was interior design, and she was well able to indulge it from Hong Kong, where she lived. Her husband's job had originally taken her to the financial hub, which bills itself as Asia's city of life. At first she'd thought she'd slit her wrists. For three months she'd done nothing but indulge in little drinkie-poos with the other trailing spouses, who were wives, to a woman – the husbands didn't trail, they blazed. It was Isabelle's own husband who'd first suggested she set up a business.

To keep you off the sauce, hon.

Should I hit him? Isabelle had wondered. *Or should I take his advice?*

She'd decided on taking his advice, and a few weeks later she'd phoned Camilla back home. Sensible, judicious Camilla was a lawyer with a top London firm, and she in turn had phoned feisty Annie, who'd been unemployed at the time – her degree in history of art had proved far less useful than even her school careers adviser had promised it would. Annie had listened to Camilla with a growing sense of excitement. *Why not?* she'd thought. Isabelle and Camilla were her friends, at university she'd taken a special paper on the classical and decorative arts of Asia, and anyway, even if she hadn't, running an upmarket Asian stuff shop had to be as good a use for her degree as any other. Thus Zenses was born. The three entrepreneurs had been very lucky. During their second month of trading a London-based Park Avenue Princess had bought *all their stock* – and what's more, she'd gushed about it in the pages of *The Loop*, a glossy, flossy magazine for the New York/London set. *I call him Billy Buddha*, the displaced Park Avenue Princess had twittered, of an eighteenth-century Burmese Buddha head. Billy Buddha had featured prominently in the accompanying photo spread of the PAP's house, and all over London, bull-market wives had fallen in love with him. Since then, Zenses had gone from strength to strength. These days, Isabelle, an Olympic-grade shopper, had a wonderful time sleuthing Asia for the merchandise. Clever Camilla did the books, and Annie did everything else.

Unpacking new consignments was one of Annie's favourite jobs; usually it was like Christmas without the stress. But this morning it felt more like the obligatory Boxing Day family row. Not that there was anything wrong with the Vietnamese lacquer. The pieces were gorgeous. All had the simplest shapes, and each was in just a single colour. Some were lacquered in smooth, glossy gold, others in a lunar silver, and others still in shiny black. But the majority were in a distinctive Asian red, somewhere between dried blood and squashed plum. Annie saw this colour every day without ill-effect, but this morning it made her feel queasy – although perhaps her queasiness had nothing to do with the colour, and everything to do with William's suggestion of a baby.

Annie had met William through friends of friends, just ten days after she'd walked out on Ming Kwan – and only a week or so after William had himself walked out on Penelope. Both of them had been dumpers, and both of them had found dumping almost as confusing as being dumped. Both of them had been in turmoil, and they'd offered each other refuge, both psychic and physical. William had been Annie's typhoon harbour, and she remained very grateful to him for that. But what woman drops anchor, permanently, in her typhoon harbour? Had gratitude led Annie to stick around when she shouldn't have done? And had her sticking around convinced William he'd won her heart?

The Zenses dragons all thought so, and they blinked their stylized eyes at human folly. Annie blinked, too. How on earth was she supposed to have guessed William would go and propose? Marriage had never properly entered her radar before he'd suggested it. She and Ming Kwan had discussed the M-word, in desultory fashion, but they'd decided against. Why bother, if you loved each other? Love wasn't ownership, so why pretend it was? What was the point of an unenforceable guarantee of property rights? That was how she and Ming Kwan had felt, so how was Annie supposed to have guessed

William wanted his certificate, his receipt, his little bit of paper?

'Will you marry me?' he'd pleaded, and Annie had only just stopped herself from laughing, but he'd been looking at her as if the sun couldn't rival her as a source of warmth and light, and his eyes had quite killed her smile.

'What?'

'Will you marry me?'

Annie hadn't had an answer prepared, and she'd felt even more panicked than she would have done in an exam, if a question had come up on a subject quite new to her. For an instant, her mind had shut down, frozen. But then the neurons had started shimmering again. *Oh, well!* they'd shimmered, *Ming Kwan has ruled himself out of the game.* He had, and, never having tried it, Annie suspected she'd make a very bad job of being single – better, she'd thought, to be part of a mismatched couple than to be on her own. She was, after all, coming up for thirty. Furthermore, there was William's house in his favour, and between her and William's house, it really had been love at first sight. Finally, there were manners; it would have been so *rude* to say no, so *mean*.

'Yes,' she'd said.

Yes? Yes? Ohmigod! The word was scarcely out of Annie's mouth before she'd started wondering how she could recall it. She'd faced technical difficulties in speaking out at once, since William had, naturally enough, stilled her tongue with his. Annie had thought that to have recalled her yes after that kiss would have been even ruder, even meaner, than saying no in the first place. So she'd remained silent, and yes had slowly solidified inside her. Now it seemed as unalterable as granite, and her wedding preparations seemed as unstoppable as an avalanche. There was no escaping it; her fate was as certain as the grave.

'Oh, shut up!' Annie spoke the words aloud, crossly ticking herself off for being melodramatic. She gulped the incense-laden Zenses air, and felt a little soothed. For the past few minutes she'd been staring into space, but now she conscientiously checked over a couple of bowls, and a box or two. One had a hairline crack in the lacquer, and she put it aside. With this evidence of diligence before her, she felt free to resume her vacant staring. Everything was already just so damned *difficult*, she thought, and now William had gone and added the extra complication of spawning. Bloody, bloody, bloody hell! Annie gave up the pretence of working, and sat back on her haunches. She had been just as stunned when William had suggested a baby as she had when he'd proposed. Wasn't it supposed to be *women* who linked marriage with babies? How many more surprises could William throw at her? Was he a closet transvestite or something? Ming Kwan, reflected Annie, had been both so much stranger to her, and also so much more familiar than William. Ming Kwan would never have said, *Darling, how about a baby?* They'd both been adamant they didn't want children. Ming Kwan had been almost ideological about it. 'We're not animals,' he'd said, 'we don't have to buckle to biological destiny. We don't have to succumb to what nature has ordained for us, and reproduce. We're free to resist base instinct.'

Annie wasn't sure about all that, but she'd never wanted children. As they left their twenties and headed out into their thirties, lots of her girlfriends were wavering. *When is the right time to have a baby?* was becoming a regular topic on their girls' night out agendas. Annie usually joked there never was a right time, or asked, rhetorically: why downgrade your glamour factor to become a mum? Then she'd zone out on her pals. Her reasons for not wanting children were more confused than Ming Kwan's. When she'd been with him, she'd worried, a bit, about whether a child would be an eternal third, excluded from their twosome. But now that she was with William, she could scarcely use this nagging worry as a reason to remain childless. Then there was fear. Some mothers didn't love their children, couldn't be bothered with their children, failed to protect them, or, worse, abused them. Suppose she turned out to be such a mother? But Annie wasn't generally a fearful person, and, in any case, she couldn't kid herself; most of her reasons for not wanting children were purely selfish. She didn't want to fade to the horizon like a bank of cloud, as mothers did. She didn't want to be patronized, as mothers were. Plus there'd be all that inescapable, deadening responsibility, all that hard work, all that slog. And what about her art gallery? She'd have to forget ambition. Also allure. If she became a mother, men would lose interest in her. Why, even William might start eyeing up the babes!

Yes, thought Annie, as she brushed yet another stray Styrofoam S from her skirt, but would William's losing interest in her be such a disaster? That was the problem with the big anti-motherhood reasons: Annie subscribed to them, but they didn't truly persuade her. Call her shallow as a puddle, but what truly persuaded her were the little reasons – the aesthetic reasons. For a start, take pregnancy. Yuk! Gross! Annie pressed her hands to her stomach. She liked her little flat belly and her pert breasts. She didn't want to be fat, or floppy. She didn't want to look grotesque, even if only for a few months. And who was to say the flab and the bulges would last only a few months? Look at all those women who still appeared six months pregnant, six months after they'd had the baby. And think of their pelvic floors! She *might* have been able to want a baby, Annie unenthusiastically supposed, if it could have been grown neatly, in a vat, but until that day – no thanks. And maternity clothes were just as bad as what happened to your body! Annie pulled a face. Catch her in jeans with an elasticated waist? Or a floral tent? Annie's moue of distaste became more pronounced – then, to cap it all, she remembered nursing bras. In her mind's eye she saw Caroline whipping open her shirt to feed one of the twins and revealing a front-opening bra, which could easily have done double duty as a minor piece of civil engineering. Frankly, the stuff that went with babies was an affront against the visual world. Of course,

Annie granted that the babies themselves were beautiful – they had to be or else no one would bother to look after them – but it wasn't even as if the effrontery stopped when the babies were born (and birth itself was something she really didn't want to think about, thank you very much). Who could deny that babies attracted ugly junk like honey attracted flies? All those hideous plastics in bright, primary colours! Baths. Potties. Toys. Annie stared around her stylish shop, and shuddered to contrast it with the image of Caroline's house she carried around in her head. How could her sister stand to see that chunky play equipment blooming in her garden, and that clunky double buggy sprouting in her hall? Not, granted Annie, that all baby crap was big and brash and primary-coloured. Sometimes it was pastel-coloured, sweet, and cuddly. Ugh! Annie made a disgusted sound – and at once felt disgusted with herself. Honestly! What sort of sister was she? Forget Caroline, she was being *so* disloyal to Liz!

four

Jo jerked away from her nightmare and found herself trussed in sweaty, tangled sheets, and terror. She moaned, and groggily thrust one hand to her belly, then swayed upright in bed as the waking world gradually reasserted itself. Her bedroom was not quite dark, and very far from silent. The neon chiaroscuro of New York filtered in through her drapes, and honks and screeches, sirens and shouts blared up from the street, ten storeys below. She even fancied she could smell the streets. New York stank in the summer; already, in May, it was heating up; already, at noon, it was wreathed in its seasonal stench of garbage and rotting corpses. But Jo's room didn't really whiff of decay. She always kept a few scented candles clustered on her dressing table, and, as she inhaled, her olfactory hallucination yielded to their scent of roses. The heady sweetness calmed her. Soon she was able to reflect that the background traffic rumble was comforting, too; these days she'd have been kept awake by silence. She lay down again, preparing to let New York's incessant racket wash over her, a discordant lullaby hullabaloo.

A *what?* A *lullaby?* Jo gasped, as her dream once again rushed in on her, as the nightmare bared its toothless gums. She remembered she'd dreamed her tummy was hugely distended, that her taut skin was stretched over it like leather over a drum – but, quite unlike leather, her living skin was rubbery and elastic. In her dream, some horror movie alien had invaded her – she had been able to feel it slithering inside her belly, and to see it wriggling beneath her tight, tight skin. The alien's hand had started thrusting outwards, the grotesque but oh-so-human, five-fingered shape clearly visible as it had pushed against her springy flesh, trying to force its way to freedom. In a movie theatre, watching splatter-effect sci-fi, Jo would have averted her eyes. Instead, she'd woken up . . . but the nightmare wasn't over. Would it ever be? Jo took a few rough and raspy breaths, gripped by a panic far greater than fear of any alien. Because this alien wasn't alien. She didn't need an analyst to help her interpret *this* dream – her body was telling her something: it had been occupied.

What? She was pregnant? Rubbish! Jo took a couple of really deep, rose-scented breaths, and rallied herself. Dreams were no more reliable as indicators of what was going on in the world than were opinion polls. People who believed opinion polls were fools – and she'd be a fool to believe her dream.

Except, was it so impossible that her subconscious mind had picked up on subtle bodily clues, and had then passed its knowledge onto her conscious mind, under the cover of sleep?

And, anyway, now she came to think of it, how subtle had the clues actually been? Hadn't she felt unwell very often over the past few weeks? Hadn't her breasts felt tingly and sore? Hadn't her clothes started to cut into her flesh? Yes. Yes. Yes. And when, exactly, had she had her last period? Jo screwed up her face and tried to remember. She wasn't sure – but it was certainly much longer ago than a month. Fuck! Pill or no pill, it was as obvious as an escaped hippopotamus in Bloomingdales. Jo flung herself against her mattress, and writhed as though in labour. Except it wasn't just her own pain that made her writhe, it was the thought of the father's, too: his pain and his rage. *Sure I love you. Sure I do.* Jo had allowed herself to believe that; despite her best intentions, she and Brett were still as much of an item as they had ever been. But were they enough of an item to deal with this? Fuck. Fuck. Fuck.

Liz was at her drawing board, working on a dinky ickle bunnikin, for a dinky ickle pram set. She'd just roughed out the bunnikin's dinky ickle bobtail, when she felt the familiar dinky ickle cramping pains. Fuck! She stood up so hastily she knocked over a jar of drafting pens. Another month, another monthly. Another cycle lost to eternity, and she must make yet another trip to the dingy office loos, to confirm, as if she needed confirmation, the power of the bloody, blood-red curse.

Fuck! thought Simon. He was in a dark and smoky, intimate and poky City pub. Not a wine bar. No, no, no. Simon liked a pint, and so did his drinking companion, Bill. Simon and Bill had joined Global Commerce Bank during the same graduate intake. Though Bill had thrusted and Simon had plodded, they'd become muckers. After a couple of years, Bill had left to join a competitor, and since then he'd been zig-zagging between employers – and zig-zagging up the greasy corporate pole. But perhaps his luck was about to run out. Bill's current chop-shop had just issued a profits warning, and its stock price had taken a hammering. It was a recipe for chop-shop chopping. So when Bill had phoned at lunchtime, sounding distressed, but refusing to say why, Simon had felt a shiver of foreboding – and since he'd seen Bill's face, the shiver had turned into a tsunami.

'What's it all about?' he asked now, as he pushed a bag of bacon-flavoured crisps towards his friend.

All around the two men, other men bellowed, swigged beer, and smoked. All these men wore suits – the City fad for casual dressing had passed, along with the fad for tech stocks and the e-economy. All these men looked in control, powerful, successful. All of them thought they had accepted that the price the City extracted for its telephone-number paycheques was zero job security. Right. Just like all of them had accepted they were mortal. And anyway, very few of them were on telephone-number paycheques. Simon never had been. And nor was Bill, any more.

Bill didn't answer Simon's question – and Simon's sense of unease deepened.

'Come on. What's it all about?' he pressed.

'You're a great guy,' slurred Bill, in reply. He'd arrived first, and had already sunk a couple of pints, and a couple of chasers. 'A good man, loyal. I'm for ever in your debt, old friend.'

'Well now.' Simon, stone cold sober, was thoroughly unnerved by Bill's words, and his maudlin tone. He opened his briefcase to fish out his mobile. Bill was clearly in need of a bender, so he'd better phone Caroline to say he'd be even later than usual – especially since he was well and truly in the doghouse, following their row about the precise definition of the word *fun*.

'I've had it, old friend!' slurred Bill.

'Come, come!' Simon put down his phone, with the call home still unmade.

'And Felicity pregnant, again. Three kids. Three sets of school fees. A huge mortgage. What'll I do?'

'Oh shit!' said Simon, giving up the pretence of ignorance. 'You've been axed.'

'Boom!' Bill made a revolver out of two fingers, and feigned shooting himself in the head.

'Shit!' repeated Simon. 'But you'll find something else, soon.'

Bill didn't even bother to acknowledge the trite falsehood. 'We'll have to sell the cottage,' he said, instead.

It was scarcely hardship for a well-fed, well-housed man to have to divest himself of his second home, and some people might now have indulged in a little gleeful gloating at Bill's expense – but not Simon. If he'd had a second home, he too would have been appalled at the prospect of losing it, and he knew how his friend loved his cottage by the sea, his walks along the beach, his sailing.

'Surely not?' he soothed. 'What about your pay-out? Investments? And don't you have insurance?'

Bill again ignored him. 'Three sets of school fees,' he repeated, then he groaned, and dropped his head into his hands.

Simon's mind lurched to Nat and Louis, and he blanched. Two sets of school fees were plenty bad enough. Even on his current salary, he'd only just be able to give his kids the leg-up of a private education, so what if his job went the way of Bill's? Not a good question. And what would Caroline say, to find herself landed with an unemployed idler? He took a long pull on his bitter, and then another. Yes, tonight he'd definitely get plastered. And not just for Bill's sake, either.

Caroline was furious when Simon staggered into bed, drunk, at 4 a.m., and tried to paw her for sex. As she fought to fall back to sleep, she let herself imagine some other, faceless man, a sex god who'd only want sex when she did, and *never* when he was drunk.

'It was Bill,' Simon explained, through his hangover, as he knotted his tie, or tied his noose, a few hours later. He'd missed the 6.20 by over an hour, and now he was shooting for the 8.05. 'He's lost his job.'

'*What?*'

Caroline sounded so alarmed, Simon couldn't face telling her how anxious he was about his own job prospects, though he wanted to.

'Yesterday,' he said, instead.

'Poor Felicity! She's pregnant, isn't she?'

Once she'd heard the whole story, Caroline forgave her husband his drunken binge. Nevertheless, the faceless sex god she'd conjured in the night lingered in her mind. She was dreaming of him still as, a couple of hours after her husband had left the house, she arrived at Lucy's for a coffee coven. The other mothers were already gathered at one end of Tabitha's big, sunny playroom, whilst Tabitha ignored Phoebe and Hector, at the other. All three children ignored the entrance of the twins, who didn't mind, but toddled happily over to the toy box, where they began to squabble over a plastic golf club.

Lucy passed Caroline a mug of coffee and a plate of home-made shortbread.

'No biscuits, thanks,' said Caroline. For once she was not in flatties, leggings and a hide-everything jersey. This morning she'd put on heels – low, but heels nonetheless – opaque black tights, a shortish black skirt she'd often worn to the office, before she'd had the boys, and a cheerful red top. She'd even put on make-up. In her pre-motherhood days, she'd not been one to prefer the natural look over its more groomed alternatives, but since she'd had the twins, she'd largely given up.

'You look nice,' complimented Emma, who was herself in sneakers, jogging pants and a sweatshirt – which dowdy outfit imparted a definite edge to her tone.

'And on a diet?' asked Lucy, pointing at the plate of shortbread.

'Yes,' accused Sophie. 'Fancy passing on biscuits!'

'D'you lot really mean: who is he, then?' demanded Caroline, correctly trusting such abruptness would distract her friends. There was general merriment.

'When would you find the time?' tittered Emma.

'Where would you find the *man*?' added Sophie. Not counting males under five, the coven members spent their days in an almost exclusively female environment – a girls' school for grown-ups, a convent, a PMT department of the soul. 'You know,' continued Sophie, in a tone that indicated she was about to make some startlingly original contribution to the conversation, 'the way we live we might as well be single mothers.'

'For God's sake!' groaned Caroline. 'Please, not that again!'

The other mothers laughed, rather than taking umbrage.

'Anyway, y'know what?' said Lucy, jerking her thumb towards the playroom wall, and also towards the house next door. 'There *are* men. We've got a new neighbour. Toby.'

A ripple ran through the little group. Caroline felt an electric current surge through her body, and only just restrained herself from crossing to the window to peer out, in the hope of spotting Toby. This is ridiculous, she told herself, crossly. How old are you? Thirteen?

'What's he like?' she asked, too casually.

'A lawyer. Nice looking. About fortyish. No sign of a family.'

'So a divorcee, then?'

'Probably.'

'Girlfriend?'

'Haven't seen one.'

'Children?'

'I told you, no sign of a family.'

The rhythm of the women's conversation was suddenly interrupted by their own children.

'Hector! Stop that!' yelled Sophie, as she spotted her son attempting to cut the playroom's brown, velveteen curtains with a pair of scissors. Lucy looked quite unperturbed.

'I hate those curtains,' she said. 'They came from Jim's mum's old house. And the scissors are so child-friendly they don't actually cut anything.'

Sophie gave her a quick smile, then got up to remove the scissors from Hector, who howled. Phoebe, never one to pass up the chance of a good roar, at once joined in. Tabitha, a timid little girl in the process of being potty-trained, was so unnerved she wet herself. Meanwhile the twins chose this moment to begin a really serious scrap over the toy golf club. What with one thing and another, it was quite a while before the mums were free to get back to Toby.

'So,' said Caroline, gloomily. 'Fortyish. No girlfriend. No family. Doesn't that suggest something to you?'

'No,' said Lucy.

'But you say he's nice looking?'

'Very nice looking.'

'*Very* nice looking?'

Lucy blushed. 'He obviously takes care of himself. Must have gym membership. And he dresses very well.'

'Riiiight,' drawled Caroline. 'And have you been inside his house yet?'

'I took him a welcome-to-the-neighbourhood cake.'

'And what was it like?'

'Chocolate orange.'

'Not the cake! His house!'

'Oh.' Lucy, who went in for Regency stripes and Regency repro, sniffed derisively. 'The style was way too modern for my taste, but very nice, if you like that kind of thing. Very smart. Glass topped tables, enormous vases, all immaculately kept.'

'I get you!' Emma spoke directly to Caroline, and her tone was glum. 'The interior design gene, right?'

'Right.'

'Is there one?' asked Sophie, looking puzzled.

'I think Caroline's trying to tell us she thinks Toby's gay,' explained Emma.

'Ooooh,' said Lucy, 'Well *that* would certainly fit. He has had a most charming young man to stay a couple of weekends.

Helped me pick up my groceries after the bag burst. I thought perhaps a nephew, or his godson.'

Caroline sighed and took a thoughtful sip of lukewarm instant coffee. So, that was Toby eliminated from her list of potential affairees. Not that she really wanted an affair. Not really, really. And not that it was a long list. In fact, it wasn't a list at all. Now that Toby had been crossed off, it was back to being the purest, most virginal, blankest of blanks.

Annie thought it was quite ridiculous, all these women marrying in white when they were virginal as the driven slush. However, she recognized this as an inappropriate thought to be having in Boodle & Hawkes' wedding dress department. She sharply told herself to concentrate on the job in hand, which was to gather ideas for her own wedding dress. Liz, who'd married in a registry office in a calf-length green and gold creation of her own design, had also come along. She could have whipped up a ballgown from a length of ribbon and a scrap of lace, and she'd volunteered to make Annie's dress, as her wedding present to her sister.

'Have you thought about the shape, yet?' she asked.

'I don't want to look like a meringue.'

'D'you think I'd let you?'

'And not an empire line.'

'A princess line? Or something straight?'

'Straight, probably.'

'And a train?'

'Perhaps.'

'Fabric? Anything but duchesse satin. Such a mistake! So stiff and unyielding.'

'Lace, I'd thought.'

'A simple column of lace?'

'Or chiffon? Georgette?'

'Mmmm,' sighed Liz, imagining cap sleeves and a kicky little fishtail. 'That'd be pretty.'

The two women paused and gazed about them a moment. The shop floor was circular, like a wedding cake, the dresses hung from racks around the circumference, and the fittings were pink and ivory, twiddly with gilt. Annie could relate to the fancy scrolls and fat little cherubs; she herself felt twiddly with guilt. Here and there other brides-to-be and their friends, or sisters, or mothers, exclaimed over sleeves, necklines, beading and bows. Why couldn't *she* summon their noisy enthusiasm? Everywhere silk and net and organza frothed and tossed like gloriously spendthrift cherry blossom. Cherry trees in full flower would have thrilled her heart, but all these dresses could do was depress her. Even if she managed not to look like a meringue, she'd still look like a bride, and she just didn't want to. It was William who wanted a traditional wedding, not her. Beautiful and blushing just wasn't her scene. Was it very wrong to wish she could wear something to make every guy in the church want to fuck her? Was it very wrong to wish she could wear skin-tight faux chainmail in silver Lurex? That's what she'd have worn for Ming Kwan, if they'd ever bothered to get married. She'd have worn something warrior-woman, something woman-man, strong and sexy and don't mess with me, mister. But as it was, she was going to look like a bride straight from the pages of a bridal magazine, all my beloved is mine, and I am his. And that, thought Annie, was a load of balls, frankly.

'Liz . . .' she began, about to reveal something of her unhappy thoughts.

'I know,' sniffed Liz, who was also feeling weighed down by emotions it was hard to acknowledge. 'So much choice is overwhelming. But come on, let's get working the racks.' She pointed first one way, and then another. 'You take that section. I'll take this.'

Liz's gloom deepened as she riffled through all the dream dresses, destined to help women fulfil their dreams of a dream-like day. But why was she feeling so sad? These dresses swished with the power and the special magic of beginnings. She thought of two shining, mythic people, just setting out, two people striding hand in hand to meet their future, both certain that love never failed, that love beareth all things, believeth all things, hopeth all things, endureth all things. Bear*eth*? Hop*eth*? Liz frowned to herself. Where had all these *eths* come from? The marriage service? Or perhaps that letter from St Paul to the Corinthians? Yes, that was probably it. She hadn't had St Paul at her own wedding – she and Zack had asked each of their guests to bring along a copy of a favourite song, or poem, or passage, and then they'd had a lucky-dip reading – but she'd listened to him often enough at other people's. Though I speak with the tongues of men and of angels. When I was a child, I spake as a child. Through a glass darkly. And now abideth faith, hope, love, these three; but the greatest of these is love.

Well, thought Liz, as she fingered a billowing skirt of finest, creamiest silk, there was no arguing with that. But hope, not love, was her real problem. Hope for the beginning which came after the marriage beginning – or before it, or nothing to do with it. But anyway, the beginning of a new life. The blazing beginning of a whole new person. Liz's baby longing, always lurking, now pounced hard. It got her in its terrible jaws, and shook its head from side to side, and all at once the billowing, creamy skirt of a woman's wedding dress reminded Liz of another sort of billowing, creamy skirt. She dropped the fabric quickly, and it sighed away from her fingers with a soft swoosh. What did women do with their wedding dresses once they'd worn them? The unromantic sold them. Others cut them down and dyed them. Or they put them away for their daughters' wedding dresses. Or – and here was the rub – they used some of the fabric for a christening gown. Liz made a little moue. True, she had never worn one of these frothy white confections, nor would any child of hers be christened; it would be welcomed into the human community with a secular party, but still. She imagined herself cradling a tiny infant. In her mind's eye she saw a baby trailing yards of daintily embroidered white silk – silk that, in a parallel universe, had trailed behind her on her wedding day. She saw a sleeping baby, lying like a tiny ghost in her arms . . . except, she thought, sniffing hard, there was no *like* about it.

But love hopeth all things, she firmly repeated to herself, as she shuffled sideways and began examining the next dress. It was in devore, long sleeved, and vaguely medieval. Liz tried to focus on the cuffs. They were buttoned, pointy and prettily cut. Acting on auto-pilot, she folded them back to see how the seams lay. Usually she loved the technical challenge of working out how a complicated dress had been cut and constructed, but today she just couldn't be bothered. Love hopeth all things and it endureth all things. Fine. But would it endureth infertility? Liz was beginning to give up hope in a baby. Was Zack, as well? And if Zack gave up hope in a baby, would he also give up hope in her?

This question had been stalking Liz for weeks; she could feel it growing, like a tumour in her head. But despite the deadly, multiplying cells of angst, she hadn't yet lost *all* sense of perspective; she decided it was time to face her fear, and talk. There could be no right time to say, *Darling, will you still love me if* . . . so she didn't bother to try to find one, nor to make one. Nor did she practise what she'd say. Nor did she prepare the setting. Instead she dished up her distress along with Zack's evening meal – fish pie and broccoli served with one hand, the centre of their emotional lives with the other.

'I went wedding dress shopping with Annie today,' she began, as she sat down to eat.

'Yes?' Zack speared a morsel of cod with his fork. 'Find anything you could copy?'

'No. And I got a bit upset, actually.'

Zack looked surprised, but his mouth was full of fish, so it was a moment before he could speak. 'Upset? Why?'

'All the dresses.'

'But you like dresses!'

'Yes. But you know what women do with wedding dresses? I mean, after they've worn them?'

Zack gave her question serious consideration for a moment or two, then gave up. 'No idea.'

'Often, they make them into christening gowns.'

'Christening gowns?' Zack pushed his plate away, and leaned back in his wooden kitchen chair. 'Ah.'

'Zack! D'you think we ever are going to have a baby?'

Zack was silent for a long beat. 'I dunno, love,' he said, at last. 'But perhaps it's time to give up on the ovulation kits.'

'But Dr Kent said . . .'

'That's what I mean. Perhaps it's time to go back to the doctor. Dr Kent. And I'd better come with you this time. I should have been there before. I'm sorry.'

'But Zack! What if Dr Kent says I just can't have a child?'

'Not *I*,' said Zack firmly. 'What if *we* can't have a child. It might be me.'

This was true: it might have been Zack; his testicles might long since have given up the ghost; his sperm might be, to all intents and purposes, inanimate. But Zack didn't believe these things, not for one single minute. *His* sperm were healthy little devils, they could have swum the Atlantic, let alone . . . whatever bit of Liz it was, precisely, that they had to swim to do their job. He'd denied these things to his wife solely out of a slightly patronizing, but loving, kindness. His wife needed reassurance, and he'd offer it, even if he didn't actually believe his reassuring words to be true. Which they surely weren't. Liz would be thirty-seven soon. Everyone knew a woman's fertility declined from . . . Zack couldn't remember when female fertility started to decline, but anyway, he was confident it dropped off a cliff after thirty-five.

So was Liz.

'I'm sure it's me,' she wailed. 'I'm not a proper woman!'

It was the same fear she had confided to Jo, and Zack, like Jo, thought it was either silly, or incomprehensible, or both.

'Proper?' He frowned. 'What's *proper*? And what's a proper *woman*?'

'A woman who works – I mean, who functions as she should. But I don't – I just don't function properly.'

Zack could patronize Liz no longer, however kind his patronage would be. Instead of condescending to her, he got up, walked round the battered deal table, and yanked his wife to her feet. Then he circled his arms round her waist before kissing her, properly kissing her, with a properly functioning kiss – an action that had the unhappy effect of reducing her to tears.

'Liz?' Zack was beginning to struggle, really to struggle. 'Lizzie?' he added, desperation clear in his voice.

'What if I can't have a child?' she sobbed into his shoulder. 'What if I can't have a child, and you leave me for a more fertile woman?'

Liz's words vibrated round the kitchen, and Zack's eyes registered stunned confusion. But he quickly recovered from his shock. He took his wife's face in his hands, the better to pinion her with his gaze.

'Darling, it's you I love. I love *you*. If you can't have a child, you can't have a child. Yes, I'd like a baby, I'd love our child, adore it, even. Of course I would. But d'you honestly think I care about the state of your ovaries? Your fallopian tubes? Of course I don't. I *don't*. Darling, I love *you*.'

The morning after her dream that she was pregnant, Jo had decided to dismiss its message, because she didn't want it to be true. Her period would surely come, she'd told herself, and surely come, and surely come. After all, the pill was 99.8 per cent reliable. Yes, but what about that sneaky little 0.2 per cent? Jo had waited for her already late period an extra fortnight now, a fortnight during which she'd continued to feel sick and tired, and ravenously hungry. A fortnight during which her breasts had swollen still further, more skirts had ceased to fit, and her sense of smell had gone completely haywire. Now she'd decided she really had to find out if pregnancy was the cause. She couldn't risk putting it off any longer, in case she missed the deadline for ending it.

Shouldn't you be the first to know the wonderful news? This was the copy line splashed across the box of Jo's home-use pregnancy test. It was a question, but Jo felt it in her guts as a lie. She hoped the rest of the copy was truthful. It promised a result in one minute. It promised the test would be a cinch to use. Jo certainly hoped so. She read the instructions leaflet twice through before she shut herself into her sliver of bathroom, where she propped it on the glass shelf in front of her mirror, above her washbasin. This done, she obediently collected her piss in a small, plastic specimen cup. Next she obediently took from the kit's box a foil-wrapped package, which she obediently unwrapped to reveal a wand-like device. This, she just knew, would never deign to obey any command she might give it. So she didn't command.

'Not pregnant, *pleeease*,' she pleaded, as she dipped the wand into her piss, and stood back to wait.

The wand didn't look like much, but it was very powerful, very magic. It told the future. It told of miracles and of disasters, and of disasters miraculously avoided. And all in sixty seconds! In sixty seconds Jo would know her fate. It was, to her, a very, very long sixty seconds. She watched the second hand on her Cartier crawl round the dial as slowly as a dying man, crawling for distant water in the desert. And she felt something of a dying man's desperation; she felt just as subject to the inevitable. And it *was* inevitable. The wand had at last done its divination, and her fate was just as she'd known it would be: a blue line in the results window; a baby in her womb.

So sod the wand! Jo snapped it in two and tossed the pieces into her bathroom trashcan. And these two pieces of chemically impregnated absorbent paper housed in cheap plastic were not all that was destined for the trash. Jo slumped to the floor and began to cry, both for herself, and for her baby . . . Except one thing she mustn't, mustn't do was think of the thing in her womb as a baby. And, in fact, it wasn't a baby. Not yet. It was an embryo. A foetus. A mass of jelly-like cells. It might be human, but it was not yet remotely like a person. Or so Jo hoped. Or so she was determined to believe. And she would get rid of this not-person. It wasn't a moral decision, it was a matter of expedience. She had no other choice. She was a single career-woman, pregnant by a married man . . .

Jo's attention flicked to Brett, and her heart briefly surged. Her attempt to dump him had been abortive. Perhaps he'd try to persuade her to abort on abortion, too? Perhaps Brett might want her to keep this ba— foetus? *Sure I'll love it. Sure I will.* Oh, how funny. Ha! Ha! Tee hee! And who could blame him, really? He was a married father of three. There was no more room in his life for a ba— an embryo, than there was in hers. It wouldn't be fair to inflict a child on him. And she had no desire for a child, either. None at all! Brett didn't need to talk her out of going through with this pregnancy, since she simply didn't want to. She liked her freedom, she enjoyed the luxury of selfishness, she didn't want a living millstone round her neck. No. She had to get on with her own life. As at nineteen, so at thirty-four. This ba— mass of jelly-like cells inside her was quite unwanted. It was doomed. It was dead.

Jo reached for a Kleenex from the box by her make-up bag, and blew her nose noisily. Then she stood up, brushed down her skirt, and determined to phone her oh bee gee why en, right away. This was a city where everybody had their own personal cardiologist, haematologist, and dermatologist, as well as their own personal fitness trainer. An oh bee gee why en, or OBGYN was as essential to a New York woman as her manicurist, and Jo intended to phone hers, at once, to book a termination. She made towards the bathroom door, but became distracted by the instructions leaflet leaning against her tooth-brush mug. More trash! She reached for it, and in doing so she glanced into the mirror, above the sink.

How dangerous mirrors can be! Instead of her own feline green eyes staring back at her, Jo saw two dark pools, and deep. These pools, these eyes, were huge and unblinking, fish-like, and damning. They were focused both on nothing, and also on Jo – who recognized them, of course. Unlike the eyes of a liv-ing child, these ancient, ever-young eyes were eternally the same. They existed outside time, and they were quite unchanged in all the fifteen years since they'd first started their sporadic haunting of their dear old mum. These eyes were the undead ghost of Jo's unborn dead. These eyes were the ghost of a future that hadn't been. Here was her past, come to haunt her. Or to blackmail her.

And here was the ghost of a future that still could be. As Jo stared into the looking-glass world behind the glass, her unborn, undead offspring's ever unchanging eyes were joined by another pair; two more dark, dark ovals slowly solidified from nothing. These eyes, too, were focused both on nothing, and on Jo. These eyes, too, she recognized at once. Old Eyes and New Eyes bore a close family resemblance – which was unsurprising, since they shared a mother, though not a father. Brothers? Sisters? Jo didn't know; she dared not hazard the sex of an unborn ghost, neither past, nor future. But she dared to hazard focusing on New Eyes. She gazed into the mirror, and New Eyes gazed out. These eyes were huge and unblinking, fish-like, and trusting. Oh, they were so trusting. And so gentle! They looked quite incapable of judging. But they were not – and Jo, their mother, knew it all too well.

five

William was sitting on a hard pew in St John's, Lesser Elsland,
trying to block out Bach, who was way beyond the ability of
the ancient organist, and the yak, yak, yak of Charles and
Clarissa's guests. He sat in morose silence between his mother
and his betrothed. Much to his surprise, Charles and Clarissa
had invited all three of them to little Edward's christening. He
could only suppose that the glittery card he'd sent had done the
trick, and secured the re-establishment of friendly relations.
What power in the paws of a blue teddy bear! Unless it was
simply that the birth of a baby always encouraged the burying
of hatchets? Certainly, Penelope must have given her blessing
to his invitation to today's celebration – and also to Annie's.
How generous she was! She must have accepted that it was
time to consign their shared past, to the past. He craned
around the church, peering past his mother's hat, sprays of
flowers, and inconveniently placed pillars, trying to spot her.
Not that he *wanted* to spot her. The thought of seeing Penelope
today filled him with a nervous, slightly excited dread. It would
be only the second or third time they'd seen each other since

the big split, and the first time she'd met Annie. He glanced sideways at his beloved – and winced at the thought of what Penelope would make of her. Such clothes! William didn't very often notice women's clothes, but he'd have had to be made of stone not to react to Annie's today, they were so completely unsuitable.

Annie didn't think she looked unsuitable; she thought she looked attractively unusual. She wasn't as skilled with a needle as Liz, but she wasn't half bad, and she'd stitched her skirt herself. It was full-length, full-wrap, and full-on glitzy. She'd conjured it from a length of fabric she'd picked up in Brick Lane – fabric that had originally been intended for a wedding sari. The cobwebby stuff of it was a heavily embroidered, heavily sequinned pinkish-brown organza – synthetic, of course, or the sequins wouldn't have held. Annie had lined it in pale pink, which flashed through the brown like salmon scales flashing through muddy water. Her cropped Lycra T-shirt was pale pink, too, and so were her high-heeled sandals, but her navel stud was gold, as were all her tiny, dainty bangles, the pretty chains coiled around her legs like snakes, and her elaborate, dangling earrings.

Annie thought this was a lovely outfit, entirely suitable for church, temple, synagogue, or mosque. But she was aware of William wincing by her side. She grinned to herself, and adjusted the position of her arms, solely to set her bangles jangling. That would teach him to look at her askance! This morning, he hadn't actually said *You're surely not going out in that?* but he had greeted her outfit with a moment of appalled silence.

'Where's your hat?' he'd demanded, at last.

Annie owned hundreds of hats. But she didn't own the bejewelled, chocolate-coloured turban, demanded by her Indian look, so she'd decided to come hatless, trusting God, if He existed, would understand the absolute impossibility of wearing the wrong hat in His house, and not much caring what anyone else thought. After all, she'd only come today because she'd been unable to think of a good reason not to – she was, indisputably, William's betrothed and, though she tried her best, she couldn't fend off *all* the attendant social obligations. But now she was actually sitting on a cold, hard pew, she couldn't think what on earth she was doing here. Granted, the church was beautiful. Its honey-coloured walls wept holiness; Annie could sense them leaching the stuff into the air. How could they not, when so many generations had prayed within them? But that this church had been a place of worship for a thousand years didn't mean she had to sit in it, today. She was an agnostic, for Christ's sake. Perhaps it was all a plot of William's. Perhaps he thought that exposure to little Edward would soften her up to the idea of babies. Well, if so, he had another think coming. Exposure to her own sister's twins had not caused her to weaken, so how could exposure to a stranger's child? And what, Annie wondered, could possibly have been going through Penelope's mind when she'd sanctioned her invitation to this do? Had the woman she'd supplanted secretly been hoping that William would take one look at her, and at once renounce the false pretender to his ruby ring?

Little Edward was duly baptized in the name of the Father, and of the Son, and of the Holy Ghost. Amen. Then he, and all his well-wishers, repaired to his maternal grandparents' place – Lesser Elsland Hall. Not that there was anything terribly lesser about it. It was a grand Elizabethan house whose beauty was not diminished a jot by the fact that it was riddled with woodworm, rising damp, sinking damp, and sideways damp. Clarissa and Penelope's parents were not the first generation entirely unable to afford the crippling upkeep. The rot had set in centuries back, not to mention the fungi and the destructive insects. But the Hall had been standing for 400 years; how likely was it to fall down now?

William, Annie, and Penelope all rather wished it would. If the drawing room's oak-panelled walls were to start to buckle right this minute, it would at least save them from excruciating small talk.

'Penelope, this is Annie,' said William, wafting his champagne flute in a vaguely introductory fashion. 'Annie, meet Penelope.'

The two women appraised each other unenthusiastically. Penelope, a sturdy lass, was in mustard yellow. Annie thought Penelope's attire was eye-catchingly hideous, and that Penelope herself was fascinatingly ugly, like Henrietta's pugs. Meanwhile, Penelope thought Annie looked like an insect who'd just buzzed in from a Bollywood set. She, on the other hand, was a kitten.

'Very glamorous outfit,' she purred.

Alas, cattiness didn't suit Penelope. She was just too nice for malice. William had been spot-on. His ex had agreed that Annie should be invited today out of generosity, and also out of the recognition that her own family, and William's, could not be kept apart for ever. There would be weddings, charity balls, Henley. She and Annie were sure to bump into each other eventually – so best to get it over and done with, like lancing a boil, and on her own territory to boot. But Annie had also been spot-on. Penelope's generosity was not unmixed. She preferred to draw a veil – a widow's veil – over her feelings when William had dumped her, and the added pain and confusion she'd suffered when he'd replaced her so rapidly. Surely, after he dumped a girl, a man was supposed to have a stop-gap fling, before he met *the one*? Penelope knew she was being too ridiculous, but she clung to the secret hope that she still had hope. Surely William was rightfully hers? He was *her* Sweet William, as sweet as the pretty, close-clustered flowers. Was it so impossible Annie wasn't the one for him? Was it so impossible *she* was, despite everything? And if these things were possible, it must also be possible that today, when William saw her beside her rival, the scales would fall from his eyes, he'd realize his terrible mistake, and the social universe would return to its natural order.

Annie met Penelope's comment on her clothes with silence.

'Well now,' said William, flapping his non-glass-bearing hand. 'Well now.'

'Well now what?' asked Annie, faux innocently.

'Er,' said William. 'Um.'

Annie and Penelope independently decided to let him flounder his way out of this one. But William wasn't up to the task. All around the polite party ebbed and flowed, but he, his betrothed, and his ex, were as marooned in their awkwardness as little Edward in his Victorian christening gown.

'Er,' said William, trying again. 'Er, Penelope, Annie's very interested in Asian art. And Annie, um, Penelope . . .' It was on the tip of his tongue to say that Penelope liked to ride to hounds, but he remembered in time that Annie had been a hunt-sab in her teenage years. So he stuttered into silence and looked at Penelope pleadingly. Not at Annie. He knew Annie wouldn't save him. But Penelope might. She had a natural kindness, and natural good manners. So often, in the past, she'd rescued him from conversational difficulty: would she help him out, now?

She would. Like William, Penelope lived in Knightsbridge, where she worked, as a PR – dear Sophie Wessex, such an inspiration – for the Walton Street shop where all her friends placed their wedding lists. But she was a country girl, at heart. She naturally assumed gardening to be a safe topic: church affairs, dogs, the village, gardening, all women were interested in these things. She gestured to the sunny outside world –

lawns and flowering shrubs and drifts of colour were temptingly visible through the French windows.

'Do you like gardening?' she asked Annie. 'Because mummy's got them looking absolutely glorious at the moment. Of course, tulips are her special thing, and they're over now. But the Mediterranean beds! And the roses!'

Annie sensed danger. Creating something from the nothing of soil and seed held as little interest for her as creating something from the nothing of egg and seed, but she knew that, in this company, hers was a minority view. It surely couldn't be long until Penelope invited her to inspect the herbaceous borders. What a yawn! And then there were her shoes. Her pretty pink sandals were designed for swaying seductively over rugs and parquet, not scrambling over grass and gravel.

'How I do love roses!' she sighed, summoning her sincerest smile. 'But now, I'm sure you two would like to catch up? Why don't I take myself off to mingle, whilst you natter?'

Annie drifted away. Granted, she'd been horribly rude, but it was such a relief to have escaped both Penelope and the risk of being dragged off to comment on Michaelmas hollyhocks, and wotnot. She took another glass of champagne, and then decided she might as well have a nosy-mosey round the downstairs rooms of the house. But she didn't get further than the deserted library, where she found a 1930s bodice-ripper and a big leather chair – a combination that proved utterly irresistible.

Back in the drawing room, Penelope and William were still engaged in chit-chat. Each managed to maintain a facade of calm, but internally each was in uproar. They began to reminisce, and Penelope giggled at a memory. When she giggled she looked remarkably pretty . . . Or so thought William.

Annie never giggled – she laughed, but she didn't giggle. And, unlike Penelope's, her face was too thin to dimple. He imagined Annie's face, not-dimpling at him. Why had she left him with Penelope? It was more than insouciant, it was almost contemptuous. Wasn't she in the least bit worried Penelope might . . . William checked himself: *Don't be a conceited idiot, of course Penelope won't make a play for you!* But didn't Annie feel even the teeniest bit concerned about the threat posed by other women? Especially Penelope. Didn't she think he was worth her jealousy? Or was she testing him? That must be it! No doubt Annie was spying on him, watching to see if he'd flirt with Penelope. The bloody silly games women played! But two could play at those games. He'd show her! He'd flirt like any matinée idol.

And Penelope would flirt right on back, like any Victorian coquette with her fan. She too thought Annie's behaviour extraordinary. What sort of woman abandoned her betrothed to his ex, so the pair of them could natter? Mummy had once left a diamond brooch lying about, and the cleaner du jour had stolen it. Mummy had been upset, of course, but she'd refused to blame the cleaner. She'd said the theft had been her fault, since she'd been the one to place temptation in another's path. Penelope gleefully seized on the reasoning: it would be Annie's fault if she now, blamelessly, took advantage of her rival's carelessness.

And, when all was said and done, it wasn't as if William had a ring on his finger. Yet. Or so argued Henrietta, as she watched her son and Penelope from across the room. Thus far, Henrietta hadn't much enjoyed the christening. Things had got off to a bad start when she'd first seen Annie's houri outfit, and then she'd had to face Penelope's mother, her old school friend, dear Serena. Dear Serena had very tactfully conveyed that Penelope had not yet found herself a replacement for William and, even more tactfully, refrained from comment on William's choice of a replacement for her own sweet girl. All this tact had heaped coals on Henrietta's head. The coals had glowed hotter to see Serena fussing over that little poppet, Edward. Serena was a grandmother! No doubt Serena's daughter would be willing to make *her* a grandmother, given the chance! And William and Penelope were just made for each other. As were she and Penelope, as mother-and-daughter-in-law. If only there weren't the complication of Annie! But complications, thought Henrietta grimly, could always be ironed out. And William and Penelope were laughing and smiling together quite like old times! Well, well, well . . .

Well, thought Simon, things couldn't get much worse. He was once again on the 6.20, snailing up to London. This morning the train had been delayed by unexpected summer rain. The waiting room at Ryleford was closed for roof repairs, so he and all his fellow commuters had got wet and cold as they hung about on the platform. Now the carriage was unpleasantly damp, and it smelled of gently steaming macs. Still, at least Simon had managed to secure himself a seat – although not, this morning, a window seat. He was squashed between a very fat man and a very thin women, and opposite a spotty youth. His *Financial Times* saved him from eye contact with spotty, although every time he turned a page, he risked jabbing fatty or skinny with his elbow.

For Simon, the pink pages of the *FT* made even less rosy reading than usual. This morning it wasn't No Name Bank focusing on core competencies and improving efficiency by responding to customer needs. This morning No Name Bank had a name – Global Commerce Bank, Simon's own employer. GCB had just published half-yearly results, and they'd made the front page. That was bad: very, very bad. Bankers weren't C-list celebs; they knew there was no upside in media exposure. So, for a bank, it wasn't often a cause for celebration to have made the front pages of the *FT*, or the *Wall Street Journal.* What it usually meant was cock-up, big financial positions blow-up, disaster, and dismay – sometimes even criminal activity.

GCB was in a mess. Simon knew the broad details but still he couldn't tear his eyes away from his paper.

GCB IN SHOCK PROFITS WARNING

GCB has shocked financial markets by announcing a 56% decline in first-half profits. Chief Executive Dick Blewit said: 'Unprecedented economic turbulence has caused GCB to report a significant decline in first-half profits, together with a more focused business strategy going forward.

Simon pursed his lips. More focused business strategies meant fewer jobs.

The centrepiece of this strategy will be a re-evaluation of all non-core and non-revenue-producing areas.

Fuck! You couldn't get more non-revenue-producing than the back office, thought Simon. The back office was pure overhead. Although, on the plus side, chaps like him were probably too cheap to bother cutting. The cost saving in getting rid of him, compared to getting rid of a trader, was minimal. Perhaps the nets would be cast for the sharks, not the minnows?

We anticipate rapid implementation, on a going-forward basis, to restore profitability and help boost the share price, by year end. While we expect challenging market conditions to continue, I am highly confident GCB will achieve significant business synergies, going forward.'

Simon lowered his paper and stared glumly at his knees. His trousers were still damp from the rain, and his spirits were dripping. Even if he kept his job, one thing was clear: on a going-forward basis, he was going to have to work even harder than he did already. He'd have to put in even longer hours, which meant he'd get even less time with Caroline and the boys. Tough on her. Tough on him. Tough on the twins. But not as tough on any of them as unemployment would be.

When Simon finally struggled into GCB, he found the place swirling with conflicting analyses of the half-yearly results, rival deconstructions of Dick Blewit's statement, rumour, counter-rumour, and fear. He tried to avoid getting dragged into the morass – in times like these, he argued, it was best to keep your head down. So instead of standing in the corridor and chatting, he headed straight for his desk, where he found the usual 3 trillion e-mails waiting for him. But he only looked at one of them. It was from HR. Nobody had a clue what HR did during the fat years, but in the lean years it was common knowledge they weren't so much human resources as human you're-out-sources, human-get-out-of-here-sources, human bye-bye-sources. Simon clicked open his e-mail with a justified sense of dread.

As part of our ongoing, going-forward programme to improve and upgrade staff at GCB, you have been selected to undergo a 360-degree performance evaluation. This will involve you receiving performance

feedback from several colleagues in the organization.
We hope you will embrace this as an opportunity for
self-improvement. This office will contact you shortly
with further details.

Simon briefly slumped forward so his head was resting on
his keyboard. In his mind's eye he saw Caroline's face, creased
with disappointment in him, and he immediately decided not
to tell her he was up for evaluation. Meanwhile, in his mind's
ear he heard his boss, Keith, smarming down the phone to HR.
Simon had never liked Keith, who not only had a smarmy telephone manner, but also a smarmy grin and a smarmy per-
sonality. Ugh! Simon could just hear him: *Have we sent the
memo on 360 degree performance evaluation to that idiot Simon
Ayrton? We need to make sure the paperwork's in place before
we fire him.*

Liz and Zack felt a little as if they were undergoing a performance evaluation. The two of them were sitting side by side
on uncomfortable plastic chairs, listening to Dr Kent – now
very pregnant, and looking even more like a Teletubby than
ever – as she outlined some of the commoner reasons why
couples might experience delayed conception. She'd already
mentioned disorders of ovulation and was now onto the
fallopian tubes.

'Tubal damage can be caused by infection, miscarriage,
ectopic pregnancy, or a number of other possibilities,' she was

saying. 'But you've never had an ectopic pregnancy, have you, Mrs Fielding? And no late miscarriages?'

'No,' agreed Liz. 'What d'you mean by a number of other possibilities?'

'Endometriosis, roughly overgrowth of the lining of the womb, but you show no signs of that. Pelvic inflammatory disease. Unknown factors.' Dr Kent paused, and shrugged expansively, using her hands and her arms, as well as her shoulders. 'But just as often as it's tubal damage, it's the man's reproductive system.'

Zack had zoned out on fallopian tubes, but now he snapped to attention. 'What?'

'Of course. Semen can be low in volume. It can be low in numbers of sperm, or in sperm motility. There can be infection present, or antibodies that attack the sperm.'

'Yes, yes,' muttered Zack, crossing and then uncrossing his legs. 'But what can be *done* about it all? What next, for us?'

Dr Kent tapped her biro on the side of her desk. Her own baby was kicking and squirming inside her. This was her third. She'd had her first at thirty-one. Age was such a factor, in these things – and her notes told her Mrs Fielding was thirty-six, whilst Mr Fielding was thirty-eight.

'This is your third month with ovulation prediction kits?' she asked.

Her patients nodded.

'Um-hmm . . . Do you have health insurance?'

'Yes,' said Zack. 'I do, through work. It covers both of us.'

Dr Kent became businesslike. 'Good. In that case, I can get you an appointment at Holy Family – the private hospital in St John's Wood. Y'know? Otherwise, I'll try the North London, but it'll be a long wait.'

'And what'll they do?' asked Liz.

'There're a number of procedures and investigations they could carry out. They'll do a blood hormone profile, to check you're ovulating. They'll also take swabs to check for infection. They might use ultrasound to scan your ovaries, and there are various ways they could investigate your womb and tubes. But all that's a bit down the line. As for you, Mr Fielding . . .'

'*Me?*' flinched Zack.

'As for you,' repeated Dr Kent, smiling at him kindly, 'they'll start with a physical examination of your scrotum, possibly blood tests, and definitely a semen analysis. They'll examine the sperm microscopically, test for fructose levels, do a separation test.'

'Why fructose?' asked Liz. 'And what's a separation test?'

Zack scowled at her. By now he just wanted to get out of the surgery; he was beginning to feel as if the ceiling were plunging down on him like the piston in a syringe.

'Fructose?' said Dr Kent. 'If semen's low in it, then it suggests a blockage below the vesicles . . .'

All Liz's guides to getting pregnant featured diagrams of the male reproductive system, and now she tried to remember them, but she couldn't.

'What are the . . .' she began, but Zack kicked her, so she shut up.

Dr Kent glanced from the pair of them to her watch. She knew she'd been hasty on fructose and the seminal vesicles, and Mr Fielding clearly wasn't accommodated to the idea that the reasons for delayed conception might lie with him. She ought to offer a quick bit of counselling. But did she have the time? She thought of all the patients outside in the waiting room – plus she wanted to get out early today, to take her youngest, soon to be her middle child, to a birthday party.

'And a separation test,' she continued, in a tone just as discouraging of Liz's questions as Zack's kick had been, 'will help determine the motility of the sperm. But don't worry, they'll be able to answer all of your questions up at the clinic. And they provide a full counselling service, too. I'll try and get you Dr Souallah. He's excellent.'

Caroline didn't allow her children to be ill, so she'd been ignoring Louis's rash for the past few days. But this morning it had come up all over his body.

'That's your *take me to the doctor, mummy*, rash isn't it?' she'd said as she'd dressed him. He didn't seem remotely ill, nevertheless she'd phoned the surgery to book the appointment, then she'd rung round the coffee coven, to make arrangements for Nat. Sophie had come up trumps – what a doll.

The waiting room was kept much too hot for summer –

although not too hot for OAPs. They sat with their backs to the walls, bundled up in heavy coats and tea-cosy hats, smiling indulgently at Louis. He was not bothered by his rash, and was happily making train noises as he pushed a toy truck across the floor. *Choo, choo, choo,* went the truck, *woo-woo.* That was him occupied, thought Caroline, but what about her? The waiting room didn't offer a toy box for adults, only a stack of ancient, mid-market, women's magazines. Caroline scowled down at a cover showing a smiling housewife proffering a tray of sausage rolls. She often felt she lived her whole life between the pages of a housewife's magazine, and she simply couldn't face reading one now. So, in sheer desperation, she reached across to an empty chair, and picked up an abandoned copy of the *Ryleford Courier.*

The *Ryleford Courier* was a free paper. The front page carried news of cats stuck up trees, and inside it was stuffed with adverts for local products and services. Once a week it was delivered to Caroline's house, and once a week she chucked it in the bin, unread. But today, with nothing else to read, she found it moderately entertaining. Did she fancy getting away from it all? Well, then, a husband and wife team of personal travel advisers lived not so far away: *Holidays, flights, short breaks. Business or pleasure. For independent, professional advice, call Jenny and Trevor.* She might just do that, thought Caroline, and she'd ask whether they could book her a holiday from her self. Or here was one that was just *so* Ryleford: *Heraldic jewellery. Gold or silver. Cufflinks, signet rings, and heraldic buttons. All engraved with your family crest. Highest quality. Reasonable prices.* Caroline chuckled, and turned the page. At once her chuckle died, for here were the personals, the lonely hearts, and, though riveting, they always made her sad.

Men seeking men and women seeking women seemed to have given up hope in the *Ryleford Courier*, which carried, so far as Caroline could see, nothing but adverts from spinsters seeking sex: *Sincere, single business lady, 40, seeks genuine, considerate gentleman, 35–45, for friendship/romance, and to share interests, theatre, galleries, etc.* Caroline sighed, although she saluted the bravery, and the common sense, of this unknown business lady. It was only practical to advertise for love if you'd been unlucky, and all the more conventional channels had let you down. *Brunette, 38, good face and shape, GSOH, well-educated, into travelling, dining out, reading and sports, WLTM tall, good-looking man, 40s/50s, with big heart.* Big heart? thought Caroline; more likely big heartbreak. *Free-spirited country dweller, 53, seeks companionable man for walks, pub lunches, and possible LTR.*

Caroline frowned and lowered the paper. Louis was now entertaining the OAPs by flying his truck through the air. 'Zoom, zoom, zoom,' he sang, 'we're going to the moon.' That was where all the lonely men must be, thought his mum. They must be sobbing for love, on the lovely, silvery moon. If not there, then where else could they be? Where were they, all the lonely, dark princes? She closed her eyes, and began to compose an imaginary ad: *Dark prince, tall and tortured, interests world peace and conservation, loves laughter, literature, stargazing, all things beautiful and weird, seeks amazing lady for adventures both close to home, and far away . . .*

Brett was not a dark prince, he was a hollow man. Jo had not yet told him she was pregnant – if she'd decided on abortion, she never would have done. But she'd decided against abortion, and it was time to break her silence. Outside, New York was stinking hot, the garbage melting into the asphalt, but inside her grey and green Upper East Side apartment, all was cool. She had the AC on full blast, and she'd dressed coolly, too, in a loose linen shift dress, just the colour of seawater, trapped in rock pools. The aquamarine complemented, and complimented, her green eyes, which themselves shone with a cool self-possession.

But her self-possession was not complete. For a start, though she had clad it elegantly enough, she felt her body was letting her down very badly. Pregnancy might have made some women beautiful, sheened them with a radiance, glossed their hair, added sparkle to their eyes and lights to their skin, but for Jo it was a disaster, looks-wise. It wasn't just the weight gain. In the last few weeks her pores had become clogged with grease, and her once glossy hair was definitely tending to the lank and lifeless. But far worse than the tricks of her body were the tricks of her soul: since her home pregnancy test, Old Eyes and New Eyes had taken to hovering, constantly, at the peripheries of her vision. The rational part of her assumed they had no more reality than the figures encountered in dreams, but to the rest of her, they seemed just as real as the furniture in her sitting room. Now she glanced up to the ceiling, where, as she'd expected, they were fluttering, held within the curve of her C-shaped aluminium track lighting as if within the palm of some protective hand. They were like two dark, soft-winged moths, she thought – moths set on unnerving her. *Let him be generous,* she fancied them to plead, *let him be understanding, and accepting. Let him be pleased.*

Brett, when he arrived, was wary and on edge. Jo, he thought, was in a strange mood tonight. He and she usually headed straight for bed, but tonight she was reluctant to strip, and had fobbed him off with a beer. Would he be forced to declare his love again? Brett groaned, inwardly. It was such a drag he still hadn't found her replacement. Could he be losing his touch? He shivered, to think it. But these days, seduction seemed to be getting harder. Just a few nights back, in a bar, a promising beauty had laughed in his face.

'You're too old for me!' she'd taunted.

Brett frowned at the memory and stared forty in the face. But it was a terrible sight, so he averted his eyes and flicked them to Jo. Ferrchrissakes! Her bloom seemed to be fading before his eyes. He'd had no idea a woman could lose her looks so quickly. Was it because he'd told her he loved her? Did she feel so secure of him she'd decided it was okay to look like some New Jersey soccer mom?

Jo inelegantly hauled her treacherous body to the very edge of her sleek, celery-coloured, suede sofa. Brett was sitting opposite her on a moss-green chair, also suede. The lovers were separated only by the flattened wooden n of Jo's coffee table, and also by the flattened wooden n of everything.

'I've got something to tell you.'

If she dumps me, thought Brett, *this time I'll let her.*

'Yes?' He took a swig of his beer.

'I'm pregnant.'

'*What?*'

'You heard.'

'But that's impossible.' Brett banged down his beer on the coffee table. 'You're on the pill!'

'It's only 99.8 per cent effective.'

'Don't give me that!'

Jo shrugged, since she had nothing to say.

'Are you sure?'

'That I'm pregnant? Yes, of course.'

'No woman gets pregnant by accident!'

Jo told herself to stay calm: shouting now would achieve nothing. 'That's not true.'

'Bullshit!'

'No, Brett.'

'And you're claiming it's mine?'

'*Claiming?*' Jo laughed, but added nothing.

Brett decided not to dispute the certainty conveyed by her laughter – maybe later, but not now.

'Ferchrissakes!' he said. 'Ferchrissakes!' He belatedly wished they'd used condoms – but they'd never even discussed the possibility. Condoms weren't for the likes of them; they were risk junkies, and the risk of AIDS, of death, had added an erotic thrill to their couplings. But there was risk, and risk – and the risk of a baby could never have thrilled him. It could only ever have inhibited him. Had he suspected the danger, he'd have run screaming from the extra-marital bed, mid-thrust. 'So, when are you getting rid of it?'

Jo did not pretend, neither to herself nor to Brett, that she felt a shocked surprise. She did not demand how he could suggest such a thing, nor did she become hysterical. She accepted that termination was the obvious termination to her pregnancy, so she said nothing, just shook her head.

'You are getting rid of it, right?'

'Wrong.'

'You're not getting rid of it?'

'No.'

'But . . .'

Jo held up a hand to silence him. 'Brett, you understand basic probability. How could I deny our baby the chance to think how astonishing it was that he . . .'

'*He?*'

Jo shrugged; *he* was simply a policy she'd hit upon to avoid the inanimate feel of *it*.

'Or she. I don't know our baby's sex, but I don't like to call it *it*, so I call it *he*. How could I deny him the chance to think how astonishing it was that he had ever been born at all, when he so easily might not have been? Imagine how he'll reason a few years hence: if mom had slept with a different man, on a different night, then no me; if one particular sperm had been pushed aside at the moment of my conception, then no me. And so on, and on, and on. He'll think himself back through my mom's mom, and your dad's dad, all the way back to those hominids in Africa, back, back, back. Back to the primordial slime. In the face of such odds against his ever existing at all, how could I – me, Brett, *me* – how could I be the one to say, *Sorry, tricked ya!*'

Jo had said her piece, and Brett was looking at her as if she'd lost her mind, but she didn't care. She hadn't really been talking to him. She'd been talking to her two little moths. And if that meant she had, indeed, lost her mind, then so be it. She gazed up to the track lighting, and Old Eyes and New Eyes gazed down. Mother and unborn offspring silently communed.

I failed, thought-said Jo, *he's not pleased, is he? Not pleased, not understanding, not generous.*

No, he's not, blinked back two pairs of eyes.

I'm sorry.

There's always you, blinked back one pair of eyes: New Eyes.

So, thought Jo, her little speech had done half its job. She had intended to reassure New Eyes: *Hush, my love,* she'd wanted to say, *mommy's here.* Clearly, she had succeeded. But had she succeeded in imparting anything to Old Eyes? And what had she intended to impart? Jo really didn't like to think about either question; they were both way too difficult, and too complicated.

Life was just so damn confusing, thought William. Annie was sleeping with her back to him, and she'd shuffled right to the far side of the bed. A few weeks ago he'd have snuggled up close, spooned his body into hers and snaked his arms around her, just for the pleasure of feeling her breathe in her sleep. But now he didn't much want to. Now he was content to lie in his own patch of bed space. Why the change? It was Penelope's fault, thought William, or, not exactly her fault, but certainly it had jolted him seeing her like that, at little Edward's christening.

For a start, he'd been jolted by Penelope's marginally podgy body. Until he'd met Annie, William had never thought of skinny girls as his type. Until he'd met her, he'd always thought he liked a bit of flesh to get hold of, a bit of squidgy softness in which to sink, or in which to surrender. At first Annie, with her jutting bones, had made him think he'd been wrong about all that. He'd taken one look at her, and he'd thought . . . he hadn't thought; that first glimpse of Annie had plunged him beyond thought. But now he'd seen her scrawny body next to Penelope's generous one, it had made him realize how badly he'd been missing curves. How badly he'd been missing fullness. Ripeness. Abundance. And he'd been missing

Penelope's good, plain common sense, too. She was in all ways such a *sensible* girl. No silly hunt-sabbing for Penelope! No laughing at the royal family! And her taste was so . . . tasteful. William remembered Annie's Chinese pictures, hanging a couple of floors beneath him, and scowled into the dark of the bedroom. He had taken Annie's side against his mother in the row about the pugtraits, because he'd felt he'd had to. A son's mother had to yield to his wife-to-be. That was just the way life was, and the sooner his own mother realized it, the better for everybody. Nonetheless, he didn't much like Annie's pictures – they were very tiring to live with. So crude! So inartistic! Penelope would never have tolerated such gaudiness. She liked hunting prints, just as he did. Prints of flowers, prints of fruit. Unpretentious stuff . . . And her dress sense was sound, too. What on earth had Annie been thinking of, going to little Edward's christening dressed like a stray from a Christmas panto? Penelope would never have embarrassed him like that. Penelope had looked delightful in . . . William couldn't quite remember what she'd been wearing, but whatever it was, it hadn't been glittery, or skimpy. It had been suitable. Just like her. And, when all was said and done, a man could do with a bit of suitability. Whenever her man ran out of things to say, a suitable girl fed him lines, she laughed at his jokes, and never cracked ones he couldn't understand. William *never* got Annie's jokes – not even after she'd explained them. She really was a strange one, when you came to think about it. And that was quite apart from her attitude to babies. She'd still not told him whether or not she wanted children. Was that normal? And even if it was: was it as normal as Penelope's uncomplicated broodiness, or his own?

Six

Liz was lying on a couch in a darkened room, which was little more than a cubicle, having her ovaries scanned by Dr Souallah. It wasn't until the nurse had asked her to remove her knickers, hitch up her skirt, and arrange her legs as though for a smear, that she'd realized the scanning device would be shoved up inside her, not gently rolled back and forth over her abdomen. This was her second consultation at Holy Family. Last week, with Zack, it had been bad enough. Dr Souallah had done what he called his fertility work-up, which had meant he'd asked them all sorts of truly embarrassing questions about the frequency and timing of sexual inter-course. But at least she'd kept her knickers on, except during her physical examination by a female nurse. Now, knickerless, and with a bit of metal and plastic inside her, a pen-like thing which was being wielded by a man, she felt she'd been stripped of all her dignity, and all her modesty. Still, she supposed an internal scan was no worse than the indignities of pregnancy – the indignities Jo would no doubt soon be experiencing.

At the thought of Jo, Liz flinched. Dr Souallah at once stopped his manipulation of the scanning device.

'Are you okay? Did that hurt?'

'I'm fine.' No she wasn't. She wasn't fine at all, she was jealous as hell. Apart from Zack, Jo was the person Liz was closest to in the whole world. Yet when Jo had phoned with her stunning news, Liz had barely been able to croak out her congratulations.

'I'm sorry,' Jo had croaked back. 'I'm really sorry.'

Liz hadn't bothered to tell her sister not to be so silly. Jo hadn't wanted to be pregnant, and was. Liz wanted to be pregnant, and wasn't. Of course Jo was sorry. And of course Liz was jealous. Still, it couldn't be helped. It was what it was; she had to accept Jo's pregnancy, just like she had to accept being stripped of her dignity. Jealousy was jealousy. Female biology was female biology. Too bad! Tant pis! Tough shit!

Dr Souallah was saying something.

'What?' Liz asked. 'Sorry, but could you repeat that, I didn't quite get it.'

Dr Souallah smiled at her in the half-light. He was a nice man, she thought, although he might have explained this procedure a little better. But he had kind eyes – chocolate brown, like his hair – and an expression that suggested he might at any moment start singing a mournful song, the type with *aye, aye, aye, aye,* as the chorus.

'There's no sign that your ovaries are polycystic. Remember, I explained you don't show any of the features typical of polycystic ovary syndrome? Well, now we can be sure. There's no swelling, either. Also, I've done the measurements, and the lining of your uterus is normal thickness.'

'Everything looks okay?'

'Everything looks fine.'

Liz should have been reassured, but she wasn't.

'So that means it's something worse?' she said, anxiously. 'I mean blocked tubes? You'll have to do a hystero . . . a hystero . . .'

'A hysterosalpinography?'

Hysterosalpinographies were not covered by Liz's guides to getting pregnant, but they were everyday stuff to Dr Souallah. He had already explained to Liz that hysterosalpinography was an X-ray technique, which involved injecting a contrast medium into a woman's uterus, thus allowing her reproductive organs to be seen, and revealing any tubal blockage.

'Yes,' agreed Liz, who thought they sounded terrifying, 'That's what I meant.'

'Let's wait and see what your blood hormone profile shows, and also Zack's semen analysis. Once we've got the results from the basic tests, we can decide how best to proceed.'

We? thought Liz, bitterly. *We?* He was the doctor, for heaven's sake, and informed consent, the patient's involvement in the decision-making process and so on and so forth could only go so far. She couldn't even remember the name of the hysterothingy, how was she supposed to be able to decide whether or not she should have one?

'Yes,' she said meekly. 'I suppose we can.'

'And the results won't take long to come through.' Dr Souallah patted his ultrasound machine. 'This is instantaneous. Your blood hormone profile should be ready by tomorrow, and once we've got Zack's semen, it'll only be another couple of days . . . He'll reschedule, as soon as he's feeling better?'

Liz and Zack had held hands through their first consultation with Dr Souallah, and they were both supposed to have been at Holy Family this morning – Liz for her blood tests and her scan, Zack to give semen for analysis. But Zack had woken up with a stinking cold, and had cancelled his appointment. Typical man! Liz had thought, as she'd dressed, this morning. Now she felt guilty about her lack of sympathy.

'Yes. When I left, he looked terrible, poor thing.'

'Paracetamol,' said Dr Souallah, firmly. 'Anyway, now we're all finished, I'll leave you to sort yourself out. Come through to the office when you're ready.'

Jo remembered her dream of her body being invaded by a space alien, and thought it hadn't been so far off the mark, after all. The face turned towards her could have belonged to a resident of the planet Zog; it was nearly all eyes, and its eyes which were almost everything were set in a high-domed, elongated skull. Jo turned her head slightly, and looked up to two *more* pairs of eyes: Old Eyes and New Eyes, her two dark moths, who were flitting in the room's semi-lit gloom. She contemplated them a moment, then turned back to the monitor, and gazed, once more, at a pair of real eyes. Did her baby gaze back? Or was it quite unaware that its privacy had been invaded? Jo suspected not. Doctors might scoff, but it seemed to her, right now, that modern medicine shaded into the supernatural. Why shouldn't she be being watched, not only from the ceiling, but also from within her womb, via the miracle of technology? She felt, very strongly, that her baby could see her and was just as interested to stare into her eyes as she was to stare into his. Or hers.

'Well, Mommy,' grinned the ultrasound operative, 'say hello.'

Jo was taken aback to hear herself described as *Mommy*.

'Hello,' she mumbled, embarrassed. How she wished this first glimpse of her growing baby could have taken place in private, just herself and the alien, without the alien presence of the ultrasound operative. On the screen, through a snowstorm of what could have been static, or could have been her body fluids sloshing, or could have been just about anything, really, her baby was performing an astronaut's outer-space acrobatics, tumbling this way and that, unimpeded by gravity.

'It's still a bit early to tell the sex,' said the operative, 'but I'll call it *he*. Purely for convenience. Don't take it to mean anything.'

'I won't,' smiled Jo. 'That's what I do, too. I call it *he*, so I don't have to call it *it*.'

The operative applied another squirt of cold jelly to Jo's exposed stomach, which was by now beginning to round out –

nicely according to Jo's OBGYN, but revoltingly according to Jo. The operative thought Jo's stomach was neither nice nor revolting, merely a medium for the passage, or impediment, of sonar. She expertly slid the head of her scanning device around her patient's navel.

'I need to get a better angle for skull measurements,' she explained.

Jo grunted, and watched as her baby kicked its stubby proto-legs, and wafted its proto-arms. It did another graceful somersault – which amazingly, she couldn't feel at all within her. A somersault, thought Jo, was the action of a child. She imagined a child turning somersaults and joyful cartwheels on a green, green lawn, in summer. The child was laughing, but Jo felt tears prick her own eyes. She quickly blinked them back, grateful for the dim light. The ultrasound operative was absorbed in taking measurements, but even if she'd glanced up from her keyboard, she wouldn't have noticed Jo's glittering eyes. Or so Jo hoped. She didn't want to cry in the presence of this kind, efficient technician. It would be as impossible as crying had now become in the presence of Brett.

At the thought of Brett, Jo moaned slightly. The two of them had barely spoken, except about business, since she'd told him she was pregnant. He'd walked away from her, and also from his child. She'd been left to tell herself both she, and his child, would be better off without him. And maybe they would. But Jo doubted it. She couldn't fool herself. Brett could walk away from her, but she couldn't just walk away from him.

True, she had tried to fire him, but now he'd gone she missed him, badly, badly. She missed the feel of his hands on her hair and flesh; she missed the feel of his hair and flesh beneath her fingers. She missed his smell, and the smell of her own body after he had finished with it. She missed the scorching heat of his body within hers. Were these things replaceable? Jo had no choice; she had to believe that they were. But a father was not. A father was irreplaceable. Jo knew her child would miss his father, just as much as she did, and also far more than she did, in ways she could only dimly imagine. It was so unfair. It was *wrong*. Her child deserved more from his own father than a blank indifference to his existence. Jo felt tears sting her eyes, again. Tears were stupid, she berated herself, and it was certainly very stupid of her to continue to want Brett. But was it also stupid of her to want him to acknowledge that the being on the screen, the being inside her body, had been half made by him? Jo knew that it was not. She wanted Brett to acknowledge his child. She wanted him to love his child, as he damn well *ought*.

The ultrasound operative quietly passed Jo a Kleenex. 'I know. It can be quite overwhelming, can't it?'

Jo blew her nose, grateful for the Kleenex, but she said nothing, and watched her baby in sad silence. Meanwhile, the operative tapped away at her keyboard a few minutes longer.

'There. I've got what I need,' she said, at last. 'And don't worry, everything looks fine; all his measurements are well within the usual parameters.' She leaned over to the wall to click on the light, which was harsh and bright after the gloom. 'I'll do you a couple of print-outs, now.'

The print-outs of Jo's baby were black and white, grainy, and overlaid with the snowstorm of static, or body fluids, or Jo knew not what. But Jo didn't care. She smiled down at the pictures, and the operative smiled at her expression.

'Well, Mommy, he's photogenic, hey?'

'Better than a movie star.'

The operative nodded, but then turned brisk. 'Wipe the jelly off with this.' She passed over a big roll of paper towel. 'I'll be outside, if you've got any questions.'

Once she was alone, Jo climbed off the examination couch and wiped her tummy. She had just started rearranging her clothes, when she glanced up to the ceiling to check on her moths. Old Eyes was fluttering, as usual, but something strange was happening to New Eyes. Jo froze, with her skirt half-zipped. New Eyes was evaporating. The ghost that had condensed from nothing in the world behind her bathroom mirror had now begun to un-condense. Did it feel banished by the power of a pair of *real* eyes? Or better: set free? Jo glanced to the computer screen, now nothing but a pane of coated glass, but so recently another mirror, of sorts: a mirror reflecting her own solitude in her baby's eyes, and her baby's solitude in hers. From the mirror-screen Jo glanced to her print-outs, which were lying on the examination couch, then from her print-outs back to New Eyes, who was still slowly dispersing into the atoms of the surrounding air. She continued to watch as, gradually, all the non-stuff stuff of New Eyes streamed away into nothing, into the void, into a blankness as blank as their expression once had been. Or else they streamed away to infinity, the destination and the origin on which they'd been fixed all along.

It was a mercy Ursula didn't know Jo felt herself to be a witness to the comings and goings of ghostly eyes. She'd have worried her daughter was losing her wits, along with her figure. Especially since she seemed to believe she was pregnant via a virgin conception.

'Who's the father?' Ursula had asked, when Jo had phoned.

'Nobody.'

Huh! But Ursula hadn't pressed. Just like she hadn't pressed Annie on the delicate subject of whether she loved her betrothed. If her girls wanted to keep their distance, she'd have to let them; she was their mother, not their conscience, or some sort of supernatural being, indwelling within them, or attendant upon them. She'd even maintained a scrupulous discretion with Liz.

'Mum,' her oldest had said, over coffee and cake, a week or so back, 'I think you should know Zack and I are seeing a fertility specialist.'

All Ursula's suspicions had been justified, and she'd felt a heavy coldness in her guts.

'Oh, darling . . .'

'Don't, Mum! I don't want pity! And I don't want to talk

about it. I just want you to know, so . . . I mean . . . I just thought you should know, so . . . and if I do want to talk, I know where you are.'

Subject closed. Ursula had said nothing, but had continued to consume her cake, whilst feeling herself consumed by sadness on her oldest child's behalf.

But at least there was always Caroline! These last few weeks, as Ursula had tossed and turned at night, worrying about Liz, or Annie, or Jo, she'd consoled herself that at least she had *one* daughter who gave no cause for maternal concern. Caroline's marriage was strong. Her husband adored her, she had two adorable sons, a house many people would have adored, and a lifestyle, ditto. Admittedly, the ratio of one out of four daughters settled and happy was not particularly good, but it was better than none out of four and, recently, Ursula had been clinging to it.

Which was why she was so distressed to have found what appeared to be jottings for a lonely hearts ad, in Caroline's handwriting.

'Darling!' she said, sharply. 'What's this?'

Caroline was at her kitchen sink, washing a lettuce for lunch. Her sink looked out over the back garden, where Jason was romping with the boys, all three of them tearing round the weed-infested lawn, yelling and wow-wowing like Native Americans. She hoped Louis's rash wouldn't come back – the doctor had explained it was a mild infant urticaria, probably brought on by house mites, or by pollution. He didn't know, really, but nothing serious. Could be pollen, perhaps? Or grass seed? And anyway here was a cream, to clear it.

'What's what?' she asked, glancing over to her mother, who was today in a purple jumpsuit.

'This.' Ursula crossed the 'flags' (stone effect lino) of Caroline's country-style kitchen, and waved a tear-off sheet of A4 under her daughter's nose. The paper was completely covered in green swirls.

'Nat's green period,' laughed Caroline. 'Last week he painted this huge piece of paper green all over, nothing but green. What a wonderful patch of green, I said, when . . .'

'No! No! No!' snapped Ursula. 'I meant *this*.' She flipped the paper over, and jabbed at it with her finger.

There was dead silence, for a beat.

'Ah!' said Caroline. 'I thought I'd destroyed that.'

'I bet you did!'

Ursula held the paper at arm's length, and mother and daughter both studied it.

Rather special woman.

Sensitive, liberal strawberry blonde.

Sensitive, warm, strawberry blonde, early 30s, WLTM
(seeks?)

Pudding. Dessert. Torte. Dolce. Sugar,
you may think you have had the real sorbet de cassis (sp?),
but I'm a Viennese truffle cake, with a side order of

*Mother, 32, bored out of her skull, seeks attractive,
athletic man, with a view to changing her life.*

Caroline took the paper from her mother, ripped it into
tiny pieces and chucked them in the swing bin. Then she
returned to rinsing lettuce leaves.

'Good job it was you, not Simon, who found that.'

'Too bloody right! What the hell were you thinking of?'
Ursula positively shrieked, she was so rattled by this evidence
of restlessness in the daughter she'd relied upon to be happy.
Her daughters' worlds all seemed to be going to the dogs at
once, and it was more than a mother could be expected to bear.

'I wasn't serious. It was just a fantasy, to keep me going.'

'A fantasy! To keep you going! Fiddlesticks!'

Caroline scowled, and crossly turned her attention from
the lettuce to a red pepper that lay waiting on the draining
board.

'My life's no picnic. I tell you, I'm bored stiff, most of the
time.'

'Poor you!' mocked Ursula. 'Poor, poor you! But that's what
motherhood's like; I've been there, remember?'

'Yeah, but the difference was, you didn't have much
choice.'

'Such a *burden* to have options.'

'Okay, so I'm lucky. But you didn't expect equality, and I
do. In your day, everybody was at it – having kids, I mean.
Staying at home. Now it's only mugs like me.'

'Mugs like you? *Equality?*'

'Nobody told me it goes out the window once you have kids.'

'Dear, dear!' Ursula's tone was still mocking, 'Dear, dear!'

'Well, they didn't.'

'So you plan to walk out on Simon, a decent man, who loves you, to prove that you're his equal?'

'No!' Caroline sliced viciously at the red pepper. 'Who said anything about walking out? I just needed . . .'

'Needed what? Infidelity has no place in a marriage, no place at all. Once trust's gone, it's gone for good. Look at Annie, and Ming Kwan!'

'Annie?' Caroline shook her head to clear it of other people's disasters. 'She's happy now. And I wasn't exactly planning on being unfaith—'

'I don't care what you were *exactly* planning. You don't walk out on the kids just because you're fed up with them. And you don't betray your husband, just because—'

'Because what? The passion's gone?' Now it was Caroline's turn to mock – and it was always dangerous to mock your mum.

'Now you listen to me, my girl! You may be thirty-two, and a mother yourself, but that ad was the work of a silly little spoilt little *brat*. You have a wonderful husband; okay he might not set the world on fire, but he loves you. He loves the boys. He does his best—'

'What? Surely you're not going to say it's not a bad best?'

'Well, it's not! Look at this house! It's what you always wanted. You're not flogging yourself to death juggling work and—'

'So I'm not allowed to be unhappy, because so many women have it so much worse?'

'Damn right! And you're not unhappy. You're just being melodramatic. And selfish, and self-pitying. You'll turn into one of those whinging, middle-aged women, who moan their husbands don't understand them, or their orgasms.'

'Gee, thanks . . .'

'Simon deserves more than that! Have you even *told* him you're—'

'Fantasizing about having an affair?' cut in Caroline. 'Now who's being silly?'

'You should talk to him—'

'Why should I say anything? He should have noticed I've been . . . distracted.'

'How can he be expected to notice anything, the hours he works? And *who's* he working for?'

Caroline knew the answer, and it made her even crosser.

'Play it *safe*?' she spat. 'Is that what you're telling me? Make do . . .'

'*Making do . . . ?*' Ursula thumped the draining board. She'd never liked Caroline's country-style kitchen. Okay, it didn't quite have an Aga, but all its distressed 'oak' (veneer) struck her as pretentious in a suburban house. 'Look at this swanky kitchen! There's no making do in here!'

Holding the Baby

'You know I'm not talking about the kitchen – and I know you despise it, by the way. You're telling me to make do with contentment. But I'm fed up with contentment.'

'Then you're an idiot.'

'So accept I haven't got . . .' Caroline was about to shout she hadn't got what she'd wanted out of life, but changed her mind at the last minute '. . . What about going flat-out for life?' she said instead, almost calmly. 'What about living to the limits? Making a grab for . . .'

'Compromise isn't always failure!'

'What is it, then?'

'Com-*promise*,' shot back Ursula, deliberately mispronouncing the word. 'It's a promise. You've promised Simon to find a middle way between your needs and his, your opinions and his, your desires and his . . . and you've promised him not to compromise all that by some silly, indiscreet action.'

'So, stick with my marriage, come what may?'

'Come what may?' Ursula as good as blew a raspberry. 'Does he beat you? Does he drink? Does he screw around?'

'But what about *me*?'

'What about you?'

'What if I feel I'm . . .' Caroline wanted to say: what if I feel I'm slowly vanishing? But even to her own ears it sounded moany: who was she to say where self-respect became egoism? 'And love?' she challenged, instead. 'What about gambling all for love?'

'Love,' repeated Ursula. 'My point, precisely. You've got

kids, now. Their needs have to come first. That's love, Caroline. It isn't as exciting or as entrancing as the other kind; it's tough, and cool, and real. And you just have to get on with it. Get on with your life, my girl. Don't do anything stupid. Don't wreck things, for yourself, and Simon, and the boys.'

What did it mean to wreck a life, wondered Annie, as she lay in bed nursing a cold, and how many ways were there to do it? Her virus-befuddled brain wasn't just idly spewing out these questions; she was thinking about Ming Kwan, and whether or not she should phone him. This morning, her battered immune system was fully occupied fighting the cold virus, and Ming Kwan had seized the opportunity to recrudesce with a vengeance.

It was all the fault of *The Loop*. Annie read it every month, ostensibly to see if there'd been a repeat of the Park Avenue Princess / Billy Buddha product-placement incident, but really to see if anyone she knew was in it, and because it was such a treat. Except this month's issue was a treat that had morphed into a trick: someone she knew *was* in it, and that someone was Ming Kwan. And Ming Kwan wasn't just in it, he'd practically taken over the issue, four pages they'd given him. Four pages! Annie flicked through the piece again, then flung the magazine onto the floor. The violence of this action precipitated a coughing fit, and she reached to the cluttered bedside table for her beaker of Lemsip. Not that she expected Lemsip to do her much good. Infection was rearing up to grab her round the heart, and she knew it would take more than hot drinks to defeat it . . . If she wanted to defeat it. But did she? Annie put down her beaker, rolled to the edge of the bed, then stretched to retrieve the magazine she'd just tossed away.

Ming Kwan had been given four pages in *The Loop* because he was unfairly handsome, unfairly dashing, and a literary agent. He represented a string of high-profile authors, most of whom were women, and most of whom were Chinese, or hyphenated Chinese: Anglo-Chinese, American-Chinese, Canadian-Chinese. Some of these women had written memoirs of growing up during the Cultural Revolution, others had written lightly fictionalized accounts of the same thing, a few had tackled Tiananmen, the problems of contemporary China, and life in the Chinese diaspora. They all wrote lit lit, as opposed to lad lit, chick lit, mum lit or any other it lit. Lit lit was always big in *The Loop*, since its readers knew they'd be called upon to discuss it at dinner parties. Then again, unfairly handsome, unfairly dashing men were always in short supply. What with one thing and another, *The Loop*'s editor had been delighted when one of her chums had said she fancied Ming Kwan rotten, so could she do a piece on him, please?

Annie wriggled to get comfortable against the pillows. She briefly cradled *The Loop* against her chest, wishing her blocked nose didn't prevent her breathing in its comforting, glossy paper scent, and the mingled scent of scents with which scent manufacturers had impregnated strips along the edges of its pages, by way of advertisement. She steeled herself a moment longer, then riffled through to the pictures of the man she'd loved, then thought she'd hated, and now . . .

Annie scowled, and concentrated hard on the photos. Here was Ming Kwan, reading, in his office. Here he was elegantly lounging on a day-bed, gazing out on the world with all the languor of a courtesan, all the hauteur of a king. Christ, he looked good! But she was not prepared to be seduced by his image. She reminded herself that, though Ming Kwan had no control over his looks – he couldn't help it if he was beautiful – his dash was far from effortless. Indeed, it was very carefully thought out. He wore his hair long, in a trademark queue, a plaited tail. This traditional Chinese style was rarely seen in modern China – but it impressed the *gweilo*, the foreign devils. And Ming Kwan's clothes were affected, too. In London and New York, he wore Chinese-style suits in black silk, the collars round and high, the sleeves flowing, the jackets fastened with intricately knotted frogging – but when he visited Hong Kong or Beijing he wore jeans and T-shirts, just like everybody else. Even his name had the teensiest hint of the showman about it. True, it had been bestowed by his parents when he was born – at University College Hospital, London – but Annie knew that for his first eighteen years he'd mostly gone by his English name, David, or even its shortening, Dave. It was only at university that he'd started using his Chinese name. Fair enough, thought Annie, since, roughly translated, Ming Kwan means bright and shining future. It must have seemed a great name for an undergraduate – although she sniffily pointed out, to herself, it might not sit so well on him when he hit middle age.

Ming Kwan, middle aged! Imagine that! Annie, still semi-resisting his appeal, tried to, but it was just too hard. Though he was in his early thirties, Ming Kwan still had something of the glow of youth about him, just as he had when she'd first set eyes on him, four years back. The two of them had met at a party. Annie smiled to herself, to remember it. A little drink, a little weed, talking, dancing, snogging . . .

Then they'd gone back to his place, where almond eyes had gazed into round ones, round eyes had gazed into almond ones, and two people had decided that eyes, of any shape, could be tunnels, tumbling them directly to the centre of the universe. Come, love, and make me null and void. Then that had been that . . . until Ming Kwan had slept with one of the scribbleatrices he represented. Even Annie's blood cells had been shocked. She'd listened, patiently, to his halting, tearful confession, and agreed with his suggestion that love required absolute honesty. Then she'd walked out on him on the grounds that love didn't require *that* sort of tolerance. It had been a mess, but the two of them would probably have sorted it out if Annie hadn't immediately met William, and very quickly, as she put it to herself with the glibness born of desperation, somehow or other ended up engaged to him.

But should she *stay* engaged? That was the question now vibrating through Annie's mucus-clogged brain. She was lying in the bed she shared with her betrothed, mooning over pictures of her ex. Was that right? Well, no. It wasn't, really. But what if Ming Kwan had found himself somebody else, these past few months? What if some drop dead gorgeous clothes horse, who also happened to be able to talk, had got her claws into him? Annie snuffled and told herself it wasn't very likely. That sort of gossip travelled fast, and she'd surely have heard something on the grapevine . . . But what if her friends were keeping information from her? Annie snuffled a bit more, dropped *The Loop*, reached for a handful of Kleenex, and began to shred them.

Should she stay engaged?

Sniff.

Should she call it off?

Sniff, sniff.

Should she at least phone Ming Kwan, before she was hidden behind the purdah of marriage?

Sob, sob, sob.

Simon, being a man, could never find himself in purdah, but he was certainly in hell. Looked at some ways, it was quite nice, really – warm and cosy, with comfy chairs, and even coffee and cake. Keith, his boss, had suggested they come to GCB's local Starbucks, for their 'little chat'. Simon had been alarmed; taking the worker bees out for coffee was such a transparent management technique. For all he knew, Keith had been to an HR seminar on it: *Take them out for coffee, to soften the blow.*

Anyway, how could a 360-degree performance evaluation be presented as a 'little chat'?

The two businessmen had bagged themselves padded, velvet chairs, and a quiet table, towards the back of the café.

'Two grande skim lattes at the bar,' yelled the barista.

'That'll be us,' said Keith, a jowly man with a receding hairline, who spoke with an unpleasant adenoidal whine. He got up to fetch the coffees, and left his documents spread out on the table. Simon tried to read them, but he was sitting opposite his boss, and, from this angle, Keith's documents were upside down. He could make out the odd word – *management, bottom-line* – but no more. Ah, well, he'd know soon enough what they said. More importantly, he'd probably know whether or not he was for the bullet. Just last week, GCB had de-hired eighty people from the London office. They'd done it cleverly, quietly, so the financial press hadn't noticed. Hardly anybody had noticed, except the de-hirees, and those who worried they might be next. Simon breathed in the coffee-scented Starbucks air, and smelled only the rankness of his own distress.

'So,' said Keith, shuffling his papers. 'Here's the self-evaluation form you filled out. I'm going to talk you through it, okay?'

No. It's not okay. Rip the bloody thing to shreds.

'Okay.'

'Let's start with the self-evaluation of this year's performance, shall we?'

'The scale of one to ten?'

'That's right. You gave yourself a nine.'

Ten had been excellent, and Simon had dared not risk that, but, on the other hand, he'd dared not give himself less than an eight. So he'd compromised on nine.

'Nine,' he agreed, nodding firmly.

'Do you really think nine's justified?'

Of course not, you idiot!

'Well, of course!'

'What have you done all year to support it?'

Simon's mind went blank. He couldn't even remember what he'd been doing that morning, let alone what he'd been doing all year. He looked at his boss, pleadingly – but pleading looks didn't work with Keith.

'And the very first question: *In your own evaluation, do you possess the skills necessary to do your job?* You answered: *Don't know.*' Keith paused, and waved the evaluation form. '*Don't know*,' he repeated. 'Simon, *Don't know* doesn't fill me with much confidence.'

It didn't fill Simon with much confidence, either. 'I didn't really understand the question,' he mumbled.

'What? But this form's designed for someone with the intelligence of a radiator! And the second question: *Do you live the values of this organization?* You answered: *Very good.* Simon, that's the wrong answer. We're talking can you recite the ten core values GCB represents?'

Simon swallowed. No, he couldn't.

'Empowerment,' began Keith, counting GCB's core values

off on his fingers, 'responsibility, excellence, diversity, dedication.' He paused, unable to remember any more. 'There's five of them, straight off.'

Simon reached for his coffee and took a sip. Had things got so bad he'd be justified in going on the counter-attack? It was risky, but if he were anyway in a lose-lose situation, he might as well fight. But was he in a lose-lose situation? Was he toast? Duh! What a question! Simon thought he might as well be a slice of white, popped into the toaster, back at home. God, what would he tell Caroline? He took another sip of coffee. Yes, he decided, best to fight.

'What about *you*, Keith? Are *you* dedicated to excellence?'

Keith leaned forward on his comfy, velvet chair. 'Listen, Simon, I'm your only hope in the organization. You need me on your side. I suggest we make this a positive, goal-orientated discussion.'

'What goals are we talking about here?'

'Our entire management team is working to accelerate significant improvements in bottom-line performance.'

'You're talking about de-hiring, aren't you?'

'Whilst GCB is undergoing some restructuring, we do want to identify the best performers, and use them to leverage the resources, going forward.'

Yeah, thought Simon, the bastard was talking about de-hiring.

*

Brett never worried about being a bastard. He worried about being a lean, mean, money-making machine. And that was Jo's problem. Or, rather, her problem was: how do you exert moral pressure on a machine? Were machines susceptible to black-mail? Jo had decided to take a leaf out of Old Eyes' and New Eyes' book, and give it a try.

New Eyes might have departed his or her mom, but Old Eyes was still trailing her everywhere. Jo glanced up to check on the position of her newly lonely moth, as she strode purpose-fully towards her boss's office door. She was carrying a folder, and though its contents made her hands shake, she was deter-mined not to succumb to nerves. Her sharp rap on Brett's door was confident enough but, as always, her loins liquefied the moment she was in his presence. It didn't help that his office lair was big, and designed to intimidate. Not, she re-minded herself, that she didn't have a right to be here; Brett was her boss, after all, and she had a legitimate business reason to talk to him.

'What is it?' he snapped from behind his bank of screens, which crouched like goblins on his huge expanse of desk.

'Tsukahara,' replied Jo, naming a high-profile Japanese client. 'They want to do a Hong Kong dollar put against the US dollar, with an underlying US 5 billion.'

Brett thought about this a moment. 'Interesting.'

'Yes. But I'll need your help getting compliance approval.'

Brett pulled over a pad, and scribbled a quick note. 'Okay, I'll get onto the lawyers.'

'Thanks.' Jo paused, to clear her brain of Tsukahara, and

the mighty Greenback. 'And I also want to show you these.' She flipped open her folder, and stepped towards Brett's desk. 'From the hospital,' she added, as she thrust her scans towards him. Brett knew what they were at once but he did not give them his attention; instead Mom and Pop looked at each other a long moment.

'What is this? Blackmail?'

'Sometimes it's justified.'

'You think? Well *I* think you're mistaken. Blackmail's as wrong as—'

'Conceiving a baby, and then—'

'*You* want to have this baby. That's your call; there's nothing I can do to stop you. But—'

'Brett, you're his father.'

'His?'

Jo felt a sense of deja vu. 'I say *his*,' she explained, for the second time, 'so I don't have to say *its*. They did the same thing at the hospital, when I had the scans. But they couldn't tell the sex, and I don't know it. Does it matter? Boy or girl, you're the father.'

'How can I say this clearly enough? I'm. Not. Interested.'

'I. Don't. Believe. You.'

'You know I'd never have agreed to a baby. I thought we were protected by the pill.'

'Well, we turned out not to be.'

It was obligatory for Wall Street bosses to keep silver-framed photos of their wives and children on their desks –

this was the men; female bosses tended not to have families. Brett now leaned forward to tap his own family's photo, a formal, studio portrait, displayed in a heavy, silver frame, from Tiffany.

'I have to think of Marcie and the girls. My primary responsibility has to be to them.'

'Don't be pompous!' Jo spoke contemptuously. She thought Brett sounded like a politician who'd been caught with his pants down. Nevertheless, she flicked her gaze to the family photo, and her contempt immediately died. To her, Marcie looked all teeth – and also all sadness. She had often daydreamed about confronting her rival, and forcing her to . . . to what? To face, openly, that she wasn't loved? To face, openly, that she'd been passed over? Jo had slept with Marcie's husband, and she'd decided to keep his baby, but she was far too much of a coward to inflict on her lover's wife the pain and humiliation of the truth. 'I don't know,' she said. 'I don't know about Marcie, or your daughters. I don't know any of it, Brett. All I know is I want you . . .' Oh, how hopelessly she wanted him, '. . . to acknowledge *our* child. To be its father in every sense.' Jo jabbed at the scans. 'Look at them, Brett. Please! Just look at them.'

This time, Brett did take the scans, and he studied the grainy images of his baby a long, long moment.

'Here,' he said, passing them back. 'Tsukahara. I'll get onto compliance right away.'

*

Zack was staring down at the pornographic images in *Stag*. It was a magazine he'd never heard of before, and never wished to see again. Not that there was anything wrong with porn – he was as fond of it as the next man – but it was all a matter of context, he supposed. And a cubicle at Holy Family was, he felt, an entirely inappropriate setting in which to be viewing pictures of naughty nurse Natalie, wielding her syringe. He sighed, and flipped the page. *Slippery When Wet*, read the new headline, above a picture of a naked lovely, sprawled in the middle of a deserted road, at night, in the rain. Oh, well, whatever turned you on. Alas, right now, it didn't turn him on at all. Zack, whose trousers were round his ankles, caressed his cock in the hope of eliciting a response. He didn't get one. Christ! Was this the onset of impotency? What had Dr Souallah done to him? He'd come to hospital to give his semen for analysis, but had the medics slipped him something to deprive him of his manhood? Or had they done something last time, after that excruciating interview, when he'd had his balls examined? You did read about these cases: doctors remove wrong kidney/eye/leg/the essence of a man.

But this was no good! Zack told himself to get a grip. He had to concentrate on the job in hand – ha! ha! – or he'd never get home.

'Use those,' the nurse had said, when she'd shown him in. 'And collect it in this.'

Those had meant the porno mags – there was a pile of them, on a shelf in the cubicle, next to a big box of tissues (did they throw away spattered mags, Zack had wondered, as an aside, or did they re-use them?). *This* had meant a small specimen jar. And *it* had meant . . .

Proper collection was important, since the highest concentration of sperm was contained in the first portion of the ejaculate. Or so it had been explained to Zack, who had felt in no position to argue. But the specimen jar alarmed him almost as much as the clinical white walls, the smell of antiseptic, and the idea of what he had to do. Once he was alone, and partially undressed, he'd tried to force the jar over the end of his flaccid cock, as if it were a rigid condom unwrapped too early. But it had looked so ridiculous, and felt so uncomfortable, that he'd given up on that idea, and decided he'd better hold it a bit away, when he . . . but would his aim be true enough? And first, there was the problem of achieving an erection. Zack turned the page on the wet-surface lovely, and came across an image of a man coming, most voluminously, over a woman's face. But this evidence of another man's prowess only depressed him further, and he snapped the magazine shut. If he were going to ring any spunk out of himself today, he'd have to try some different strategy. But what? Zack shut his eyes. He supposed that since all else had failed, he might as well try imagining his wife. He pictured Liz, doing nothing much, just spread naked on their bed, and himself kissing her tummy, then rolling her over and running his tongue up her spine . . .

It didn't take long. Which was a good thing, Zack

supposed. Although, on second thoughts, perhaps not? In his defence, he reminded himself he'd refrained from sex for the recommended four days, since every ejaculate reduced sperm numbers by one third. Or so he'd been told. He emerged from the cubicle looking furtive and sheepish.

'Get anything?' bellowed the pretty young nurse in the busy reception area.

Zack glanced round. Yes! Everyone was looking at him.

'Mm,' he squeaked.

'And left the jar on the examination couch?' roared the nurse.

Yes, thought Zack, people were definitely winking and nudging.

'Mm.'

'In the insulation wrap, to keep it at body temperature?' The nurse had a good pair of lungs on her, that was for sure.

'Exactly as instructed,' hissed Zack, and then he scuttled to make his escape.

Seven

After her row with Ursula, Caroline had muttered and mumbled to herself about bloody interfering mothers. Nevertheless, she'd decided her mother was right: she should count her blessings, buckle down to the life she had, and be grateful for it. But a girl had to have *some* dream to keep her going, through toddler-filled days. Caroline had replaced her dream of romance with a dream of herself looking edible. She'd abandoned her sketchy sort-of-plan to have an affair, and replaced it with a solid plan to shop, shop, shop. Why shouldn't she splurge on some new clothes to cheer herself up? You'd think she and Simon lived on the breadline, the way they scrimped and saved. But Simon had a good City job; he could certainly stand her a spree, once in a while.

For a mother of pre-school twins, the logistics of retail therapy were tricky. But once again the coffee coven had come up trumps, for Caroline – what a wonderful group of women they were, she thought, as she pointed the Volvo towards Ryleford's twiddle-dee-dee town centre. This morning, her driving was even worse than ever. The twins, though only two, already acted as her lookouts on the road, and without their warning shouts from the back, she almost collided with a delivery van as she daydreamed about her transformation from hen to chick. She wanted to buy herself some new lingerie. Back in her glory days, such as they had ever been, she wouldn't have been caught dead in a bra saggy and grey from too much washing, or in knackered knickers. But since the twins had come along, pretty underwear had gone the way of a good night's sleep. First the grotty underwear of late pregnancy, then paper knickers and nursing bras, now twanged elastic. Caroline's head was so filled with visions of seductive satin, luscious lace, and raunchy ribbon that she accidentally put the car into reverse at the traffic lights.

No damage was done. Hurrah! The prospect of a huge garage bill would not prevent her credit card glowing bright, today. She'd buy herself a new dress, too. Something vampy, trampy, and divine. A red-hot mama, that's what she was! She'd buy herself something clinging, and plunging . . . once she'd dealt with the parking. Caroline couldn't park to save her life, but she eventually found a likely-looking space, big enough to drive in front-ways, and began the horrible business of getting into it, whilst pedestrians stood and shook their heads in disbelief.

Although she intended to make straight for *Le Baiser*, Ryleford's only lingerie shop, Caroline allowed herself to become distracted by Timmy Lissle, a shoe shop masquerading as a temple, or vice versa. The place was a shoe fetishist's dream. Kinky shoes and jinky shoes winked from the racks. They slinked. They slank. They slunk. All the heels were high, all the toes were pointed, and all the leather smelled of flesh. Timmy Lissle wasn't a cobbler; on his lasts were conjured objects of desire, both carnal and consumer. They cost a bomb. Caroline could just imagine Simon's face if she pulled out a pair of Timmy Lissles: you got them *where*? You spent *how much*? Still, if she indulged, she'd tell him she'd wear her new shoes to bed; that should shut him up.

The recession was biting, and Timmy Lissle was quiet this morning. Despite the fact that she was the only customer, Caroline felt ill at ease in her dowdy dirndl skirt, her shabby cardy, and shoes she daren't even look at, not in here. She couldn't have felt more out of place if she'd turned up at an NCT meeting in Chanel. Still, she refused to be completely overwhelmed, and firmly ignored the snooty manageress – who, in turn, firmly ignored her one and only customer.

After two circuits of the shop floor, Caroline came to a stop in front of a pair of insubstantial sandals: silver and spangly, with spiked heels. Not a wife's shoes at all – well, quite, that was the point. They reminded Caroline of a pair of shoes she'd had when she was sixteen. Totty shoes to make her totter. She remembered tottering down a driveway, at night, in those long-gone heels, tottering towards a party, where she'd met this boy, who . . .

But no! She had to stop this. She had to stop this nostalgia, and this regret. Caroline quickly replaced the sandals. Their spangles and their silver suddenly seemed tarnished. Look where regret had nearly got her! Into an affair – that's where. Or, rather, she might have been at risk of an affair if she'd met a man to have an affair with, but that she hadn't, wasn't the point. Her mum had been right, having an affair now would be stupid. Not that Ursula had been right about everything. Caroline simply couldn't accept Ursula's cavalier attitude towards equality. True, Ursula had phoned to apologize. 'We're not sub-human,' she'd said. '*Of course* I'm a feminist! It's just I worry about you, that's all.' Still, her mother hadn't seemed horrified by the idea that a woman could turn herself into a 1950s-style mousewife, just by having children. But it *was* horrifying. Though probably inevitable. But even if it was inevitable, thought Caroline, you could still fight it, like you could still chuck drugs at terminal disease. God forbid she should ever get cancer, but if she did, she'd *have* to chuck drugs at it, to buy herself time, for the twins. She couldn't give in, gracefully or otherwise; she was a mother, so she'd have to resist. Caroline picked up a second pair of sandals, these ones in mauve, also with heels capable of grinding out a man's eyes. That was what made her cross about herself, she decided. She'd given in to motherhood. Given in, and given up. And also to wifehood. Here she was, spending her husband's hard-earned dosh, when she really ought to be out earning her own, and spending her own . . .

Not that she was prepared to stop spending Simon's money, yet. Once again, Caroline imagined Simon's reaction to a pair of Timmy Lissles. She smiled, to think of her husband. Really, he was so good, and so good to her. He let her be. And shouldn't she try to be better for him? It wasn't quite what she'd meant but, willy-nilly, she found herself giving more serious consideration to her earlier, jokey idea that she'd wear shoes in bed, for her husband. Caroline pursed her lips, and replaced the mauve sandals. Then she walked over to a shelf of ankle boots, and picked up a severely laced pair in black patent leather. All that stuff she'd gone on about to her mum. All that stuff about living life to its limits, and reaching for the stars. Well, okay . . . but when she held Simon, didn't she already hold a star?

The shop manageress finally deigned to acknowledge Caroline's existence. She graciously slid out from behind her till, and glided over to the display of ankle boots.

'Can I help you?'

'Yes, I think you can.' Caroline put down the ankle boots, and walked back to the shelf holding the sparkly, silver sandals.

'I'd like to try these on, please, if you have them in my size.'

They did. And Caroline bought them. As she left the shop, carrying her distinctive, burnt-orange Timmy Lissle shopping bag, she reflected that Simon was in for a treat tonight. And so was she.

Henrietta and Penelope were also on the spend, although not together, and not as extravagantly as Caroline. They were both, separately, heading for the haberdashery department in Peter Jones. Henrietta wanted some skeins of wool for her needle-point, Penelope wanted to look at patterns, and they both wanted to fossick through the remnants box, which sometimes held the most simply marvellous bargains.

Penelope arrived first. Today she was in her habitual uniform of navy skirt, striped shirt, and pearls, with her hair scraped back by an Alice band. But this was high summer, and she had it in mind to make herself something long and cool, like a Pimms. She was fed up with looking wholesome and nutritious. Milk was fine in the nursery, but she wanted a minty, thirst-quenching dress to make a man long to drink. And not just any old man, either. She knew it was naughty, since he was promised to another, but Penelope couldn't help it if she had a particular man in mind. She found herself a place at the long, wide counter where the pattern books were kept, and began flipping through them. One dress quickly caught her eye: it was ankle-length, and sleeveless, with a scooped neck. Penelope could just imagine it in, say, a pale green linen. She could just imagine herself wearing it, in a punt, lazily trailing her hand in the water, her face mysteriously shaded by a wide-brimmed hat, whilst William did all the sweaty work with the pole . . . But the dress, though it looked to hang quite straight, was cut on a triangle, and took three yards of fabric. Three yards! Such extravagance, for a sun-dress! And, on reflection, Penelope wasn't sure about going sleeveless, since the tops of her arms were decidedly flabby.

By now, Henrietta had also arrived in the haberdashery department and was perusing the skeins of wool, which hung along one wall, the colours melting down it like candle wax, tint into tint, tone into tone – all the reds grouped together, all the oranges, all the yellows. As she perused, she thought fondly of Penelope. On winter evenings, she and Penelope had often sat in companionable silence, working on their needle-point. Once, a few years back, they'd even recovered the dining room chairs from her own Hampshire cottage. Henrietta sighed to think of it, then sighed again to think that she would never share a nice, quiet hobby with Annie, then sighed a third time to think that nothing seemed to have come of Penelope's and William's flirtation at the christening. It was too bad! Surely William realized girls like Penelope didn't grow on trees, she was sure to be snapped up, soon, unless . . .

'Why, Penelope!' Henrietta was so startled to spot the woman she'd been beatifying, that she exclaimed out loud, and made another shopper stare.

Penelope was imagining herself with firm, sculpted upper arms – and also the hideous effort of achieving them – when her thoughts were interrupted by Henrietta.

'Penelope, my dear!'

'Henrietta!'

The two women air-kissed, as warmly as air-kissing

allowed, and then stood back and looked at each other a long moment, each of them thinking: if only . . .

'How *are* you, my dear?' asked Henrietta. 'I'm so sorry, I meant to catch you at the christening. But every time I glanced your way, you were absolutely *engrossed* in conversation.'

She raised one eyebrow, clearly alluding to Penelope's lengthy, giggly chat, with William.

'Yes.' Penelope's smile was arch. 'It was a *lovely* day, wasn't it?'

'Delightful . . . And how is that darling Edward?'

'Such a poppet.'

'And Clarissa?'

'So happy.'

'I know your mother is absolutely thrilled.' Henrietta couldn't keep the wistfulness from her voice, she did so long to be a grandmother.

'I'm thrilled, too!' Penelope also spoke wistfully. 'It's simply wonderful to be an aunt.' This was true, but Penelope's face plainly said she thought it would be better by far to be a mother. Both women imagined Penelope cuddling a baby – not her nephew, but her own baby, which was also William's baby, and Henrietta's grandchild.

'And life in general?' asked Henrietta, after a beat. What she was really itching to ask was: if William came crawling back, would you have him?

'Oh, y'know. Not too bad. And you?'

Pride momentarily distracted Henrietta from her scheming.

'Didn't your mother tell you? I've just been made president of the Knightsbridge chapter of the National Association of Flower Arrangers.'

'Gosh!' Even Penelope was stunned. But she quickly recovered herself. 'Congratulations.'

'Thank you. William was so delighted for me.'

It was the deliberately offered opening for which Penelope had been hoping. 'And how is William?'

Henrietta patted her hair, self-consciously. 'He talks about you all the time.'

'He does?'

Well, no, he didn't, actually, but Henrietta *wished* he did. And what Henrietta wished was almost as good as fact, in her own mind, at least.

'All the time,' she repeated. 'It does *so* infuriate Annie!'

Penelope pursed her lips at the mention of her rival.

'It was most *interesting*, to meet her.'

'So exotic!' said Henrietta, carefully.

'Exotic, yes,' agreed Penelope.

Neither woman dare come right out and say she thought Annie was frightful, but each knew that was what the other meant.

'But absolutely sweet, of course,' said Henrietta, her voice dripping lemon juice.

'Oh yes, absolutely sweet!'

The wanabee in-laws looked at each other, united in a

single thought: all was not yet lost. Henrietta remembered the Peter Jones café. She smiled, and took Penelope's arm.

'If you're free, my dear, why don't we have a coffee, and a little chat?'

And do a little plotting, she might have added, but didn't.

Brett felt aggrieved, the victim of a get-Brett plot, and the plotter was Jo, forever parading her swelling flesh around the office, forcing him to confront the fact that he was to become a father for the fourth time.

Brett hadn't been particularly keen, the first three times. But Marcie had wanted kids, and he'd let her have them, to shut her up. That was his policy towards his wife: give her what she wanted, to shut her up. It was part of the reason he'd married her, but only part of the reason. A successful man had to have a wife. That was as true on Wall Street in the twenty-first century as it had been in medieval Europe. A man had to have a wife, to make him look good in the eyes of other men. His wife had to be thin, beautiful, *very* expensive to maintain – there was no more show-off value in a wife who didn't go in for conspicuous consumption than there was in a plain woman – and an all-round social asset. She had to know where to order flowers, and where to order coke, or call-girls, should those things be required. She had to know how to fascinate her husband's fellow businessmen. Her cleavage helped enormously in this task, and so did her air of culture. She was a patron of both the Metropolitan Opera, and the Metropolitan

Museum, and her conversation with boring men was always about art, or books, or opera, even if her interlocutor were colour-blind, illiterate, and tone deaf. She attended openings, viewings, and even, God help her, *vernissages*, literally varnishing parties, which sounded like they should be to do with nails, but were actually to do with flogging pictures. Which she bought, by the yard. But only if they went with the decor, either in her Manhattan home, or at her place in the Hamptons. She threw big parties, and regularly chaired organizing committees for charity balls. But she only offered her services to the right charities – AIDS was always good; old people, never. She knew how much to spend on the dresses she wore to the charity balls she organized, and she knew there were rules about these things. She knew all the rules. She knew the ropes, and could tie them, very skilfully. If you needed a noose, for whatever purpose, Wall Street Wife was your woman.

Marcie had ticked all the right boxes. In the eyes of the world, she'd been a catch. So Brett had married her. Simple. He'd assumed his lack of feeling had been reciprocated. Marriage was a financial transaction, and Wall Street men knew one rule Wall Street wives stuck to, rigidly, was: never marry a man if you can spend his money faster than he can earn it. Brett had assumed what his bride had mostly wanted from him was diamonds – a wife's insurance policy. He'd assumed she'd regarded him as first-husband material. Which had been fine by him; a wife wasn't for life, a wife was for until she got too old to be a trophy. If, before that time, she voluntarily transferred her allegiance to another, richer man, it would save her (first) husband expense and energy in the divorce courts. Not that Brett's and Marcie's marriage hadn't had legs. It had lasted, now, much longer than many Wall Street marriages. Ten years! In the eyes of the world, it was counted a success. And they had those three pretty little princesses to prove it!

Brett now leaned forward to pick up the family photo, which was displayed so prominently on his vast desk. Its silver frame was heavy, and felt cool in his hands. He brought the image close to his face and examined it, carefully, for the first time since Marcie had given it to him. She herself was smiling her slightly manic smile, and her head looked too big for her body, as heads always did on near anorexics. She was still, thought Brett disinterestedly, a looker. She did the gym thing. Of course she did! She did Botox, detox, hair-dye, fake tan, make-up, manicure, pedicure and, for all he knew, face, boob and body lifts. Still, even in this picture, which was a couple of years old now, she no longer looked *young*. Especially when so cruelly juxtaposed with her daughters, who would, in only a few short years, eclipse her entirely. Maybe. Or maybe not? Brett sighed. Avery, Chelsea, and Jenna were all big disappointments to him, face-wise. They all took after their mom: blond, blue-eyed photocopies of the original – but so much less vibrant than Marcie. None of them threatened beauty, or even much above a bland prettiness. In this photo, Avery was in forgettable pigtails, Chelsea was in danger of disappearing behind her shy smile, and Jenna just looked nondescript. They all looked shifty. Had they been scared of the camera? Brett rolled his eyes at what he supposed to be the girls' silly fears. Jenna, Avery and Chelsea often made Brett roll his eyes. His disappointment in them didn't stop with their faces. To their daddy, these girls were mostly pretty dresses and pink bedrooms, and frills that threw tantrums. And what tantrums! Brett remembered their piercing yells and their screwed up faces. Oh, boy! Still, he gave them all they needed. Their pink bedrooms foamed with toys: Barbies, scores of them; bead sets; Little Miss America cosmetics; Little Miss America dress-up; Little Miss America notebooks, desk tidies, pens, pencils . . . anything branded Little Miss America and packed in that hard, candy pink, he bought his girls. His policy towards his daughters was the same as it was towards his wife: give them what they wanted, to shut them up.

Would it have been different if he'd had a boy? Brett pursed his lips, and tried to imagine a boy's face superimposed over his daughters'. He tried to wraith their wraith-like images with the wraith of a boy without existence – but he couldn't quite manage it. The best he could do was a fuzzy haze smeared over Jenna. This boy presence didn't have a face, but it quickly acquired a name. Brett bestowed that name, with his blessing: I name you Little Brett. And though Little Brett hadn't a face, Brett Senior knew for sure he wouldn't have been scared of the camera; he'd have stared boldly at the lens. Nor would he have looked forgettable, or in danger of disappearing, or nondescript. Little Brett would have blazed in shining glory. He would have been a kind of god, and Brett Senior would have brought him presents, not to shut him up, but as gifts of gratitude, or of propitiation, or of expiation, or of entreaty. Or, at the very least, he'd have bought presents for Little Brett to make him shout and whoop: *Yea! Yo! Dad, this waddever toy is like todally cool!* Brett smiled to imagine it, and smiled down at the fuzzy boy-haze spread over Jenna's features. As he watched, faceless Little Brett began to develop a face – Brett Senior's own face. Brett, The Verminator, The Extra-Terrestrial, watched entranced as his own nose, mouth, and chin materialized in the air, conjured not from photographic paper, and dark-room chemicals, but from somewhere deep within his own psychic hollows. He gazed down upon the apparition with all the wonderment of which he was capable. Little Brett was . . . Little Brett was . . . Little Brett was himself, consecrated to the future.

Brett blinked back tears, sighed, and prepared to face something that had been bugging him ever since Jo had thrust her scans under his nose. What if she were carrying a boy? What if she were carrying Little Brett, a being who was himself in miniature? Distorted echoes of bad-tempered conversations came back to him:

'Brett, you're his father.'

'His?'

'I say his, so I don't have to say it.'

'His?'

'They called him a boy, at the hospital.'

No they didn't. The ultrasound operative had used the word *he*, not the word *boy*, and Jo had said, *They couldn't tell the sex, and I don't know it.* But Brett wanted to forget Jo's precise words, so he did. Why not? He knew for sure that Jo had said the hospital had called their baby a he, and would skilled, experienced medics do that unless they really did think it was a he? No way! It would be unethical. And then there was Jo's own choice of words. She'd said she called their baby he to avoid calling it *it*. But why had she chosen to call it he, and not she? That surely was no casual choice? That surely reflected her unconscious – or perhaps even conscious? – feminine intuition? No, Brett corrected himself, not her feminine intuition – her maternal intuition. Intuition wasn't something he knew much about, but mothers surely communed with the babies in their wombs? Whatever she said about it, Jo must have a mother's intuition of the sex of the baby she was carrying. She must. No question. It stood to reason. She had divined the sex of her baby, even if she hadn't recognized that fact. And she had chosen to call her baby he, not she. Therefore, argued Brett, her baby, – their baby, his baby – was a he. It must be so. It was only logical.

Brett prided himself on his logic, and, as he gazed down at a picture of his wife and daughters, he continued to employ it. If his home was an oestrogen-drenched harem, he argued, then he should leave it, to set up a more manly one, a testostoden, with the mother of his son. And his home *was* an oestrogen-drenched harem. Therefore, he should leave it.

On the other hand, Jo wouldn't be a catch in quite the way that Marcie had been. Not in the eyes of the world. Jo knew the business – the financial business – far too well to flatter men whose grasp on the markets was not as sure as hers. And she was already too old to be a true trophy. Even if she hadn't been, pregnancy was stealing her looks.

But on the other, other hand, counter-argued Brett, whatever Jo's shortcomings, there was still his son to think about. His male heir, a boy worthy of his father. *If* he left home, Brett mused, *if* he did, it would not be for his own sake, or for Jo's that he acted, but for Little Brett's, and Little Brett's alone . . .

If Annie left William, she'd do it solely for her own sake. Nothing ventured, nothing gained, she thought, as she stood with the phone pressed to her ear. She was by now back at work, completely recovered from her cold and grateful that Zenses was, yet again, empty of customers. If only it would stay that way for the next ten minutes!

'Hello,' said a bored-sounding woman on the other end of the phone. 'Bingham and Bingwell, literary agents. How can I help you?'

Annie took a deep, steadying breath of the incense-laden air.

'Ming Kwan Li, please.' Her voice sounded much squeakier than she'd have liked. It was at last free of the ugliness imparted by a bunged-up nose, and she'd been hoping she'd be able to sound seductive today. But perhaps not? She glanced pleadingly down to Toad. Toad was a toad, who guarded the Zenses cash register. Not a real one, but wooden. He was a splendidly warty fellow, carrying a bronze coin in his mouth. Annie's business partner, Isabelle, had sent him over from Hong Kong, where he and his kind were regarded as lucky symbols. Now Annie gave him a quick pat as she hung on for Ming Kwan.

'Please, Toad,' she said. 'I need all the help I can get.'

'Excuse me?'

'Ming Kwan?' Oh, God! He'd answered just as she'd been talking to a wooden toad!

'*Annie?*'

Three miles away, in his cluttered, book lined office, Ming Kwan found himself fighting for breath. Annie's voice had winded him as surely as a punch in the stomach; it was just as shocking as a random attack, coming, as it did, out of the blue. He and Annie hadn't spoken at all since she'd phoned to say she'd got engaged – and that was a conversation he preferred to forget, just as he preferred to forget so much of the last few months. What a fucking idiot he'd been to screw Shee Chee! And what a worse idiot to have confessed!

Shee Chee Chen might have contributed to the collapse of Ming Kwan's emotional life, but he hadn't been able to rid himself of reminders of her. Other things aside, theirs was a professional relationship: celebrity American-Chinese author, paired off with Anglo-Chinese agent. A whole shelf in Ming Kwan's office was devoted to her books. Her first, *China Fun*, had picked up an important literary prize; her second, *Bamboo*, had been less well received by the critics, nevertheless it had been a bestseller on both sides of the Atlantic; her third, *Terracotta Army*, had been made into a smash hit movie – on the back of which she'd moved from New York to LA. Despite her glitzy image, her London agency had always been sleepy old Bingham & Bingwell, where Ming Kwan had inherited her when the agent who'd represented her for the previous ten years had retired. His bosses had decided Shee Chee and Ming Kwan would be a natural fit. And they'd been right. The first time author and agent had met, they'd ended up screwing.

And screwing up, big time. Or so Ming Kwan now thought. He gritted his teeth to prevent himself groaning down the phone to Annie, and asked himself, yet again, the question he'd been asking ever since he'd climbed out of Shee Chee's hotel bed after his afternoon of fun: why had he done it? Shee Chee's fame had been a factor, of course. Not that she was Hollywood famous, or anything. Despite her LA address, Shee Chee could walk down any street, anywhere, unpursued by autograph hunters, unhindered by the paparazzi, quite unnoticed. But in Ming Kwan's cosy, everybody-knows-everybody world, she was a star. And he was a starfucker. Literally. Well, she *had* offered . . .

'Oh, come *on*,' she'd drawled, 'shame is *so* bourgeois. Embarrassment is *so* humdrum.'

Bingo! The last thing queue-toting, black-silk-wearing, Ming Kwan-monikered Ming Kwan had wanted was to appear humdrum. He'd had to demonstrate to Shee Chee, and to himself, that he was a sexual sophisticate. So he'd gone for it.

Oh, God, the guilt! Of course he'd confessed. Forgive me, Annie, for I have sinned. What a fucking idiot! And what a fucking idiot Annie had been to have overreacted quite so badly to his confession, and then to have gone and got engaged to the first jerk she'd met, after him. Now, at the sound of her voice, Ming Kwan wanted to suck her down the phone, clamp his mouth to hers, and gorge on her soul – but, alas, he simply couldn't bring himself to be civil to her.

'What is it this time?' he snapped. 'Are you pregnant, or something?'

For a split second, Annie was so cross she almost hung up. But it wasn't a completely unreasonable question. Ming Kwan couldn't read her mind, certainly not down the phone. Why would she have phoned him, now, as he must think, that she was lost to him? Last time they'd spoken, she'd said she was going to marry another man. Why should he now anticipate a stab at reconciliation?

'No,' she said gently, 'I'm not pregnant.'

'Then what is it? And be quick, I'm supposed to be on my way to a meeting.'

'Okay.' Annie looked at Toad, and Toad looked back encouragingly. 'D'you want to meet up? I mean for coffee, or . . . I mean so we can talk.'

'What do we have to talk about?'

'Everything. We have everything to talk about.'

'Everything?'

'Don't you agree?'

Ming Kwan leaned back in his chair, and briefly closed his eyes. Was Annie offering him hope? And if so, of what? When he spoke again his tone was sad and tired, but no longer confrontational. 'Yeah . . . Yeah, of course I agree.'

'I thought you would. I mean I . . .' Annie faded out.

Yes, thought Ming Kwan, this was definitely hope. 'You did?' he asked.

'Mm.'

There was silence, for a very long beat.

'I'm going on a trip in two days' time,' said Ming Kwan, at last. 'You know August's not a proper working month, so I'm off. Part business. Part pleasure. New York, then San Fran – *not* LA. Then Beijing, Hong Kong – God, it'll be hot – and home. I'll be away the whole month.'

'A month?' questioned Annie. Such a desert! Such a wasteland! 'So how about we hook up the week you get back?'

Liz and Zack both sensed cruel time stretching before them and before them and before them: bleak time, devoid of children's laughter, and of children's tears. Their test results had come through, and they were in Dr Souallah's office, listening as he killed their dreams.

Dr Souallah didn't look a bit like an executioner. He wasn't in a black cloak, but a white coat, and he looked like a sad but kindly local pharmacist, about to dispense a bottle of cough syrup. His office had nothing about it of the gallows; it was quite unremarkable, except for the photos on the walls. Dr Souallah's successes – couples who came to him as patients, and left as parents – very often sent him snap-shots of what he called his 'take-homes', by which he meant all the babies conceived under his supervision, either through routine fertility treatments, or through the various methods of assisted conception, or through artificial insemination. The snaps of take-homes were a joy to behold: babies in the bath, babies asleep on their fathers' chests, babies being breast-fed, bottle-fed, or force-fed mashed banana. They would have brought a smile to anyone's face – anyone who wasn't under Dr Souallah's supervision, and wasn't, yet, one of his successes. They made Liz and Zack feel terrible, as if they were being mocked, like fat dieters locked into a chocolate factory by thin people as a prank.

Dr Souallah was far too kind ever to contemplate such cruelty. Today his sad eyes seemed sadder than ever, their expression indicating that the chorus of the song he was all set to sing had changed from aye, aye, aye, aye, to one long, inarticulate wail of misery.

'You do understand what I'm saying?' he checked, as standard professional practice.

'Yeah,' said Zack, in a robotic voice that made Liz shiver to hear it, 'you're saying it's me.'

*

The world had ended. But the world kept spinning, and moneyed Manhattan had spun itself en masse to the glorious beaches of Long Island. The fabled Hamptons! Wadda blast! Wadda scream! Wadda scene! Brett and Marcie's place was at East Hampton, one of the ultra-modern villas right on the shore. As Marcie knelt, under the vaulted ceiling of the huge master bedroom, preparing to worship at the groin of the great god husband, she could hear the rollers of the Atlantic crashing and thundering in the background. She knew for certain that there would be no crashing and thundering going on in her own body tonight, and she was just as indifferent to that fact as she was to what she was doing. She took Brett in her mouth, and caressed him with her tongue, but her mind was elsewhere, with Hart, her heart.

Brett was wrong to think Marcie had never loved him; she had done, in her own way, once upon a time. She'd loved his good looks, and his great technique, and the sense that, with her husband, there was nothing there. As a bride, she'd intuited that Brett's head and his heart were void, and she'd found his vacancy peaceful. Some of her past boyfriends had wanted to consume her, but not Brett. From the very beginning, he'd left her alone to do her own thing. Not that her own thing had ever amounted to much – just drifting round, existing, mostly – but she'd enjoyed it. And even as a new wife, she'd left Brett alone to do *his* own thing. Which was to play the field. She'd always been tolerant of that, not because she didn't care, but because she understood the need to be alone, and she thought Brett, her hollow, empty husband, probably found solitude in his hollow, empty affairs.

The birth of her three girls had shattered Marcie's own solitude. After she'd become a mother, she'd found herself caught in a web of constant, background, non-verbal communication with her children. It was like white noise – the white noise of maternity. And Marcie had been glad to have had her peace so thoroughly destroyed. She'd always wanted children, both with the same unthinking acquisitiveness with which she'd always wanted pink diamonds, a porsche, her house in the Hamptons, but also in ways she couldn't compare to anything else, and which she couldn't name. Not that she had ever wanted the shlepp of looking after kids. The day-to-day details of childcare had never interested her, and she'd always been happy to leave the boring bits of motherhood to babysitters from the Islands. Why not? It was what all the Wall Street wives did, and what any mother would do, if only she could afford it. Still, Avery, Jenna, and Chelsea were *her* girls, she thought. Not hers and Brett's, just hers. Brett had let her have them, in the sense that he'd consented to their conception, and after that, he'd made it plain that he intended to let her have them in every other sense, too. It was soon after she'd begun to understand this that Marcie had begun to teach herself not to care for Brett, or about him. After all, how could she love a man who didn't love her daughters?

Hart, Marcie reassured herself, did truly love her girls. And her girls already loved Uncle Hart, the warm bear of a man they played with every now and then – not *too* often – Marcie didn't want suspicions raised, neither theirs, nor the neighbours', nor Brett's. Hart made her daughters laugh. He gave them piggy-backs. He called Jenna, Jiggle; Avery, Very Berry, or just Berry for short; and Chelsea, Chelsee-saw – or just See-saw. Brett had never given her girls silly nicknames. Nor had he ever showed them how to toast marshmallows on sticks over a bonfire, nor had he tried to teach them how to fly a kite. But Hart had done these things, and more, on snatched afternoons on the beaches, mid-week.

Her lucky girls, thought Marcie, and lucky *her*. How Hart energized her! From the moment she had met her Hart, his own white noise had crackled and hissed through her like voltage, arcing all around the white noise of her daughters. Hart was shocking. Fizzing. There was nothing vacant about him; he was all presence – loud, brash, and very, very big, both tall and broad. Marcie marvelled at just how much space he filled, at how much there was of him – and at the astonishing way in which his presence made her feel more present to herself, in the world.

And then, of course, there was his money, his moolah. Well, Marcie was a Wall Street wife, after all. Money-lust was a part of her, just like her liver. She needed a man who could pay for her and for her girls. Hart could pay and pay, and pay. He had made his squillions from the gold rush of the internet boom; he'd kept them because he'd had the good sense to get out before boom turned to bust, and paper gold to dust. Now he was semi-retired, which was why he'd managed to spend the whole summer in the Hamptons.

Marcie had spent the whole summer in the Hamptons because it was what Wall Street wives did; they decamped from Manhattan, a sweaty, bad-tempered oven at this time of year, and parked themselves, their children, and their babysitters, in the Hamptons for the golden months between Memorial Day and Labor Day. Meanwhile their cash-machine husbands continued to whir in the banks, and trekked out from the city only on weekends.

Hart was not a husband. He had been, once – a brief starter marriage, which had ended amicably enough, and without the complicating factor of children. Marcie, a semi-detached wife and Hart, a semi-retired non-husband, had first met at a barbecue thrown by one of their neighbours, right at the start of the summer.

'Hey there!' Hart had said to Marcie as he'd passed her a burger.

'Hey!' she'd replied, and for both of them all the atoms of the world had suddenly danced themselves into new and exciting patterns.

Marcie thought about that meeting now, as she continued to kneel before Brett, naked but for her heels and her diamonds. She thought about the way Hart had said he'd been touched, to see her naked for the first time. Had she ever touched Brett? . . . *He* certainly wasn't touching *her* now. He had his hands hanging loosely, by his sides. Marcie reached up, took one of her husband's hands in hers, grasped it hard, and felt nothing. When she touched Hart, she burned. And when Hart touched her, he really did *touch* her. Hart need only place his finger, briefly, to her arm, and she'd feel as if he and she were one body, without any intervening space. He need only place his finger, briefly, to her nose, and she'd be washed all through with tender feelings, or even angry ones, but feelings, anyway. He need only place his finger, briefly, to her lips, and she'd feel a little crazy. Hart's touch touched her to the quick. Marcie closed her eyes and flicked her tongue over her husband's flesh: my Hart quickens me, she thought.

'I'll make this quick,' smarmed Keith down the phone into Simon's ear. 'I need to see you, in my office.'

'I'll be right through.' Simon kept his voice steady, but he felt hope receding as surely as his boss's hairline; twenty-five of his fellow office grunts had already lost their jobs today. He swept his eyes over his desk, his fiefdom, then stood up and slowly made his way through the open-plan area, to Keith's office. A sacked man walking, that's what he was. He refused to meet anybody's eye. He didn't want to see sympathy etched on his colleagues' faces, nor did he want to see relief: phew! It's Ayrton, not me! He wanted to use these last precious seconds, before the guillotine did its slicing, to prepare himself to meet the blade like a man.

Simon pushed through Keith's office door without knocking. His boss was sitting behind his desk as usual but, most unusually, two flunkies from HR were perched primly on his office sofa – these were the buboes, signalling death. Simon felt like a revenant. Which meant he didn't feel at all. He walked zombie-like to the chair facing Keith, and sat down.

'I'll keep this short,' said Keith, his adenoidal whine pronounced, his jowls wobbling from the strain of the day. 'You know, of course, that I've been fighting head count battles? And some of them, I've lost. Simon, we need to talk about your future . . .'

Simon tuned out. Whatever words Keith chose to use, his boss was telling him he was a failure at Global Commerce Bank. And hence redundant. And hence a failure as a provider. And hence a failure as a husband, and as a father. And hence, with whatever dignity he took this news, a failure as a man.

Eight

Liz was at her drawing board in the Noodle O'Doodle offices, working on a little lamb for the *My Very First Snuggly* range. Snugglies, a cross between sleeping bags and snow suits, were not yet on the market, but they'd gone down very well with the focus groups, and Noodle O'Doodle planned to introduce them in selected shops next autumn. The hope was that within five years, every newborn in the country would be swaddled in a snuggly. Liz had been asked to come up with a character to brand the range. She always defaulted to lambs when she was too tired to think of anything else, but even she could see that this particular specimen of her art, though cute in his own way, completely failed to gambol across her drawing board. The poor wee thing lacked the joie de vivre necessary if he was to do his job properly.

Not that Miranda noticed when she waltzed into Liz's office, looking dreamy.

'Little lamb, who made thee?' she gushed over Liz's shoulder, as she gazed, most uncritically, at her animal designer's work-in-progress. 'Dost thou know who made thee,

/ Gave thee life, and bade thee feed / By the stream and o'er the mead?'

'Heavens!' said Liz, quickly pulling at the clips that held her drawing in place. 'I'm so sorry, Miranda. You should have warned me. I didn't have time to . . .'

'Oh, don't bother to clear him away,' laughed Miranda, 'I'm fine about your work, now. Really I am.'

Liz lowered her head, trying to hide her confusion at her boss's change of heart towards the work she'd so recently found upsetting.

'Gave thee clothing of delight,' sighed Miranda, 'softest clothing, woolly, bright.'

'Miranda?' said Liz, faintly. 'What is it?' As if she didn't know. There could be only one reason why a woman previously unable to look upon big-eyed baby animals intended for big-eyed babies should suddenly start quoting poetry at them.

Miranda pulled up a stool, sat down, and wriggled to get comfortable. She was clearly readying herself for a long, girlish heart-to-heart.

'Guess what?' she crowed.

'I can't begin to,' said Liz, who could do, all too well.

'I'm pregnant!' exulted Miranda, patting her tummy. 'At last!' she added, as an afterthought. 'I've known for a couple of weeks now. I wasn't going to say anything until the third month, but I'm just too excited to keep the news to myself, and I knew you'd want me to share it!'

What Liz wanted to do was to shoot out rays of black radiation from her eyes and shrivel her boss on the spot. It was almost as bad as how she'd momentarily – momentarily, thank God – felt about Zack, when she'd learned his spunk was spunkless. Spiritless. Hopeless. That was how she'd put it to herself, although it hadn't been how Dr Souallah had put it. He'd sat in his white coat, surrounded by all those happy family snaps of babies, and gone on and on about sperm, sperm, sperm. Who would have thought there could have been so much to say about them? He'd kicked off with something about fewer than 10 million sperm per millilitre of semen.

'10 *million?*' Liz had blurted. What an unimaginably large number! But not enough, apparently.

'Low sperm count has literally dozens of causes,' Dr Souallah had continued. 'Hard to say what the cause might be in your case, Zack. It could, of course, be temporary.'

'*Temporary?*' Liz had leaned forward eagerly, whilst her husband had sat by her side, still and silent, and waxy as a corpse.

'Yes. But sperm quality is as important as sheer numbers.'

Alas, Zack's sperm was low quality. Low grade. Trash. Well, Dr Souallah hadn't actually used the word *trash*, but Liz had thought it. Her husband's sperm had poor motility, and poor morphology. Some of them wriggled sluggishly, others couldn't travel in a straight line. That meant they had difficulty invading . . .

'Invading?' Dr Souallah really had used the word, and Liz had been startled.

'Invading,' Dr Souallah had repeated, 'your cervical mucus, and penetrating your eggs.'

And as if that wasn't bad enough, it then emerged that of Zack's few, sluggish wrigglers, very many had distorted shapes. Very many had round, enlarged heads.

'Which indicates an early unravelling of genetic material,' Dr Souallah had said. 'You do understand what I'm saying?' he'd checked, as his two patients had looked at him blankly. Liz had had no grip at all on unravelling genetic material, but she hadn't had time to ask.

'Yeah,' Zack had said, in an eerie, terrifyingly mechanical voice. 'You're saying it's me.'

And that, thought Liz, was that. Despite all the medical jargon, what Dr Souallah had been saying, really, was that Zack was firing blanks . . . Or at least, she supposed that's what he'd been saying. But perhaps there was still room for optimism that the blanks might be mixed with live bullets? After he'd broken his dreadful news, Dr Souallah had launched into a brief overview of what she and Zack might now expect from reproductive technology – a branch of healing that was evidently a world away from her cosy, bedside-manner understanding of medicine. She'd listened in silence as Dr Souallah had explained that for her to achieve pregnancy she would almost certainly have to undergo artificial insemination. She had wanted to ask: where will the sperm come from? However impossible the odds, she had clung to the hope that some could be harvested, or retrieved, or extracted from Zack. But with Zack sitting right beside her she'd been unable to ask, and Dr Souallah hadn't explicitly addressed the problem; instead he'd handed her a leaflet: *Reproductive Technology: your questions answered.* Zack had been so distressed that Liz had hidden it, unread, in her knickers drawer the minute they'd got home.

Despite her dejection, there was no way Liz would unburden her troubles on pregnant Miranda.

'Congratulations,' she said, in a most uncongratulatory tone. 'Fantastic news.'

'We're so thrilled. Especially after *so long.* Rob's completely over the moon. Y'know, for a while there . . . I haven't told you this before, but years back, not with Rob, before I was married, I had a miscarriage. So, y'know, we thought it couldn't be me. So, for a while there . . .'

'You thought it was Rob?'

'We did. *Rob* thought it was Rob. Christ, he was in a state. But now . . .' Miranda flung out her arms, 'everything's just wonderful.'

Liz forced herself to smile. 'Great. I'm so happy for you both. It's marvellous. But now, if you don't mind, I really ought to . . .' She tapped her lamb with her pencil.

'He is meek,' said Miranda – it was certainly true of Liz's lamb – 'and He is mild, / He became a little child.'

'Quite,' said Liz, 'but marketing want him by Thursday, and you can see he's nowhere near finished yet.'

Rosie Milne

'Y'know what the best thing is?' asked Miranda. 'I mean, *one* of the best things. It's the sex! Pregnant sex! Nothing to beat it. I feel fine, which helps, no sickness or anything. So we're free to . . . we've had so many months of doing it to order, and worrying, worrying. Now all that's behind us, and it's almost as if we've only just met, if y'know what I mean?'

Liz decided that come the glorious day when her eyes did – hurrah! – develop the power to shoot out killer rays of black radiation, she'd focus them on Miranda's toes, and then slowly, oh so slowly, move them up her body, increasing and prolonging Miranda's agony, and her terror. She herself dare scarcely think about sex at the moment. Zack hadn't reached for her once since that horrible interview with Dr Souallah, and, though she'd wanted to, for both their sakes, she hadn't reached for him, either. Recreational sex had been fine when they hadn't been trying to procreate. But now that they were so desperate to procreate, and procreation had, it seemed to her, become so far divorced from their two human bodies, and from any human expression of love, recreational sex seemed quite impossible . . . And why was that? Because, thought Liz, it *was* impossible. Right now, sex for her and Zack could not be recreational. Right now its point would be restoration, restitution, even resurrection.

'You do know what I mean?' pressed Miranda. 'About Rob and me feeling like newly in-loves?'

'Of course I do,' said Liz. 'It's fabulous for both of you. And I'm so glad you've not been feeling sick.'

Miranda rolled her eyes. 'Mind you, it's such a *bore*. No smoking. No drinking. No sushi, or brie.'

'Poor you. Very dull.'

'And I've been getting sooo tired.' Miranda stretched and yawned expansively. 'Utterly knackered.'

Liz saw hope. She glanced at her watch – five to four.

'You should be looking after yourself,' she said. 'Why don't you knock off early, since there's nothing special going on.'

'Y'know, I might just do that. I do have to think of myself first and foremost, these next few months.'

'Of course you do. You go home, and have a nap.' To Liz's great relief, Miranda stood up. 'Bye, then,' she added, as further encouragement for her boss to leave.

'Bye!' Miranda blew a kiss to Liz, and then turned, and blew another to the lamb on the drawing board. 'Little lamb, God bless thee!' she trilled. 'Little lamb, God bless thee!'

Simon could have done with a blessing, preferably from Caroline. He was thinking of her as he trudged glumly towards the Dog & Gun, with his hands thrust deep in his pockets and his shoulders hunched. He didn't often drop in to his local, but tonight he'd simply had to flee his home; he'd been forced to run from his wife by the knowledge that he was deceiving her. He wanted to 'fess up, he really did, but it was very hard for a salary-man to admit to no salary – so Simon hadn't admitted a thing. He hadn't yet told Caroline he'd lost his job. GCB had made deception easy by giving him a month's notice, and a month's grace. All this past fortnight he'd been getting up at 5.40, just as usual, putting on a suit, just as usual, catching the 6.20, just as usual. He sometimes wondered what he'd have done if GCB had made him clear his desk and leave the minute they'd fired him? Would he have continued to suit-up, and then to have left the house to hang around parks and shopping malls all day? Perhaps, since he felt that the alternative – telling Caroline what had happened – would be telling her that her defender against the world, her protector, champion, and knight, the man who put the bacon on her table and the frozen peas in her freezer, was a dud, a duffer, and a fraud.

Simon came to the traffic crossing opposite the Dog & Gun, and waited for the little red man to change to green. In some ways breaking the news to Caroline would be especially difficult, just now. She'd been so crabby for so long, but now her mood seemed to be improving. More than improving! Shoes in bed? Blimey! Simon briefly felt jaunty enough to kick a discarded Coke can into the gutter. But his joy passed in a second. Telling Caroline now that he'd lost his job would be like saving up news of a death, only to announce it at a party. Mind you, he knew he would have to jeopardize the happy mood at home – and soon. How much had Caroline's shoes cost? He was unemployed, or would be, once his grace period was over. With hubby on the scrapheap, wifie would have to curb her impulses to extravagance for a while.

The Dog & Gun was a swirly red carpet on the floor and horse brasses on exposed oak beams sort of pub – none of those fruit machines, or other noisy wotnots. The atmosphere was relaxed and cheery, boozy and beery, smoky with good will. Almost as soon as he pushed through the swing door Simon was spotted, and summoned to the bosom of the bar.

'Simon, my man!' called one of the Jims, waving him over with a friendly gesture.

Simon could never get the Jims straight. One of them was married to Caroline's friend Sophie, and the other to Emma. Or was it to Lucy? And whichever of the three women wasn't married to a Jim was married to Benedict – no, Simon corrected himself – to Barnaby. As he crossed the swirly red carpet, he repeated the name to himself a couple of times. He didn't want to offend his acquaintances by getting their names wrong, or by getting their wives muddled up.

But social niceties were neither here nor there. Far more serious problems were about to engulf poor Simon. The City's tom-toms had been beating. Barnaby, who was in fact Emma's husband, worked for a vile man called Kevin. Before he'd moved firms and taken it upon himself to start tormenting Barnaby, Kevin had worked at GCB, where he still had many contacts. Simon's soon-to-be-ex boss, Keith, was one of his best muckers. Keith had kept his friend and former colleague in on the scuttlebutt concerning job losses at GCB – not the nitty-gritty, but the broad details. As was his wont, Kevin had used the scuttlebutt to put the frighteners on his own staff.

Barnaby sipped his pint and watched Simon sip his. Both men lowered their arms, simultaneously.

'So then,' said Barnaby, 'sounds like your shop's really in a mess.'

'GCB,' snorted Jim one. 'The anti-Teflon bank. Problems stick.'

'Not funny!' snapped Simon.

'Big job losses, I heard,' mused Barnaby, gazing down on his beer as if it were an oracle. 'You're in Keith Pickford's team, aren't you? Retrenching, isn't he?'

Barnaby and the Jims didn't know Simon had lost his job, and if they had, they wouldn't have been such dolts as to probe. But Simon wrongly assumed those City tom-toms had been beating out the rhythm of his redundancy far more accurately than they had. He assumed the two Jims, and Barnaby, were all in on the secret he was so desperate to keep from his wife. And also, he now all at once realized, to keep from the world. In his fragile state of mind, he angrily assumed that his amiable drinking companions were mocking him.

'For God's sake!' he shouted, banging his pint down on the bar.

'Oi!' said Jim two, who was in the splatter line.

Simon didn't pause to apologize. Instead, he barged out of the pub, and headed for home at a jog. Then he remembered why he'd escaped to the pub in the first place: at home, it was impossible not to confront the knowledge that he was deceiving his wife. He slowed his pace to a walk. Once again, he thrust his hands deep into his pockets, hunched his shoulders, and submitted to gloom.

William wasn't one to be deceived, tricked, or bamboozled by manipulative females.

'I say!' he said, opening and closing his mouth like a fish. 'I say!' But he didn't, in fact, say anything. He just stood there, staring furiously at his mother, and at Penelope. The two women were sitting at his dining table, calmly looking at him, whilst they spread paté de foie gras on dainty triangles of toast. Did they think he was stupid? He could tell at once what had happened. They'd been scheming. Mummy had obviously invited Penelope to lunch, knowing that Annie would be at Zenses, and that he'd turn up for feeding, too. And Penelope had obviously accepted, knowing these same things. They were obviously hoping they could manoeuvre him into . . . into . . . into something or other. Were they hoping for the overthrow of Annie the pretender, and her replacement with Penelope, the true Queen of Hearts? But that sort of thing only happened in silly soap operas! It was too ridiculous.

Mind you, thought William, he was being damnably rude to both of them, standing here like this. It just wasn't on. And he *was* hungry. Foie gras. How yum. And he could smell roast beef, too. And hadn't Mummy muttered something about steamed chocolate pudding as she'd passed him on the stairs earlier this morning? William had never been able to resist steamed chocolate pudding, smothered in sauce. Then again, however adroit his mother and Penelope might be, he was more than a match for their artful ploys. He was far too adroit himself to be woman-handled into doing anything he didn't want. So he would be civil, the rules of society demanded it.

'Penelope!' he said. 'What a surprise! And how delightful to see you.'

Penelope half-rose from her chair, and William stepped forward, preparing to air-kiss her. But he tripped over one of the roots that spread over the floor from his mother's latest flower arrangement. He winced as it sheared away from the peculiar trunk of its foliate mother tree, snapping him painfully on the ankle as it did so.

Henrietta had rather allowed her elevation to the chair of the Knightsbridge chapter of the National Association of Flower Arrangers to go to her head. She had decided that a floral designer in her position had a duty to update her skills and ideas, so she was currently experimenting with post-modern styles. Postmodern flower arranging largely dispensed with flowers as constituents of arrangements, in favour of found objects, metal, wood and foliage. And postmodern flower arrangements were not delicate or shy. Huge pieces, they were, great sculptural things, or even architectural, far too big to be placed on a table or a shelf, or in an empty fireplace; these pieces demanded floor-space, and got it. The arrangement currently gracing William's dining room could have been an offshoot of Yggdrasil, the World Tree of Norse mythology.

William bent down to rub his ankle, and to pick up the

tentacle of rope and wire and moss and vine, all embedded with chunks of glass, which his clumsy foot had severed from its place. He lifted it, and straightened, holding it like a python, draped across his outstretched arms.

'So sorry!' he said to his mother.

'How unlucky,' said Henrietta, who was thinking how lucky it was that her son had provided her with an excuse to leave him alone with Penelope so very early in the luncheon. 'Let me take that.' She stood up, walked around the table, and relieved her son of his snake-like burden. 'I'll just take it down to the conservatory, and look out some more Gomphrena Fructicosa, and a couple of Ligularia leaves. Watch out for stray chunks of glass!'

With this imperious command, she whistled to Bonnie and Clyde, who'd been snuffling about under the table, then both mistress and dogs were gone. William and Penelope were left to descend into an embarrassed silence, or to flirt, or to have a slanging match, or to snog, or to do whatever they liked, really.

'Hello, William,' said Penelope.

What a nice voice she had, thought William; low, like Annie's, but not so rasping. She sounded reassuring and competent, like his old nanny. Annie never sounded reassuring. She usually sounded as if she were living in the middle of a hurricane.

'Hello, you,' he said.

Penelope was thrilled by the intimacy of that *you*, and blushed as she and William at last air-kissed.

'You look positively blossoming,' said William, as he slid onto his seat.

Penelope, too, sat down. 'Blossoming?' she asked, doubtfully. She'd suffered agonies, deciding what to wear today. She hadn't wanted to look as if she'd made *too* much effort, but she did want to impress. To strike the right balance, she'd abandoned her candy-striped shirt in favour of a plain one with a pie-crust collar. The collar poked out, teasingly, from the round neckline of her jersey – scarlet, and decorated with a motif of geese. Her skirt too was scarlet, not her usual navy. She hadn't expected William to inundate her with compliments, but then, nor had she expected *blossoming* to be offered as a description of her person, and of her attire. What could it mean?

'Jolly,' clarified William. 'You look jolly.'

Penelope took another bite of her foie gras. Honestly! Jolly sounded worse than blossoming!

No it didn't, not to William. To him, jolly sounded beautiful. He gazed on Penelope's jolly geese motif, and thought how rarely Annie looked jolly. Rarely? Huh! Annie *never* looked jolly. She didn't do jolly. She did sharp-tongued wit that he didn't get. She did mystery, she did pity. But she didn't do jolly. There was no merry-making about her, no festivity, no fun. But a jovial man such as himself could do with a bit of jollity, now and then. He was a convivial fellow, hearty, and good-humoured. Was Annie hearty? She was not. As indicated by her far from hearty appetite.

'More foie gras?' he pressed Penelope.

'Please,' replied Penelope, comfortably.

And that was something else a man could do with, thought William. A bit of comfort. Annie offered carnal delight, but she didn't offer comfort. Not like Penelope. Penelope would really look after a man's wellbeing. She would save him trouble, and promote his content. Annie never fetched his slippers, as it were, but Penelope would attend to his creature comforts. Hot water bottles. She would bring him a hot water bottle on a cold winter's night. And, mused William, she'd gladly deal with other bottles in the night, too, the sort that had to be sterilized, and then made up with formula. Yes, he sighed, there were far worse things in life than being comfortable.

One of them was being infertile. Zack was lying on the Indonesian day-bed, staring at the telly, which was off, and worrying, worrying. Unlike Liz, he hadn't bothered praying any of his sperm could be salvaged. Dr Souallah had asked: *You do understand what I'm saying?* And Zack had understood, at once, that he would never father a child. He had half-heard Dr Souallah drone on about artificial insemination, and he hadn't needed to ask: where will the sperm come from? He had understood, at once, that they would come from a donor. He had understood, at once, that if Liz conceived a child, it would not be genetically related to him . . .

Except he hadn't understood these things at all. These facts were inassimilable, and he had, for the moment, given up trying to assimilate them. Instead, he was anxious about Liz. He knew he must be threatening to overwhelm her with his own needs, which made him feel terrible – especially when her needs were so pressing. And one of them, one of his wife's most basic needs, or desires, would not now be met by him. He could scarcely blame her for taking herself off in a huff tonight. She'd said she'd had enough – of what? of what? – and then she'd marched upstairs, where he'd heard her running a bath. He hoped it was hot and bubbly. Hot and bubbly was good, he supposed, though hiding from him most definitely was not. And what did hiding from him herald? He remembered Liz telling him, when they'd both still assumed their problems in conceiving a child had something to do with her body, not with his, that she'd felt as if she wasn't a proper woman, because she didn't work, she didn't function as she should. But she did. And he didn't. He'd not fully understood her state of mind back then, but now he knew, from the inside, what it felt like not to function properly. And he understood, from the inside, one of the fears that went with not functioning properly. Liz had said to him: *What if I can't have a child, and you leave me for a more fertile woman?* He'd said: *As if, darling.* But what if Liz left him for a more fertile man, because he couldn't father a child? What if she did? What then? It would be a bereavement as bad as the one he'd just suffered.

Liz wasn't thinking about death, but about life. Her bath *was* hot, bubbly, and soothing, just as Zack had hoped. She'd tipped almost a full bottle of peach bubble bath into the water, and now scented white foam was everywhere, as if her bathroom had been the site of an explosion at a soap factory. As well as bubbles and hot water, she'd also furnished herself with a glass of white wine, why not, since she clearly wasn't going to get pregnant any time soon? Not without assistance. Tonight, the marvel of medical ingenuity was much on her mind; she was at last reading the leaflet Dr Souallah had given her and Zack.

Reproductive Technology: your questions answered was little more than an A4 photocopy. It hadn't been designed to stand up to bath reading, especially not to extravagantly be-bubbled bath reading. It was already a bit soggy. Liz warned herself not to let it get any wetter; she didn't want it disintegrating in her hands, just as she'd found the relevant bit: artificial insemination, and the source of the requisite sperm.

What is artificial insemination? she read, through the scented steam coming off her bath.

Artificial insemination (AI) places sperm directly in the cervix (called intracervical insemination) or uterus (called intrauterine insemination, or IUI). It is useful under the following circumstances:

Liz quickly scanned the list, and two bullets jumped out at her.

- *When the male partner's semen contains very low numbers of sperm*
- *When donor sperm are required*

Liz began to cry, but told herself, sharply, that tears just wouldn't do. She waited for her vision to clear, and then continued reading.

The Artificial Insemination Procedure

The AI procedure is as follows:
- *A woman usually (but not always) takes fertility drugs in advance*
- *The man must produce sperm at the time the woman is ovulating*
- *The sperm are subject to certain so-called 'washing' procedures (see box, preparing sperm for IUI and assisted reproductive technologies, below)*
- *The sperm are then inserted into the uterine cavity through a long, thin catheter*

To distract herself from images of long, thin catheters, Liz tried to find the box outlining the so-called washing procedures Zack's sperm would undergo, if any could be saved from the addled and raddled mess of his ejaculate. Washing sounded almost motherly. It sounded gentle, and tender. What a cruel bit of jargon! Liz gave up looking for the box on washing procedures, and miserably returned to her reading.

AIH and DI

AIH (artificial insemination by the husband) involves inseminating the woman with her partner's sperm. It is appropriate for couples in which the woman's body makes antibodies to her partner's sperm, destroying them before they reach the egg.

So not her, then, thought Liz, wiping a damp strand of hair off her face.

DI, donor insemination, involves inseminating the woman with an unidentified donor's sperm. This method is appropriate for cases when the male partner is impotent, or has defective sperm.

Liz read the final sentence through again: *This method is appropriate for cases when the male partner is impotent, or has defective sperm.* Where would sperm for her insemination come from? Liz now faced what she'd have known all along if only she'd dared be honest with herself: sperm for her insemination would come from an unidentified donor. Here was confirmation of the truth she'd tried to evade. Here was her future, laid out for her, in cold type. She dropped the leaflet in the bath, where it quickly turned to mush, quite unregarded, since she had begun to cry in earnest. True, reproductive technology was wondrous, an amazing human achievement. True, it offered her and Zack hope . . . or, Liz checked herself, perhaps it only offered *her* hope? No. She rejected the question almost before she'd fully formed it. Granted, donor insemination held out no hope to Zack's *genes* – they would die with him – but Zack, thought Liz, was more than his genes, and DI genuinely offered her husband hope. It offered him the hope of fatherhood, just as it offered her the hope of motherhood. But still, she didn't like the sound of it. How could something that offered so much hope sound so desolate? How could something humans had come up with in order to continue the human race sound so veterinarian? And how could conception be made to sound so devoid of love?

In any case, it was all very well to say Zack was more than his genes and that DI offered him the hope of fatherhood – but that was bollocks, really, wasn't it? It *was* all about genes. And even if it wasn't, how would Zack feel to watch her belly swelling, and to know that the child growing within it had been fathered by another man? How would he feel to know he'd been cuckolded by Dr Souallah and his team? And how would *she* feel to have growing within her a child not fathered by Zack, not conceived in the night during an act of mutual adoration, but during the day, during an act of clinical routine? Most important of all, how would a child conceived from donated sperm feel about his or her conception? Should such a child be told how it had been conceived? As an adult, would it want to trace its biological father? Could it even do so? Liz wasn't sure whether sperm donation was anonymous. Did hospitals keep records on their 'unidentified' donors? And did it matter? Whether the biological father was traceable or not, she could easily imagine the feelings of displacement, bitterness and loss a child conceived by sperm donation might feel as an adult.

Liz lay back in her bath and tried to relax her way out of this quagmire. She told herself to breathe deeply, and shut her streaming eyes, determined to visualize some pretty scene. A beach, perhaps, fringed with softly waving palms, and lapped with a turquoise sea. Instead she saw herself in a surgical gown, lying on a hospital bed, and Dr Souallah jabbing at her with a syringe loaded with an unidentified donor's sperm. Suppose she were successfully inseminated, like a cow, or a pig, or a sheep, down on some dreary factory farm. Suppose a being took hold inside her. It would be a true little stranger, a little stranger who had nothing at all to do with Zack, or with her and Zack, but only with her, and Dr Souallah, and his syringe . . .

Jo was in a surgical gown, lying on a hospital bed, and a doctor was coming at her with a syringe. She was thirty-four. In New York, where everyone believed in human perfectibility, amnios were standard practice from thirty-two, and Jo was about to have hers, although she wished she wasn't. For a start, she wasn't sure *why* she was having an amnio. Sure, everybody did it, but what was the point? Okay, amniocentesis identified the sex of the baby, and Jo badly wanted to know that. Sure, she referred to her offspring as he, but that was only a linguistic convenience; what if it was actually of the she variety? Mom didn't know, one way or the other, and this lack of knowledge offended against her trader's aversion to uncertainty. So yes, Mom wanted to know, for sure, her baby's sex. But amniocentesis also identified foetal abnormality.

And why identify foetal abnormality? Well, thought Jo, if ever there was a question which wasn't a question, that was it. Whether a he or a she, her baby had quickened, now. A few days back, she'd felt the squirm of life within her for the first time, and she'd felt as though her soul had swooned. So suppose her baby had Down's Syndrome, or something? What was she going to do? Abort it? Jo glanced up, to her sole remaining little ghost, who was, as usual, fluttering against the ceiling. She met, and held, the haunting, old, old eyes of Old Eyes. These were eyes no face would ever grow into, thanks to her – so no she wouldn't abort her baby.

Oh, come *on*. Of course she would. Otherwise she wouldn't be here.

Why submit to a test if she intended to ignore the results? Informed choice, that was the thing. Should it be necessary, she wanted to give herself the option of . . . Jo met Old Eyes' eyes, again, and couldn't complete her sentence, even in the privacy of her head.

Anyway, assuming everything was all right, what peace of mind she'd have won for herself by submitting to this quick test! True, she was about to have a needle jabbed in her tummy, a needle that would pierce her flesh, and also her baby's amniotic sac, so that fluid could be removed for analysis. True, she'd be nagged by worry for the next three weeks or so, before the results became available, but then, assuming everything was okay, she could relax for the rest of her pregnancy. Fifteen or sixteen weeks of serenity, in exchange for a bit of fear now, didn't seem such a bad exchange.

Nevertheless, Jo shivered. She'd read all about the failure rate of amnios. She'd read they carried a one per cent chance of miscarriage, which was one per cent too high for her, however risk-hungry she was on Wall Street. But her American-born and American-trained OBGYN had assured her the figure was a worldwide average, taking into account amnios conducted in China, Africa, India, all the places where, her doctor had implied, nobody had a clue. In New York it was different. At *this hospital*, it was different. This hospital was on the Upper East Side, in 10021, the wealthiest, most powerful zip code on the planet. It would have been sued into oblivion if it had ever lost a baby. The doctors here were highly, highly qualified, and very, very careful. Still, Jo was trembling slightly.

And then there was the syringe. It was enormous. How much fluid were they going to take out of her?

'Right,' said the doctor, 'I want you to keep very still.'

Jo immediately spasmed with fear.

'No,' said the doctor. 'I said keep *very* still.'

'Sorry,' Jo muttered, meekly. She wished she had a male hand to squeeze, but Brett, of course, was absent. She'd have to make do with psychic communion with Old Eyes. She looked to where she'd last seen her lonely moth fluttering, but even he, or she, or it, seemed to have deserted her.

'Okay,' said the doctor. 'We're ready. You'll feel it, but it won't hurt.'

He'd already used ultrasound to determine where, on Jo's tummy, he'd insert his needle, and now he checked the screen one last time. Then he did his jabbing.

He'd not lied; it didn't hurt, exactly, or rather it did, but not in a way Jo had expected pain to feel. She thought she'd never felt anything quite so disgusting, and her whole body jolted, which filled her with fear that she'd ripped her baby's amniotic sac, and had killed it, through her own weakness of body, and of will. But she hadn't, and forty minutes later, she was on her way, off home to bed. Again she longed for a man who'd squeeze her hand – and a man who'd do something or other about the way she was feeling. Which was truly rotten. She got as far as the hospital lobby, when she was certain she was going to faint. Luckily, she found an empty seat, and after a few minutes of sitting with her head between her knees, she felt better. But she'd come to a decision. If this was how she reacted to an amnio, when it came to giving birth, she'd elect for a C-section. She could do that, since she was in New York, although she suspected that in the UK medics might be sniffy about it. So, thank goodness she wasn't in London. No seismic heaving in her body, no earthquake in her insides, no loss of control – especially without a male around to . . . do whatever males did in the labour room. Apart from the male doctors who delivered the babies, of course. Jo resisted the temptation to roll her eyes at the uselessness of non-medical men, and instead considered whether to ask Liz to come over for the birth. But no, that would be cruel, given her sister's problems. So should she ask her mother? Ugh! What a thought! Jo shuddered. Just as when she'd lost her virginity Ursula would have been the last person she'd have wanted as a witness. Mum could come over to help out once she got her baby home – it was traditional, after all – but not for the birth itself. The C-section. Swift, clean, and comfortable. And, of course, a C-section would be another way of minimizing uncertainty and surprise.

Caroline had had a C-section, because she'd been told to – it was safer for twins – but also because she so much couldn't abide the wise-woman, spirituality-drenched pregnancies some women went in for, that she'd decided to go as technological as possible in rebellion. And anyway, who wanted to be turned into an animal? Animality in the bedroom was one thing, but animality in the labour room was quite another. She could do without it, thanks all the same. She could do without being reduced to biology, and without spiritual birthing experiences, to boot. So she'd had her C-section – but all that was nearly three years in the past and, in the present, the twins were, as usual, driving their mother nuts. She'd managed to bundle them as far as Sophie's front door, but then – disaster! First Nat and then Louis had decided to have a bawl, in Sophie's porch.

'Home!' sobbed Nat.

'Home!' added Louis, quick to offer fraternal support.

'Boys!' cajoled Caroline, in what she hoped was a kindly, patient tone. 'You're going to have a l-u-r-v-e-r-l-y playdate with Hector, and Tabitha, and Phoebe!'

'No!' wailed the boys, in unison.

'But I don't understand. What's the problem?'

'No!' The boys stamped their feet for emphasis. 'No! No!'

Caroline sighed. It could be anything; they could have taken against the colour of Sophie's front door, for all she knew. She rang the bell, quite hopeful that the cheery ding-ding-a-ding-dong-ding-dong-ding would distract her boys. And it probably would have done – but it didn't need to. Sophie flung open the door after the first two ding-dings, so quickly and violently that she stunned Nat and Louis into immediate silence. Or perhaps it wasn't the violence of her actions that did the trick, but the violence of her galvanized interest and distress, feelings which were plainly etched on her normally placid, somewhat bovine face.

'Sophs!' cried Caroline, alarmed to see her friend looking so stricken, and so excited. 'What on earth's the matter?'

*

What was the matter was that following the incident in the Dog & Gun, Barnaby had tackled his boss, vile Kevin.

'What exactly's going on over at GCB? I know this bloke, Simon Ayrton. Has he been canned?'

Vile Kevin had got on the blower to his mucker, Keith. 'This bloke Simon Ayrton, have you given him the bullet?'

'You know I can't comment on the record, but recently we let some people go. Simon's performance was sub-par. We gave him a 360, but he was a lost cause.'

Kevin duly reported back to Barnaby. 'Yeah. Your mate got canned. And there's more of that coming, not just at GCB, so watch it yourself, boyo, in these uncertain times.'

Barnaby had naturally let his wife, Emma, in on the scuttlebutt, and Emma had just passed the scuttlebutt to the riveted young witches of the coffee coven.

'Oh, you poor darling!' crooned Sophie, stepping forward to hug Caroline hard. 'But don't worry, we're here for you.'

Caroline disentangled herself from Sophie's embrace, and took a step back. 'Here for *me*?' she repeated, with a slightly strained laugh. 'Er, Sophie . . .?'

Sophie's mouth fell open in a wide O. 'Ohmigod!' she said. 'Simon hasn't told you, has he?' Her hands flew to her face, and her eyes were huge, staring.

'Ohmigod!' Caroline not only echoed her friend's exclamation, but she echoed her body language, too. 'Is he having an affair?'

Sophie dropped her hands from her face. 'An affair?' she asked, in a more normal, slightly puzzled tone.

Caroline realized it wasn't infidelity – and that lingering guilt at the thought of what she'd half wanted to do had made her too quick to jump to conclusions.

'Silly me!' she giggled. 'Of course Simon's not having an affair! So what else hasn't he told me?'

Sophie didn't answer, at once. Instead she shooed the twins into her messy and welcoming hall.

'You two run up to Hector's room. The others are already playing. I'll bring you juice and biccies, in a bit.'

Biccies always did it for the boys. Sophie and Caroline watched as they happily scampered up the stairs, their mysterious tears forgotten.

'So,' said Caroline, when they'd disappeared into Hector's bedroom. 'What's this all about?'

Sophie took her friend's arm. 'Come in, my dear. Lucy and Emma are waiting. And like I said, the coffee coven's here for you at times of crisis.'

Zack felt as though he were in mortal peril, although he knew he wasn't, because he was already dead. He was the end of his own line. Zack-the-last. And that's what being dead was: having no possibility of any future. Everything was over, bar the breathing, and he didn't seem able to do much about the breathing. His soul was spent, but his body seemed determined to get him through the days: his chest just went on rising and falling, rising and falling, independently of his will. Each time his lungs took a great gulp of petrol-laden air, the taste of autumn coated his tongue. It was September, season of mists and bitter fruitlessness. This morning, Zack had woken up and felt melancholy pressing in on him. He had decided to take a mid-week mental health day, and had opted for a stroll through his local park, hoping nature would be restorative.

Not that nature stood much of a chance in Zack's neck of the woods. This park was little more than a scrotty field of cigarette butts and candy wrappers, here and there overgrown by patches of feeble grass. The few trees were blasted, the paths were tarmac, and the flowerbeds were planted with the prettiest broken bottles. Still, the pigeons liked it, and the winos. And there was a nice, safe, fenced-off playground for the kiddies. Mums in this part of London were not mums, but working mothers, very concerned that their little darlings should receive appropriate stimulation throughout the day, and lots of doses of healthy fresh air. This morning, as every morning, the playground was swarming with nannies, chatting, and their pre-school charges, cavorting.

Zack didn't know how it could have happened, quite, but just as his chest kept on rising and falling of its own accord, so his feet had trudged him to the perimeter of the playground. Now he was outside the high, wire-mesh fence, yearning after the children inside, yearning, yearning, and attracting nervous glances from the nannies, who were always on their guard for paedophiles.

There was nothing abhorrent about Zack's yearning. He yearned for the nannies' charges as a mystic might yearn for a vision of God. As he stood beyond the pale of the playground fence, he truly, truly loved the kids within. How he loved these kids, in their jeans, and their Kickers, and their infant joy. He could feel love beating out of him in great waves, almost as if his body were dissolving, and his energy, and his being, were becoming one with theirs. How he loved that little boy, whooshing down the slide, and yelling. See how his face scrunched up as he laughed. See how his small, blond head glinted in the sun. How he wobbled, as he ran! Watch him hare back around the base of the slide, to the steps, so eager for another go . . . whoopsie! The boy slipped, fell, and began to cry. Zack made as if to go to him, but bumped his nose on the fence. He watched, enviously, as the little boy's nanny picked him up and gave him a cuddle, then he transferred his attention to a baby girl, toddling along, pushing her doll before her in a toy wheelbarrow. She was fat, almost round, like a little India rubber ball in her red coat and red boots. Zack wanted to hold her – not physically, but psychically. He wanted his soul to keep hers unspotted, to keep it safe, to keep it from all the hideous dangers of the world.

Two nannies were sitting on the wall of the sandpit, within which their two charges were digging holes as if their lives depended on it. The nannies had been keeping half an eye on

Zack, and now one of them shot him yet another troubled glance. She had recently read something in the paper: a paedophile had told his counsellor that to stop him snatching a child it would have to be chained to its mother – and if it was, he'd take the mother, too. The nanny shivered, to remember that. She nudged her friend, and nodded towards Zack.

'He's been loitering plenty long enough, don't you think?'

'Yiis,' twanged her friend – they were both Aussies, both big, strapping lasses, who looked as if their attitude to wrestling crocs would be: no worries!

The first nanny stood up. 'Keep an eye on him!' she said, nodding to her charge.

'Excuse me?' Crocs-don't-bother-me stood with her legs and arms akimbo, and challenged Zack through the wire mesh of the playground fence.

'Huh?' Zack jumped, surprised out of his reverie, and alarmed to find himself faced by this intimidating creature.

'Who're you with?'

'What?'

'Which kid is yours?'

'None of them,' shrugged Zack, with the honesty of innocence. 'They're none of them mine.'

'So what're you doing here?'

'Nothing. Just watching.'

'Watching?'

'Isn't it allowed?'

The Aussie nanny curled her lip. 'We know your sort,' she snarled. 'I think you'd better clear off, mate. Just clear off.'

Nine

Jo, by now very obviously pregnant, was in her OBGYN's interior-designed, expensively furnished office, looking at her interior-designed, expensively furnished OBGYN, who was grinning broadly, showing her interior-designed, expensively furnished teeth.

'So,' she said. 'Good news!'

'My amnio?' asked Jo, and the nagging worry she'd been feeling about the results at once vaporized in the fierce, white light of her doctor's smile.

'Uh-huh. Everything's fine.'

'Oh *good.*' Jo swallowed hard to contain her relief.

'And good for you! Now, next question. D'you wanna know the sex?'

'Yes, please.' Jo spoke without a second's hesitation. 'Yes, please,' she repeated, 'I do.'

The OBGYN paused, for dramatic effect.

'It's a girl,' she announced. 'A little girl. Congratulations, Mommy, you're gonna have a daughter.'

Jo completely forgot to be irritated, as she usually was, by the way medical personnel insisted on calling her Mommy. It was a girl! A little girl! Congratulations, Mommy, you're gonna have a daughter! Jo glanced up to Old Eyes, who'd settled on the fussy pelmet above her OBGYN's office window. For once, Old Eyes did not seem to be judging her, and if she'd been alone with him, or her, and the her in her belly, Jo would have laughed out loud and crooned something silly to both her offspring. But she wasn't alone.

'That's great,' she said, folding her hands over her swelling tummy. 'Just great.'

'So much easier, if you know for sure,' said her OBGYN. 'Now you can start decorating the nursery and choosing a name.'

In her pre-pregnancy days, Jo had scarcely been aware of the babies knocking around New York, but over the last few months she had begun to notice how rigidly Americans enforced the pink for girls and blue for boys rule. On weekends, the parents strolling round Central Park with their offspring slung round their necks, or pushing their preciously occupied jogging buggies as they jogged The Loop, all stuck to a strict colour coding: blue blankets and babygros for one variety of infant, pink for the other. The snowsuits already ranged in the babywear shops were similarly coded. Jo now supposed it must be the same for paint effects and soft furnishings.

'The nursery?' She smiled to picture her minute spare bedroom. 'I think I'll paint it black.' She wafted at her jacket. 'Get her started young.'

Jo's maternity clothes were all in deepest black. Like Jo, and like ninety per cent of women in New York, the OBGYN was also dressed from head to toe in black, but she didn't crack a smile. She just looked at Jo with a kind but puzzled expression.

'And a name?' she asked. 'Have you thought about a name?'

Very early on in her pregnancy, Jo had made a few preparatory lists, but then she'd stopped, since naming a child had begun to seem as awesome as conceiving one. How could it be done, she'd wondered, until the child was actually born, and could be seen? But even as her OBGYN asked the question, it was answered. Jo, who for so long had been seeing ghostly eyes, now heard a ghostly voice sighing inside her body, inside her belly, and inside her head. 'Maaadddiiisssooonnn,' rustled the voice, in the way leaves rustle words in the wind. 'Maaadddiiisssooonnn.'

Madison? Jo pursed her lips. It wasn't a name she'd ever considered, but it sounded right, somehow. After all, her daughter had been conceived, and would, God willing, be born and brought up in Manhattan. She would be an all-American girl, so of course she'd want her own American moniker. And hadn't Somebody Madison taken part in drafting the US Constitution? Or was it Madison Somebody, and the Bill of Rights? Freedom anyway, thought Jo a little wildly, a break with outdated ways of thinking, a future untrammelled by the past.

'Madison,' she said firmly. 'Her name is Madison.'

Ming Kwan, whose name, roughly translated, meant bright and shining future, was back in town, and Annie, who was starkers in preparation for putting on the glam, just for him, was hoping his name, roughly translated, spoke truly. Luckily, William had taken himself off somewhere for the evening. Annie neither knew nor cared where he'd gone, but she was grateful for his absence, since it meant she didn't risk raising his suspicions, as she prinked to betray him. She smiled to herself as she contemplated her wardrobe. The dresses hanging there were like so many versions of herself, but bodyless, or they were like memories made cloth: I wore this skirt for that wedding; I made this dress for that party. Annie liked her cloth memories, and she reached out to caress them. At her touch, velvet, silk, and cotton whispered tips on how best to enchant. Annie listened to their whispering, and decided on a tight, pale-pink halter neck over wide, floaty, rose-pink trousers. A few moments later, she was twisting this way and that in front of her pier glass. The pink was very pretty. Too pretty. Tonight she didn't want to look pretty, she wanted to look dangerous and ethereal – a sorceress in modern guise. She wriggled out of the trousers, yanked off the top, then flung them both on to her and William's bed. Next she tried her black crushed velvet; the bordello fabric was slinky and tactile . . . and somehow reminiscent of a lampshade in Ursula's sitting room. Annie had never before noticed the similarity, but now she had, she knew she'd have to get rid of this dress. Oh well. Her loss was Oxfam's gain. She wriggled out of her bordello black, too, and chucked it on the bed, where it sighed down onto the rejected halter neck, like a lover swooning into an embrace – rather as she hoped to swoon into Ming Kwan's embrace later tonight, if only she could first find something to wear.

Annie finally settled on a tight, low-cut minidress of Thai silk. It was exactly the deep blue-black of the Thai sky as the sun daily yielded to the moon, or so thought Ming Kwan, who knew Thailand well. He didn't mean the filth-smeared Bangkok sky, but the blue-black sky over the jungly tribal lands where the silk-weavers lived. When they looked up at night those tribal weavers must see the stars undimmed by light pollution, they must find them so irresistible they stretched up their hands to snatch them down. Or so Ming Kwan fancied. The weavers must weave stars into their silks. How else to explain that Annie, as she moved, flickered with silver? He watched, hypnotized, as one of the waiters led her across the floor of this swanky East-West fusion place, which he'd chosen solely to impress. He hoped the food would live up to the decor, which was delicate, and vaguely Japanese. Annie was taking her time crossing the tatami mats, probably deliberately, he thought. She was letting him have an eyeful. But why? He hoped he knew the answer to that question, and gave himself up to yearning, as memories of joy in her presence, and desolation at her loss shimmied through him, in tempo with the shimmy of her hips.

Annie finally arrived at Ming Kwan's table. She willed herself to remain cool as crystal as she stood, staring down into his doe-like, almond eyes. And Ming Kwan, as he stared up into Annie's round, green eyes, mysterious and entrancing as jade, found he couldn't stand to greet her. Annie smiled, and he felt her smile as a painful pricking of needles all over and all through his flesh. He gulped, and shifted in his seat.

'So how've you been?' he asked.

It was a question Liz and Zack needed to ask each other, too. They were lying back to back, at opposite sides of their bed, when Liz became aware that Zack was weeping.

'Zack?' she said, rolling over and reaching for him. 'Zack?'

'This girl thought I was a paedophile,' sobbed Zack into his wife's hair.

'What?'

'In the park. I was watching the little kids in the playground, and this girl told me to clear off.'

'*Oh, Zack!*' said Liz, drawing away from him just a little, in order to brush her hand across his face. She had begun to trace his tears with one fingertip, when Zack's own hand shot up from under the duvet to grab hers, hard, around the wrist.

'You won't leave me, will you?' he pleaded. 'Because I'm impotent?'

'*Oh, Zack!*' repeated Liz. '*Oh, Zack!*'

Happiness of the body was not possible for these two, yet. But they could offer each other consolation of the body, and they did.

Ironing was valium for Caroline's soul. Or so she tried to kid herself as she worked her way down the pile of fresh laundry. She had set up her ironing board in the small den off the kitchen, because it held the telly – and telly stupefied her boys as surely as ironing stupefied her. Nat and Louis were snuggled on the battered old sofa, watching a cartoon about a cat and a tiger, and she was smoothly moving her iron back and forth, back and forth, over a sheet. And as Caroline's hand moved back and forth, her mind moved back and forth over the problem that had been occupying it all morning: what she thought about Simon's redundancy.

This was not the same as trying to decide what she thought about his failure, or his inability, to confide in her. Her husband's silence had jolted her. It had come so soon after her own flirtation with the idea of having an affair. Could she and Simon have been in really serious danger of drifting? She was his *wife*. Why hadn't he brought his troubles to her? On the other hand she understood his reluctance to speak. He'd claimed it was because he hadn't wanted to worry her, and no doubt he'd been sincere. But equally importantly, his self-image had been at stake.

'Simon, is this true?' she'd asked.

'I've let you down!' he'd said. 'And the boys!'

'No! No!'

'But I'm a working man.'

Caroline had known exactly what he'd meant, since she, too, was a working man, beneath her oh-so-effective disguise of female flesh. Her poor husband! The loss of status, and the loss of self-esteem! He'd looked so woebegone, so sad, so hang-dog.

Worse, much worse, he'd looked at her as if he'd expected her to throw a hissy fit, and his expression had threatened Caroline's *own* self-image. Now she scorched the sheet – luckily on its last legs, anyway – swore, and blamed her iron, which was old and temperamental. How ghastly to be the sort of woman whose husband expected her to throw a hissy fit. Was that the sort of woman she'd become? And if so, when? The coffee coven had obviously expected a hissy fit, too, or, if not a hissy fit, some other variety of hysteria. Caroline chuckled to remember the last meeting of the coven. True, at the time it had been horrible for her, but her friends had so transparently enjoyed being the bearers of bad tidings. They'd been concerned for her, distressed, and quick to offer help – but they'd *so* relished the drama of the morning, too.

Her mum, that prize drama queen, had also been quick to offer help. Ursula had, predictably, gone into a complete flap when Caroline had phoned to tell her. But it had been a generous flap.

'If you need any financial help . . .' she'd said, in amongst all the ohmigods and what'll y'dos.

'Absolutely not,' Simon had said, when she'd relayed her mother's offer. Caroline hadn't really expected him to say anything else. She'd known his pride wouldn't stand for family handouts, except in cases of dire need, and they weren't on the poverty line, yet. Okay, they might have to live off baked beans for the next few months, but the mortgage was insured for a year, and Simon would get a redundancy package . . . Jo and Annie had both been much calmer in the face of her news than had Ursula. They'd both seemed to think a spot of joblessness was par for the course.

'Job security?' Jo had scoffed. 'Come off it!' Caroline half-frowned, half-smiled, to think of her pregnant sister. She couldn't help gloating, slightly, at the thought of the shock in store for glamorous, high-flying Jo, when motherhood clobbered her. But that was a base thought! And beneath her. Caroline did a bit of vigorous ironing, flattening her mean streak along with the creases in the tatty, much-mended, and now scorched sheet. It was so strange to think that Jo was blowing up like a balloon, and yet she, Caroline, would never see her pregnant. Next time she saw her sister, she'd meet her niece, too. Madison. Strange name, but that was Jo's business. Or had it been the father's choice? Now Caroline really did frown. Neither she, nor Annie, nor Mum had yet got to the bottom of the mystery of Madison's father. Liz had, perhaps; she'd always been so close to Jo, but if she had, she wasn't telling. Caroline paused in her ironing a moment, and groaned for her eldest sister. She hadn't yet told Liz and Zack that Simon had been fired. Why bother them with the need to pretend to care?

Caroline began to fold the sheet. In truth, it didn't look all that much better than when she'd begun to iron it, but then, that was ironing for you. She put it on her 'done' pile, and reached for a pillowcase from the laundry basket. Once again she began her rhythmic sliding of the iron. So, she internally summarized, she knew what the coffee coven thought of Simon's redundancy, and what Mum, Annie, and Jo all thought, but what did she herself think? Well, what did she? Caroline paused in her ironing. A small smile danced its way into her eyes, and then slid down her nose, to her mouth. Oh dear! What she felt, in the face of this disaster for her husband, was glee.

Annie and William were steeped, for the moment, in cosy domesticity. Henrietta was out, lecturing her flower arrangers on postmodern influences on the disposition of foliage in mass sculptural designs, and the two lovebirds were having a quiet night in, companionably sitting on either side of one of the fireplaces in William's big drawing room. Tonight there was no flower arrangement in the fireplace – unless a fire counted as a postmodern flower arrangement. Though it was only October, there had been a chilly snap, and a fire had been deemed the thing. It should have had an old cat stretched before it in a smudge of feline indolence, but all it could manage was Bonnie and Clyde, who were heaped together on the rug in front of the marble hearth. Their grunts and snuffles, and the crackle and spit of the fire, were the only sounds, apart from the soft rustle of pages being turned. Annie was reading chick lit, and William was reading an illustrated history of the Boer War – he had a thing about military derring-do, so long as it was safely distant. But his mind wasn't on slaughter, it was on Penelope, who, he realized, was threatening a subjection so much more dangerous than the sword.

William had met Penelope for lunch twice more since the encounter she and Henrietta had so artfully engineered. Their liaisons had been chaste; both their kisses and their conversations had been limited to the social. They'd firmly kept a lid on their feelings, and firmly talked about mutual friends, the everfascinating doings of the Royal Family, and the shocking behaviour of the Royal staff, who were, through the tabloids, currently providing the nation with glimpses behind the veil of majesty. Not that either William or Penelope had read this rubbish. Or so each of them avowed, to the other. Now William remembered Penelope's flush as she'd so soundly denounced a Royal butler. How far down her body had that flush extended? He pictured the melon mounds of her breasts, flushing, beneath her jersey (had she been wearing a jersey, that day? He couldn't quite remember). He pictured the generous curve of her tummy, but sternly kept his inner eye from wandering any lower. Instead he imagined the great shelf of her derrière, and himself cupping his hand around one of its plump cheeks, and . . . at this moment, he coughed.

'All right?' asked Annie, glancing up from her novel.

'Fine.' William ostentatiously turned a page. 'You?'

'Fine.'

They both returned their eyes to their books, and William got back to his reverie. Voluptuous, that was the word for Penelope. She was a voluptuous voluptuary. Look at the way she relished her food! William remembered her tucking in to foie gras, to venison, to sticky toffee pudding. He grinned to himself, and looked surreptitiously at Annie. Annie more or less lived off soup and salad, and that bloody muck, tofu. But, given the chance, Penelope gorged on red meat, game, offal – just like him. What an appetite! And what an appetite for . . . William half thought *life*, but changed it at the last moment, and completed the thought with the very image he'd self-censored, a few moments back – Penelope's front bottom, and his stepping stone into the arms of the goddess of love. He coughed again, crossed then uncrossed his legs, and barked a silent command to himself to concentrate on the Boers.

Meanwhile, Annie hadn't the foggiest what her novel was about. It had a jaunty pink cover, but all she could think about was Ming Kwan, who clashed with pink as surely as did orange, or lime green. In her mind, Ming Kwan was red, the Chinese colour of happiness, and the western colour of sex and danger. Dinner with him had certainly been sexy and dangerous – although they hadn't actually *done* anything, Annie reminded herself regretfully, except talk.

'Come on, Annie,' Ming Kwan had said of his short-lived

dalliance with Shee Chee. 'It was a one-off bit of lunacy. It meant nothing. It just meant . . .'

'It meant you have no willpower. It meant you wrecked my trust.'

'It was just sex. And not even very good sex.'

'And if it had been good sex . . .?'

'It couldn't have been,' Ming Kwan had said, soulfully, 'because it wasn't with you.'

Annie had laughed at that. 'Nice try,' she'd jeered. 'Nice try.'

'And true.'

'Huh! And, of course, Shee Chee didn't want it to continue.'

'She could have been begging at my feet, and I'd have said no.'

'What? Piss off, Shee Chee, I've got better fish to fry?'

'Yes.'

'Balls.'

Ming Kwan had met, and held, Annie's eye. 'We wouldn't be here,' he'd pointed out, 'if you didn't believe I loved you.'

Annie hadn't argued. 'And what about willpower?' she'd said, after a beat. 'There'll always be temptation. You gave in to temptation once. Why not again? And again? And again?'

'It was . . .'

'I'm not the sort of woman to stand for that. The embarrassment. The humiliation.'

'I'd never ask you to. There were . . . special circumstances.'

'*Exonerating* circumstances?' Annie had snorted. 'Such as?'

'Think who she is, Annie!'

'Some two-bit author who—'

'She's famous, and—'

'World famous on the literary pages. And so she can get a table in any restaurant she likes? So long as it's in Soho. And so she can screw who she likes? So long as he works in publishing. Lucky her!'

'Please, Annie!' Ming Kwan had beseeched. 'Think! What would you do if a movie star offered you a one-night stand?'

'A *movie star*? Shee Chee's not in that league! She's not even—'

'It's only a difference of degree, not of kind. Tell me, what would you do if a movie star offered you a one-night stand?'

Annie hadn't deigned to answer Ming Kwan's question over dinner, but she was wondering about it now, as she pretended to read her book. She'd always dismissed Hollywood stars as designer plastic: plastic bodies, probably, quite literally plastic bodies, or silicon, given the way they all went in for surgery; plastic eyes; plastic souls. But what if one of them were actually to show up on a quiet day in Zenses, and say, *Hey, babe, how about it?*

Annie giggled, and William looked at her, enquiringly.

'So funny,' she said, tapping her book. Luckily, he didn't

press for details of the joke. Hey, babe, how about it? Annie had to concede his point to Ming Kwan. She knew she'd have spread her legs before the star's question was even completed, so eager would she have been to boast about it afterwards.

Liz was about to be exposed to the full boastfulness of pregnancy.

'So, what d'you think?' asked Miranda, holding up a navy two-piece from Sally P, a trendy maternity-wear shop, recently opened by the eponymous Sally.

Liz glanced up from her drawing board.

'Very nice,' she said shortly.

Miranda smirked and patted her tummy, which was not yet visibly swollen. 'Surprising how early on you start to feel the need for roomier clothes.'

'I'm sure.'

'I thought, why not treat myself?'

'Mm. Why not.'

'So hard to tell how the bump will grow, over the next few weeks.'

'Mm.'

'I'm calling it Bug, y'know, cos it's such a darling little minibeast.'

Aaaarghhh!!! thought Liz, in italics. She resisted the urge to point out that a bug was something that bothered, or annoyed, or caused disease. This afternoon she was working on a cute kangaroo, and now, with great ferocity, she erased its 'ickle ear. She did know, of course, that pregnancy must be one of the two or three most wonderful things ever to have happened, or ever likely to happen to Miranda. And she did know, of course, that her and Zack's problems were making her ungenerous and sour. But still, was it only jealousy that made Miranda appear to be enveloped, for the moment, in vanity, smugness, and selfishness? Did this transformation happen to all pregnant women? Would it have happened to her? Had it happened to Jo? Had her own sister started simpering, as well as swelling? Liz paused in her erasing – she couldn't see it, somehow, and Jo still sounded normal enough, on the phone. Plus she hadn't named her bump – ugh! – but named her *baby*. Madison. So pretty! But Bug? *Bug?* Liz could only hope that Miranda's husband, Rob, saw his wife's current tooth-rotting sickliness as sweet. Despite her mood, she sincerely hoped so – if not, her boss's marriage was in for a rough ride over the next few months. Smirking? Simpering? Silly, conceited smiles? These things were enough to put you off pregnancy all together.

And there were other routes into motherhood, after all, thought Liz. She had read, somewhere, perhaps in *Reproductive Technology: your questions answered*, or else in one of the other leaflets she'd picked up since that one had turned to mush in her bath, that a couple in which one partner had been diagnosed as infertile should attempt to determine alternatives to the treatment process as early as possible, to reduce anxiety and feelings of hopelessness. Alternatives had turned out to mean having no children – gee, thanks – adoption, and surro-gacy. Liz had always thought surrogacy was barking mad, and she hadn't changed her mind just because she and Zack had found themselves so desperate. In any case, it was a last-ditch measure for women who'd found they were unable to carry a baby to term, or who were unable to conceive in any medi-cally assisted way. But there was no reason why she shouldn't be able to conceive, with sperm from a donor . . . and if she didn't want to be impregnated with sperm from a donor? Well, that left the no-option, gee-thanks option of no children. Or adoption.

Liz picked up her pencil, and started to re-draw her kangaroo's ear. She could half-hear Miranda prattling away in the background – by now she was on to yoga in pregnancy. Miranda hadn't seemed to noticed she was talking to herself, and Liz tossed out the odd *mm-hmm*, or *yes of course*, or, *oh, I know*, to maintain the illusion that she was paying attention. But really she was thinking about adoption. Could it be a route into parenthood, for her and Zack? How would *he* feel about it? And how did *she* feel? She had misgivings about using donor sperm. She had misgivings about carrying within her, and mothering, a child not fathered by Zack. So how would she feel about mothering a child that had not grown within her *at all* and, genetically, had nothing to do with either her or Zack? Would she be able to love it? Would she be able to love it *as her own*?

Except, loving an adopted child as her own wouldn't be

good enough, thought Liz. She'd have to love an adopted child *better* than her own. Suppose its blood mother, its birth mother, had died? Then she'd always feel the ghost of a dead woman hovering at her back, watching her every move. Or suppose she and Zack adopted a child whose blood mother was still living? After giving birth, a woman would only become childless by surrendering and sacrificing her baby to adoption if *compelled* to do so by some truly calamitous circumstance. She'd know she'd lose her baby to adoption as surely as she would have done to cholera – and no woman would *choose* that. So, suppose, thought Liz, she and Zack took advantage of a woman's so-called choice, which wasn't a choice at all? In that case she, Liz, would be haunted by a living woman, as surely as she would have been by a dead one. If she adopted a child, whether its blood mother were living or dead, she'd feel herself in the presence, always, of a yawning absence. *You must do better as a mother than I would have done*, that absence would challenge, *you must be better than I would have been. And my child must be better, and do better, than either of us have been and done.*

Liz shivered. Could she live with – live up to, and surpass – that challenge? And what of the challenging absence's blood child? The child for whom she, Liz, must be better, and do better, than the absence would have been and done. If they adopted, she and Zack would certainly not tell their child he, or she, had been delivered by a stork. Their child would get the truth. And would the truth shade their child's life, as an oak tree shaded the ground beneath it from the sun? Suppose she and Zack had to say: *Your birth mummy is probably still alive. She sacrificed you because . . .* Would *any* child be able to see surrender to adoption as a sacrifice, or only as an abandonment? What pain, what rage, what confusion her adopted child would surely feel. But would pain, rage, and confusion prevent her child from longing for its blood mother? No. There would always be the chance, however slim, that her own darling child would turn its eyes on her and spit: *But my real mummy. But my real mummy would have loved me more/taught me more/wanted better for me. You've been nice, Mum, you've been kind. I love you. But not as much as I could have loved my real mummy. My real mummy would have known me, all through, in a way that you just never will, and I could have known her all through, too. And it's never too late! So now I'm off to try to find her. Byeee!*

Liz's hand froze over her drawing. How would she feel if she adopted a child and then, at twenty, her child decided to search out his or her real mother? And how would Zack feel about a real father, hovering somewhere in the background of his child's life? And how would Mum feel about real grandparents doing likewise? And what would her sisters make of real aunts? And what if her child one day demanded: Are these people really my family? What's my relationship to them?

Liz gulped. She tutted, and tried to return her attention to her kangaroo's ear, which was now lopsided.

'So what d'you think?' asked Miranda, from the other side of the drawing board.

'Oh, I agree,' said Liz, vaguely.

'Lavender then?'

'Lavender,' said Liz, more firmly. She assumed Miranda was talking about dyes, or colour swatches – but she was actually talking about aromatherapy oils, in pregnancy.

'But sometimes I prefer geranium.'

What?

'Oh, so do I.'

Liz once more tuned out on her boss's chatter. She got back to wondering about the ties of blood and love. Were the ties of blood truly as sticky as she had just supposed? Wasn't your family whoever loved you? If she and Zack adopted, surely they would be able to fill their child with enough love to last it a lifetime? They'd charge their child with love, as a capacitor with electricity. And, thus filled up with love, their child's light would shine, and shine, and shine. What was a *real* parent, anyway? The real, thought Liz, was anything that wasn't imaginary. And she and Zack were not that! They were solid. Their bodies existed, solidly, in space and time. Then again, why should the ghost of a blood mother be alarming? Why shouldn't it be gentle, and encouraging? Motherly, even? As she sacrificed her child to adoption, surely any birth mother must pray, to whatever god, or gods, or forces she believed in, that her child would find a loving home, relative wealth, an education, and hope. Liz knew that she and Zack could provide these things to an adopted child, should they choose to do so. And should they choose to do so, why shouldn't they see their action as undertaken not only for their own sakes, and for the sake of their child, but also for the sake of their child's ghostly blood mother, and her sacrifice?

Ghosts always stalked the mean streets of Gotham, but only once a year were they openly acknowledged. Happy Halloween! The day of the dead was approaching, the dust of the grave blowing off it. New York was everywhere decked in the festival's jolly colours: orange and yellow. In shop windows skeletons danced, and witches grinned their witchy grins. And in Brett's office at United American Bank, Jo felt herself to be haunted not only by her familiar Old Eyes, but also by the ghosts of New Eyes' ghostly presence. Could ghostly eyes have ghosts? Jo didn't know, but everywhere she looked this morning, she saw eyes keeping Old Eyes company. The way the light reflected in two points off the window behind Brett's head looked, to her, like eyes. The decorative globe he kept high up on a cupboard looked, to her, like an eyeball. Even the curve of his chair back looked like an eyebrow. Why had all these eyes taken a bead on her? Easy. Jo knew the answer to that one. The eyes, the ghosts of New Eyes, were all joined in pleading on Madison's behalf: *Win her father for her*, they begged, they charged, *win her father for her*.

Brett was focused on the unreal world of cyber-cash, scried in his computer screen. But he looked up at Jo's knock and watched her intently as she moved her big body into his office. She looked ludicrously distorted, yet he paused to wonder: should he, or shouldn't he? Should he leave Marcie and her daughters for Jo and his son? His boy. Little Brett.

This time Jo hadn't even got a pretext. This time there was no story about Tsukahara. As when she'd tried to dump Brett, she decided her best policy was to come right out with her news. She used the same formulation her OBGYN had used, to her.

'Congratulations, Daddy, you're gonna have a daughter.'

'*What?*'

'That's what I came in to tell you. I had an amnio. Our baby's a girl. Madison. I'm sure you don't mind I didn't consult you on her name? I know: You're. Not. Interested. But still, I hoped you'd want to know. I hoped it for Madison's sake.'

'A *daughter*?'

'Madison.'

'Madison? A *girl*?' Brett's dreams of Little Brett, of himself in miniature, shredded into blue confetti, as did any idea of leaving Marcie in order to live with Jo. 'A *girl*?'

'Yes.'

'Not a boy?'

'No.'

'But you were so sure!'

'Sure? Of what?'

'You called it *he*.'

'Oh, that!' Jo laughed. 'I told you, it was meaningless. Just convenience. I told you, I didn't know the sex.' She paused. 'Also, I didn't care,' she added, pointedly.

'But maternal intuition!'

'What?'

'You called it *he*. You must have known it was a boy!'

'Maternal intuition? About Madison's sex?' Jo shook her head. 'Sorry!'

'You told me the hospital said it was a boy!'

Jo frowned in puzzlement. 'You must have misheard!'

'So it really is a girl?'

'Madison, yes.'

'But I wanted to call him Little Brett.'

Old Eyes and all the ghosts of New Eyes now turned on Jo: *You've failed!* She was as shocked and distressed as they were. She was appalled. Sure, she knew there were lots of places where the birth of a son was greeted with joy, whilst the birth of a girl was greeted as though it were a funeral, a disgrace, the grounds for suicide or divorce. She'd read about those places in concerned pieces in the *New York Times*. India. China. Bangladesh. But in America? On *Manhattan*? Then again, it wasn't just any girl whose existence Brett was belittling, it was *Madison*'s. Her own daughter's. And his. Brett should be whooping for joy and, to Jo, the fact that he clearly valued his girl less highly than he'd have valued a boy was far more shocking than his suggestion of abortion had been, when she'd first told him she was pregnant. Abortion was gender-blind, at least in her part of the world. Everybody, including herself, had abortions. And *what* was aborted? She glanced up to Old Eyes. Though sad about what she'd done, sad for the being to whom she'd done it, sad, indeed, for all the unwanted products of conception, she didn't think she'd killed a person – a fellow member of the moral community – she thought she'd put a stop to a flesh bag of potential. Not that being a member of the moral community was the be all and end all of everything. But the thing was: it felt to Jo that Madison had joined it now. She was *actual*. She was kicking, lustily. Jo could feel her daughter's feet jabbing hard up under her diaphragm. Madison was making the mound of her stomach jerk as if it had a life of its own. Which it did. Rejecting Madison now, it seemed to Jo, was little different from infanticide.

'Madison is a girl, yes,' she repeated, way too calmly.

As she spoke, all lingering desire for The Verminator, The Extra-Terrestrial, died within her. At that moment, she was finally set free from the slavery of sex, by solidarity with her daughter, and she understood something she'd never understood whilst she'd been enthralled. Okay, sex with Brett had been enough to bind her in rope, and chains – but all *Brett's* intensity? All *his* vehemence? All *his* violence? Too right it had been *his*. Intercourse? Ha bloody ha! All that energy had been focused on him, all along. Not her. She'd been disarrayed, but she hadn't been noticed. The previously hidden truth, now acknowledged, was instantly as insistent as toothache. Toothache needed no evidence of its reality, beyond the fact of pain

– and nor did her new knowledge. But, oh, the pain! Jo felt it in her chest and throat, behind her eyes, and in her guts. Pain spread down to her fingers, to her toes, to the innermost hollow of her body . . . where Madison felt it, too, and stopped her lusty kicking, stunned into stillness by her mother's sorrow, and her own.

Ten

Liz always found Christmas shopping a harrowing experience – the crowds, the fake jollity, all the rubbishy stuff destined to go straight from the stocking to the bin. This year she knew it would be worse than ever, and she'd decided to get the hardest part over with first. Shopping for children. It had to be done. An uncle's infertility, thought Liz, was no excuse for an aunt to give up on her present-buying responsibilities. This was why she was in a vast, windowless, warehouse wandering up and down aisles stocked solely with toys. Toys seemed to stretch away from her for miles in either direction. Toys were stacked to the rafters, on cheap wire racking. This could have been Santa's grotto, if it hadn't been quite so grotty. Liz had started coming here when the twins were born. It was where everyone came, once they acquired children, or nieces, or nephews. Liz had never actually *liked* it – in her professional opinion, the store's emblem, Happy Harold, a hippopotamus, had something chillingly manic about him; if it were up to her, she'd have redrawn his eyes – but it had never struck her before quite how grim this place was. The staff were all spotty youths, dull-eyed and dispirited despite their jaunty red and yellow uniforms. Shoppers such as herself, unaccompanied by children, looked dispirited, too, whilst those with children in tow – or being towed along by children – looked harassed. Even the store's attempt to generate some Christmas spirit had backfired, or so it seemed to Liz. Piped children's voices piped in the background. At the moment, it was 'Oh little town of Bethlehem': *Oh holy Child of Bethlehem,/Descend to us we pray./Cast out our sin, and enter in,/Be born in us today.* Though an agnostic, Liz was annoyed. How dare they? How dare they take a hymn to a newborn child, and turn it into a sales jingle? The decorations irritated her, too. Tinsel was everywhere. Even Liz, with her vibrant, eclectic taste, didn't like the clashing colours. The store's many plastic fir-trees were also in clashing colours – every colour, except green – and they were flashy with multi-coloured lights. Who were the shop managers trying to fool? This place wasn't overflowing with joy, but with greed.

Still, Nat and Louis had to be furnished with *something* to open on Christmas Day. And Jo's C-section was booked for 15 December, so this year Liz would have to think about Madison, too. But Madison was easy. Madison would get a range of outfits from Noodle O'Doodle, each of them decorated with her aunt's own animal designs. But what about her nephews? Nat and Louis already had just about every toy Liz could think of. They had a veritable menagerie of cuddly animals. They had a train set. They had building blocks, craft supplies, puzzles, books and tapes – even a few strictly educational computer games, which Liz thought was quite ridiculous for two-year-olds. She wouldn't dream of giving them action men, or toy guns, so what was left? Meccano? Did they have that? Or was it old-fashioned? She stopped in front of a toy garage. Nat and Louis certainly had toy cars – but did they have a garage? Liz fished out her mobile – she'd call Caroline, and find out.

At that moment, the piped music changed to 'Away in a Manger':

> *Away in a manger, no crib for a bed,*
> *The little Lord Jesus laid down his sweet head.*
> *The stars in the bright sky looked down where he lay,*
> *The little Lord Jesus asleep on the hay.*

To Liz, these words, when sung by children, were like the words 'I love you', when spoken sincerely by a man to a woman – nothing at all could make them crass, or corny. It didn't matter that she was hearing the carol over a PA system, in a shop. It didn't matter that she was listening to tinny voices with mid-Atlantic accents. Liz could have been in a cathedral, listening to the unbroken voices of unbroken boys, soaring. Or she could have been at a kindergarten nativity play, listening to tiny tots lisp out the words from inside their costumes of dressing gowns and towels. Liz could see those children, felt she could almost reach out and touch them and, in that instant, when these imaginary children were so real to her, she became certain she'd never bear a child. All remaining doubt was banished. Artificial insemination might be full of awe but, to Liz, it still seemed as veterinarian, and as impossible *for her*, as it ever had. Conjuring a baby from a stranger's sperm wasn't her idea of reproduction. But that she didn't want to put herself through the medical procedures didn't stop her crying; sorrow at the loss of her non-existent child wrung tears from her eyes, and set her chest heaving.

> *The cattle are lowing, the baby awakes,*
> *But little Lord Jesus no crying he makes.*
> *I love thee, Lord Jesus! Look down from the sky,*
> *And stay by my bedside till morning is nigh.*

Nobody stopped to ask Liz if she was all right. The toy warehouse was as devoid of sympathy as a vacuum – either that, or her fellow shoppers themselves felt so depressed they thought it was entirely normal for a woman to break down in front of a rack of toys.

> *Be near me, Lord Jesus; I ask thee to stay*
> *Close by me for ever, and love me, I pray.*
> *Bless all the dear children in thy tender care,*
> *And fit us for heaven, to live with thee there.*

Liz sobbed and sobbed. She was bereaved, and bereft. Grief washed over her and through her like water, but it didn't leave her feeling cleansed; it left her feeling drowned. She thrashed about and fought for breath against the momentum of her tragedy, which was such an everyday sort of tragedy. Hers was an ordinary tragedy of bad luck. Liz knew that, and railed against her knowledge. There was nothing singular about her state. She sobbed for herself and, though she railed against her lack of singularity, she also sobbed for all the other unwillingly childless women of the world: infertile women; women whose husbands were infertile; women whose children had died; women who'd had their children taken from them by cruel regimes; women who had given up their children to adoption.

Adoption? As the idea of her own child waned in Liz's mind, the idea of taking in another woman's child waxed stronger. And as it waxed, she found herself sobbing for the tragedies of the world's disadvantaged children as well as those of the world's disadvantaged mothers. Her own blood child would never sing, dance, play, or infuriate her beyond all endurance. Her own child would never be, it would never exist. But the world was filled with children who were filled with existence, and empty of much else. Liz thought of children all around the world who had lost their mothers, or bits of themselves, to war, or to disease, or to starvation. In her mind's eye, she saw a montage of old news clips. She saw African children, their faces skulls, their bellies hugely distended from malnutrition. She saw a Brazilian street child, lying dead in a gutter. She saw Thai child sex workers, hanging about brothel doorways.

She thought of all the dangers children faced: men with guns, and men with pricks, but no compunction; viruses; landmines; drought.

In Liz's psyche, anger began to replace sadness. How could she have allowed herself to sink into self-pity! Child sex workers? Landmines? She sniffed hard and wiped the scratchy sleeve of her heavy woollen coat across her eyes. Here she was, surrounded on all sides by toys, toys, toys. Dolls and balls, skipping ropes and teddy bears. Electronic gizmos. No landmines. No nasty surprises in amongst the frisbees. Ka-boom! Oh dear! A leg gone, or an arm. And these toys would be bought by indulgent parents, or aunts, or uncles, for children like Louis and Nat, who already had so much. And all over the world there was this vast oversupply of cheerless, toyless babies . . .

So? The world had never been fair, and never would be. There was no point in whinging about unfairness, thought Liz.

Yes there was! And it wasn't as if she were powerless to do anything! *She* wasn't a third-world woman at the mercy of bad politics, bad economics, and ignorant men. She and Zack were rich – at least by the standards of Africa and Asia, if not by the standards of south-east England. They had a comfortable, family house, which lacked a family. And would always lack a family, unless she had a change of heart about artificial insemination, or Zack's sperm miraculously flipped from low-grade to four-star. Or she and Zack offered refuge to a tiny foot-soldier from the world's lost troops of children.

Caroline was way too young to have been in the vanguard of feminism, and now feminism was dead. Gender as an issue was out, not in, cold, not hot, as far from being the new black as a rainbow. Or so she'd read in one of the Sundays. The woman journalist who'd written that should have come round to her house, Caroline thought, as she took up her rolling pin, and her feather duster, in order to join the fight. Or, rather, as she shoved her rolling pin and her duster at her recently de-hired husband. De-hired in the jobs market, re-hired at home. Surely that was fair enough? Tonight, she'd asked Simon to bathe the twins and put them to bed, which was a start, though a small one. Her ambitions were much greater.

'Simon,' she said, when he eventually returned to the den, looking shattered, 'I've got a plan.'

'Nat weed in the bath,' said Simon. 'And Louis threw an absolute fit.'

Caroline pictured her sons in the bath together, and laughed. 'Louis's so fastidious,' she said.

'And then neither of them would let me clean their teeth!'

'They never do! But did you hear me?'

'Hear you?' Simon slumped onto the collapsing sofa next to his wife and used the remote to click on the telly.

'Turn that off!' said Caroline, very sharply. 'I said I've got a plan.'

Simon glanced sideways at her, but didn't click off the telly. 'A plan?'

Caroline reached for the remote, and the screen went dead. 'A plan,' she repeated. 'I'm going back to work. You're going to stay at home and look after the kids.'

Simon considered this for a moment. 'Am I?' He shrugged, humouring his wife. 'Fine by me. You know I've always felt I was missing out, and that the boys were missing out, too, on having me around. And I don't mind kiddy slog, really. It's fun, even when it's a struggle, like tonight . . .'

'Fun!' snorted Caroline, always irritated by the word. 'Try dealing with both of them throwing tantrums in the supermarket at the same time. Or both of them—'

Simon grinned, and held up his hand. 'I'm sure it's hell,' he agreed – and dropped his act. 'Anyway, sweetheart, it's not much of a plan.'

'Ha! So dismissive? Just like that?'

'You'll never earn enough, round here. How many times have you said it yourself? There's nothing in Ryleford, bar tea caddies and chocolate boxes, blown up into boutiques and twiddle-de-dee shops.'

'Who says I intend to work in Ryleford?'

'Well, don't you?'

'Of course not! I want to be in London,' Caroline flung out her arms, 'with the brightest, and the best.'

'London?' Simon was bemused. 'What about the commute?'

'You did it.'

'But you're a mother . . .'

'And you're a father.'

'I know. And parenting's a shared responsibility. Quite. I earn – sorry, earned – the dosh, and . . .'

'I do – sorry, *did* – the housework and all that crap.'

'Yes, but *all that crap* means looking after the boys! And if you start commuting, you'll never even *see* the boys.'

'Don't you want your turn at seeing them?'

'That's not the issue. D'you want a turn at *not* seeing them?'

Caroline wrinkled her nose. 'I'll be up front about my commitments. I'll get something that's strictly nine to five. And I'll make sure I stick to the hours.'

'Huh!'

'Not possible?'

'No.'

'We'll see.'

'And will you be able to get anything? Have you considered that? In this economic climate, jobs are hard to come by.' Simon sighed. 'As I'm discovering,' he added regretfully.

Caroline reached out and took his hand. 'I know, love,' she said. 'But even in a bear market there's a need for corporate communication specialists, if only to convey bad news.'

Simon pictured the two HR buboes, who'd sat in on his sacking by Keith. 'D'you *want* to convey bad news?'

Caroline was silent.

'Of course you don't! Nobody does – not even berks like Keith. D'you really want to leave the boys *all day*, so you can do some crappy job, for some crappy company?'

Caroline looked at him, defiantly. 'Yes,' she said. 'I do.'

Husband and wife glared at each other a long moment.

'Okay,' said Simon, at last. 'Okay, we'll both work. We'll hire a nanny. If your pay won't cover it, I'll chip in. After all, why should paying for childcare be solely your responsibility?'

'I agree,' said Caroline. 'I mean, I agree we could get a nanny, and that both of us could go back to work. Of course we could. Easy! But I thought you'd *want* a spell as Mr Mum? I thought you'd want to spend a bit of time – quantity time, as well as quality time – with your sons?'

'Think of it – *one* salary?'

'We always survived off one salary before.'

'Yes, but it was *my* salary. You know you won't be able to pull down anything like what I was earning – and will earn again, when I find something.'

'If you—'

'Honestly, d'you think we could live off your earnings?'

'Not without cutting back . . .'

'Cutting back? What about the mortgage? Once the insurance stops?'

'Couldn't we give it a try?'

'What about school fees?'

Caroline smiled serenely as she prepared to challenge one

of Ryleford's most cherished holy cows. 'The state serves millions of people well enough.'

'Our sons aren't millions of people, they're *our* sons!'

'Indeed.'

Simon was taken aback. If his wife wasn't swayed by school fees, nothing would sway her. He stared at his shoeless feet, for a long moment, steadying himself to make a concession. 'I s'pose I could think about it.'

'Excellent! Because I've already rung round a few head-hunters.'

Penelope was a sort of headhunter. She had William in her sights and, by now, he and she had progressed from meeting for lunch to meeting for tea. The café on the top floor of Peter Jones was their chosen venue. This afternoon they'd managed to bag a table by the window, and the roofs of Knightsbridge were spread before them – they would have been pretty as a Christmas card, if only they'd been dusted with snow. Still, the borough lights, just coming on in the mid-afternoon winter gloom, glinted and glittered with seasonal festivity. As did the shop. Peter Jones was as much in the throes of Christmas as any edge-of-town toy warehouse – but its decorations were far more tasteful. No tinsel had been allowed inside its hallowed halls, which were decked with artificial greenery hung with blue ribbons and tiny, silver lights.

'I do so love Christmas,' sighed Penelope, as she ran her

tongue along a stripe of chocolate icing, and then bit into her éclair.

William, who had chosen a piece of blueberry cheesecake, as yet untouched, watched her suck at the gooey delight. 'There's cream round your mouth,' he said.

Penelope ran her tongue around her lips. 'I never have been able to resist sweet things.'

'Me neither.'

They smiled at each other, and William slowly took in the ample proportions of Penelope's body. She'd never dieted them into nonentity, and never would; her body was a mansion. He watched her take another bite of the sticky, oozing pastry. He waited a moment to give her time to swallow, and then, in silence, he leaned towards her. In silence, she leaned towards him. The next moment they were kissing.

Sweet William! thought Penelope. The sweetest cream I ever tasted.

Steamed pudding, thought William. He was gorging on sticky toffee, lemon ginger, and his very favourite, chocolate, smothered in hot sauce.

But this was Peter Jones, after all, and the café was filled with matronly ladies, up from the Shires for a spot of shopping. Both William and Penelope could sense disapproving eyes on their backs, and they quite quickly broke from each other.

'You taste of éclair,' said William.

'I expect I do,' agreed Penelope, and then they both turned their attention to their cakes, as if nothing at all had happened.

Once again Marcie knew nothing at all would happen in her body. Once again, she was worshipping at the groin of the great god husband. Once again, she was giving head. And, once again, her head couldn't have cared less. Her head was too filled with Hart to notice Brett's cock in her mouth.

'Don't you think it's time?' Hart had asked.

'Time?'

'To move in with me? You, and the girls?'

Yeeesss! Marcie would have punched the air for glee if she hadn't been otherwise engaged. She felt no scruples about leaving the marital home – this plush triplex, in a low-rise, at 83rd and Madison – and she felt no scruples about causing the marital husband pain. Did Brett even feel pain? She nibbled him, hard, and he didn't wince. But she *did* have social scruples. She and Brett had a slew of black-tie obligations coming up, and no Wall Street wife, including herself, ever looked kindly on those who would flatten the seasonal fizz. So, no way could she walk out before Christmas. Anyway, she thought, as she tickled with her tongue, she had her daughters to consider. She had obligations to them, as well as to society. How would her girls feel, to lose their father? Marcie glanced upwards to Brett's face. He was staring straight ahead, as if he were out on the sidewalk. The girls, she reminded herself, were hers, not his – and this was by his choice. Then again, Hart loved them, and would treat them as his own. Still, best to wait until after the holidays before she explained to the girls how their lives would change. Brett was, after all, their dad. It counted, even though it didn't. Let them have one final Christmas at which the illusion of family unity was maintained, if only for a day. This year Jenna, Chelsea, and Avery would tuck into turkey. They would unwrap presents – lots of them. They would have a tree, stockings, decorations, candy, all just as usual. And then, in the New Year, she'd whisk them down to TriBeCa.

They'd like their new nest. Hart was remodelling his vast loft to accommodate them – three small bedrooms, all ensuite, were being carved out of one corner of the echoing space. It would be such an adventure for her girls to live amongst exposed brick, concrete pillars and industrial ironwork rather than the swags and frills of this Upper East Side home. Then again, the Upper East Side might be urbane and suave, but TriBeCa had a buzz, a chutzpah. Not that her girls would be *educated* in the badlands of the urban frontier. They'd still go to School on 92nd Street – Hart's driver would drop them off and pick them up. Downtown living, Uptown schooling. Her girls, gloated Marcie, would get the best of both worlds. Yes! Yeess!

Yeeesss! Annie and Ming Kwan were ravishing each other, in his bathroom. So many mirrors! They were both naked, and Annie was propped half in, half out, of Ming Kwan's sink. She had stopped noticing how painful it was to have taps jabbing into her back. True, she was moaning, but not with discomfort. She had surrendered to Ming Kwan's velvet kisses, his silken taste, his satin scent, his skin. Oh, his skin, that cloth of gold. Annie clawed for her lover's flesh, and lost herself in its rich folds. She arched her back at the touch of tapestry, and of her lover's fingers, and of his tongue. She stretched her mouth to her lover's, and her mouth was stuffed with the mystery, and the power, and the sinuous beauty of a rippling Chinese dragon embroidered in rainbow silks on an emperor's robe. Men were only genitals on legs? What did it matter if those genitals were caramel-coloured, or pastry-coloured? Annie's mind was, at present, incapable of considering these questions, but her body was fully capable of answering them for her.

Simon imagined his wife, surrounded by mirrors at the hairdresser's.

'Can't possibly meet fancy, London headhunters with this no-style, mumsy style,' she'd said, when she'd announced that he'd be holding the fort at home this afternoon.

'It looks fine to me,' he'd objected.

'Never trust a man, on hair!' Caroline had sniffed. 'Although I do admit I'm nervous I'll emerge looking as if I've been the victim of a scissors-wielding psychopath.'

Simon smiled to remember that, and fervently hoped his wife would return having been coiffured into the very image of a professional woman.

Hang on! What *was* the very image of a professional woman? Simon was doing the post-lunch stacking of the dishwasher, his ears alert for screams from upstairs, where Nat and

Louis were playing in their bedroom. Now he paused to consider his own question and realized, with a rueful shrug, that he was really thinking about Caroline's plan. Yet again.

The more Simon thought about Caroline's plan, the more disquieting he found it. On reflection, he was deeply shocked by his wife's ideas. He picked up a plate, scraped the remains of spaghetti bolognese into the bin, and remembered asking his wife whether she really wanted to leave the boys all day, so she could do some crappy job, for some crappy company.

'Yes,' she'd said. 'I do.'

He could have understood it if she'd proposed abandoning the boys to do cancer research, or to get back to solving deep mathematical puzzles, or so that she could return to her career as a physicist, or as a social worker. Something that really mattered, that made a difference, or that really contributed. But being a corporate communications specialist was just a job. Caroline knew that. Yet she'd still rather be a corporate communications specialist than a mother. Or, at the very least, she'd rather spend her days doing whatever corporate communications specialists did than looking after her own children. Did that make his wife, the woman he loved, the woman at the centre of his emotional life, a total shit, beneath her lovely skin? Or did it just make her one hundred per cent normal? After all, his job at GCB had only ever been a job; nothing he'd ever done had changed the world, or our understanding of it, and yet he'd valued that job, and he'd still be doing it if only he hadn't gone and lost it.

Not that he would be jobless for ever. Simon began to scrape leftovers off another plate. It might take time, he reassured himself; he might have to consider a change of direction, retraining, or taking a lower-paid, lower-status job than the one he'd had at GCB, but he'd find something else, eventually. He *would* . . . And if Caroline also wanted to work? Well, he'd spoken truly the other night: if her salary wouldn't stretch to a nanny – or to childcare of some other sort – and yet getting back to work meant so much to her, then he wouldn't mind subsidizing the expense, for a bit.

On the other hand, there were all the arguments Caroline herself had used before the twins were born. He remembered she'd talked about nannies as flighty, ill-educated girls, who'd mostly be interested in finding men. At the time, that had struck him as a slur on nannies, not that he'd argued. He'd assumed Caroline hadn't meant it – just as he'd assumed she hadn't meant it when she'd suggested she should return to work whilst he stayed at home, as Mr Mum. He'd been flippant about that. *Fine by me*, he'd humoured her. But was it fine? He was a man. A breadwinner. A provider. He should shield his family from the dangers of the world – not send his wife out to do daily battle in the dangerous big city whilst he remained safely cocooned at home. And if he did accept wimpish safety, how would it feel to be supported by his wife? How would it feel to be a kept man? Not just a kept man, either, but an honorary *mum*, treated as a mum by other mums and, even worse, by other *men*?

'Oh, for fuck's sake!' Simon admonished the dirty mug he was about to place in the dishwasher. 'Stop being such a bloody dinosaur!' The mug, a cheerful ceramic affair, ignored his instruction. But Simon took note of it. He'd never counted himself a New Man. Indeed, he didn't quite know what was meant by the term – unless it described earnest, vegetarian males who rode bicycles, sported beards, and used moisturizer? But he did know there was more to life than MOTs, DIY, sport, and outdoor survival.

'What does it matter if a man's kept by a woman?' he asked the mug. *What does it matter*, he added silently in his head, *if a woman is the one doing interesting things out in the world, whilst her man stays at home to stack the dishwasher?*

Simon placed the mug in its allotted space and lifted out the cutlery basket. He placed it on the draining board and began filling it with dirty knives and forks. Forget what the world might think – did he himself want to be Mr Mum? . . . W-e-l-l, no. Not really. Of course, Simon reassured himself, it would only be for a few months. A year or two, at the very most. Not for ever. It would be a career break, rather than the end of his career. And think of the advantages! Caroline had invoked quantity time, as well as quality time with the twins. Quantity time had to count, didn't it? Think of the boys – nearly three already! In three more years his boys would be six and, three years later, nine, and then twelve, and then fifteen, and then gone. Bye, bye! That was his role as a father, thought

Simon, as he carefully poured dishwasher powder into its slot; his role was to prepare his sons for independence, and then to wave them off as they embarked on all the delights, and all the disappointments of adulthood. That was his job – but he didn't want to do it. He really didn't. He wanted to keep his boys small and dependent, for ever. He wanted cuddles at bedtime – or any time, really – he wanted his boys' faces to light up when they saw him. He wanted to be told all their news, in a stream of only semi-comprehensible but un-self-censored chatter. These things happened now, but for how much longer would they continue to happen? How much longer until his sons were rolling their eyes and patronizing him? How much longer until they were keeping secrets from him? Lying to him, even? How much longer until they were off? Simon sniffed a little to think of it, and submitted to a piercing nostalgia for a past that had not yet been. He wanted *time* with his boys. Time to teach them all he knew about love, and about being a man – which wasn't much – and time to learn from them all they knew about love, and about being boys. He should have known, of course, what it was like to be a boy, but he'd forgotten.

And he wanted to remember. He wanted to remember innocence, and the thrill of seeing quite ordinary things as new and strange. He wanted to recall excitement, and wonder, and the misplaced certainty of endless, endless possibilities. Simon banged shut the dishwasher, harder than he'd intended, and decided he wanted to be granted the great gift of recollection.

*

Liz had not been able to forget the world's lost troops of children. They pressed in on her with pleading faces and pleading arms outstretched as she stood at her work surface, chopping vegetables for a soup.

'So,' she said, 'I've been thinking about it some more.'

Zack was sitting at the kitchen table, staring into nothing. 'About what?' he asked – then immediately wondered why he'd bothered. How many topics were there between his wife and himself, right now?

'Reproductive technology. Artificial insemination. Donor sperm.'

'Oh, that.'

Liz's hand froze, her knife poised over a stick of celery. 'I've decided it's not for me. I just don't like the sound of it. I don't like the sound of it being done *to me*.'

Zack remained silent. What could he say? His dreams of biological fatherhood had all been shattered – now his wife appeared to be shattering his remaining dreams of family life. But whether or not to get herself inseminated was her call. If she didn't want to accept another man's sperm into her body, he could scarcely force her. Rape, he was sure, was a blasphemous comparison; nevertheless, it sprang to mind.

'It's too much technology, where no technology ought to be.' Liz recommenced her slicing, and addressed the stick of celery. 'I know it's worked for lots and lots of couples, and they're ecstatic. I know their children are delights. I know it makes sense, of course it does, to seek help if you can't

279

conceive naturally . . . but *this type* of assisted conception? Like an animal? I mean, I know I *am* an animal, a mammal, but . . . I don't know, Zack. I just don't know.'

'And I can't tell you,' said Zack. 'There aren't any answers.'

Liz gave up on her vegetables and sat down at the kitchen table opposite her husband. 'Answers? I don't even know what the *questions* are, half the time. But here's one I *can* answer: do I want to carry within me a child that's not yours?' She vigorously shook her head. 'No, I don't.'

Husband and wife looked at each other a long, long moment.

'Thanks, love,' said Zack. 'Thanks.'

Liz gravely blew her husband a kiss. 'It's not just you,' she said. 'It's also the child. We all want to know who we are, and where we come from. What would we say to our child?'

Zack ignored her question. 'But what about you?' he asked instead. 'The whole baby thing? Pregnancy. Birth. You won't experience them.'

'It's just biology.'

'Bollocks. You'll miss all that's involved in having a child of your own.'

'Just think of the heartbreak if we kept trying and failing . . .'

'Raised hopes, then dashed hopes?'

'Yes.'

'I'm sure we could cope with all that, if you wanted to try.'

'But I don't. I want us to think about other alternatives.'

'Other alt . . .?'

'Adoption. Not as a last ditch, last resort, but as a positive choice.'

Zack was still focused on all his wife would miss if they ruled out donor insemination. 'It seems so selfish to deprive you of—'

'Shut up! I've thought it all through.' Liz thrust out her chin and spoke defiantly. 'Sure, an adopted child might not stand much more chance of knowing where he or she came from than a child conceived with donor sperm. Sure, there might be issues of displacement, and loss – but those children already *exist*. That's the difference. The need to provide a stable, loving, nurturing childhood overrides the need to provide a provenance, as it were.'

Zack didn't argue. He said nothing.

'I know there aren't many white babies,' Liz continued, less aggressively. 'But so many unlucky children in the world who need homes.'

Zack leaned back in his chair and briefly closed his eyes. Just as his wife had done in the toy warehouse, he saw a montage of old news clips on his inner TV screen. Those starving, bashed-up children were so often unwelcome, he thought, as the images spooled. Unwanted. Unloved. Except that was probably despicably unfair. Surely Liz was right, and the only appropriate word was unlucky? If only those children had been born in wealthier parts of the world, or to wealthier or more educated parents . . . God! Life was such a lottery. Zack sighed both at his and Liz's bad luck in being unable to conceive, and also at their almost incredible good luck in being white, western, wealthy. Could they help spread that good luck around? Should they? He pictured himself cradling an African child, or a Romanian one, or a sloe-eyed Asian baby. But who would have the better luck here? The child? Or himself, given the chance to father it? The luck, thought Zack, would mostly be his. Yet his good luck would have to be a mother's bad luck – and probably, a father's too. Zack imagined himself glancing up from an African baby's entranc- ing, pocket-watch face, only to meet a pair of adult eyes: haughty brown eyes, hard with scorn, glassy with disdain. Zack couldn't imagine the face in which these eyes were set, but he knew to whom they belonged. They belonged to the African child's biological father. Zack heard that man's voice in his head: *They said it was for the best interests of my child. But my child is not your child. My child is mine. I can't help it that you are infertile. That doesn't give you the right to take what's mine.*

'No!' cried Zack, to the imaginary man. 'No!'

'What?' said Liz, startled. 'You don't agree the world is filled with children in need of homes?'

'Of course I agree!' said Zack, impatiently. 'I meant . . . I meant you're right. I meant we have so much to offer.' He swept his arm around the untidy kitchen. 'This home.' He pointed to Liz's tray of chopped vegetables. 'That food. Education. Financial stability.'

'Love?' suggested Liz.

'Love,' agreed Zack. 'Love,' he repeated.

Eleven

Jo's C-section hadn't been quite as clean and crisp and controlled as she'd expected. She'd had an epidural, not a general, so she'd been fully conscious of a pain, which, like the pain of her amnio, had hurt in a way she'd never expected pain to hurt. Not that she'd been able to feel anything, exactly – and she certainly hadn't been able to *see*, since the lower part of her body had been screened off – but she'd been aware of a yanking in her insides, or of an uprooting. It had been a dislocation, or a dislodging, or an enforced discontinuity, both terrible and wonderful, and she'd wept throughout. Then afterwards she'd shaken. And shaken, and shaken.

'Hormones,' a midwife had said, kindly.

But Jo hadn't believed her. This shaking hadn't been hormones. It had been . . . whatever it had been, it was over now. Jo was sitting up in her narrow hospital bed, dressed in a hideous blue hospital gown. She was still attached to an IV line, and she was still pumped full of painkillers. But did she need the drugs? Or would euphoria have killed her post-operative pain? Perhaps, since she was gazing deep into a pair of newest of new eyes, imprinting them both onto, and with, her own eyes. The eyes she gazed into were empty and full, absent and present, blank and bewitching. They were vessels to be filled up with memory, and their colour was a blue as dark as oblivion. Their focus was both on nothing and on Jo, who had recognized them, and remembered them, the first moment she'd seen them.

Jo, the new mother, and the neophyte, gazed on the goddess she cradled in her arms. She gazed on Madison's tiny, wrinkled face with adoration. Such a nose! And surely it had come from her? Such lips! The softness of such new, new skin! She lightly stroked Madison's cheek with the tip of one finger, then lifted her baby higher, wincing at the motion. But though it hurt to lift her baby, she held Madison close against her face. She wanted more than just to imprint her gaze on Madison's, and Madison's on hers. She wanted to breathe in the breath of life, which was air that Madison had breathed out. She wanted to breathe in her baby's milky breath, and the smell of her, which was also the smell of her self. And she wanted Madison to inhale the air that she had exhaled; she wanted her daughter, for nine long months a part of her body, to breathe in her mother's self.

Madison was swaddled in the hospital's cellular blankets; they were bound around her tightly, tightly, although they did not press on her as tightly as her mother's womb had pressed, so very recently. Her eyes were not nearly so empty of memory as they appeared. She had recognized and remembered Jo's green eyes immediately, as surely as Jo had recognized and remembered her own blue ones. Madison knew nothing of the miracles of technology. But she knew there could be windows between different worlds; her mother had observed her eyes, through a technician's screen, and she had observed her mother's eyes, likewise. Now, once again, she gazed just as intently on her mother as her mother gazed on her. She, too, wanted to breathe in the breath of life. She inhaled her mother's exhaled breath, as greedily as her mother inhaled her own exhaled breath. She breathed deeply, and her mother's exhaled breath held the scent of her mother, which was also the scent of her self. *Perhaps I can adapt to this world, after all,* she thought. Her first impressions had not been reassuring. The light! The cold! The noise! These things had been both terrible and magnificent, as had been her certainty that they foreshadowed other types of terror and of magnificence that she'd encounter in her new, most emphatic of worlds. But in this moment, neither terror nor magnificence intruded; for Madison, all was smell. *I'm safe,* she thought, and with that thought, she fell asleep.

But what of Old Eyes? Today, Jo had given birth. What of the baby she had denied actuality, all those years ago? As Madison slept peacefully in her arms, Jo raised her eyes to the ceiling, and to Old Eyes. Mother and unborn, undead ghost regarded each other over the body of a living baby, and exchanged a look, which properly sunk in on both sides. Or so Jo fancied. She felt suffused with peace; her spirit had fallen quiet. She would not forget, she would never forget her child who existed outside time, but today, on its sister's birthday, it could go. She released it. She watched, solemnly, as Old Eyes began to un-condense, just as New Eyes had un-condensed. Like New Eyes, Old Eyes began to diffuse into the atoms of the surrounding air. All the non-stuff stuff of its moth-like presence slowly streamed away into nothing, into the void, into blankness. Or else it streamed away to infinity, the destination and the origin on which it had been fixed all along.

Infinity was a loud and popular bar in Covent Garden. There was a large, aluminium Möbius curve suspended from the ceiling. This curve had only one side and one edge, and it could have had something to do with the mathematical concept of infinity, although nobody in the place was sure. Still, both Liz and Annie thought its strange sinuousness was intriguing. The curve was pregnant with meaning beyond their comprehension, which seemed appropriate, since they were at Infinity to celebrate Madison's birth, and she too was pregnant with mysterious meaning.

Cocktails were back in fashion, and both sisters had ordered Cosmopolitans, although they'd toyed with the idea of Manhattans. The atmosphere was very smoky – too smoky for Liz, who'd begun to cough. She and Annie had bagged themselves a semi-circular booth, upholstered in purple velvet, on a raised dais to one side of the small dance floor. Nobody was dancing, yet, although later there would be live music and lots of wiggly-jiggly.

Annie raised her glass, which came complete with a glacé cherry on a cocktail stick and a tiny paper parasol. 'To Madison!' she grinned.

'To Madison!' repeated Liz. She coughed some more, and then she burst into tears.

Annie put down her glass. 'Oh dear,' she said. 'Oh dear.'

'Sorry,' spluttered Liz. 'So sorry. This jealousy is quite ridiculous.'

'No it's not. It's only natural.'

'It's ghastly. It's pathological.'

'Rubbish!'

'I'm delighted for Jo, really.'

'I know. And she'd understand.'

'Of course she would! And I'm delighted for myself, too. What a *wonderful* thing, to have a niece!'

'It *is* wonderful,' agreed Annie. 'Hang on to that. A little girl for all of us to love, and to share.'

'I know.' Liz took a swig of her Cosmopolitan, which was intended for polite sipping. 'And anyway, Zack and I will have our own family one day.'

'I'm sure you will,' said Annie, warmly. 'I'm sure of it!'

'So are we. Guess what?'

'What?'

'We've decided to adopt.'

'Well,' said Annie forty minutes later, when Liz had finished speaking, 'if you're going to adopt from the developing world, why don't you think about China? Ming Kwan is forever saying—'

'*Ming Kwan?*' interrupted Liz. '*Is* forever saying?'

Annie blushed. She had not yet told anybody that Ming Kwan had reappeared in her life. Now she inwardly cursed herself for carelessness around her sharp-witted sister. She twiddled her cocktail umbrella, and looked shifty.

'*Aaannie?*'

'No,' said Annie, very firmly. 'It's too new. And too private.'

Liz leaned back against the purple velvet, and took a sip of her Cosmopolitan. 'I see,' she said. She remembered Annie and Ming Kwan as they once had been, vibrating in a kind of forcefield of attraction. She thought of William, her prospective brother-in-law, who was nice enough, but . . . 'I see,' she repeated.

'Maybe you do,' giggled Annie. 'And maybe you don't.'

'You're really not telling?'

'No!'

'Okay,' smiled Liz. 'Fair enough.' She took another sip of her drink. 'So, what is it that Ming Kwan *is* forever saying?'

'Oh, yes.' Annie's attention snapped back from the complexities of her own life to those of her sister's. 'Well, perhaps forever was a bit of an exaggeration, but he does go on about it – did you know China has millions of superfluous girls?'

'Vaguely. I've read about it, a bit.'

'It's because of the one-child policy. Y'know? China's attempt to curb its population growth?'

'Its *staggering* population growth.'

'That's right. They have to feed them all, and educate them. So, only one child per family, in an attempt to combat poverty and improve quality of life all round.'

'I always wondered: what happens if a couple has *two* children?'

'A fine, I think.' Annie took a handful of peanuts from the bowl in the middle of the table, and nibbled on one. 'The second child doesn't legally exist.'

'Oh,' said Liz. 'So what happens to somebody who doesn't legally exist?'

'Dunno.'

'And what's it got to do with all these . . .'

'Superfluous girls?'

'Yes.'

'Ah!' said Annie. 'W-e-l-l, there's this huge cultural preference towards sons.'

'Meaning?'

'It's illegal to abandon a girl, of course.' Annie shrugged, faux off-hand. 'And selective abortion's illegal, too, but ultrasound is easy, and cheap. Ming Kwan says it's simplified the quest for a male heir no end. Female infanticide's not legal, either. Then again, if a girl falls sick, why call the doctor? Medicine's expensive.'

Liz blanched, and her skin took on a greenish tinge in the subdued light.

'Think of the pressures,' said Annie. 'Social, economic, political.'

'There's no excuse.'

'And they *are* trying to do something about it. Campaigns and so on. Daughters are as good as sons. Ming Kwan was telling me that's the latest slogan.'

'Is the message getting through?'

Annie avoided the question. 'It's mainly economics,' she said. 'Boys are the Chinese social security system. Parents rely on sons for support in old age. When girls marry, they become part of their husbands' households, often living with their husbands' families.'

'So it's *his* parents, who receive *her* care?'

'You got it! In rural areas, a wife's expected to be totally dedicated to her husband's family – they paid a bride price for her, after all. And if a girl's only going to end up marrying out of the family, why devote resources to her? But it's not just that; on farms boys are needed to work – fetch water, guard the orchards, bring in the harvest. And inheritance passes from father to son. Not just goods, either. The Chinese go in for ancestor worship – and they need boys to inherit the ancestral name.'

'Fucking hell!'

'Anyway, that's why the Chinese, especially the rural Chinese, prefer Little Emperors to Little Empresses. Little Emperors. That's what they call the millions of only boys, spoiled rotten by their parents and grandparents.'

Liz looked across at Annie, and thought also of Caroline, and of Jo.

'Imagine!' she said. 'No sisters!'

'And no brothers, either. It's all leading to terrible problems – mostly couched in terms of the *poor, poor* men, unable to find brides. Abduction of women's already a big issue.'

'There's already such an imbalance of the sexes?'

'Yes.'

'Because the girls have all been got rid of?'

'Aborted. Got rid of. Abandoned – that's what I'm getting round to.' Annie paused a moment. 'The abandoned ones go into orphanages,' she said.

The sisters met each other's eyes. Liz leaned forward.

'Orphanages?' she repeated, carefully.

'Pretty grim places, often. I'm sure the staff try to do their best, but you can imagine, it must be so difficult for them . . .'

Both Annie and Liz had by now finished their drinks. Annie waved over the waiter, and ordered another round. Only once this was accomplished did she return to China's lost girls. 'The orphanages represent mothers trying to do their best. According to Ming Kwan, abandonment's an adoption plan. Mothers bundle up their spare girls and leave them somewhere near an orphanage, hoping they'll make it to America.'

'What? Americans are allowed to adopt from the orphanages?'

'You don't have to be American. China's adoption policies are a haven for . . . for . . .'

'Infertile couples,' completed Liz, sadly.

'Yes,' agreed Annie, gently. 'Rich ones, from the West. It's what the girls' mothers hope for. Especially America.'

'Zack and I can't offer America.'

'No. But I expect those mothers would settle for the UK.'

The sisters fell silent, each imagining Chinese mothers of peasant stock settling for the UK, and each imagining the pain of those shadow-mothers of shadow-children, flitting in a distant land of shadows.

Fletchor & Mellor was an American-owned multi-national specializing in the manufacture of what it called household pharmaceuticals, although many of its products leaned more towards the janitorial than the pharmaceutical. It was a huge company, a cog in the engine of capitalism, which was itself the engine of the West. Not that Caroline was thinking of Fletchor & Mellor in quite those terms; she was thinking of it in terms of a job.

The house was blissfully silent. Simon had agreed to a spell – a spell, not a lifetime – as Mr Mum, and had put his own search for a job on hold, at least until the spring, whilst his family adjusted to the reincarnation of Caroline's career, and of Caroline. This morning he had taken the twins to play footie in the park. Meanwhile, Caroline was in her country-style kitchen, sitting at the deal table, taking a call from a top London headhunter. Well, she thought, the salary the headhunter had just mentioned was certainly most attractive. And F&M was bluest of blue chip.

'Sounds interesting,' she said. 'Let me just run through the details again.' She drew her pencil down the sheet of A4 lying on the table in front of her. It was covered with notes in her spidery writing. 'Their share price has taken a hammering . . .'

'. . . down sixty per cent in six months.'

'So they're going to be undertaking a root and branch review of their entire European operation?'

'Everything will be up for negotiation.' The headhunter was a middle-aged man whose voice oozed greasily down the phone from his office in Mayfair.

'They want to consolidate, and focus on three core areas? Cosmetics; laundry powders; household cleaning products?'

'That's it.'

'Cosmetics doesn't seem to sit very well with the other two.'

'You'd have to ask them about that. I didn't get into that level of detail. Just big-picture stuff.'

'And the big picture's that they want to sell off personal hygiene products, their baby-care range, and aerosols?'

'No. Not get rid of aerosols, completely. They want to maintain a filling function. And novelty soaps, they want to hang onto that division.'

'Right,' said Caroline, who thought she'd better avoid the ins-and-outs of aerosols. 'Novelty soaps. And they're going to relocate their European head office to Frankfurt?'

'That's the plan.'

There was silence for a beat, as both Caroline and the headhunter considered how news of a move to Frankfurt would go down in West London, where Fletchor & Mellor currently had their European head office.

'So,' sighed Caroline at last, 'they want someone to explain to their staff how their lives will be affected by decisions beyond their control?'

'A corporate communications specialist, yes.'

'We don't just deal in doom and gloom,' demurred Caroline, a little miffed.

'It's all there is, at the moment.'

'Do you mean there's only bad news at the moment? Or that this job is all you have to offer me?'

'Both. And you're a perfect fit. Your qualifications match their requirements exactly. So, if you agree, I'd like to fax them over your CV. Shall I do it?'

Caroline took a deep breath. Crunch time. Was she going to put her CV where her mouth was? Was she going to get out there and communicate corporately? Or was she going to stay at home, singing 'The Wheels on the Sodding Bus'?

The sodding bus was the clincher. Caroline was fed up with the language of the domestic; she wanted complex thought. Simon was wrong. He'd said to her, Yours was just a job. In other words, hers wasn't a career. But it was and laundry powder *wasn't* trivial! Imagine life, for women, without laundry powder, and washing machines to put it in. Imagine life without bleach, and scouring powders. For that matter, imagine the drabness of life without lipstick.

'Yes, please,' she said firmly. 'Fax them my CV. I think you should do it, right away.'

Nobody's curriculum vitae was finalized until death. Henrietta knew that, and her head was filled with dreams of a new entry on hers: a grandchild. She gleefully, and very deliberately, took her time bossing her long-suffering butcher about her Christmas order: a *brown* turkey, not a white, a honey-*pineapple* roast ham, not a honey-orange.

Meanwhile, Annie, whose CV was also in flux, was at Zenses, so the wedding cake house in Knightsbridge was deserted but for Bonnie and Clyde, who were snuffling about in the kitchen, and William and Penelope, who were snuffling about in bed.

Both the humans were sated with pleasure. William's satiety came from sex, and Penelope was confident she had given a pretty good impression that so had hers. But really it came from ice-cream. Dolce de leche. Caramel. Caramelo. Sweet syrup of love. Penelope and William were tucking into a post-coital tub of the stuff.

'God,' said William. 'I've had way, way too much.'

'I could never get enough,' giggled Penelope. 'Vanilla ice. Sugar cream.'

William took the spoon they were sharing from her hand, and fed her a sloppy, melting, mouthful or two.

'Such sweetness,' he said, licking a dribble of golden toffee from her chin. 'Such a glut of riches.'

'Mmm,' sighed Penelope, wriggling happily at this gentle gratification of her desires, and then wriggling some more at the prospect of the gratification of other desires, still to come. She reached out a sticky hand to caress William's hair, and as she did so she imagined their wedding day.

Penelope would marry William at Saint John's, Lesser Elsland. Much the same people would attend as had attended darling Edward's christening – only Annie would be absent. She would marry on a glorious summer's day. The ancient little church would be decked with roses. Her Sweet William would be in top hat and tails, and under his tailcoat he would wear a jolly silk waistcoat – green, perhaps, embroidered with golden bees, or blue, embroidered with silver moons? She herself would be the most bride-like bride ever to grace an aisle. Her dress would be of duchesse satin – so smooth, so sheeny – ivory, or cream, with a very full skirt. The heavily beaded bodice would be chaste, the sleeves long – even puffed, perhaps? She'd wear a veil, of course, so romantic, so demure. Her bouquet would be a waterfall of lilies and roses – later, she'd toss it to her guests.

'You next!' she'd tease the woman who caught it. By then, of course, she'd have changed into her going-away outfit – a neat little silk suit, for sure. Lilac, perhaps, with a big, ostrich-feathered hat? William would so proudly hand her, and her hat, into his car.

'Mine,' he'd say. 'Mine.'

Of course, his chums would have tied tin cans and balloons to the car bumper. What larks! They'd have sprayed a heart on the rear window, and scrawled the news: *Just married.* If they'd been really naughty, they'd have hidden a smelly kipper somewhere under the bonnet, and William would curse when he had to stop to remove it. Then they would reach the hotel where they were to spend the first night of their honeymoon . . . And then that would be that, for a year. But twelve months later they'd be back in St John's.

'One of my success stories,' the rector would boom as he christened her and William's first child: a son, Bertrand, after William's father. She'd be deft and skilful round the baby, William would be protective – and they'd both be *so* proud. And darling little Bertie, the object of their pride, would wear a gown of duchesse satin, cut down from the skirts of her wedding dress . . .

Liz had not changed her mind on the merits of christening a child versus throwing it a secular party – especially if the child in question had been plucked from a land of Buddhists, Taoists, Confucians, and communists. For the moment, she thought about the Buddhists and the Taoists, rather than the communists. Could it be that her consciousness was flowing into a great, universal river of energy, as her body hesitated outside Global Adoption Links, in Golders Green?

Global Adoption Links, or GAL, was an agency specializing

in placing Chinese baby girls with British couples. Its logo, prominently displayed on a board by the front door, was a globe encircled by children holding hands, as if they were dancing ring-a-roses round the planet. Beneath the logo was the agency's motto: *Because every child deserves a family*. Despite its worldwide ambition, the agency was housed in a bog-standard, converted semi, tucked behind a railway bridge. The prosaic nature of the surroundings soon put a stop to Liz's mystical wool-gathering; this house seemed very far from China, and from a daughter. She gave herself a mental shake, then pushed through the gate, and headed towards the front door.

The reception area was hung with Christmas cards, and the receptionist looked like an elf. He was a weedy young man, dressed in green, sporting rimless specs and a goatee.

'Have you had one of our information packs?' he asked Liz.

'No. We've just seen your website.'

The receptionist reached beneath his desk and pulled out a shiny blue folder stamped with the agency's globe-and-dancing-children logo, and also with its motto.

'I can't make you an appointment until you've read it and completed all the forms.'

Liz took the folder. Once more her mind wandered Eastwards. Could cosmic energy flow through printed paper? Could yin and yang be contained by shiny blue card? Why not? These things were no more mysterious than baby girls riding the trade winds West, along with cheap electronics, cheaper plastic toys, and the cheapest of cheap fake everything.

'Because every child deserves a family,' Zack read aloud from the blue folder's front cover. He and Liz were huddled on their kaleidoscopic day-bed learning what it would take for them to *earn* a family. The notes supplied with GAL's information pack explained that if their application to become parents were to proceed, they would have to complete a series of psychometric tests, which had been supplied with the folder. Zack gloomily pulled out a four-page leaflet and flicked through it. Inside, it was printed with multiple-choice questions, and the entire front page was devoted to a daunting rubric.

'It's like an exam!' he said.

'It *is* an exam,' said Liz.

Zack grunted, and again read aloud, this time from the rubric. '*Psychological inventory: definition of scales.*' He looked directly at Liz. 'Do we want to undergo a psychological inventory?'

Liz was no more enthusiastic than her husband. 'Do we have any choice?' Zack didn't answer. '*Responsibility,*' he read, '*the extent to which one believes that life should be governed by reason and order, and that one should be concerned with civic responsibility.*' He paused. 'Do you accept that as a definition?'

'Dunno.'

'Me neither . . . *Socialization, the extent to which one believes in adhering to social norms and standards of propriety.*

Self-control, a measure of self-discipline, and the control of impulses . . . It's so unfair! Natural parents don't have to go through all this bullshit!'

'Perhaps they should,' said Liz, tartly, 'seeing how lousy some of them are. A licence to become a parent isn't such a bad idea!'

'No? I think it's a *terrible* idea!'

'We have to be better than natural parents, remember?'

Zack once again saw an African father's eyes, hard with scorn, glassy with disdain. As he watched his inner screen, those eyes changed shape. They retained their dark brown colour, but they flattened, and curved, and slanted, as though their possessor were squinting against a sandstorm. Zack knew he was now staring into a Chinese man's eyes. Though he was terrified, he was not cowed. It was like when he'd fallen in love with Liz, he'd been terrified then, too. But he'd jumped. Thank God. And he would jump now. He would accept the challenge laid down by some unknown, unlucky child's blood father, and he would also accept the risks – of loss, and of pain – that such a challenge would bring . . . or rather, he would accept both the challenge, and the risks, if only GAL allowed him to. Zack smiled at his wife.

'So, have you got a pencil?' he asked.

'You want to get started on the forms right now? Right away?'

'Why not?' Zack tapped the leaflet. 'If we're going to do it, we might as well get stuck into this bloody exam.'

Jo, an entirely unlicensed mother, was still in a hideous blue hospital gown, although she'd lost the IV line by now. The latter-day Madonna was nursing her child, and Madison was really guzzling the milk, thought Jo, who was not yet used to the strange tugging sensation. Nor was she used to the transformation of her tits from breasts – objects of beauty, and of delight – to mammary glands – objects of mammalian utility. She was besotted with her daughter; nevertheless, as she gazed down upon Madison's little puckered lips sucking and slurping, she couldn't help remembering far pleasanter tongue to nipple contact. But perhaps, she mused, this was only because these last few days her thoughts had so very often circled back to Brett. Madison's father. Her fury with him had not abated, and nor had desire reignited. But Madison her darling daughter was also *his* daughter. There was the rub. Should she try, once again, one last time, to *force* Brett to take an interest in his offspring? True, she wasn't keen to welcome him back into her life and he might not want to be welcomed into Madison's, but what Mom and Pop wanted was neither here nor there. What Madison *needed* was the point. Jo frowned down at her greedy daughter. 'I can feed you,' she said, 'but I can't show you what it's like to be a member of the other half of the human race.' A father could do that – sort of, vaguely, a bit. Did Madison need a father? Did she need Brett? What could she learn from him? Could he teach her anything useful, or only unhappy lessons, about the unthinking exercise of power? Would it be better for her daughter to have occasional contact with a father who wasn't much interested in her, than to have no father at all? Jo didn't know. She just didn't know.

'What do you think?' she asked Madison. 'What do you think, little girl?'

Madison paused in her greedy guzzling, and turned her huge blue eyes upwards, upon her mother. She longed to speak. *I do not want to share you,* she longed to say. *And I do not want you to share me, however lopsidedly, with any man, but especially not with a man who does not want me because I am a girl.* She stretched, in Jo's arms, and yawned prettily, a little mouse-like yawn. *We're two against the world,* she wanted to say,

Two against the world is just as it should be.
I is fine
We two is fine
We many is fine
But we three?

Madison frowned, out of sadness for her father. *We three?* She wanted to ask her mother. *You, me, and a man whose best friends are dollars?* Alas, Madison could not speak. However hard she struggled, she could not form the words. She had no teeth against which to curl or click her tongue; she could not force her lips into the shapes of the English language. Discounting lusty screaming, her immature mouth locked her into silence. So Madison said nothing, but turned back to her mother's nipple, and once more began to suck.

*

Simon was easing himself into his new role just as gently as Caroline would allow. This morning he'd willingly given the twins breakfast, but he'd far less willingly brought them round to Hector's for one of their regular playdates. Caroline had cried off the coffee coven because the Mayfair headhunter had sent her a fat file on Fletchor & Mellor, and she wanted to read it. Simon had been most reluctant to come in her stead. Spending time with the boys was one thing, but being initiated into the secret society of mums was quite another, and he wasn't sure if he was ready for it, yet.

The first half-hour had been just as bad as he'd antici-pated. Once Nat, Louis, and the other children had been plonked in front of a Christmas video, the coven mums had sat staring at him, smiling falsely and clearly wondering what to make of a man in their midst. But Sophie, a foodie, had made mulled wine and mince pies. Her comfortable house was deliciously scented with spices and, by now, Simon was deliciously scented with good cheer – in other words, tipsy. As were the mums. Everyone had relaxed, and the mums were beginning to treat Simon as one of their own. They had already given him a few hints on where to buy winter pyjamas for the twins, a deeply important subject in which Caroline, though a dear, had never shown the slightest interest, and also on what to look for when buying mangos. Ditto. Now they were explaining how to make chocolate truffles. Simon was delighted to be given the lesson; never in his married life had he eaten a homemade chocolate truffle, but this Christmas it would be different! This Christmas, the Ayrton household would feast on the things – and he would have made them!

Simon had made his recipe notes on the back of the dread envelope containing his and Caroline's scarlet electricity bill – he'd had it in his pocket, since he intended to pay the damn thing, sometime.

'So let me check I've got this,' he said, glancing down at his jottings. 'Fifty grams *chopped* almonds. One hundred grams *ground* almonds. One hundred grams plain chocolate. Two tablespoons double cream. Seventy-five grams sugar—'

'*Castor* sugar,' corrected Lucy.

'Seventy-five grams castor sugar. Vanilla essence. Grated chocolate, for coating.'

'You could use chocolate vermicelli instead,' said Lucy.

'Such a simple recipe,' smiled Sophie. 'All you do is brown the chopped almonds lightly, under the grill. Break the chocolate into small pieces and melt it in a bowl over a pan of hot water. Add all the other . . .'

'Remove the bowl from the pan, first,' interrupted Lucy anxiously.

'Well obviously!' said Sophie. 'Add all the other ingredients . . .'

'Except the coating chocolate.'

'Lucy! He's not stupid.'

'Yes I am,' said Simon, flashing Lucy a quick smile.

Sophie snorted. 'Mix to a stiff paste,' she said. 'Balls it up . . . that's a technical term – pastry chefs use it. Balls it up, into small balls, and roll them at once in the coating chocolate. Put them into paper sweet cases to serve.'

'Bob's your uncle!' said Emma brightly. She was a hopeless cook. Her idea of cooking, even for Phoebe, was to open a carton of some frozen ready-meal, cut a slit in the centre of its film cover, zap it in the microwave, and then stir before serving.

'Where do I get paper sweet cases?' asked Simon.

'Anywhere,' said Sophie airily. 'But I can let you have some, if you'd like?'

Simon laughed out loud. 'I love my wife, dearly,' he said. 'But she must be nuts to want to go back to work, and miss out on all this fun with you lot!'

Annie and Ming Kwan were not having much fun; they were too conscious of the clock. Five through seven, the hours between the end of work and the beginning of the evening, the shadow hours consecrated to couples jointly in on betrayal, were *so* brief. Both of them wanted to be in bed, but instead they were in Soho, in a noisy wine bar. They'd managed to claim a small table for themselves, against stiff competition from the after-work crowds. A copy of the *Standard* lay between them, and they bickered over the headlines as they drank their white wine.

Conceptual Brit art had displaced the economy, health policy, and the clapped-out Tube from tonight's front page. A young turk had just won an important prize for *My Desk*, a sculpture of his desk, cluttered with books, papers, an alarm clock, a couple of paperweights, a mug, a spoon, pens, Post-its, a telephone, and a computer. There was nothing extraordinary about this – except *My Desk* was sculpted from the artist's frozen urine, and had to be displayed in a refrigerated glass cabinet.

'It's just junk,' declared Ming Kwan. 'They might as well give me a prize for *my* desk, from the office.'

'It's not made of your piss!'

'Something's not made of piss, so it shouldn't get a prize?'

Annie took a sip of her wine. 'W-e-l-l . . .' she said, quite the history-of-art graduate struggling to be fair, 'art these days is mostly autobiography, and . . .'

'Autobiography?'

'Y'know, everything seen through the lens of—'

'I know what autobiography means,' objected Ming Kwan, the literary agent.

'Sorry!'

Ming Kwan laughed, but then his laughter died, and his face became suffused with sadness.

'What about *our* autobiographies?' he said. 'What about the stories we're making of our lives?'

He and Annie looked at each other a long moment. Annie remained silent.

'You do know, don't you, that you've got to call it off with William?'

Annie glanced away. Her fingers busily twisted her ruby

engagement ring, whilst her eyes stared blankly at the *Standard.*

'Well?' pressed Ming Kwan.

'Of course I know it,' snapped Annie. 'Of course I do.'

'Good.'

'Yes.'

'So now it's just a question of . . .'

'Delivering the blow?'

This time it was Ming Kwan's turn to remain silent.

Annie reached across the table and slowly traced one of his stiletto cheekbones with her beautifully manicured finger. 'I'll tell him in the New Year,' she promised. 'Nobody likes to be alone at New Year. I just couldn't do it to him.'

'*I'll* be alone at New Year.'

'That's different. You'll know you won't be alone for long. You'll be waiting for me. And when I'm free to come to you, we'll celebrate our own New Year.'

Ming Kwan reached up and took Annie's hand. He lifted it from his cheekbone to his lips, and kissed it.

'Okay. We'll celebrate the lunar New Year.'

Annie knew both that the Chinese lunar New Year fell a few weeks after the Western, solar one, and that the Chinese gave years the names of animals.

'What is it, next year?'

'The year of the monkey.'

'The monkey?' Annie's tone made it plain she was doubtful about monkeys.

'The monkey,' nodded Ming Kwan, 'possessor of super-natural powers, legendary source of assistance in trouble, creature of the moon. There's a poem about two monkeys on a riverbank: *A pair of monkeys are reaching / For the moon, in the water.* That's us. We're two monkeys, reaching for the moon.'

Annie leaned over to kiss him, briefly.

'Monkey woman.' He smiled, when they broke. 'Monkey woman.'

Ursula was a pack animal. She had flown out to the States carrying sixteen million pieces of luggage, one of which had contained her own bits and pieces of this and that, the rest of which had been jammed with gifts from the family for Jo and for Madison. She had arrived the day before her daughter and her new baby granddaughter had left hospital. Once they were home, she had thrown herself into the part of willing domestic drudge – shopping, cooking, and cleaning. But this role was already beginning to pall, and she was by now desperate for Jason to arrive. Only one more day to go! He was flying out for Christmas week, and, new baby or no new baby, she and he planned to take advantage of all the seasonal attractions New York had to offer, however tacky: The Nutcracker at the Lincoln Center; the ice rink and the tree at the Rockefeller Center; The Rockettes at Radio City, and so on and so forth.

'And in between we'll baby-sit, I promise,' she cooed, to Madison.

Jo was asleep in her bedroom, and Ursula and Madison were having their own private getting-to-know-you session in Jo's sleek, minimalist sitting room. The suede sofas and chairs, thought Ursula, wouldn't stand up very well to Madison's attentions once she was old enough to wreak destruction. And her own pink angora sweater wouldn't stand up very well, now, to Madison's baby regurgitation. This morning Ursula had sensibly swathed herself in white linen cloths. She knew it would have been even more sensible to have changed the angora sweater for something more practical, but she had done her stint as practical, in her own days as a mother. Her body might be elderly by now, but she was free, once more, to dress as frivolously as a girl, and she didn't intend to relinquish that freedom.

'Won't we have fun together?' Ursula continued to coo to her granddaughter.

Fun? Thought Madison, *The world is too serious for fun.* She expressed her disagreement with her grandmother by turning down the corners of her mouth, in preparation for a good wail. Ursula hastily moved to pick her up from the pretty crib where she was lying.

'Hush, now!' she said, giving her a cuddle. 'We don't want to wake Mummy, do we?'

On balance, Madison decided she probably didn't. She regarded her grandmother solemnly. And Ursula solemnly regarded her. Two eternal souls looked at each other, across the blink of sixty years.

Madison gazed up, with eyes drenched in knowledge. Ursula gazed down, with eyes drenched in wonder. She found herself wondering, especially, about her granddaughter's eyes. Of course, they could not focus yet, although they could probably detect changes in the light. Such big eyes, like a bush baby's! At the moment they were way too big for Madison's tiny face. And what a colour! They were the clear, deep blue of an unpolluted sky. But that would change, thought Ursula. And when it did, would Madison find herself growing into her mother's mysterious green eyes? Or into her mysterious father's even more mysterious eyes? Or into eyes which were entirely her own?

Except, Ursula corrected herself, nobody had eyes which were entirely their own. All her daughters had their dad's eyes. She herself had her own mother's eyes – eyes the same shape and size and blue as her mother's had been, and sometimes just as steely. But Ursula knew what went on behind the still surface of her own eyes, and she'd never known what went on behind her mother's, just as her mother had never known what went on behind hers. Ursula sighed as she remembered the greedy, needy woman whose shadow she'd spent so many years trying to flee. Still, the first time she'd gazed into Liz's eyes – her firstborn daughter's eyes – she had forgiven her mother everything. And she didn't try to fool herself she'd made any more success of being a mother than her own mother had done. Where her mother had been too needy, she'd no doubt been too remote; where her mother had wanted a suffocating closeness, her own keenness not to pry had perhaps led to a distance that went beyond the merely discreet? Ursula sighed. She didn't expect her childless daughters, Annie and Liz, to have forgiven her those shortcomings, but what of Caroline, and what of Jo?

Ursula stroked her granddaughter's soft cheek with her bony finger, and wondered whether Jo had forgiven her everything when first she'd gazed upon Madison, just as she herself had forgiven her own mother when first she'd gazed upon Liz? Not that forgiving up the generations led to understanding downwards, alas. Her own girls, with their father's magical green eyes, had sometimes seemed to her as alien as bats – creatures that navigated the world not by the familiar sense of sight, but by the bizarre sense of sonar. Would Jo and Madison similarly be strange to each other? Or would each let the other look in? Ursula continued to stare down into Madison's blue depths, and she sighed at the mystery of communion, and its lack.

Madison also sighed as she stared right back. Again, she longed to be able to speak. *Our eyes are two-way magic mirrors,* she longed to explain to her grandmother. *They are magic mirrors on the past and future. I am you, when you were young. You are me, grown old.* Although perhaps there were mercies, in her inarticulateness? Madison knew her grandmother would have found the thought of her, Madison, grown old, scarcely bearable. But Madison was not afraid of growing old. She had not yet forgotten the land of blank, of not-being, whence she had come, and whither she would one day return. *My eyes contain my mother's eyes*, she wanted to say to Ursula. *Yours. Your mother's. Her mother's. So many women, stretching back, and back. And so many women, stretching on and on, into the future. My daughter, and my daughter's daughter, and her daughter, all those women will hide me, and my mother, and you, in their eyes.*

So many women.

All of us living secret lives.

All of us hiding each other in the reeds of our lake-like eyes.

Twelve

It was a New Year. All over the world, people were hoping for a new start. All over the world, people had already packed in their resolutions. Liz and Zack hadn't bothered to make any. They needed all their resolution to face their exam to become parents. Despite their scepticism towards psychometric tests, they had scored highly on Global Adoption Link's multiple choice. They'd passed with flying colours, and now they had been invited into the agency's headquarters for an oral. Patricia, their case lead manager, was a thin, nervous woman whose intensity both Liz and Zack found unsettling.

'You must think of yourselves as my clients,' she instructed them.

The instruction wasn't so hard to follow. In one sense, Liz and Zack truly *were* Patricia's clients – they were her dependants. Their hopes of a child were at the mercy of her will. Not that this truth could be acknowledged openly. Someone at GAL had decided it would be a good idea to try to mask the inequality between its case lead managers and its clients with a stab at cosiness. Liz and Zack, both saturated with nerves, sat side by side on a sofa in what the agency called its community room, although it might equally well have been labelled a probationary holding cell. Patricia sat opposite them in a comfy armchair, beneath a tatty poster of a kitten. But she looked neither comfy, nor kittenish – she looked severe. She had a short, severe hairstyle, wore severe tortoiseshell glasses, and was dressed severely, in a mannish trouser suit.

'Have you brought the documentation?' Patricia demanded.

'Yes.' Zack's hands shook as he passed over two lives, in bumpf. 'Copies of our birth certificates, our wedding certificate, medical reports, character references, and financial records . . . Have I missed anything?'

'I don't think so.' Patricia took the pile of paperwork and frowned at her clipboard, which held her notes 'You've been married five years?'

'Yes. Our certificate—'

'Good.' She glanced from Liz to Zack, and both of them thought her astute, assessing eyes looked very large behind her square-framed spectacles. 'Then let's just talk through your character references, shall we?'

Caroline felt like she'd just had a blindfold removed. How long was it since she'd last been able to look around the world? She gazed about her with frank interest. The Fletchor & Mellor reception area was both quite unremarkable and as fascinating as some exotic temple. Black leather seats on aluminium frames! A glass-topped table, spread with newspapers! Potted plants! A couple of bored-looking receptionists sitting behind the broad curve of their desk! Caroline sighed with satisfaction – and sighed, again, to think of the picture she must present to the receptionists. She'd made herself up very carefully this morning. Why not, since she knew she was going to be interviewed by a panel of men? Her haircut had been successful – hurrah! Now she sported a short, neat bob. Her suit – her suit of armour – was well cut, and sleek. Her legs were encased in sheer stockings, and her feet were so beautifully shod! She pointed her toes, the better to admire her new, patent leather slingbacks, which hit exactly the right balance between provocative and professional. She thought of Simon stuck at home, and felt a triumphant glee. When she'd hurried out this morning, the kitchen had looked like the site of a small nuclear explosion. After the huge success of his chocolate truffles Simon had decided he was a natural cook – and Caroline wasn't about to disabuse him of this erroneous idea. She'd much rather eat slightly peculiar glop cooked by him than slightly peculiar glop cooked by herself. This morning she'd left him baking oatmeal and raisin cookies with the twins. Supposedly. What actually seemed to have been happening, so far as Caroline had been able to see as she'd backed hastily out of the kitchen, nervous about oatmeal on her skirt, was that the boys had been making oatmeal pancakes on the floor whilst their dad had been knocking up a catastrophe in his mixing bowl.

'Boys?' she'd heard him ask hopefully, as she'd made her escape through the front door. 'Who wants a stir?'

Caroline smiled to think of the state the twins' clothes must be in by now. And their hair was probably spiked with cookie mixture, stiffened into punkish Mohawk styles. Oh, well. Let them have their fun. It wasn't *her* who'd have to wash their clothes, or bathe them.

'Caroline Ayrton?' asked one of the bored-looking receptionists. Caroline snapped out of her reverie.

'Yes?'

'They're ready for you now.'

Caroline took the lift up to the twentieth floor, where a secretary met her and showed her into a harshly lit meeting room, done up in neutral tones, and wood-effect plastic. Mitch, Ron, and Brian, the three execs who would interview her, were already waiting. All three were much taken by her legs – and her CV wasn't half bad, either, if you were prepared to ignore the hiatus following the birth of her children. Luckily, Mitch, Ron, and Brian were all fully prepared to turn a blind eye to the blank period. The great, empty crater in Caroline's CV meant Fletchor & Mellor would get her cheap, if Fletchor & Mellor wanted her at all. And cheapness was important when the economy was staggering, especially to a company undertaking a root and branch re-evaluation of its business, in order to decide where best to chop.

'So,' said Mitch, the most senior of the three execs, and an American. He tapped Caroline's CV, which lay before him amongst some other papers on the big conference table. 'You were with Holland, Blaine and Murphy when they merged with Haskey Twigge?'

Everyone in the room knew that 'merger' was a euphemism for 'takeover', which was itself a euphemism for 'large-scale sackings'.

'I was,' agreed Caroline, leaning forwards slightly.

'Difficult time, I should imagine?'

Now everyone in the room knew that Mitch was asking Caroline if she could negotiate the territory: the casual cruelty, the lack of kindness, of corporate might.

Caroline nodded crisply: the crisp businesswoman, well able to manage power, from her neatly bobbed head, to her patent leather toes.

'In that job, as in all my others,' she said blandly, 'my role was to take a mass of complex information and then convey it to the people directly affected in simple, easily comprehensible terms.'

'A big challenge, during the upheavals of a merger?'

'Corporate communication is always a challenge. I see a company as having the structure of a barbell.' Caroline traced a barbell in the air with her hands. 'Management *here,* and the employees *here*. Whatever the issue, my role, as corporate communications specialist, is to act as the strut between the two.'

'A barbell?' Mitch was impressed. Caroline clearly had at least one of the skills essential to a corporate communications specialist: she could speak, without saying anything at all. 'Okay,' he said. 'Perhaps you'd like to walk me through some of the strategies you employed at Holland, Blaine and Murphy?'

Jo knew all about the despotism of corporate might, but she wasn't worrying about it, this lovely morning. She was worrying about her daughter. Madison was strapped to her chest in a sling, suspended face out to the world so she could look around at her surroundings. If she so desired. But Madison didn't so desire. She was more interested in the internal landscape of her dreams than in the pastoral dream which was Central Park, and she had fallen asleep. Mother and daughter were taking a stroll through the glades of Manhattan's mock-rural heart, dodging traffic, both human and vehicular, as they went. They were heading downtown, and Jo could see the midtown skyscrapers sharply delineated in the clear air. It was a glorious day, but freezing, the sky was an ice-blue arc, and both she and Madison exhaled clouds of congealed breath. They were both well bundled up against the cold, and so was Brett, who walked beside them: Mom, Pop, and baby, the perfect family group . . . Except the emotional atmosphere between Madison's parents was as freezing as the day.

'Of course I'll pay,' said Brett. 'I'll make her an allowance.'

'I'm not talking about money!' snapped Jo. 'I don't want your dollars.'

'But I don't understand what it is you *do* want!'

Jo lifted her gloved hand and placed it, briefly, on the hood of Madison's bulky snowsuit. 'I want her to know the man she comes from, so that she can know herself. Even if you can't, yet, say you love her . . .'

'That's unfair!'

'. . . I feel sure you will be able to say you love her, very soon.'

Brett thought of Jenna, Avery, and Chelsea, and scowled.

'Jo . . .' he began.

'And imagine her in twenty years' time, if we – you and I – let ourselves slip away from each other. She'll despise me for losing you. And she'll despise you for losing her. Could you live with the knowledge of your daughter's scorn?'

'What d'you want me to do? Have her live with me?' Brett had long since forgotten he'd ever considered asking Jo and his putative son to do just that; the memory had been wiped by his daughter's femininity, like a song from a tape, by a magnet.

'No . . .'

'Good! So we're straight on one thing. You *know* the realities of my life.'

'Marcie. And Jenna. And Avery. And Chelsea.'

Brett said nothing, but composed his face into a wounded expression.

'Why?' flashed Jo. 'I mean: why would accepting your duties towards Madison interfere so badly with your fulfilment of duties to your existing family?'

'This is ridiculous!'

'It's deadly serious.'

'No man should have fatherhood foisted upon him.'

Jo agreed, and agreement made her furious. 'Have you looked at Madison, properly looked at her, even once, today?'

Brett kept his eyes focused forwards. 'You're trying to blackmail me, again.'

'*What?*'

'I can't split myself in two. I can't devote myself to her. I have too many other, conflicting responsibilities.'

'What I'm saying is—'

'And what *I'm* saying is you claimed your right to choose, and so do I. You should have thought about all this before you got pregnant . . .'

'It was an accident!'

'Or when you decided not to get rid of her!'

Jo stopped dead. Madison was strapped to her chest. If he so chose, Brett could now kiss his daughter, he could tickle her, he could blow raspberries on her tummy. Yet still – *still* – he talked of getting rid of her. Some remarks were irrevocable, gone beyond recall. And so were some actions. Jo performed an irrevocable action now. She wheeled about and started walking, fast, heading uptown. Brett, too, was gone, beyond recall.

Jo walked past bare flowerbeds, past lawns glittering with frost, past leafless trees. She walked past dog-walkers, and joggers, and moony young lovers – all with unseeing eyes. At last she came to the children's boating pond, drained, now, for the winter. Here she claimed an empty bench, circled her arms around her daughter, and sat and stared into the pond's concrete shallowness, trying to focus on the texture of its lining, the cracks and bumps in the concrete. But her vision was bleary. Her tears were not for herself – she could now truthfully say she was glad to have cleared the landscape of her own life of Brett's pestilential presence – but for Madison, who would grow up without even the most good-for-nothing of good-for-nothing fathers. Her irrevocable decision was *right*, Jo insisted to herself; it was *right*. She would not regret her action . . . it was just that everything was so wrong, wrong, *wrong*.

Madison woke up and also stared into the empty pond. Though she'd been sleeping all morning, she divined, at once, what had happened between her parents. She felt sorry for them both, especially for Brett. If only she could express aloud her pity for her father, his wasted life, his dullness. She wanted to say: *I am made desolate by his purposelessness, and by his banality,* but she could not. Nor could she offer her mother the reassurance she knew she craved. Madison wanted to tell her mother that she too would be happy to wander through the fields and woods and valleys of her life, unencumbered by Brett. True, he might have been redeemed by love if she had been a boy. But she wasn't. That was his bad luck, his sad luck. Madison ached for it, but still she wanted to say: *Daddy is a man gone wrong. He has squandered his life, but I will not squander my own. I will not. Nor will I be scarred by him. He will not mar the beauty and the brightness of my life.*

Don't worry, Mum, I'll be fine! She struggled hard to force air over her voicebox, and to control her tongue, but despite her desire all she could produce were whimpers.

If Liz and Zack's daughter was out there, anywhere, she was thinking in Putonghau, which is Mandarin for 'Mandarin'. But had fate picked out a baby girl, just for them? Granted, Patricia, that latter-day goddess of destiny, had bestowed her blessing – but it was only a conditional blessing; it let them progress to the next level of GAL's exam for would be parents. They'd passed the multiple choice, they'd passed the oral, now it was time for the practical: the completion of a home study. Over the past few days, they'd cleaned their house from top to bottom, tidied up the garden, fixed a few loose floorboards, and mended a broken tap or two. This morning, Liz had placed fresh flowers in every room and baked a chocolate cake to give the house a child-friendly smell.

Patricia was not fooled by the smell of baking – such an obvious trick, the stuff of estate agents, and house vendors. But, just like an agent, she was impressed by the proximity of Liz and Zack's house to the local park, shops, the library, and a well-thought-of state primary school.

'Great location!' she said, as Liz helped her out of her coat.

Liz dared not let herself be swept away by relief. 'Yes,' she said. 'It's very convenient.'

Zack emerged from the kitchen. 'Hi!' he oiled. 'How about coffee, before we start?'

Patricia was once again in a mannish trouser suit, and today she carried a big, impressive-looking briefcase.

'No thanks,' she said briskly, 'I'd prefer to get straight down to business.'

'Shall we show you round?'

'Not yet. I need to run through a few questions first. Where shall we sit?'

Liz and Zack took Patricia into their sitting room, where she was startled by the riot of pattern and texture. Still, interior design was none of her concern. She sat down on an armchair draped with a patchwork throw, and pulled a questionnaire, a note pad, and a pen from her briefcase. Meanwhile, Liz and Zack settled themselves on their brightly becushioned day-bed.

Patricia glanced down at GAL's standard questionnaire. 'Central heating?' she barked, to set the ball rolling.

'Yes,' said Zack. 'Gas.'

'Damp? Structural defects? Roof problems?'

'It's a sound house.'

'Number of bathrooms?'

'One. But two loos.'

'And it's obvious you don't share cooking facilities.'

'No. We don't.'

'Fridge?'

'What?'

'Do you have a fridge?'

Liz and Zack glanced at each other, amazed. 'Yes. We have a fridge.'

'An adopted child could have her own bedroom?'

'Yes!' said Liz, eagerly. 'Even a playroom! We have three bedrooms. We can show you.'

'Later.' Patricia glanced out of the back window. 'And I can see you have a garden. No direct access to the street?'

'Oh no,' said Zack. 'It's quite safe to play in.'

Patricia peered at him over the top of her glasses. 'If you are accepted,' she said, 'there'll have to be a separate safety audit later. Stair gates. Window locks on upper-storey windows. That kind of thing.'

'Of course!' said Liz. 'We understand.' She decided she'd risk a very small joke. 'We're even prepared to put padlocks on the loo seats, if we have to!'

'Good.' Patricia nodded, without smiling. Liz and Zack both shifted uncomfortably and felt their hopes shift too.

After twenty minutes more of this, Patricia brought the interview to a conclusion. 'It's time for me to look around. D'you two mind waiting here? I'd prefer to assess your house on my own, if that's all right with you.'

Liz swallowed hard, and smiled as brightly as she could.

'That's fine,' she lied. 'Absolutely fine.'

Annie felt far from fine. The year of the monkey had not yet arrived, but its predecessor, the year of the ram, was tottering towards the horological abattoir. Annie couldn't wait for it to go. Ming Kwan had told her that in China the ram was an emblem of a retired life, and one of the six sacrificial animals of legend. For a full year, Annie had retired from life – but now she was back, a monkey-woman scampering and chittering in the land of the living. And, in her guise of monkey-woman, she was dead set on taking a knife to her ram. Except it wasn't quite as simple as that, she thought, as once again she began to stand up, then changed her mind and plopped back onto the sofa.

Henrietta had taken Bonnie and Clyde down to her Hampshire cottage for the weekend, and William and Annie had the Knightsbridge house all to themselves for two whole days. What a golden opportunity! Annie had decided she simply couldn't let it pass her by . . . and William, too, had decided he must seize the day. They were now in the big drawing room, locked in one of passion's inversions. Each was preternaturally aware of the other. Each was as unable to sit still as the other. Two hearts were pounding, two mouths were dry, four palms were sweating, and two people were in a proper tizz.

'Oh, God, William,' said Annie, jumping up at last, her eyes wide with distress. 'There's no easy way to say this, but . . . but . . . but.'

William also jumped up, flapped his arms a bit, and then sat down again. 'Yes?' he asked. 'Yes?'

Annie felt as though she couldn't breathe, as if her ribcage were being crushed, as if the walls of the drawing room were collapsing in on her. 'Oh, William,' she gasped. 'I'm so sorry, but I've simply got to end it. I can't go through with it! I can't marry you! I'm so, so sorry. I . . .' She stopped, and gawked at William, jaw agape. 'You're *smiling*!' she accused. She rejoiced. She puzzled.

William quickly got his face in order . . . for about a tenth of a second. Then his grin broke through again. 'Oh, Annie, thank you,' he said.

'*Thank you?*'

'From the bottom of my heart!' William clasped his breast theatrically. 'I wanted to end it, too!'

'*You did?*'

'I'm such a coward!'

After a moment of stunned surprised, Annie began to laugh. William quickly joined in – but then began to look uncomfortable. 'Could I ask,' he began, shiftily, 'is there . . . um . . . anyone else?'

Annie swallowed, and looked solemn. 'Yes, actually.'

'Thank goodness!' William started beaming again.

Annie blushed scarlet. 'It's Ming Kwan . . . and you have someone too?'

'Penelope!'

'Who else!'

They looked at each other a long moment.

'God,' said Annie, 'we're so *wrong* for each other. How the hell did we ever manage to get into this thing together?'

'You're very beautiful,' replied William promptly,

chivalrously, and truthfully. 'Beautiful, and sexy, and funny, and charming.'

'Yeah, yeah,' said Annie, who'd noticed that he hadn't mentioned enchanting, or bewitching. Which was fine. 'And you're so *kind.* You're kind, caring, generous, and . . . much too nice for me.'

'Rubbish!'

'No.' Annie took a couple of steps towards the man whose ring she still, for the moment, continued to wear, and looked up at him very seriously. 'Thank you, William. I'm so grateful. You were so good. When . . .'

'No!' interrupted William, with a very hammy leer. '*You* were so good.'

Annie hit him, lightly, on the arm. 'When we first met, I was in such a state, and . . .'

'You were good to me, too,' said William, 'and good *for* me. I . . .' He caught himself about to stray into territory that should be absolutely private between himself and Penelope: his once-upon-a-time fear of commitment; his once-upon-a-time fear of fatherhood. 'You helped me sort out some things in my mind,' he finished.

'We were both disorientated by walking out on people we loved,' said Annie.

'We were probably both disorientated by the *speed* of things.'

'We didn't collide, we crashed.'

William clapped his hands together. 'Bang!' he said.

'Quite the wrong sort of write-off,' laughed Annie. 'But I'm glad we acted madly, now that we know it won't be permanent.'

'Me too!'

The newly un-betrothed smiled into each other's eyes. Each leaned towards the other. They wrapped each other in an embrace and kissed as meaningfully, though not as hungrily, as on the day they'd met.

Brett didn't know the meaning of kissing, but Marcie did; Hart had reminded her what it was all about. Hart, to whom her own heart flew, and to whom she was now busily preparing to fly. Packing was such a bore. It was a chore Marcie rarely undertook. But this morning she hadn't felt able to instruct her housekeeper to do it, since she hadn't confided in her housekeeper that she was leaving. Nor had she confided in Maria, her daughters' weekend babysitter, who was, at this very minute, chaperoning Jenna, Chelsea, and Avery round the dinosaurs and the dioramas at the Museum of Natural History. Marcie had arranged to pick up her girls on the steps outside at one. Her plan was to take them for pizza, and then to break the news: for a week or two they would be staying in a hotel, where Uncle Hart – they remembered him, didn't they? From the summer? He was so thrilled to be seeing them again – where Uncle Hart would visit them, often. Then, once they'd all got reacquainted, there would be an exciting move down to TriBeCa, and a big, big loft where three cool new bedrooms were all ready and waiting for the three coolest little girls in the whole, wide world.

Marcie hummed as she packed. Hart, her dearest Hart, had given her a full set of crocodile-skin luggage in which to convey her choicest chattels to him. The choicest of her choice chattels were to be found in the safe, at the back of one of her many closets – this was where she kept all the insurance jewellery Brett had given her down the years. She was groping in the furthest reaches of the safe, double-checking she hadn't missed a stray ring, or brooch, or emerald or diamond, when Brett, the source of all these costly baubles, walked in to her dressing room, freshly returned from his regular Saturday-morning session at the gym.

'Good workout?' asked Marcie, without looking round.

Brett froze, mid-step, as he took in both the scene and its implication. Why would any Wall Street wife be emptying her safe? And there was a giveaway set of cases – new cases, ones he hadn't seen before – stacked against the wall.

'I've been out two hours.'

'Yup.'

'You've packed.'

'Yup.'

'You're emptying your safe.'

'Yup.'

'What do you think you're doing?' Since he knew the answer, Brett's Noo York accent was made more pronounced by aggression: *Whaddaya thing you doin'?*

Marcie turned to her husband. She knew she looked good. She was one of the few women on Manhattan who didn't habitually wear black. *Great style,* Hart had complimented her, soon after they'd met. *Black's sooo borrring.* Today she was in powder-blue. *Baby-blue, for my baby,* Hart had said, when he'd given her this pretty dress.

'Goodbye, honey.' Marcie blasted her husband with her tyrannosaur smile. 'And have a nice day.'

Liz and Zack were having a terrible day. Patricia had been satisfied they did not live in a lice infested slum, and had duly instructed them to report to GAL's Golders Green offices for the next part of their parenting exam. Once again, they were sitting side by side, on the community room's sofa, with Patricia sitting opposite them in a comfy armchair, beneath a tatty poster of a kitten. She was composed, as is proper for an invigilator, but the poor candidates both felt shivery and sick. It was as if Liz and Zack were facing their finals. And these finals were far more final than the undergraduate kind. These finals were final. They both knew that if they fucked them up, they'd fuck up their chance to be parents.

Patricia had kicked off the interview by asking her clients if they were pursuing international adoption because Caucasian babies were so hard to come by, and things were going rapidly downhill, from there.

'So,' she lectured, 'transracial adoption is not for every-one. You must think about whether building an interracial, multi-ethnic family is a fit, for you. Adopting transracially means your family will be interracial for generations. What do you know about your extended family's response to people of different racial and ethnic backgrounds?'

She looked at Liz and Zack, expectantly, and they froze, caught between offence and terror. Liz cleared her throat. Annie had phoned a few days previously, giggly with the news that she'd called off her engagement to William and was now, once again, with Ming Kwan; it was official.

'My sister is dating an Anglo-Chinese man.'

'I see.' Patricia looked interested, and made a note.

'Yes. In fact, she was the one who first suggested adopting from China.'

'I see.'

'Nobody in the family has ever batted an eyelid.'

'What if your sister and her partner had children? Would your family be accepting?'

'For God's sake!' flashed Zack.

Liz laid a restraining hand, on his arm. 'She's always insisted she doesn't want children. But if she ever changed her mind . . .'

'Our daughter would have mixed race cousins,' interrupted Zack dryly.

'And everyone in the family would be delighted,' added Liz. 'Delighted.'

Patricia made another note. 'I see,' she said again. 'So your family would be supportive.'

'Sure,' Liz shrugged. 'Me,' she pointed to herself. 'Him,' she pointed to Zack, 'our baby. We'd just be a normal family.'

Patricia shook her head. 'You might see it that way, but to many you'd be a family with an adopted Chinese daughter. A blended family . . .'

'Blended?' cut in Liz. She imagined colours blending on her drawing board. Red into mauve into blue into green into yellow.

'Yes,' Patricia nodded. 'The issues would be in your face, day in, day out. How would you feel about getting a lot of public attention, positive, and negative, from people in shops, on the bus, at the park, and so on?'

'Positive would be fine,' said Zack. 'Negative?' He flushed. 'I'd tell them to . . .'

'We'd treat it with contempt,' Liz jumped in hastily. She wasn't sure how Patricia would react to Zack saying *fuck off*. Was it politic to swear, if your suitability as parents was being assessed?

'What about playground teasing? Do you have the interpersonal resources necessary for appropriately coping with the hurt, fears and anger that will come as a result of prejudices towards your daughter? Do you have the resources necessary to help your daughter build the resiliency she will need to cope with these prejudices?'

Liz and Zack just stared at their counsellor-inquisitor-invigilator.

Patricia unbent, slightly.

'I'm posing some very difficult questions for you to consider. We are in desperate need of families for Chinese girls; however, adoption is a life-changing event for you and for the child. We must be absolutely sure you are willing to take on the challenge.'

'We'd tell our daughter she was wonderful,' said Zack. 'We'd tell her she was pretty and clever and lovely. We'd tell her she was creative, intelligent, artistic, brave. We'd tell her if anyone failed to look at her, but judged her according to some stupid, stupid stereotype, then –' he slammed his fist into the palm of his other hand, and spoke with an urgent force –'she should beat the shit out of them.'

'No!' shouted Liz. 'No,' she repeated, more quietly. 'We'd tell her there are no such things as stereotypes. We'd tell her –' she searched around for counsellor-speak – 'we'd teach her appropriate methods of conflict resolution . . . we'd teach her to argue, and to persuade. We'd teach her prejudice was born of ignorance, often poverty. Deprivation. She should feel sorry for those people.'

'I see,' said Patricia. 'I see.'

What did Patricia see? wondered Liz. What did Patricia see that she and Zack couldn't?

'Your daughter would look different from you,' Patricia went on. 'She would be bound to notice the differences. How would you explain them?'

Liz imagined cuddling a girl with saffron skin, and amber eyes.

'I'd say: yes, darling, you have black hair because your birth mother—'

'Your tummy-mummy . . .'

Liz baulked at Patricia's phrase, and exchanged a glance with Zack. No daughter of theirs would get condescending kiddie-speak. They would assume their daughter was their intellectual equal – no, their superior. In the brains department, thought Liz, she and Zack would never be able to hold a candle to their child.

'Your tummy-mummy,' she continued, after the tiniest of pauses, 'was Chinese. But Daddy and I are English. And you, darling, are *both* English and Chinese.'

'You are a beautiful hybrid,' added Zack, 'like a rose.'

Zack wasn't a gardener and Liz, surprised by his analogy, looked directly at him. So, she thought, for her their daughter would contain a rainbow, for Zack she would be a rose – but Patricia didn't allow much time for romantic musing.

'How comfortable would you be with maintaining your daughter's racial and cultural identity?' she demanded quite sharply.

'Very comfortable,' said Zack.

'Yes, but what d'you *mean* by that? You *know* adoption comes from loss . . .'

Liz and Zack both cast down their eyes, each thinking of their own losses. In silence, Liz reached out, took her husband's hand, and laced her fingers into his.

'The adoptee suffers loss at every turn,' continued Patricia, who was not oblivious to her clients' pain, but could not allow it to detain her. 'Her life starts with the loss of her biological parents, but it's not just that. You have to let her grieve and mourn the loss of her heritage, too, and you have to let her do it over and over again.'

'Yes,' said Zack. 'We understand.'

'We'd learn as much as we could about China, for her sake,' added Liz.

'We'd learn Mandarin.'

'We'd celebrate Chinese festivals – I'm sure my sister's partner would help explain things.'

'When she was older, we'd be happy to take her to visit her home province.'

'All that's fine,' said Patricia, 'but *could* you maintain her cultural identity whilst still feeling that she was yours?'

Again, Liz and Zack just looked at her: what was she asking them?

Patricia sensed their incomprehension and tried again.

'Would you be willing to allow a child to become her own person, even though she might be very different from you?'

'Oh, come *on*,' said Zack, who was not picking up at all on Liz's keep cool vibes. 'That's a problem for *every* parent. Every parent has to let a child become their own person.'

'I see,' said Patricia, making another note. 'I see.'

Thirteen

Annie could have sworn that when she'd moved out on Ming Kwan, she'd had only a box or two, plus her pictures. But now she was moving her stuff back in again, the boxes seemed to have reproduced. And box begat box. How could she have acquired so many things, over the last year, with William? It was junk, mostly, she thought, as she began to unpack in Ming Kwan's small sitting room which was also, once again, her own sitting room. She glanced around, feeling a slight twinge of regret for the gallery-sized walls of Knightsbridge. Her pictures would look cramped in here. Still, she'd just have to learn to live with that – after all, she'd lived with it before. She could still see lighter-shaded squares on the ochre walls where her pictures had once hung, and would hang again, when they'd been crated up and sent over. Pictures couldn't just be bundled into boxes. Annie had arranged for them to be delivered from William's, next week. Henrietta would be *so pleased* to get rid of them, she thought, fondly. Now that she knew she'd never have to live with the old bat, she was quite warming to her. How quick Henrietta would be to re-hang those risible pugtraits! And pugraits, thought Annie, weren't all Henrietta would be smiling about, these coming weeks. Hen and Pen! How happy those two would be together!

Annie grinned, and knelt on the rug to unpack a box of books. Books, she thought, were the last things she should have brought into this flat, which was already overflowing with the damn things. It was like the butter mountain, or the wine lake, except it was the book mountain, and the word lake. Annie once again felt a brief nostalgia for Knightsbridge and its sumptuous bookshelves. Except that was silly, since Ming Kwan's books were so much more interesting than the gardening guides of Knightsbridge. Annie leaned over to a higgledy pile of books, magazines, and DVDs, lying on the floor next to the sofa. She picked up a hardback at random: *Crime Does Pay: How Asian Crime Novels Differ From Western Mysteries*. Annie didn't read many crime novels, nor mysteries, either. Still, this book was intriguing. She flipped it over, intending to read the back-cover blurb – but then reminded herself she had a job to do. She replaced the book. Even unread, it had proved her point: Knightsbridge's gardening guides had nothing on Hoxton.

And nor did Knightsbridge. Hoxton was great. A bit too self-consciously trendy these days, what with all the artists, and the sandwich shops selling panini and ciabatta. Not that Annie, with her history-of-art degree and her pictures, had anything against artists, and she'd much rather eat ciabatta than the industrially air-puffed flop that wasn't really bread. And she enjoyed swilling beer in the Czech bar, and hanging out at the jazz club. She might even suggest to her business partners that they open a branch of Zenses round here. Although what would the Buddha heads think, if all they had to contemplate, through their serenely slanted eyes, was Old Street round-about? Perhaps it would be fairer to them to open Zenses in Clerkenwell, just up the road? That was another great thing about Hoxton, thought Annie; she and Ming Kwan could walk anywhere from this flat. Into the City. Up to Islington. Twenty minutes to Chancery Lane, another twenty to the West End, the river, the South Bank. Who wanted the garden squares of Knightsbridge? Annie would miss having access to a lawn, but the building that housed this flat had a great tar beach on the roof, perfect for idling away the dog days of summer.

Ming Kwan came into the room carrying two steaming mugs of tea – not English tea with milk, but Chinese chrysan-themum tea, which was a clear, pale yellow. He negotiated a dispirited potted plant just inside the door, placed there according to the dictates of Feng Shui, in the hope that it would deflect arrows of negative energy. Ming Kwan had never had much faith in the powers of this plant; it looked far too etiolated to do its job, and he glanced at it disparagingly as he passed the tea to Annie. He couldn't get very far into the room because of all the boxes, so he perched on the arm of the sofa, from which vantage point he surveyed his beloved, who was still kneeling on the floor, although most definitely not at his feet.

'How're you getting on?' he asked.

'Slowly.'

'That's okay. There's no hurry.'

Annie looked up, and Ming Kwan gazed down. The two of them stared deep into each other's eyes.

'Annie?' asked Ming Kwan. 'Will you marry me?'

'Nope.'

'Will you have my kids?'

'Nope.'

'Good! Just checking.'

'I wouldn't mind a spot of tantric sex, though,' grinned Annie, and then she turned away and got on with unpacking her bloody boxes.

Tantric sex wasn't often on the agenda in Ryleford, where Simon was running a few errands. Meanwhile, Caroline was at home, alone with the twins. Chaos had descended. The dishwasher had just flooded the kitchen. What was it with domestic appliances, wondered Caroline; was it personal? Did they have it in for her? She was trying to mop up the mess, and the twins were trying to surf on the mini-flood when the phone rang.

'Hello?'

'Caroline?'

Caroline jolted. It was the greasy-voiced headhunter, calling from London. Presumably, he had heard from Fletchor & Mellor.

'Yes,' she said, trying to make her voice sound decisive and businesslike. 'It's me.'

Alas, decisive and businesslike didn't mix with small boys who'd just turned three. At that moment, Louis slipped in the water and plopped down on his bottom. He wasn't hurt, even though he was now potty-trained and no longer benefited from the padding of nappies, but he was surprised, and his trousers were wet. Naturally he started to roar. Nat joined in, to keep him company.

'Good God!' said the headhunter. 'What on earth's going on?'

'Just murdering my children,' trilled Caroline. 'Hang on a sec.' She used her shoulder to crunch the cordless phone to her ear, and batted at the boys, trying to semaphore to them to shut up. It didn't work, so she walked over to her larder, where she fished out an unopened packet of chocolate biscuits, slit the packaging, and tossed it to her twin raptors. They fell on it just as keenly as she'd anticipated, and silence was restored. 'Okay,' she said. 'I'm free to talk.'

'Good,' said the headhunter. 'And good news . . .'

Ten minutes later Simon walked into the kitchen carrying an armful of packages. He dumped them on the table and burst out laughing.

'Blimey!' he said, and then remembered one of his New Year's resolutions had been to watch his language around the twins. Was blimey allowable, or not? 'Crumbs!' he amended, in case. His surprise was understandable. His wife and children, all three of them soaked, were doing the boogie-woogie round the flooded kitchen, singing a jazzed-up version of 'The Wheels on the Bus', at the tops of their voices. Caroline had given it a rock 'n' roll beat, and had worked in far more a-wop-bop-a-loo-bop-a-wop-bam-boos than the words could strictly stand. Never mind. The twins weren't music critics. The twins were entirely uncritical of their mother.

'Mummy got her job,' sang Louis.

'Her lovely job,' added Nat.

Simon whooped, and kissed his wife. They too did the boogie-woogie.

'But honestly, love,' said Simon, a few minutes later, pointing to the broken dishwasher, and gesturing round at the flood, 'do you really think you're qualified to talk to anybody about washing powders?'

'It was the dishwasher, not the washing machine!'

'Same difference!'

'Are you saying I'm not domesticated?'

'Nobody could ever accuse you of being a domestic goddess!'

Caroline laughed. 'Washing powder's not the point,' she said. 'And, anyway, they call it *laundry* powder. Now shut up, and crack open the champagne.'

'I can offer you milk,' teased Simon. 'Chocolate milk, Ribena, apple juice, or water.'

*

Mineral water, coffee, and soda were the preferred tipples on Wall Street, but Jo quite fancied a bloody Mary. This was her first morning back, and she felt in need of alcoholic fortification. In New York, hardly anyone drank in the European sense of the word, and women often returned to their desks two weeks after giving birth. Jo had pushed it to two months, partly so that she could spend the time with Madison, partly to avoid seeing Brett. She and he had had a series of terse conversations about how they would, or wouldn't, resume a professional relationship once she returned to United American Bank. The upshot had been that Brett, newly rid of Marcie, Jenna, Avery, and Chelsea, and not too worried about access visits to his daughters, had decided to relocate to the London office. People did that all the time on Wall Street. Transatlantic to-ing and fro-ing was quite unremarkable. Nobody at UAB had been suspicious, but in case they'd been tempted to speculate, Brett had put it about that he was going for family reasons – and then explained, soulfully, that Marcie had left him.

Thank God, thought Jo, that The Verminator had absented himself from her immediate environment. With or without a bloody Mary, she wanted to be free to concentrate on the impersonal ups and downs of the markets, not on personal clutter. And the markets were certainly very volatile. Jo pursed her lips as she stared at her screen. Yen down overnight, Aussie dollar up. At the moment, nobody could make money in Japan; the conditions were just terrible. But what about down-under?

Was it too late to get into the Aussie dollar? And the rand was doing well, too, although only compared to an all-time low, and only because of South Africa's gold mines. But gold, which had surged in value recently, surely couldn't go much higher? So nor would the rand. What to do? Buy? Sell? Hedge? Jo decided to worry about it all after she'd checked in on Madison and Carmen.

Carmen was the Latina babysitter Jo had hired for Madison. She was a warm and gentle middle-aged mother, whose own children were now grown. She was quick to laugh and quick to soothe. Her references were of the highest order, and she had a slew of first-aid qualifications as well as a cookery qualification. The Cohens, her previous family, had hung onto her for eight years, but the youngest of their three boys was now thirteen, and they were no longer strictly in need of a full-time babysitter. Mrs Cohen had told Jo she'd liked to have kept Carmen on as a housekeeper. But Carmen wasn't keen. She loved working with little ones; it was time, she thought, for a change.

Jo was more than willing to offer her one. Right from the first minute of the first interview, she had felt at ease in Carmen's presence. And so, she thought, had Madison. And so, in fact, had Madison. Madison had wanted to say: *Carmen, I fly to you as an iron filing to a magnet*, but she had settled for wriggling joyfully and waving her arms and legs. Then, all last week when her mother and her new nanny had shared the responsibility of looking after her in preparation for today,

Mom's back-to-work day, she'd been a little angel: no screaming, no poops so voluminous they'd soaked through both her diaper and her vest, no projectile vomit, and nothing but sweet co-operation at dressing, bath and changing times.

Carmen answered the phone. 'Hola?'

'Hola,' said Jo, a little self-consciously, since her Spanish was lousy – another great thing about Carmen was that she'd be able to teach Madison the language spoken by so many New Yorkers. Jo thought of the few kiddie-relevant snatches she knew: *Mas leche por favor. Zumo de piña para la niña.* Not that she'd be using that one just yet; Madison was still a bit little for juice. But her daughter had a chance of growing up bilingual. What a wonderful thing!

'Don't worry,' said Carmen, in lightly accented English. 'She's asleep.'

'She took her bottle?'

'Six ounces.'

'Bowels?'

'Everything's fine. Nothing to worry about. Da nada.'

'Good.' Jo paused. 'You'll take her to the park when she wakes up?'

'I thought the zoo, to see the polar bears.' The polar bears in Central Park zoo were city-wide celebrities amongst the under fives. 'And then I'll take her over to Andrea's, so she can get to know Nicholas.' Andrea was another Latina babysitter, and Nicholas her charge.

'Great,' said Jo, who was pleased to think of Madison being

locked in to the babysitter network so young. 'You'll ring me if there's any problem?'

'Of course.'

Once she'd reassured herself that Madison had not undergone infant meltdown at her absence, Jo thought she'd be free to turn her full attention to work: assessing probability, balancing risk. It was what she did best, work-wise. But life-wise? Jo leaned back in her chair, and sucked on a ball-point. She congratulated herself she was doing pretty good, life-wise, too. Whatever her circumstances, she knew she'd never have consented to be anything but a working mother, and she refused to be cowed by the idea of bringing up a child entirely on her own in New York. Single motherhood, unlike working motherhood, wouldn't have been what she'd have chosen, but she was confident both she and Madison would be fine. Money helped. Jo, who was paid better than most men, including most men on Wall Street, fully acknowledged that. She knew she earned her paycheque, and that UAB wouldn't pay it if she didn't. She also knew she was extraordinarily lucky. Unlike most single mothers, she could afford childcare that was beyond the best. Madison wouldn't be deprived, it was just that she'd have a mommy and a nanny, instead of a mommy and a daddy. In a sense, she'd have two mommies. Mommy, and Mommy-Carmen. Jo was delighted about that, not jealous. She was confident her daughter would grow up as loved and secure as any doubly parented child.

Jo smiled, and returned her attention to the screen. Okay,

the Aussie dollar. She frowned a moment. She'd have liked to have talked to United American Bank's Sydney economist, but Sydney was closed at this hour, so she'd have to make do with advice from London, where the markets were still open. She placed a call.

'Sanjeev?'

'Jo? You're back!'

'Evidently.'

'How's the baby?'

'Fantastic. Wonderful. Gorgeous. Don't get me started!'

'And you?' laughed Sanjeev.

'Raring to go.' Jo took a deep breath; it was time to dive into the markets once again. 'Listen, Sanjeev, can you tell me, are we still bullish on the Aussie?'

Were the bulls charging, or were the bears roaring? Had Liz and Zack been accepted into GAL's programme? Or had they failed their finals? They were about to find out. The postman had just delivered a bulky, registered letter, and the envelope was stamped with a globe, around which children were playing ring-a-roses. Zack had signed for the letter, but now he thrust it at his wife.

'You open it! I can't!'

Liz sat down at the kitchen table. 'Pass me a knife,' she said, her voice strained.

Zack did so, and then he also sat down. They looked at each other a moment, then Liz slit the envelope.

A photo fell out and landed face up on the table. It was passport-sized, and black and white. Though it was grainy, to Liz and Zack, it blazed. To them, it seemed to absorb light from all around it, so it shone, in its own golden halo, against a background of deepest black. It was incandescent, with the energy of the baby whose image it held. To a casual eye, this baby could have been either a boy or a girl. But Liz's and Zack's eyes were not casual. They both knew, for sure, that the photo was of a girl. She had a shock of black hair, almond-shaped buttons for eyes – and, unsurprisingly, a world-weary expression on her little round face.

A photo could mean only one thing: acceptance. Liz and Zack both wept at this first glimpse of their daughter. It was some time before Liz picked up the documents that would spell out the practicalities of their new parenthood. She quickly scanned the covering letter.

'They called her Fé Fé, at the orphanage. And her medical records are enclosed. If we don't want her, we have to say so, now.'

GAL undertook rigorous screening of children entering its adoption programme, and, in any case, Liz and Zack knew that the majority of superfluous Chinese girls were healthy. And if by some terrible chance their own daughter wasn't? So be it.

'Fé Fé?' repeated Zack. 'Fay? Or Fifi?'

'Fay,' said Liz firmly.

'Yes,' agreed Zack. 'Fay.'

'She's six months old. She was found in Chongqing.'

Zack raised himself half an inch from his chair, all ready to go to fetch an atlas. But then he decided maps could wait, and sat down again. 'When can we collect her?' he asked.

'Paperwork's got to be completed, both here and in China.'

'I thought the agency took care of the visas?' Zack was anxious. Could the Foreign Office still bar his and Liz's path to parenthood?

Liz re-read part of the letter.

'I don't think we need worry. It says we should be able to travel in three to four months. We'll have to be in China for about two weeks.'

'In Chong – what was it?'

'Chongqing. I assume so, yes, although it doesn't actually say.'

Zack was still anxious about his daughter's visa. 'And we'll have to go to the British Embassy?'

'I don't know.' Liz turned to a second sheet, and read a moment longer. 'It doesn't say that, either. But only one of us has to travel.'

'Oh no,' said Zack, shocked. 'No! Of course we'll both go.'

Liz leaned across the table and took his hand. 'Yes,' she agreed. 'We'll both go.'

Then the two of them burst out laughing, for sheer joy.

Epilogue

It was spring, once again. Liz, Jo, Caroline, and Annie were all together for the first time since Annie and William's extravagant party for their doomed engagement. This time, their cause for celebration was genuine: Jo had brought Madison over to England, to introduce her to her aunts. It was lunchtime, and the four women, and the one infant, were sitting at a circular table in Metro, a wildly fashionable restaurant in Covent Garden. The matches in the giveaway boxes were the fattest things in the place, and all the staff were drop-dead gorgeous movie stars in waiting. Unlike any other diner here, Madison was on milk – her mom kept a bottle to hand – and like all the other women in the room, her aunts were nibbling on exotic leaves.

'What's that?' they'd asked their dreamboat waiter, of a particularly twizzly red leaf.

'That's lettuce,' he'd replied, with the sort of shrug that said: well, I can do method acting . . .

The sisters had thought his reply hilarious – but then, their hilarity could have been a result of all the champagne

350

they'd been swilling, and which they happily continued to swill.

'Can I give her a tiny sip?' asked Annie.

'Go on then.' Jo was eating with one hand, and cradling Madison against her shoulder with the other. Now she swung her daughter round and watched as Annie leaned across the table to give her niece a tiny taste of the wine.

'Much nicer than milk,' smiled Jo.

'To you,' said Annie, gently touching her glass on Madison's nose.

'To Madison,' echoed Caroline, and the four sisters all clinked glasses.

'And to Fay.' Jo shot Liz, her closest friend, a quick smile.

'Let's see the picture again,' demanded Caroline.

Liz fished it out of her purse and passed it around for the second or third time.

'She's beautiful,' sighed Annie. 'We'll have a party for her, too, when you've brought her over.'

'Only six weeks now!' beamed Liz.

'To Fay.' Jo raised her glass, and the sisters clinked again.

'Don't forget mine!' said Caroline.

'How could we?'

'To Nat and Louis.'

'To the boys.'

'And what about to *mothers*?' asked Annie, who still never intended to become one.

'Okay. To mothers.'

Once again, four glasses clinked.

'To Mum?' proposed Caroline.

'Of course!'

'To Mum!' chorused her daughters, toasting Ursula in her favourite tipple, champers.

Liz looked serious for a moment. 'To Fay's birth mother?' she hazarded. 'We should remember her. But it seems wrong to toast her in champagne.'

All four sisters thought of some unknown peasant in a distant land, very sad, but also, they hoped, hopeful for her daughter's future.

'Of course we'll toast her!' said Jo robustly. 'And we'll toast you, too. We know you won't let her down.' She once more raised her glass.

'To Liz, and to Fay's birth mother.'

'No,' said Liz, before the others had a chance to raise their glasses. 'To Fay's birth mother, and to me.'

'To Fay's birth mother, and to Liz,' sang three very merry voices.

'What about *me*?' asked Annie. 'I feel a bit left out in this mother–baby lovefest.'

'Okay,' said Caroline, promptly. 'To you.'

'No!' objected Annie. 'I'm an independent woman! I raise my own toasts.' She raised her glass dramatically. 'To me!'

'And to me!' echoed Jo.

'And to me!' echoed Caroline.

'And to me!' echoed Liz.

And to me! echoed Madison, who'd very much enjoyed her first taste of champagne. But she still couldn't speak, and her toast came out as the softest, bubbly, baby sigh.

Join Hands with China's Children

In 1997 Jenny and Richard Bowen, who live in Berkeley, California, adopted their first Chinese daughter, a toddler from Guangzhou. She suffered from both physical and cognitive delays. But after just one year of individual attention, love, and nurture, the little girl was transformed. 'I thought about the things parents do by instinct, and I saw how she blossomed as a result,' said Jenny Bowen. 'I thought: what if we could do this for other children in the orphanages who are waiting for families, or who will never be adopted? I wanted what had happened to my daughter to happen to other children.'

This was the idea behind Half the Sky, a charity Bowen set up to work with disadvantaged children in China. Mostly, the charity works with girls, who make up ninety-five per cent of healthy children in China's welfare institutions. This fact explains the charity's name, which comes from the Chinese saying 'Women hold up half the sky'.

Half the Sky's mission is to enrich the lives and enhance the prospects both for children who are waiting to be adopted, and for those who will spend their childhoods in orphanages.

It has trained nannies, teachers, and other caregivers to deliver three distinct programmes: Baby Sisters; Little Sisters; Big Sisters.

Baby Sisters

Through caring interaction, Half the Sky nannies provide nurture and stimulation to infants, helping them to bond, and to form loving attachments. Half the Sky nannies are called zumu, Mandarin for grandmother. One zumu cares for between three and five infants.

Little Sisters

When babies reach eighteen months, they go into the Little Sisters programme. Half the Sky pre-school teachers carefully cultivate and guide the intellectual, emotional, and social development of young children through active learning, a free rein on artistic expression, and physical play. Many of the children's activities are documented, including transcriptions of their remarks, video journals, photographs, and examples of their work. Each of the Little Sisters thus has a memory book to take with her beyond the institution. Each memory book creates a personal history for a child who would otherwise lack one.

Big Sisters

This programme caters for children and teenagers aged twelve to eighteen, who would face an uncertain future without help.

Rosie Milne

The services Half the Sky provides are tailored to the needs of the individual, and have the potential to turn a girl's life around: remedial tutoring; middle school tuition; music, computer, language or vocational training.

Half the Sky operates in welfare institutions throughout China. It does not have the resources to offer its programmes in every orphanage, but it hopes to have a trickle-down effect. It plans to work with two orphanages in each province with a significant number of children living in institutions. The chosen orphanages, one in the provincial capital, and one in a small city, will come to serve as regional models and as training centres for other institutions. Half the Sky has met great openness and sympathy from the Chinese Government, especially the Ministry of Civil Affairs, through which it distributes a colourful training manual.

Twenty-five per cent of the royalties from this book will be donated to Half the Sky, so by buying it, you have already joined hands with disadvantaged children in China. If you would like more information, or if you would like to make a donation, please visit **www.halfthesky.org**

Acknowledgements

I am very grateful to Jane Camens, Teresa Chris, Shay Griffin, Charlotte Harper, Nicky Hursell, Sophie Hutton-Squire, Neridah Murray-Douglass, and Imogen Taylor. All these women were generous with their time, and made useful criticisms.

During the writing of this novel, Hong Kong was hit by SARS. I would like to thank Dr Rachel Williams and Dr Graeme Wilson for long-distance advice. Also during the writing of this novel, my family briefly relocated from Hong Kong to Tokyo, where the ground has an unnerving propensity to shake. I would like to thank Liz Case and Louise Simester for long-distance support in the aftermath of earthquakes.